Chenarcor

The Adventures of Alex & Toby

B. Heather Mantler

Mantler Publishing Prince George

Copyright © 2013 Heather Mantler

Copyright of Cover Photo © 2012 The Antique Photo Parlour

All rights reserved.

ISBN:1927507065
ISBN-13:9781927507063

Library and Archives Canada Cataloguing in Publication

Mantler, B. Heather, 1987-, author
Chenarcor : the adventures of Alex & Toby / B. Heather Mantler.

ISBN 978-1-927507-06-3 (pbk.)

I. Title.

PS8626.A676C53 2013 C813'.6 C2013-904113-3

I dedicate this book to those people who produced, directed, and starred in the western movies which inspired this story. Also to my family who have to live with me immersing myself in other times and places for my stories.

I would like to acknowledge the people who helped with editing of this book: Frances Manter, Sarah Dahlmann, and Ellen Mantler. They have all worked hard to help me get the story smooth, the grammar correct, and the historical facts straight. All errors left are my fault. I also would like to acknowledge Ian Mantler and Ashley Mitrega for being the models for the cover and The Antique Photo Parlour in West Edmonton Mall for taking the picture. The ladies there were very helpful in making it look so great.

INTRODUCING ALEX
CHAPTER 1

Toby

It was late in the afternoon, but my head was still pounding from whatever this man had been pouring down my throat last night. Jacob Wescott was seated across the table from me and busy telling me about the deal we had struck last night. I remember him as one of the players when I joined the poker game, but after that I barely remember winning that last hand. The job we agreed to do together, I don't remember. Now he was going on about a third man that was would join us. He was so into what he was talking about that he hadn't noticed that I wasn't listening.

He looked like a gunslinger. The softer hands, the hat pulled low, the gun in the holster on his hip. The job was to guard someone, which was the type of job a gunslinger would take. But Jacob's brown eyes said that he wasn't a gunslinger. My guess is that he'd shoot if you gave him a reason, but it had to be a good reason.

I had left the farm to become a gunslinger and had hoped to get a job as such. Jacob didn't seem to be quite what I was looking for. However, I thought I'd go along with the job because the trip this far had drained my money down to the point of not having enough for a hotel.

We both jumped when the kitchen door banged shut. I looked up to see a man dressed like a gunslinger with jeans, black jacket and black hat. His gun sat in the holster that rested snuggly on his hips in easy reach. He was a foot shorter than me and skinny but I wouldn't bet that he couldn't handle himself. By the looks of him he had just ridden into town.

"Alex," Jacob was surprised.

"You were expectin' Nadine?" Alex asked. There was no humour in the question.

"Alex Turner, Toby Lawton," Jacob introduced us. Alex offered his hand and I shook it. His handshake was firm and his green eyes were muddy. I noticed several scars along his throat.

We all sat down, Alex taking the chair at one end of the table.

"You said somethin' 'bout a job," Alex said to Jacob. Alex took his hat off and ran his fingers through his short, brown hair.

"Guard duty," Jacob said, "A man wants three guards to escort him an' his wife from here to Dustcloud."

"Very specific instructions," Alex said.

"It sounds like he's done this before," Jacob replied.

"When's this s'posed to happen?" Alex asked.

"Tomorrow mornin'," Jacob answered, "Probably not too early. He said he'd pay fifteen hundred at the start and end of the journey."

"You got time an' place tomorrow?" I asked. Jacob frowned as if he didn't like the question.

"I was goin' to confirm those details today," Jacob answered.

"It's getting' kinda late in the day, maybe you should be getting' those details soon," Alex suggested, "This man might've hired someone else for the job."

"I'll go now," Jacob said as he stood up. He put his coat on and stomped out of the house. Alex turned to me; it felt like he was studying me.

"How'd Jacob talk you into this job?" Alex asked.

"I was drunk," I answered. A light that looked like it should have been accompanied by laughter flickered in those green eyes, then it was gone.

"Sounds about right," Alex said, "Jacob will do practically anythin' to get his own way once an idea gets into his head."

"What about you?" I asked.

"He helped me out a couple years ago an' every time I've tried to say no since he reminds me of it," Alex answered, "Someday it won't work."

"You've been doin' this kind of work long?" I asked.

"Three years," Alex answered, "Seems longer when you're on the move. I'm guessin' you were a farmer 'fore you headed out on your own."

"If you listen to my father I still am a farmer," I replied.

"Ever plan on goin' back?" Alex asked.

"Only if I'm the only one left to claim the land," I answered, "My father, brother an' brother-in-law are workin' the farm. They don't need another mouth to feed."

The kitchen door opened and a woman stepped inside. She wore a brown and white work dress with cream shawl. Her diryt-blonde hair was pulled back in a loose bun under her hat. Alex slowly got to his feet.

"Nadine," Alex said.

"Alex," Nadine said as she came over and gave Alex a hug.

"Good to see you," Alex replied. He awkwardly hugged her back. After taking a step back, Nadine took off her shawl and hat. Alex sat back down as she hung them up.

"Will you be stayin' for supper?" Nadine pulled out a pot to start cooking.

"No," Alex answered.

"Decided you don't like my cooking?" Nadine asked.

"I was offered a seat in the poker game tonight when I dropped my stuff off at the hotel," Alex answered.

"You can't survive on whiskey alone," Nadine said turning her deep brown eyes to Alex.

"I will eat at some point," Alex replied not looking at her.

"What's the job this time?" Nadine turned back to making supper.

"Guard duty," Alex answered.

"Must be the job for Lord and Lady Bennett," Nadine said.

"Lord and Lady Bennett?" Alex asked.

"They have been on a sight seeing tour, so that they can go home an' tell their friends all about roughing it," Nadine answered, "Been around for 'bout three years. I thought it was a scam 'til I met Lady Bennett."

Jacob entered the kitchen and sat down. He removed his hat and set it on the table.

"We're to be outside the hotel just after sunrise," Jacob said.

"I'll see you there," Alex said putting his hat back on. He stood up and started for the door.

"Be on time," Jacob told him, "Otherwise, we don't get the job."

"Yes sir," Alex said half turning and giving a mock salute before leaving. As Nadine cooked supper Jacob told me all the details of the job for about the fourth time.

The next morning, sunrise found Jacob and me outside the hotel. The coach and driver were also waiting. The hotel was on the main street, as were most of the businesses. The other streets were mostly houses, all of which were quiet at this time of the morning. There were only a few people out.

"Where is Alex?" Jacob muttered checking around.

Ten minutes went by before a horse and rider came down the street. As they came closer I recognized Alex. He was riding a beautiful, bay coloured Morgan, the type of horse that you'd pay a couple thousand for from a breeder. My black Kentucky Mountain saddle horse paled in comparison. Jacob's chestnut coloured quarter horse looked downright beaten up.

"Where the hell have you been?" Jacob demanded once Alex had stopped beside us. He looked like he was just waking up.

"I just got up," Alex replied, "The poker game lasted half the night."

"Perhaps you shouldn't have gone," Jacob said.

"Then I wouldn't have any money at all," Alex replied.

"And what were you doin' before you received my message?" Jacob asked.

"I wasn't playin' poker," Alex answered.

"Then what were you doing?" Jacob asked. Before anyone could say anything more a man and lady stepped out of the hotel. Lord Bennett was tall with blond hair and expensive tastes in clothing. Lady Bennett matched him in her style of clothes, which went well with her dark red hair and hazel eyes. The man escorted the lady to the coach. Once the lady was inside he turned to us.

"I'm glad to see you are here," he said. His blue eyes had a sparkle in them. He pulled out a stack of bills and handed them to Jacob.

"Glad to take the job," Jacob said taking the bills.

"I should hope you are better than the last men," Lord Bennett said, "I was just about shot."

"Gettin' the client shot is bad for business," Alex said, "We prefer to get you safely to your destination. Keeps our reputations intact."

"I like your logic," Lord Bennett smiled before turning and getting into the coach himself.

"Some logic," Jacob said.

"If you don't want me along for the job, don't invite me," Alex said with a shrug.

"Just don't fall asleep," Jacob said. The coach started moving. The rest of us moved into our positions; Alex on the left, I on the right and Jacob taking the rear.

We left town.

Cartwheel was built in the middle of a forested area with only the townsite bare of trees. Once out of that area there was mostly small vegetation along the road.

We passed only a few other travelers on our way. Jacob was on constant alert, but Alex looked like he was half asleep.

It was close to noon when we passed a man sitting on a horse beside of the road. The man had his hat pulled low, hiding his face as we went passed. He nodded slightly to the driver's hello. It was a full minute after we had passed before the gunshot. By the time I had wheeled my horse around and had my gun out, Alex had tumbled off his horse and had returned the shot. The man fell off his horse and the horse bolted. The man didn't move. The coach had stopped, so had Alex's horse. He must have trained that animal well.

"Is everything all right?" Lord Bennett asked poking his head out the window.

"Yes," Alex answered.

"We'll be movin' again shortly," Jacob said. Lord Bennett nodded and withdrew into the coach. Alex went over to the body. He kicked it over on to its back. He leaned down for a minute, before straightening up and headed back to his horse.

"Well?" Jacob asked as Alex got back on his horse.

"Gunslinger," Alex said as we started moving again.

"And?" Jacob asked.

"I'm sure someone will find him an' bury him proper," Alex said.

"Did you recognize him?" Jacob asked.

"Gunslinger," Alex said with a shrug. Jacob sighed, but didn't ask anything else.

About mid-evening we arrived in Goldbrick. We stopped in front of the hotel. Lord and Lady Bennett got out. Lord Bennett turned to us.

"See you at sunrise," he said.

"Yes, sir," Jacob said. Lord and Lady Bennett went into the hotel. We followed the coach as it moved to the stable. Each of us tended to our animal before paying for the night and leaving the stable. We found a place that sold us a meal and a place to lie down for the night. Alex went off after leaving his stuff giving no indication of his intentions. I went straight to bed.

I opened my eyes. It was still dark outside the window. I sat up. Jacob was already up and dressed. Alex was dressed, but also still asleep.

"When did he get in?" I asked Jacob as I got ready.

"After I fell asleep," Jacob answered, "Alex needs to learn that mixin' business with pleasure is goin' to catch up fast. One more night of this and Alex won't be of any use to anyone."

"I came in shortly after you fell asleep," Alex opened his eyes, "You had just started to talk in your sleep."

"What no poker games in town?" Jacob asked.

"Never looked," Alex said as he sat up. He ran his fingers through his hair before putting his hat on. Jacob looked like he was about to ask more questions.

"We better get out there," I said pointing to the window. The sky was turning pink. We all grabbed our stuff and headed for the stable. We arrived at the same time as the coach driver.

We hadn't been waiting long, when Lord and Lady Bennett came out of the hotel. Once the coach was moving everyone moved into position.

Today Alex seemed a lot more alert than yesterday, but Jacob seemed to be spending more time glaring at Alex than paying attention. Mid-morning we made our way through a set of hills. At the place where the road narrowed, two men rode into sight, blocking the road. We stopped.

"Hand over all your valuables," a third man ordered from on top of a rock, "Or we'll kill you." Alex, Jacob and I each had our guns out and the driver was reaching under his seat for his rifle.

"Come down here and get them," Alex shouted back. He shot at the man and missed. The two men on horses pulled out their guns, but the driver took one out and I hit the other before they had a chance to shoot. Four more men came out. One of them was the man who yelled at us. They began shooting at us. Their aim was terrible; most of their bullets hit the ground near us. I took out one bandit. Jacob took out another. Alex shot at one, but fell off his horse before he could shoot again. The driver fired and missed. Jacob hit the third and the fourth man went down from a bullet that came from Alex's gun. The driver reloaded and put his gun back. Jacob and I put our guns away. Alex didn't appear.

"Alex?" Jacob called.

"I'll be fine," Alex replied, "Just give me a minute."

"Did you fall off your horse?" Lord Bennett asked from the coach window.

"Somethin' like that," Alex answered. Jacob rolled his eyes, but left Alex alone. Five minutes passed. Jacob started to tap his fingers against his saddlehorn. Two more minutes passed. Jacob was about to say something when Alex pulled himself into the saddle. I could tell by the way he was sitting that something was wrong. He seemed to be favouring his left side.

"Let's go," a weariness had crept into Alex's voice. We started moving again. Jacob hadn't noticed anything strange about Alex as he was back to watching our surroundings. I kept an eye on Alex.

We stopped about noon. Alex was white and looked like he might fall off his horse. Jacob looked through his bags for the food. Alex slid off his horse and slumped to the ground. I rode around to Alex. The left side of his shirt was covered with blood. He looked up at me.

"Jacob isn't going like this," Alex muttered, but other than that didn't move. I got off my horse. Bending down I examined the wound. The bullet had missed anything life threatening, but if the wound wasn't sewn up soon he would be dead.

"Jacob," I called as I stood up.

"What did Alex do this time?" Jacob asked.

"You got a sewing needle?" I asked. Jacob came around Alex's horse and saw him lying there.

"We should've dealt with this before you bled for the last few hours," Jacob told Alex before going back to his horse.

"Is something wrong?" Lord Bennett asked.

"We need to rest for about ten minutes," Jacob told him, "Alex needs it."

"Then we'll have lunch and perhaps a chance to stretch our legs," Lord Bennett said. Jacob brought a packet over. Alex shrugged off his jacket.

"Got any alcohol?" Jacob asked.

"No," I answered.

"Right saddlebag," Alex said through clenched teeth. I went around and pulled out the bottle of whiskey. Going back around the horse, I handed the bottle to Jacob. Alex's shirt was open to the wound, but no farther up. Jacob poured whiskey on the wound and Alex hissed. Jacob poured whiskey on the needle before starting to stitch the wound together. I saw Lord and Lady Bennett get out and wander a little way away from the coach. Once the stitching was done Jacob washed the area.

"Are you done yet?" Alex asked. Jacob didn't answer; he just bandaged the wound.

"Done," Jacob said standing up. He washed his fingers with the water before putting everything back in the packet. Alex stayed still for a minute before trying to sit up. Jacob got the food. He handed it out. Alex ate a little.

"You gonna be able to ride?" Jacob asked.

"Yeah, just give me a minute," Alex said.

"You'll need to see a doctor when we get to the next town," I said.

"Survived worse without one," Alex said, "No point wasting their time." Alex stood up slowly. He reached down and grabbed his jacket. After dusting it off he put it on.

"Bath would be nice though," Alex muttered. He got back on his horse.

"Are we ready to get under way again?" Lord Bennett asked.

"Yes," Jacob answered. Everything was put away and we all mounted our horses. Lord and Lady Bennett got into the coach.

And we started moving again.

Night was falling as we entered the next town. Plantville is the smallest place I've ever seen that was called a town. There was a short main street with a boarding house serving as the hotel and a general store occupied the lobby. The stables were on the other side of the street. Lord and Lady Bennett walked from the stables to the boarding house. The rest of us put our horses away before going across the street. The woman, who met us at the door, gave us a once over and told us that there weren't any more rooms and sent us back over to the stables to sleep in the loft. Jacob managed to beg some supper before she turned us out. We were rushed through to the kitchen, where we each received a bowl of soup and some bread. Alex ate two or three mouthfuls of soup and two bites of bread before giving the cook some money and heading off. The coach driver, Jacob and I finished the meal, paid our share and then went to the stables. Alex wasn't there.

"Probably went lookin' for some place to bathe," Jacob answered, when the driver asked where Alex went. I left them as they got ready to go to sleep.

Most of the buildings were dark, the exceptions being the sheriff's office, the church and a small shack. From the noise I guessed that the shack was the town saloon, but I didn't see Alex through the lighted windows. The light in the church was a lit candle in one window. The light in the sheriff's office showed a man sitting at the desk working and another man sleeping on a cot against the wall.

I started to wander back. I had just passed the closed up blacksmith shop when I heard a moan. I went toward it. Alex lay, half propped up by the side of the building.

"What happened?" I asked bending down.

"I pulled a stitch," Alex muttered, "Doctor is down the street. I asked the cook. She said the white house. I collapsed before I got that far."

"Here, let me help you," I said helping him up. Once we were both standing we started for the doctor's house with me supporting most of his weight. He was light enough that I could probably have carried him, but I figured he wouldn't go for that option. At the end of the main street there was a white house standing alone. We went up on the porch. I knocked. A moment later a light appeared in the window. The door opened. A man stood there blinking at us through his spectacles. He was in his nightshirt, but had pulled pants on under it.

"Can I help you?" he asked rubbing a hand through his short, dirty-blond hair.

"Are you the doctor?" I asked.

"I am," he answered.

"Fitzgerald?" Alex asked.

"Alex?" the man said. He opened the door and we entered the small office.

"You moved up in the world," Alex commented, blinking at the brightness of the room.

"What're you doing here?" Fitzgerald asked.

"Pulled a stitch after Jacob patched me up," Alex answered. I guided Alex over to the bed. He sat down.

"Someone shoot you or something?" Fitzgerald asked, gathering the supplies he thought he might need.

"Bullet's gone already," Alex said, "Last time I saw you, you were drinking yourself dead."

"I got tossed on a wagon, along with other men destined for someone's field," Fitzgerald said, "They got this far and I fell off the wagon. The town took me in once they found out I was a doctor. But to continue living here I gotta stay dry."

"Nice," Alex commented before slumping over.

"What are you doing here?" Fitzgerald asked.

"Jacob got a job guarding a lord and lady," Alex said, "Toby here an' I got dragged into it."

"You deserve the bullet?" Fitzgerald asked.

"Common bandits," Alex said.

"I need you to sit up and remove your jacket and shirt," Fitzgerald said. Alex sat up and shrugged out of his jacket. Then slumped over again. This time his eyes closed.

"Passed out," Fitzgerald muttered, then spoke louder, "Help me lay him out." I helped move Alex so that Fitzgerald could tend to the injury. Fitzgerald unbuttoned Alex's shirt and started to deal with the wound.

I'm no doctor, but I do know what anatomy men are supposed to have and what women are supposed to have. And from looking at Alex, I would have to say that for a gunslinger she is good for her gender.

Once he was finished Fitzgerald buttoned up Alex's shirt, tossed a blanket over her and signaled me to join him in the other room. The room was a kitchen. We each took a chair at the table.

"From the look on your face I would say neither of us knew that Alex was female," Fitzgerald said.

"I only met Alex a couple of days ago and every indication was that she was male," I said, "'Specially her voice."

"Her voice box might have been damaged during whatever happened that caused the scars on her throat," Fitzgerald said, "I've known her for two years and I never knew. She was good at hiding it."

"The question is what now?" I asked.

"We can tell her we know, but I think this should stay between us," Fitzgerald said, "Jacob must have known this. He keeps claiming that he trained her."

"Then probably," I replied. A groan came from the other room. We both stood up and went into the other room. Alex was awake, but hadn't moved.

"I repaired the pulled stitch," Fitzgerald said, "But you need to rest."

"Have to be able to leave tomorrow," Alex said.

"Then rest tonight," Fitzgerald said. Alex closed her eyes and seemed to drift off to sleep.

"Don't tell, please," Alex muttered.

"We won't," I told her and she was asleep, "I better get back."

"Fine," Fitzgerald said. I left the house and walked back to the stable. When I got there Jacob and the driver were fast asleep. I made a bed a little way from them and lay down.

The sky was the pinkish purple when I opened my eyes.

"Time to get up," Jacob told me.

"I'm movin'," I said sitting up. He was ready to go.

"Where's Alex?" Jacob asked.

"Let's go," the driver called down. I grabbed my stuff and went down to get my horse ready. Jacob's horse was ready and waiting. I was just about ready when Alex came into the barn. She looked like she hadn't had a good sleep, but she was standing without favouring her side.

"Who'd you spend the night with?" the driver asked with a laugh.

"The doctor for company, but in separate beds," Alex answered going to her horse. The rest of us went to wait for Lord and Lady Bennett. Alex came out a moment later.

"This sunrise stuff is too much," Alex said.

"Whatever it takes to get the job done," Jacob replied.

"If you find me another job that means I have to get up before sunrise, I will shoot you," Alex told Jacob, "I can find jobs that don't require early rising all the time, why can't you?" Jacob didn't respond.

Lord and Lady Bennett came out and entered the coach. We took up our positions as the coach started moving. Fitzgerald was out on his porch as we rode passed.

"Was that Fitzgerald?" Jacob asked once we were passed.

"He's the local doctor," Alex answered.

"He can remember that much medicine?" Jacob asked. Alex was silent, but the type of silence that filled the air with many insults unspoken. No one said anything as we continued our journey.

There were no more incidents during our journey to Dustcloud, but both Alex and I were ready to hang Jacob by the time we got there.

Dustcloud was a bustling city. It had every kind of store you could think of and any kind of business you could want, not all of them ethical. And it was filled with people from many places. It was noisy but it didn't smell as bad as most cities.

We stopped in front of the hotel in Dustcloud. Lord Bennett got out of the coach and came over to us.

"Here is the rest of the money," Lord Bennett said as he handed Jacob another stack of bills.

"Pleasure doin' business," Jacob said. Lady Bennett had gotten out of the coach as well and was waiting for Lord Bennett.

"Perhaps we can do business again," Lord Bennett said.

"Any time you are around, just drop in," Jacob said.

"I will," Lord Bennett said, then turned and started toward his wife. The gunshot came from somewhere behind us, and then Lord Bennett fell forward. Alex wheeled her horse around and was chasing after someone. Jacob was off his horse and running over to Lord Bennett, though Lady Bennett was already there. I wheeled my horse around and went after Alex. I caught up with her on the next street. There was a man running along the boardwalk with a gun in his hand. Alex was following him and I joined her. The man turned down the next street; we were just a moment behind him. But when we turned the corner he was gone. We slowed down. Alex got off her horse and handed me the reins. She went up on the boardwalk and started looking in shops and looking at the various people along the boardwalk. After ten minutes she gave up and mounted her horse.

"We lost him," Alex said.

"Let's get back," I suggested. It was a depressing walk that took us back to the hotel. Jacob and Lady Bennett were still there, but Lord Bennett was gone. We got down off our horses, tied them to the hitching post and went up to them.

"He's dead," Lady Bennett said, "The doctor has already taken him away."

"I'm sorry," I said.

"Did you catch him?" Jacob asked.

"He managed to slip away," Alex answered, she looked at Lady Bennett, "I'm sorry."

"I know that you were expecting to go home now," Lady Bennett said, "But I hope you will stay. I want my husband's killer to pay for what he did."

"Lady Bennett, I know you are upset, but that is not a good idea," Jacob sounded like he was trying to be calming.

"I will pay you," Lady Bennett's tone was firm.

"Once you're secure in your room, I'll continue my search from where I left off," Alex replied.

"Alex, this isn't a good idea," Jacob scowled at her.

"Jacob, help the lady or go home," I told him. Lady Bennett nodded. "I'll escort you to your room. Are your bags already up there?"

"Yes," Lady Bennett said. She allowed me to escort her up to her room. I checked it to make sure there was no danger and then went back down to Alex. Jacob was gone.

"What's his problem?" I asked as Alex and I took the reins of our horses.

"He doesn't like revenge jobs," Alex answered, "But I'd say the person who shot Lord Bennett purposely waited 'til we were paid off."

"We get paid off, leave and Lady Bennett is a widow without answers?" I asked.

"Most people don't wait around for the next job, they get paid an' leave. If they stayed it would be with the promise of more money than before," Alex explained.

"Apparently I need more practise as a gunslinger before I'll understand it," I said.

"You're doin' good so far," Alex said. We reached the stable. We paid the stable owner and left our horses with him. We went back to the boardwalk where we had lost the man.

We went up one side of the street and down the other side; checking both streets off of it and the alleys behind the buildings. We couldn't find the shooter and no one remembered seeing a man that Alex described has having a fresh scar that ran across his right cheek. We had hit a dead end.

"You'd think with the way we chased him down the street someone would remember him," I said.

"We'll check the rest of the town tomorrow," Alex said, "I need to rest." She looked tired and was starting to favour her side again.

"You gonna be all right?" I asked.

"Yes, I just need to rest," Alex answered. I spotted a cheap hotel and we stopped. They had one room left and we took it. I went back and got our saddlebags from the stable. By the time I got back Alex was lying on the bed fast sleep. I left her alone and went to the dining room and had supper.

I had just finished and paid the bill when I saw a man wearing the same clothes as the man who shot Lord Bennett walk through the dining room. He had a fresh scar across his right cheek. I followed him. He went through the kitchen and out the back door. Once in the alley he went into the back door a few buildings down. If I remembered correctly the building was a ladies clothing store from the front. I waited a moment before opening the door. From the little bit of light shining inside, it looked like a storeroom, but I couldn't see any farther. I backed out and closed the door behind me.

I knew Lady Bennett was counting on us to find her husband's killer and any good gunslinger would probably just walk in and deal with the problem. But one, I'm not a professional gunslinger or even much of a gunslinger. I'm a farmer that can hit eight times out of ten. Two, my backup has no idea where I went. And three, I had hoped to see my mother at least once more before I died.

I headed back to the hotel room. Alex hadn't moved. I borrowed a blanket and pillow. Lying down on the floor I slowly drifted off to sleep.

The sun was shining in the window and I had managed to find the one spot on the floor where it hit. I sat up instantly and finished waking up as I looked around. Alex was still asleep. Leaving her alone, I washed up and went downstairs. The desk clerk gave me a message. It was from Lady Bennett hoping that we could come to breakfast with her so that she could learn the latest developments. I went back upstairs. Alex was sitting up and rubbing the sleep out of her eyes.

"Lady Bennett wishes to speak with us over breakfast," I told her.

"Gimme a minute, I'm still asleep," Alex said. I left the room and went down to the lobby. Alex came down ten minutes later. She looked better, the tiredness was gone and she had found some clean clothes.

We walked over to Lady Bennett's hotel. The hostess ushered us to a private dining table. Lady Bennett was waiting for us, with breakfast already laid out. We each sat down. Lady Bennett didn't say anything until half way through breakfast, which was about the time that Alex stopped eating anyway. Alex filled her in on everything we did yesterday while I ate.

I finished eating just as she completed. Then I told them what I had seen last night.

"Apparently you found the right hotel," Lady Bennett said when I had finished.

"I was thinking it might be a good idea to go back an' look around during the day," I said.

"You said it was a woman's clothing store?" Lady Bennett asked.

"Yes, one of the fancy places," I answered.

"I need a dress for my husband's funeral," Lady Bennett said,

"And I'm sure they wouldn't run off a paying customer."

"Then Toby will go with you and look around," Alex said, "I'm going back to where we lost the man the first time. I keep getting the feeling I missed something."

"Excellent," Lady Bennett said as she stood up. Alex and I followed her out of the dining room. Out on the street Alex went one way and Lady Bennett and I went the other.

I was correct that it was a women's clothing store in building that the man had gone into. Lady Bennett sailed through the door, like only a noblewoman could do, and I followed her inside. The clerk was there before Lady Bennett stopped.

"How may I help you?" the woman asked.

"I need two black dresses," Lady Bennett said.

"Are you sure that you want black?" The clerk asked, "At this time of the season, it isn't the best choice for dresses."

"They are for my husband's funeral," Lady Bennett said, the tone of her voice dropping several degrees.

"I'm sorry," the clerk said. "What style were you looking for?" Lady Bennett's tone lightened as the clerk led her over to a pile of pattern books; they started talking about dresses. I put a bored look on my face, which wasn't hard after a minute of their gibberish, and started to wander the store. Apparently we were the only ones in the store. The front part of the store took up half the building with its displays, dressing area, counter and pile of bolts of material. Behind one of the screens in the dressing area was a doorway. Lady Bennett had the clerk's full attention, so I stepped through the doorway. It opened to a stairway. I went up to the second floor. It was a bare room with several tables, all with sewing machines on them. The room was the length of the building. I went back downstairs to the main room. The clerk hadn't noticed that I had disappeared. I sat down in one of the chairs reserved for men, who were shopping with their wives.

We were there for a good two hours while Lady Bennett and the clerk talked the dresses over. The only thing out of the ordinary that I noticed was that no one else came in the whole time we were there.

When they were finished Lady Bennett started for the door. I stood up and followed her out.

"I hope that was as useful to you as it was for me," Lady

Bennett said once we were halfway down the street.

"It was somewhat informative," I replied.

"Meaning?" Lady Bennett asked.

"The shop isn't connected to the warehouse that shares the other half of the main floor," I answered.

"Just the main floor?" Alex's voice asked from beside me, causing Lady Bennett and me to jump, "Sorry, I finished before you and figured I would wait for you outside the shop."

"The second floor is a workroom and storage space for the clothing shop," I replied.

"Then we'll have to check the warehouse," Alex said.

"What did you find?" Lady Bennett asked.

"A short cut into the alley," Alex answered, "And an old man who says the man we are looking is a thief. I also talked to the sheriff."

"And is he doing anything to help catch my husband's killer?" Lady Bennett asked.

"He and his deputies have their hands full with a massacre outside of town," Alex answered, "Otherwise he would be telling us to back off and leave it to the law. But the sheriff said that if we bring the man in he'll make sure the man gets hung proper an' legal."

"And if we have to shoot him?" I asked.

"He and the doctor will deal with it," Alex replied.

"I should get back so that you two can get on with things," Lady Bennett said. Alex and I escorted Lady Bennett to her hotel, before heading back to the building. This time we went to the door in the alley.

The door opened when I twisted the knob. Alex stepped inside and I followed her. It was dark like the night before, but once I had closed the door I could see a light on the far side of the room. There were piles of crates in neat rows with paths through the piles. Alex and I moved toward the light. When we got close enough I could see that it was lamp sitting on a crate. There wasn't anyone near the crate.

Alex held her hand up as if to ask me to stay still. I froze and listened. All I could hear was my own breathing. Alex scraped her boot against one crate. The sound seemed to echo in the quiet. Then all was silent again. A minute passed, then two.

"I think we're alone," Alex said. She started toward the lamp. I hesitated, and then followed her at a slower pace.

Alex started searching through everything around the crate.

"He sleeps here, but doesn't eat here." Alex picked up the lamp. "I wonder what's in all these crates."

I stepped close to her and lifted one off the pile. After setting it on the floor, I pulled the lid off and Alex shone the light in. The gold reflected the light back. Each brick was carefully laid in the straw in a row. Based on the one row of bricks, I would say that there had been another row on top of them.

"Looks like he's selling them," I said. Alex took one out and examined it.

"Lord Bennett's stamp," Alex said turning it over and pointing out the markings.

"He stole gold from Lord Bennett and then shot him?" I asked, "That doesn't make sense."

"Let's put everything back," Alex suggested, "And go back to Lady Bennett… see if she knows something about the gold being stolen."

"Do you think she did this?" I asked.

"No, I don't believe she had her husband killed, nor do I believe she was involved with any thieves," Alex answered, "But she may have more information than she knows."

Alex put the brick back. I put the lid back on the crate and placed it back on the pile. Alex placed the lamp on the other crate. We left the building and went back to Lady Bennett's hotel.

We asked for her at the front desk and were escorted up to her rooms. She was sitting at a table, having tea.

"Did you catch the man?" Lady Bennett asked.

"He wasn't there," I answered, "He seems to only sleep there."

"Then what did you find?" Lady Bennett asked.

"Gold bricks, "Alex said, "with Lord Bennett's mark on them."

"Looks like the man has been selling them one at a time," I said. Lady Bennett sighed.

"We came from the old country because Patrick inherited the deed to a mine after his brother died," Lady Bennett said, "We were going bankrupt in a hurry and his father asked us to remove ourselves from his household. In the old country nobility cannot take just any job, they must take a job that befits their title. Which means they need money. Coming here we were treated like royalty, but no one thought twice when my husband worked the mine. In three short weeks he had enough money from the mine to hire other workers. After three years we had enough to move back to the old country and live the rest of our lives like kings. Patrick gave the mine to his foreman and we departed to travel the land we now called home.

"About a year ago a shipment of gold was hijacked. Patrick wanted justice, but no one was willing to do much. They claimed that the robbers were long gone and unless the bars started to turn up there was nothing they could do. So, Patrick started to look into it. He tracked all the gold that showed up in a couple towns back to their source. He found three of the four robbers. He knew that the last one was here somewhere."

"But the robber found him first," Alex said.

"From what you said, yes," Lady Bennett replied.

"Some of this would've been nice to know before we took the job guarding you," I commented.

"Patrick was worried that Jacob might demand to protect him as he searched for the robber. Another person could have put Patrick in more danger instead of less," Lady Bennett said.

"I'm gonna see if Jacob is still in town," Alex said.

"To see if he'll help?" Lady Bennett asked.

"Not quite," Alex said, "We'll deal with the robber when he goes back to the warehouse for the night."

"Thank you," Lady Bennett said, "If you come back and tell me he has been caught, I will pay you."

"See you tomorrow morning," I said and then Alex and I left. We left the hotel and started down the street the way Jacob had gone the day before.

"What do you want to see Jacob about?" I asked.

"I thought I might punch him," Alex answered.

"I'm not sure it would help or even make him understand," I said. Alex didn't respond.

She stopped at a cheap hotel down the street from Lady Bennett's hotel. I followed her inside. Alex stopped at the front desk.

"Excuse me," She said to the clerk. He looked up. "Do you have a Jacob Wescott staying here?" Alex placed a bill on the desk.

"Sure," the clerk answered, his eyes on the bill, "Room 104."

"Do you know if he's currently in his room?" Alex asked keeping her hand on the bill.

"Yeah, he came in after lunch and hasn't gone out since," the clerk answered. Alex slid the bill to the clerk then we started upstairs.

Alex stopped at room 104 and knocked on the door. There was no answer. She twisted the knob and the door opened. I followed her inside. Jacob was passed out on the bed, snoring.

"And he was complaining about your habits," I commented.

"He doesn't mix business with pleasure, but the minute business is finished pleasure takes over," Alex said, "Probably played poker an' drank until just before he came back to the hotel."

"So, what now?" I asked. Alex didn't respond, just stood and looked at Jacob.

After a moment she started to take his boots off. I wasn't sure what she was doing until she checked the boot over. She pulled the other off and did the same thing, his hat was next and then his pockets. From his shirt pocket she pulled out a wad of bills. She counted out a certain number and handed them to me. I put them away. She counted out the same amount for herself. Once she had put her amount away there was only ten dollars left.

"Makes you wonder if he was going to pay us," I said.

"My guess is he took the three thousand and played poker with it and we just took his winnings," Alex said, "He's done it to me before. Never did get paid for that job." Alex slapped the last of the money on to Jacob's chest. He grunted, but didn't wake up.

"I know he can win at poker, but he has to stay sober to do it," Alex said as she stepped out of the room. I followed her and closed the door behind me.

"Does Nadine know 'bout his gambling an' drinking?" I asked as we went downstairs.

"He usually does it when traveling, so she may not," Alex answered. We left the hotel.

"Then we have something over him," I said. We started down the street toward the saloon.

"Hell, at this point I'd just tell her," Alex said, "Maybe he'll shape up after that." We stepped inside. We each ordered a whiskey and then Alex found the poker table. I stayed at the bar and watched. She was good. I am good enough to tell who was cheating, but Alex was winning against them. It was getting into the evening and the other players were leaving for supper when Alex decided it was time to quit.

She came over to where I was leaning against the bar.

"That was a good game," she said as she put the money away.

"Not bad," I commented.

"Let's see you do better," Alex said.

"Is there anything you aren't good at?" I asked.

"Yeah, but I stay way from them," Alex answered. I nodded then straightened up. We left the bar and found some place serving food.

After supper Alex and I went back to the warehouse. Going inside we checked and found no one there. We sat down in a dark corner and waited. I was just about asleep when the door opened. The thief came in and headed straight for the lamp.

Alex didn't move. I was wondering if she was even awake when she signaled not to move. The thief moved around out of sight before the lamp went out. I sensed that Alex still didn't move. We waited until we could hear the thief snoring. Then Alex lit a match as she started to move forward. I followed until the match went out. When Alex lit another she used it to light the lamp. The thief was still sleeping. I recognized him as the man that killed Lord Bennett. Alex used some rope to tie the thief up. He must have been a heavy sleeper because he was still sleeping when she had finished and she wasn't being gentle.

"Now, we go find the sheriff," Alex said. We left the thief and headed to the sheriff's office. The sheriff was on his way out of his office when we got there, but he stopped when he saw us.

"Did you catch him?" the sheriff asked.

"Without much shooting, unfortunately," Alex answered.

"But fortunately for me," the sheriff said, "Show me."

We led him back to the thief.

"I recognize him," the sheriff said, "This fellow will steal anything that isn't tied down."

"That must be what's in these crates," I said.

"You didn't look?" the sheriff asked.

"We looked in one," Alex answered, "It contained gold bricks with Lord Bennett's mark on them."

"Let's see what's in the rest," the sheriff said. Each of us took a pile and started to open crates. Alex's pile held fancy dresses and expensive looking material, the sheriff's held guns, and mine held assorted valuables like candlesticks, silverware and jewellery.

"Quite the collector," the sheriff commented, "I think I even recognize where some of this stuff came from."

"Then you can return it," Alex said.

"I will, but first we need to put this thief in prison," the sheriff said. He went over to the thief and grabbed one arm, I grabbed the other and we carried him to the sheriff's office. Alex followed us.

Once there the deputy opened doors so that we could put the thief directly into the cell. After the thief was locked up Alex and I went back to our hotel. In our room Alex wrapped herself up in her bedroll and I lay down in the bed.

"What are you gonna do now?" I asked Alex.

"Move on," Alex answered, "Not much else to do. What about you?"

"I don't know," I answered, "I was drifting when Jacob hijacked me."

"You're not bad for a partner," Alex said, "You can come along with me if you want. It tends to get lonely out there."

"Sounds good," I replied.

"We'll see how you feel when it's you against thirty," Alex said.

"Two people means fifteen each, not too bad for odds," I said.

"I meant thirty each," Alex said then rolled over as if to end the conversation.

"Could be worse odds," I said closing my eyes.

"I hope not," Alex said. I smiled and went to sleep.

I woke up before Alex did. I got out of bed, trying to be quiet. I washed up and went down stairs. I had just been served breakfast when Alex came down. She sat down across from me and was brought breakfast shortly.

"I thought you'd sleep longer," I said.

"I'm a heavy sleeper when I first go to sleep and by morning I'm only sleeping lightly," Alex replied, "Your moving around woke me."

"Sorry," I said. Alex shrugged. We didn't say anything through the rest of breakfast. Afterward we headed for Lady Bennett's hotel.

Jacob was sitting in the lobby waiting for us.

"There you two are," Jacob said getting up and coming toward us.

"Don't tell us, you found another job for us," Alex said.

"You stole from me," Jacob said.

"Only as much as you owed us," I answered, "We tried to wake you, but you were too drunk."

"Fifteen hundred times two is three thousand," Alex said, "Three thousand divided by three people is a thousand each. If you choose to gamble your thousand away that's your problem."

"That doesn't give you a right to enter a man's room and take his money," Jacob said.

"We did the work, we wanted the pay," Alex said, "By the way, does Nadine know that you have problems with drinking an' gambling?"

"I don't have problems with drinking an' gambling," Jacob said.

"Shall I tell her and see if she agrees?" Alex asked.

"You won't," Jacob said.

"Not if you drop the matter," Alex replied. Jacob looked like he was going to argue, but finally he moved around Alex and walked away.

Lady Bennett was standing at the bottom of the stairs watching us.

"Is something wrong?" she asked.

"No," I answered.

"Jacob didn't look too happy," Lady Bennett said.

"We caught your husband's killer," Alex said, "He is currently sitting in prison awaiting trial."

"Do you think he'll be hung?" Lady Bennett asked.

"Murder on top of robbery is hard to explain away," I answered.

"I will have to go to the sheriff's office and find out when the trial is," Lady Bennett said. She waited as if expecting us to tell her it wasn't a good idea for a lady to go to the trial. She wasn't gonna hear that from us.

"Anyway, thank you both for your help," Lady Bennett said, she took out her wallet and handed each of us some bills.

"You're welcome, Lady Bennett," I answered.

"If you ever need us again, we'll be around," Alex said.

"Lady Grace, if you don't mind," Lady Bennett said.

"Yes, Lady Grace," I said then Alex and I left the hotel. We headed for the stable.

THE BANK JOB
CHAPTER 2

Toby

Once we were out town I let Alex lead. She seemed to know where she was going. We retraced our steps to the town before Dustcloud. After eating lunch we headed off in another direction. We left the trees and went into the desert, but we traveled the edge of it so the trees were never far from sight. We came across a village about mid-afternoon. Alex stopped briefly to study the bulletin board in front of the general store before we continued.

When night fell we hadn't reached the next town, so we set up camp. I fell asleep the minute I closed my eyes.

It was before dawn when I woke up. Something had woken me, but I couldn't figure out what. There was the sound again. I sat up and looked around. There wasn't much light to see by, but I couldn't see anything that would make that sound. It was almost sound like a whimper. It came again, this time I figured it was coming from somewhere close to Alex. I stood up and stepped close her. She tossed in her sleep and whimpered again. The first streaks of light came across the sky and I could see Alex's face. She looked like she was in pain.

"Alex," I said touching her shoulder. She jerked awake. The fear in her eyes faded as she looked around.

"You were having a nightmare," I said.

"Not unusual." Alex rubbed the sleep out of one eye, "But since we both seem to be awake, we can get moving." She started getting up. I went back over to my stuff and started packing up. Alex did the same with her gear. In ten minutes we were packed and back to riding.

"Have nightmares often?" I asked.

"They come an' go," Alex answered, "I don't usually get back to sleep after I've woken up from one." I nodded and we rode without talking.

We traveled for two more days, stopping for the night where we could camp. There weren't any signs of civilization until the third day. Then we saw five buildings standing in the desert. Three of them were private homes and the other two were the hotel and the stable. We left our horses in the stable and got rooms at the hotel.

After being there two days Alex said she had found us a job, which in this hole-in-the-wall was some accomplishment. So I didn't question it and met her at the stables when she told me to. The rain had started that morning; it looked like the yearly storm. Alex was standing just inside the stables that were across from the hotel. Her horse was ready. She didn't say anything to me as I passed her, so I got my horse ready.

I went back to where she was standing.

"What is it?" I asked.

"Second floor, third window from the left," Alex said, her eyes not moving from what they were looking at. I looked at the window she indicted. I could see that there was a man standing there, but I couldn't see any details.

"He's been there for an hour," Alex said, "I noticed him when I came in and he didn't move the whole time it took to get my horse ready."

"Must be waiting for someone," I said.

"But who?" Alex said. Four men came in to the stable, they looked like they had ridden into town after a week of traveling and hadn't bothered to get cleaned up. All of them had long greasy hair, long beards, hats pulled low against the rain which soaked through their pants and jackets. The leader had two gunbelts across his chest in an x, a scar across the right side of his mouth, and black hair. The two looked like brothers with their matching dark brown hair, blue eyes, and Winchesters strapped on their backs. The fourth member of the crew had two guns in a black holster, his brown hair was streaked with grey and a round scar on his left cheek that looked like a bullet wound

"There you are," the leader said, "What're you two ladies waitin' for, the rain to stop?" I immediately didn't like the leader; if this was the job then I hoped I would get to shoot him afterward.

"Waiting for you four to get your dresses on," Alex answered as she headed back to her horse. I went to mine as the four men laughed. We all mounted our horses and rode out of the stable together. As we left town Alex and I dropped back a pace from the rest. I wanted to ask her about this job, but I didn't say anything.

It rained all night, so we rested the horses and just kept going. These men seemed to be either laughing at horrific jokes or silent. Alex kept silent.

The next night we found shelter and slept around a fire. By the morning it had stopped raining as we continued on.

It was afternoon when Alex slowed down to put more space between us and the four men.

"What is it?" I asked.

"The man from the window is following us," Alex said.

"Then who is he after, us or them?" I asked.

"I don't remember seeing him before, so unless you have, it's unlikely to be us," Alex answered.

"What's the job anyway?" I asked.

"Robbing a bank," Alex answered.

"What?" I asked a little louder than I should have. The men didn't notice. Alex took a few minutes to compose her answer. I waited impatiently.

"These men rob banks," she said, "They lost two men in the last job an' they need two men to help with this one."

"Us," I said.

"Yes," Alex replied.

"And what're we suppose to do?" I asked.

"Go into the bank, see what the set up is," Alex answered, "And report back to them. Then after they have pulled the job, we send the sheriff in the opposite direction."

"Is this the kind of job you usually do?" I asked, "Because if it is, I should have gone with Jacob."

Alex didn't respond, didn't even look at me. Either I read her wrong or something else was going on here. I guess I would just have to wait and see.

As dusk started to fall the four men stopped and headed for a cave. Alex and I kept going. We reached town just after the sun went down. We found a stable for our horses before heading to the hotel. We got the last two rooms. After putting our gear in our rooms Alex and I found a poker game. Alex stayed back and watched while I played.

There were three other players, all of them had greying hair and pressed clothes. The man across from me wore the star of the sheriff's office.

"So, what're you strangers doing in town?" he asked as the cards were dealt.

"Looking for a place to rest for the night," I answered as I looked at my cards, not bad.

"You waiting for the gold train?" the man to the right of me asked.

"Gold train?" Alex asked.

"Yeah, caravan that comes through monthly, takes the gold from the mines to Dustcloud," the man answered as the sheriff glared at him over his cards, "Stops though here to exchange guards."

"We're just stopping to rest," I answered. The sheriff's hand topped mine.

"You two look like you would be good at that kind of thing," the man said, "If you need a job you could probably get one guarding the gold train. Pay is good. You just have to go see Mr. Black."

I nodded as I looked at my new hand, even better than the last one.

I was just collecting my winnings when a man entered the bar. I could tell Alex recognized him. My guess was that he was the man that had been following us.

The sheriff saw him and stood up to greet him.

"Marshal," the sheriff said, "Good to see you." The marshal's eyes moved over the group, then stopped to rest on Alex. Alex met his gaze and the marshal's eyes moved back to the sheriff.

"Yes, I suppose it is good to be back," the marshal said. The sheriff sat down after shaking the marshal's hand. The marshal's eyes went from Alex and then to me and back at Alex.

"I recognize you two," the marshal said. The sheriff loosened his gun and looked at us suspiciously. "Weren't you in the company of four other men?"

"Better to ride in numbers," Alex said, "Less likely to get robbed."

"True," the marshal said, "But I don't see the other four men in town. Perhaps, they are wanted men? And you're here to tell them when the train is coming?"

"They don't know about the gold train," the sheriff said, "Spencer had to explain it to them."

"Then what are you here for?" the marshal asked us. I kept my mouth shut, I figured Alex could answer this time.

"To check over the bank for Henry's crew," Alex answered, straight faced directly to the marshal. The man on my left exhaled his drink onto the table. The sheriff's gun came out of its holster.

"I didn't catch your name," the marshal said.

"I'm Alex Turner, and this is my partner, Toby Lawton," Alex replied.

"Turner," the marshal said, "As in working with Thomas?"

"Should have shot him in the other leg," Alex replied. Now I was not sure if I should feel relieved that we weren't going to help rob a bank, confused at what was going on, or betrayed that Alex didn't tell me this before. Once again I thought I'll wait this out.

"Thomas won't be walking any time soon as is," the marshal said.

"Good, keeps him from tripping over his own feet," Alex replied, "Would've caught Henry's crew months ago if it wasn't for his feet."

"Now you're working for them?" the marshal asked.

"Only until I can get them caught," Alex answered, "They killed three men at the last bank."

"Thomas said you took off," the marshal said.

"Had to do a favour for an old friend," Alex replied. The sheriff had put his gun back and the cards had been dealt out again.

"When are Henry and his boys supposed to hit the bank?" the marshal asked.

"Tomorrow night," Alex answered.

"Then we'll catch them tomorrow night, and then maybe we can recruit you both to help with the gold train," the marshal said, "We lose too many good men trying to protect the gold and the government isn't in any hurry to put the railway out here."

I gathered up my winnings then started shuffling the cards.

"Fine with me," I replied. I dealt out the cards.

"I guess that's what we'll do," Alex said.

"Good," the marshal said. Then he had a drink and left.

I continued to play poker for another hour before I had decided it was time for bed. As I left the room Alex followed me.

"I was going to explain it to you," Alex said, "I just didn't want to do it where we could've been overheard."

"And once we were away from them?" I asked.

"I was going to tell you tomorrow and then we could go to the sheriff," Alex said, "I was working with a marshal, but he got shot and now all I have is the desire to hang these men without any authority to do so."

"Well, now you'll get to," I answered.

"You didn't have to volunteer us for the train job," Alex said.

"Since we're on that side of the law and they need help, I didn't see any problem," I said.

"I might be on that side of the law, but that kind of guard duty is tedious," Alex replied.

"Call it revenge for not telling me the whole story about the bank job," I said, before walking away.

I went up to my room for the night.

The next morning at breakfast I was half-finished when Alex came down. She sat down across from me.

"Why didn't you tell Jacob what you were doing?" I asked.

"Jacob likes certain kinds of jobs, specifically guard jobs for private citizens," Alex answered, "Bringing men in for the bounty on their heads is not something Jacob considers…honourable."

"And you do it because?"

"They're scum. They deserve hanging."

"Not much for mercy, are you?"

"Sure, I am, but only if the person deserves it. If the person killed innocent people for the fun of killing innocent people then no. If they were caught up in something without understanding the consequences then maybe."

"And Henry's crew?"

"Rob banks because they enjoy the rush and the more people they kill on the way in and out the better. Thomas came looking for me to help him catch them."

"No money attached?"

"The bounty, usually."

A plate of breakfast was set in front of Alex. She ate a little, leaving the rest.

Once I was finished we headed for the bank. The marshal was leaning against a post in front of it.

"So?" Alex asked.

"The bank manager knows, the sheriff is ready," the marshal answered, "You check out the bank, report to Henry's gang and we grab them when they show up to rob the bank tonight."

"All so easy," Alex said.

"You don't sound like you have confidence in this plan," the marshal said.

"Been trying to catch this gang for six months," Alex said, "If anything appears to be out of place then the job's off and we are headed for another town. And there's the possibility of us getting shot, because we tipped off the law."

"We'll get them," the marshal said.

"Thomas was cocky to start with too," Alex said before brushing past the marshal. The marshal looked at me; I shrugged. I followed Alex inside. Alex was standing to one side, watching the people work. The bank manager acknowledged us, but went on with his work. I let Alex work, because I had no idea what to look for. She stood there and watched for a full ten minutes before turning and leaving. I followed her out. The marshal was still outside. Alex was going to move past him, when he touched her shoulder and pointed down the road. I followed his finger. A cart drawn by a single horse was coming down the street. Alex shook her head.

"Slow as usual," Alex said.

"He followed them," the marshal said. The man saw us and stopped in front of the bank. The man was in his fifties with grey hair going white. His hat was white and his suit matched the redish-brown dust that had accumulated on it.

"You're late, Thomas," Alex told him.

"When you're lame it takes you longer to get to places," he replied.

"I hope they didn't recognize you on your way in," Alex said, "Otherwise they might turn tail and run before anyone has a chance to catch them."

"They may have shot me, but it was dark and I barely recognized them," Thomas said, "They don't know me from any other traveler. What happened to you?"

"Had to do a favour for an old friend," Alex answered, "But I was still on Henry's trail faster than you were. Even when you can't walk you are still behind, Thomas."

"But you haven't caught them yet," Thomas said.

"No, they hired me and my partner to check out the bank for them, since we got two of their men at the last bank," Alex said. Thomas looked at me.

"So, another attempt to stop them," Thomas said turning back to Alex.

"The marshal here thinks it'll be easy," Alex said.

"Sheriff in on it?" Thomas asked.

"Yes," Alex said.

"Then while you report to Henry, the marshal and I will talk to the sheriff," Thomas said, "Maybe I can save this situation by telling them the mistakes we've already made."

"Sounds good," Alex said. Thomas started toward the sheriff's office and the marshal followed on foot. Alex and I headed for the stable. We saddled our horses and rode out to where we had left the other four robbers. We left our horses outside the cave and went in. The four men were gathered around a fire just around the bend from the entrance.

"So?" the leader said.

"Vault's in the back," Alex said, "Only problems are the sheriff and a marshal who is passing through."

"A marshal?" Henry asked.

"Stopping to get the latest news an' drop off the latest wanted posters," Alex answered.

"Maybe we should wait," one of the other men said.

"No," Henry said, "We go tonight. The marshal isn't there for us. We'll go in the back of the bank and be out before he wakes up. Even the sheriff won't realize we've been there 'fore morning."

"You want us to wait until morning and mis-direct them?" Alex asked.

"They won't know which way to look," Henry said with a laugh, "You stay until morning, then you head west. We'll be waiting to split the loot an' then you go your separate way."

"Fine by us," Alex said.

"You trick us an' we shoot you," Henry said pointing his finger at us.

"Fine," Alex said. We left the cave and got back on our horses.

"Do you think they suspect anything?" I asked when we were half way back to town.

"No, if they did we wouldn't have been given a warning," Alex answered. Back in town we put our horses in the stable and headed for the sheriff's office. The sheriff, the marshal and Thomas were sitting around. Alex and I took the other two seats.

"Well?" Thomas asked.

"They're hitting the bank tonight, going in and out the back," Alex said, "Promised not the wake the neighbours."

"There's no way to rob the bank without making noise," the sheriff said.

"We thought that too once and we skipped a town," Thomas said, "Then we heard that they had hit the bank and no one knew till the next morning."

"And if we don't get them tonight?" the sheriff asked.

"They said to meet them west of here to give us our share and go different directions," Alex said, "That means you have to wait until the next robbery."

"Why?" the sheriff asked.

"Because they'll be trying to shoot us," Alex answered.

"Tonight we need to be in dark places and silent about it," Thomas said, "If they sense anything is wrong they'll turn an' run."

"We know what to do," the sheriff said.

"You also have to find the places before it's dark and no one can see you entering them or see you while you're there," Alex said, "Otherwise it won't work, it's been tried."

"Have people see you turn in early, then sneak to the place you have picked out," Thomas said.

"That seems extreme," the sheriff said.

"Yeah, but if it wasn't necessary this crew would have been hung already," Alex replied. Alex stood up and left the office. I followed her.

We found a private place and started playing poker. We were well matched, but she could beat me if she tried.

"Why a gunslinger?" I asked as she finished dealing out the hand.

"Why not?" Alex responded.

"Why not get married and settle down?" I asked.

"Like a proper lady?"

"Many ladies settle down and get married and I wouldn't call all of them proper."

"See my scars?"

"The ones that look like someone tried to slit your throat with a dull razor several times and failed?"

"Yeah, those. Those are the reason. Jacob picked me up, bloody and beaten, and with Nadine's help got me healthy again. But those first few days going out, I was still a lady and got looks from the people as if they had never seen a lady with a scar before. Jacob had been teaching me to shoot. So I decided I could be a gunslinger. I went back into town with the same scars, but this time as a male. No one looked twice, no one gave me extra room. No one cared or thought it was unusual."

"So you became a gunslinger?"

"Not much choice, lots of other jobs for men require things I can't do. As a gunslinger, people leave you alone and don't ask personal questions."

"Ever going to settle down?"

"Even men used to scars don't want their women to be a scarred as I am. Besides that would mean giving up this life, I enjoy my work."

"If you don't mind me asking, how did you get those scars?"

Alex was silent for a while; I thought she might not answer.

"I was raped by the man my parents wanted me to marry."

"And you didn't go back and confront him?"

"I was scared, I barely remember going in the opposite direction from town. Jacob found me where I had passed out after going as far as I could."

"Which is why you can't say no when he asks."

"Yeah, but some days it would be nice."

"Ever gonna go home and confront the man?"

"Maybe if the opportunity presents itself, otherwise no."

I nodded, but didn't ask any more questions. Alex left the quiet alone. We played poker until it was dark then we snuck to our hiding places.

I didn't know if anyone else was out there watching, but I was ready. It was a couple hours later when the four men came into town on horseback. They didn't talk to each other. They reached the back of the bank and went inside. Five minutes later they came out with bags of money.

"Stop!" a shout came from the other side of the street. The men started shooting at the voice and four guns shot back out of the darkness, including mine. After three bullets Alex's gun was silent. I thought maybe she had been shot by the men that were now shooting at all of us, but soon I could hear her gun going off. I stopped long enough to reload and started firing again. One of the men managed to get on his horse and ride off. Alex grabbed one of the other horses and rode after him. The rest of us took down the other three. We killed two and the third was wounded. The doctor was called and tended to the man once he was in a cell at the sheriff's office. I helped move the bodies to the mortician's then went back to the sheriff's office. We all sat waiting for Alex to come back. At some point I fell asleep in my chair.

I had just woken up when Alex rode back into town shortly before noon. She had the reins of the second horse in her hands. And slung across the back of the second horse was the main robber.

"Well, Henry, we caught you," Thomas said once Henry was taken down. Henry spat at Thomas, hitting his boots. Alex dismounted and tied the horses to the hitching post. She had a cut on the right side of her face, it wasn't deep but the blood had run down her chin.

"I don't like the plural there," Alex said to Thomas, "It sounds like you were there for the fight." Henry smirked.

"This's why I'm so hard to catch," Henry said, "The law can never agree with itself."

"I hope we agree that you need to be hung," Alex said.

"That we agree on," the marshal said before dragging Henry

inside the sheriff's office.

"The bounty," Alex said turning to Thomas. Thomas went back into the sheriff's office; Alex and I followed. He went through his pack and pulled out an envelope. He handed it to Alex. Alex took it and then we headed for the hotel. She stopped at her room and turned to me. She pulled out half of the money and offered it to me. I shook my head.

"You chased them, you're the one that got Henry," I said, "I only tagged along."

"You gonna do this every time?" Alex asked.

"No, so enjoy it while it lasts," I answered. Alex nodded, put the money back in the envelope and then went into her room. I went into mine. I put my hat on one of the bedposts, my jacket on the other and pulled my boots off. Lying down I closed my eyes and fell asleep.

I woke to a knock on my door. I sat up. It came again.

"Toby," Alex's voice called. I pulled on my boots and then opened the door. Alex was standing there. She had cleaned up and looked ready to get on our way.

"The riders for the train came in this morning, we're supposed to meet everyone else at the sheriff's office," Alex said.

"Right," I said turning back to my room. I put on my jacket and hat before grabbing my gear. I followed Alex down to the street. We went to the stables and saddled our horses and then went to the sheriff's office.

"Glad you two could make it," the marshal said seeing us.

"Would you have left us behind?" I asked.

"Only if necessary," the marshal answered. He moved on to talk to the next person. When everyone was ready each guard was given a position and the gold train started moving. The gold train was horse drawn wagons full of crates of gold with two guards on each side of a wagon. There were about fifteen wagons in all.

Because of the spacing no one talked as we rode. When night fell we stopped and made camp. The first guard shift was picked and the rest of us went to sleep.

Someone woke me up for the third shift. Everything was quiet.

At dawn everyone was woken up and the caravan started moving again.

Several men guarding the caravan were miners, some others farmers or just men that owned guns. Alex was right, this kind of guard duty was tedious. You stayed in your position and made sure nothing got close enough to touch the wagons. There was talking during meals, but otherwise there was little interaction between the men.

The third evening out, I volunteered to take the first shift. I was wandering along one side of the wagons when I heard a ripping sound. No one else seemed to have heard it. I moved quietly to the other side of the wagon. There was a dirty man trying to pull one of the crates out of the wagon, where he had cut the canvas. I walked over and tapped him on the shoulder with the barrel of my gun. He turned to look and stared down the barrel of my gun. He gulped.

"That isn't your property," I said.

"They would never miss one box," the man pleaded.

"Stealing is still stealing," I replied. The man let go of the box. One of the other guards came around the other end of the wagon, probably attracted by the sound of voices.

"I'll leave," the man said seeing the other guard.

"Did you take anything else?" I asked.

"No, just tried to take the box," the man said, "I swear."

"Then get out of here," I said, "And next time don't be stupid enough to try and steal."

"Yes," the man said nodding vigorously. Then he ran for it. The other guard came over.

"Why'd you let him go?" the guard asked, "He tried to steal a crate."

"If you want to go after him and shoot him go ahead," I said, "He was just looking for something he could sell for money." I pushed the crate back into place. When I was finished the guard fixed the canvas.

"Think he'll be back?" the guard asked.

"I doubt it," I answered. We went back the opposite way along the wagons. When the end of the shift came, the next person stood guard and I went to sleep.

In the morning we headed on our way. The ride had been quiet when six men suddenly came out of the trees around us on horse back with their guns drawn. The caravan stopped.

"No one has to get hurt if you do what you're told," one of the men near the front said. There was a gunshot from Alex's position and the nearest man to her fell off his horse. I shot the closest one to me. And the marshal shot the man that spoke. The other three men were having trouble getting their horses under control, as were a few of the guards. One man managed to get his horse under control enough to ride off. The other two men were shot. Once everything had calmed down some of the guards buried the bodies on the side of the road before we continued.

The rest of the day was quiet. Once again I volunteered for the first shift. I didn't hear or see anything strange.

The next day was also quiet with nothing happening other than the caravan steadily moving closer to Dustcloud. The two days after that went the same. On the afternoon of the third day we arrived in Dustcloud.

We entered the town and went to a warehouse guarded by several men. Once all of the wagons were inside, the marshal went over to the receiver who had a table set up outside the warehouse.

"It's all there," the marshal said.

"Once again thank you, marshal," the receiver said. He pulled some bills out of the metal box and handed them to the marshal. The marshal took them.

"See you in a month," the marshal said then walked away. One at a time the train guards went up to the man and collected their pay. Then they headed home to their families. Alex and I were the last ones to collect our pay. We mounted our horses. And once again Alex and I left Dustcloud without a direction.

"What now?" I asked.

"We ride," Alex answered, "Adventure happens when you aren't looking for it."

ADVENTURES IN GUNSLINGING
CHAPTER 3

Toby

We reached the next town, where Alex played poker for an evening. Not much happened, aside from one of the other players shooting the man that was cheating. The sheriff asked a couple questions, but everyone else was left alone. The next morning we moved on.

"What kind of jobs are you looking for?" I asked once the town was behind us.

"Good ones," Alex said, "Jacob only likes guard jobs. I will take ones where they hire you for your gun. Bounty hunting is more of a hobby; you do it while you are on other jobs. And I usually take the jobs for the side that has been wronged."

"Unless they're scum," I said.

"That's right," Alex said, "They may not pay as well and be more dangerous, but I can't seem to walk away from them."

"And you play poker if you need money," I said.

"If I need large amounts of money or if I'm bored, usually," Alex answered, "Been thinking about entering the tournament, but I 'm never there at the right time."

"The big one out at Riverside?" I asked.

"The biggest one I know of," Alex answered.

"You think you could get in?" I asked.

"Just have to play the qualifying rounds and find out," Alex answered, "But it’s seven months away."

"You need about two thousand dollars to enter the tournament," I said.

"I have one thousand," Alex said, "It’s the other thousand I need."

"Which means jobs that cover more than your living expenses," I said.

"That’s right," Alex said, "Do you have any goals in life?"

"Stay off the farm, do something interesting, and be good at whatever I decide to do," I answered, "So far, I'm not bad as a gunslinger."

"Seen worse that survived to retire," Alex said.

We reached the next town just before noon, so we stopped for lunch. On our way back to our horses, we saw one man shoot another in the middle of the street. Alex stopped and leaned on a post to watch. One of the men fell before he could draw his gun. The one on the ground was dressed in filthy coveralls and a dusty hat. The man still standing was dressed in a custom tailored pinstriped suit with grey hat. His black gunbelt had a shine to it and the silver revolver gleamed. The brown hair was slicked back, the grey eyes arrogant, and a body that had never done hard work in his life.

"Earl!" a female voice cried out and the woman rushed over to the man lying in the street. The shooter went to the far side of the street and into the saloon there. The woman was holding the man and crying. No one moved to help her; in fact most people went on their way. The woman looked up at the people.

"Help me," she cried out, but no one stopped. Alex stepped into the street and over to the woman. I followed. The woman looked at us in surprise.

"Where’s the doctor's office?" Alex asked her. The woman pointed out a building farther down the street. I picked up the body by slinging it over my shoulder. Everyone stopped to stare now. We walked to the doctor's office, the woman followed. Alex knocked on the door. There was no answer, so she tried the doorknob. The door opened. She held it for me and I entered. I went over and put the body on the bed. The doctor came in from the other room to see what was going on. Alex and I started for the door.

"You can't leave him here," the doctor said once he had identified who had been set on the bed.

"Couldn't leave him in the middle of the street either," I answered.

"Then take him somewhere else," the doctor wrung his hands, "Don't leave him here."

"He's dead," Alex said, "Bury him and then he'll be out of your office."

"I can't do that," the doctor said.

"Why? Someone made sure you can't use your hands?" I asked.

"You're new in town, aren't you?" the doctor said.

"Stopped in for lunch," I answered.

"The doctor is scared of Cutler," the woman said, "Earl was the only man in town who would stand up to him. Even the sheriff is too cowardly to do anything about Cutler's reign of terror." Alex shut the door, so that we were all inside.

"Reign of terror?" Alex asked.

"He shoots people for no reason, starts fights because someone looked at him wrong and believes he can have any woman," the woman said, "Earl stopped Cutler from molesting me."

"Enough talk, get this corpse out of my office," the doctor said.

"You will bury him," Alex said.

"Mister, you don't seem to get it," the doctor started.

"I got it alright. You're scared that Cutler will shoot you for burying the body. You forget that Cutler isn't likely to shoot the town doctor; he might need a doctor someday. I, on the other hand, don't need you." Alex pulled out her gun and pointed it at the doctor. "And I will shoot you if you don't put this man in the ground." The doctor went white.

"You can't do this," the doctor said.

"And what's stopping me?" Alex asked.

"It isn't like it's a big thing," I said, "Unless you really like having a rotting corpse in your office."

"We'll make sure Cutler doesn't shoot you until the job is done," Alex said. The doctor glared at us, he was scared and didn't want to give in. Finally he got his equipment together. I picked up the body and followed the doctor out of the office. Alex and the woman followed. People stopped and stared but left us alone as we made our way to the cemetery.

"So, who was Earl?" Alex asked the woman.

"He came into town a month ago and stayed when he found a job at the stables," the woman answered, "He had a gun and knew how to use it, but he seemed to prefer working in the stables. A week after getting here he started to mess with Cutler's business. And then a week and a half ago he stopped Cutler from molesting me. Today Cutler called Earl out of the stable and shot him before he even had a chance to defend himself."

"Earl ever give a last name?" Alex asked.

"Not that I know of," the woman answered. We reached the cemetery and the doctor went to the far corner and started to dig. I placed the body nearby. Alex and I stood and watched the doctor work. The woman stayed for a while, but then she had to get back to work. The sun was starting toward the horizon when the doctor had finished digging the grave. He placed the body in it and started shovelling the dirt back in. Night had fallen by the time he had finished. The doctor jammed a white cross at the head and went back to town.

"What do you think?" I asked.

"Better than leaving him in the street," Alex answered, "But I don't think his business is finished."

"What're we gonna do?" I asked.

"Go back to the saloon and see how much trouble we can get into," Alex answered.

"After you," I said. Alex started back into town; I followed her. She headed straight for the saloon that Cutler had gone into earlier. I followed a couple steps behind her. No one seemed to notice our entrance. We went to stand at the bar. There was a poker game going with Cutler sitting there winning everyone else's money. It looked like they should have just handed it over before they ever sat down. The barman came over.

"Whiskey," I said. He poured one and slid it over to me and looked at Alex expectantly. Alex ignored him and he went back down the bar. I poured the whiskey down my throat. Alex seemed to study everyone in the room before moving toward the poker table. I stayed at the bar.

Cutler looked up as he waited for the person to deal. He looked at Alex.

"You're the one who helped move the body," Cutler said.

"Had to do something, couldn't just leave him there," Alex said.

"Oh, you could have," Cutler said, "Would you like to join the game? I'm sure someone could move."

"No," Alex said, "I don't like playing with cheaters." Half of Cutler's mouth twitched.

"I don't cheat," Cutler said.

"Offering to shoot people if you don't win every other hand counts as cheating," Alex said. The rest of the saloon was becoming very quiet.

"You seem to have a purpose here," Cutler commented.

"I'd like to talk to you," Alex said, "Outside."

"And if I choose otherwise," Cutler asked as he loosened his gun.

"You won't," Alex said then walked out of the saloon.

"Excuse me," Cutler said pocketing his winnings and getting up from the table. He headed for the door. I followed giving him space as he went outside. Alex was standing where Earl had fallen. Cutler grinned as he started toward his end of the street. No one else came out of the saloon.

"You think you can beat me?" Cutler laughed. The first shot went off, from Alex's gun and Cutler's leg collapsed under him. Alex started to walk over to him. Cutler pulled out his gun to shoot back. I took it away from him. He turned to stare at me.

"Two against one, now that's cheating," Cutler said.

"You cheated Earl out of his life by having your gun already drawn," Alex said, "He never had a chance. And all he wanted was a quiet life."

"How do you know?" Cutler asked.

"Titus Earl could draw and could shoot, but cared nothing for those abilities," Alex said, "I met him one day about a year ago. All he wanted was somewhere to live a quiet life; to live where no one knew his reputation. He would have left you alone."

"Then he shouldn't have messed with my business," Cutler said.

"You make everyone else's business your business," Alex said, "He couldn't have stayed out of it when you made it include him. You saw a challenge, which is rare for you, but he wasn't taking the bait,"

"Now he's dead," Cutler said.

"And you think anyone is going to mourn you when you pass

on?" Alex asked, "Or do you think you'll be left in the middle of the street because no one wants to deal with you? Because I'm willing to bet there won't be anyone crying over your dead body. At least Titus Earl had that."

"So, what're you gonna do?" Cutler asked. Alex shot him in other leg, this time hitting him in the kneecap. Cutler screamed.

"No one has come running," Alex said, "This is strange in a town this size. No one to help you, no one to mourn you, no friends, not even the sheriff to charge me with murder."

"I don't need any of those," Cutler said.

"Good," Alex said, "Then we'll continue on and you can lie here in the middle of the street."

"That's it?" Cutler asked.

"No, but I prefer to save the best for last," Alex said pulling out some rope. I helped her tie his hands behind his back and gag him. Then we went to our horses and started out of town.

"Well, that was fun," Alex said.

"Did you really know Earl?" I asked.

"Yes, actually," Alex answered, "Miserable son of a bitch, but he was pretty much harmless. He had been talked into the job by some man. I was broke and looking for a job. He watched as someone challenged me to a shoot out. I won. I took the challenger's money, bullets and any else that was worth taking. So Earl offered me a chance to help with his job. Which as it turned out was to sit back with a frown as I did all the work. We got back to the man who was paying for the job. He only gave Earl half of what he said he would pay. I shot the man in the foot. The man was hopping around cursing at me. And I offered to shoot the other if he didn't pay the rest of the money. He paid up and I shot him in the other foot. Earl was killing himself laughing as we walked away. First and only time I ever heard him laugh through the whole time. Then I found another job and went off on my own."

"And shooting Cutler in both legs?" I asked.

"Seemed fitting for Earl and tying him up helped him feel what it was like to lie in the middle of the street," Alex said, "The best solution for the situation."

"I bet he's going to hold a grudge," I said.

"Can't wait to see what he thinks of to do next," Alex replied.

"You're not even a little bit worried?" I asked.

"If I worried about every enemy I've made I would never leave Jacob's house," Alex said. We rode in silence as the night wore on.

Alex was starting to fall asleep when the next town came in sight. This one looked closer to being a city with its many streets and buildings. People were just starting to get up. Some people were out in the streets already. Alex seemed to wake up a bit more as we rode into town. She stopped in front of the sheriff's office. We both got down and tied our horses to the hitching post. A man came out. He was large with full beard and had two guns, one each hip. He wore a silver star on his chest.

"Didn't think you would ever make it back here, Turner," the man said.

"Was in the area and thought I should stop in," Alex replied, "This is my partner Toby. Toby, this is Sheriff Nelson."

"Good morning," I said.

"Nice to see a gentleman," Nelson said, "What other than trouble brings you here?"

"Need another thousand before I can enter the Riverside tournament," Alex said.

"I'll see what I can do," Nelson said, "But I haven't heard much for news lately."

Alex and I followed him as he went into his office. It was the biggest sheriff's office I had seen and it had all the modern comforts one could ever ask for. Nelson sat down behind a solid oak desk and opened one of the drawers. He pulled out a stack of papers and started to go through them. He separated out about five before putting the papers back in the drawer and closing it. Nelson held them out to Alex and Alex took them. She looked through them.

"Works," Alex said.

"You look like you need a good night's sleep," Nelson commented.

"We stopped in the last town, but never got to stay," Alex said.

"What happened?" Nelson asked. He put his feet up and waited for her to start the story. Alex sat down in the chair across from him and I sat down in the chair beside the window.

"We had stopped for lunch and we got a show of this fellow Cutler shooting Titus," Alex said.

"Titus Earl?" Nelson asked.

"Yeah," Alex answered.

"I've heard of Cutler, all 'round bastard," Nelson said, "Likes things that way. Heard he had taken over a town, but didn't know which one."

"Well, Cutler went back into the saloon and no one was willing to remove the body for fear Cutler would shoot him too."

"Foolishness," Nelson said.

"Toby carried the body to the doctor's office, where the doctor refused to have it left; too scared of Cutler. I inspired enough fear in him that he agreed to bury the body. Nothing as fancy as a box and nothing more than a cross marking the grave, but Titus got buried."

"And Cutler?" Nelson asked.

"We left him lying in the middle of the street, shot in both legs, bound and gagged," Alex said, "It was night by the time we dealt with him. After that we left."

"And you rode all night and just got in," Nelson said.

"Pretty much," Alex said.

"Hotels aren't taking guests yet," Nelson said.

"I know," Alex said.

"But I'm willing to offer a cell with two bunks," Nelson said with a smile.

"What do you think?" Alex asked.

"Any bed is fine," I answered.

"Well, I guess you get to lock us up," Alex said. Alex and I stood up. We went outside and got our gear before going back inside. This time Nelson led us into the cells. There were six, three on each side containing two bunks each. They were empty. Nelson unlocked the first one on the left. Alex dumped her stuff by the door and climbed up on the top bunk, I dropped mine with hers and lay down on the bottom one. Nelson closed and locked the cell door. I was asleep the moment I closed my eyes.

I woke up to someone cursing. Nelson was escorting a man down to the last cell and the man was fighting him. Two of the other cells had prisoners in them. Nelson threw the man into the cell and locked the door behind him. On his way back to the office he stopped when he saw that I was awake.

"Need anything?" Nelson asked.

"Food, please," I answered.

"I'll see what I can find," Nelson said before going into his office. I stood up and stretched. Alex was still fast asleep.

Ten minutes later Nelson was back. He unlocked the cell door and held it open for me. I stepped out of the cell and he locked the door again. I followed him into the office. There was a tray of food on the table beside the deputy's cot.

"You'll have to excuse me," Nelson said, "But every saloon in town has been having troubles with fights breaking out."

"You have a job to do," I said with a shrug. Nelson nodded and left the building. I ate and then pulled out a deck of cards to play solitaire.

I was half way through the sixth game when Nelson and someone that looked like a deputy dragged a man to the cells. The man looked like he had had too much to drink and was barely aware what was happening. I heard a cell door close and then both men came back out.

"Sounds like a busy night," I commented.

"Three brawls and one murder," the deputy answered. Nelson looked like he was going to say something.

"Sheriff!" a voice called from outside. The deputy went to the window.

"It's Joe's brother," the deputy said, "And five of his men."

"And here I didn't think the night could get any worse," Nelson said. Nelson opened the door and stepped outside; the deputy followed. I looked through the open door. Five men were standing in the street with their hands at ready on their guns. The leader was the middle man in a matching suit, while the men on either side looked more like ranch hands with their muudy clothes and chaps.

"Let my brother go," the leader told Nelson.

"Can't," Nelson answered, "Murder isn't a charge we drop in this city. And he did it when there was a deputy standing there and not to mention the crowd of people watching. Joe isn't going free."

I stood up and walked closer to the doorway.

"I'm not leaving without my brother," the leader said. The man to the side closest to me pulled out his gun. I slid mine out of its holster. The man cocked his.

"Walk away," Nelson said, "Then no one gets hurt and I don't have to arrest any of you." The man quickly brought his gun up to fire, but I fired first. The man dropped his gun with a curse and held his hand. Nelson pulled out his two guns and the deputy pulled out his gun. The other crew already had theirs out, but everyone was looking at the man, who was holding his hand.

"You need better men," Nelson said, "Ones that don't have their guns going off in their faces. Now I suggest you leave, before I arrest you for disturbing the peace." The men started to move away. Since it didn't look like there would be any more action I put my gun away and sat back down at the table.

The deputy entered first and then Nelson came in closing the door behind him.

"We got lucky," the deputy said.

"For now," Nelson said, "Go do another round. I'll be following soon."

"Yes, sir," the deputy said, then left the office.

"You shot the man," Nelson said to me.

"I could have let him shoot you," I replied.

"How long have you been traveling with Alex?" Nelson asked.

"About a month, I think," I answered.

"If you hadn't shot that man there would have been far more shooting," Nelson said, "Alex would do something like that."

"I didn't see any reason to let them shoot you, that's all," I said. Nelson nodded and then left the office. I went back to playing solitaire.

The rest of the night was quieter. Nelson and his deputy were in and out of the office all night trying to keep things quiet. They both took turns sleeping on the deputy's bed when it was quiet.

Morning came with both of them asleep; the deputy in his bed and Nelson in his chair. I went outside to stretch my legs. I wandered down the street from the sheriff's office. Most of the shops were just opening their doors. I stopped at a restaurant that was open and went inside. I was immediately seated and offered my choice of breakfast.

While I waited I watched the people come in. Alex came in about the time my food arrived. She saw me and came over to the table.

"He let you out?" I asked as she sat down.

"He wasn't gonna leave me in there," Alex answered, "He had his fun yesterday. Though if that drunk hadn't woken up an' started screaming I might still be asleep."

"Screaming?" I asked.

"He woke up, found himself in prison and started screaming that he didn't do anything," Alex answered, " Nelson came back looking like a bull that had just been disturbed and told him impolitely to shut up. Then when he saw I was awake, he let me out. He didn't sound too happy."

"He an' his deputy were up most of the night dealing with brawls in the saloons," I said, "Then the drunk was locked up for murder. After that the drunk's brother showed up to get his brother out."

"Sounds like a busy night," Alex said.

"So, what now?" I asked.

"We go after these," Alex said, pulling out the papers that Nelson had given her yesterday. I took them and looked them over. They were all hand-drawn portraits of men with prices on their heads.

"Bounty work?" I asked.

"We can find other jobs while still doing these," Alex said, "I usually keep some on me. I just don't usually get jobs here, unless they are bounty work."

"Why not?"

"There's a feud going between the family that owns the land on one side of the city and the family that owns the land on the other side of the city. If you get hired by either side, the other side will shoot you if they ever see you, even if you only took one job a long time ago."

"Domestic disputes are dangerous to get involved with anyway."

"Pretty much."

I handed the papers back to Alex and she put them away. The leader of the group from last night entered with a man that seemed familiar. The hair brushed to one side of his face, the squint of the eyes and the bent nose. Alex noticed that something had caught my attention; she turned to look. Then she turned back.

"Samuel Johnson," Alex told me, "It's the Johnsons and the Millers that are feuding."

"The man with him that looks like a professional gunslinger," I said, "I think he's on one of those papers."

Alex did another check over her shoulder then pulled out the papers again. She pulled out the third one and stuffed the rest back.

"Wanted alive," Alex said, "For shooting up half a town an' killing six people."

"One for every bullet in his gun," I said.

"Probably," Alex said. She stuffed the paper away.

"What should we do?" I asked.

"Wait," Alex answered, "There isn't much point in challenging him here. He'd win and we would be at fault."

"Samuel Johnson tried to shoot Nelson last night," I said, "The drunk who was screaming this morning is his brother. He's in there for murder."

"That's interesting," Alex said, "We'll have to go back and talk to Nelson."

"I'm finished," I said. We stood up and left the restaurant. We headed back up the street to the sheriff's office. Entering, we found Nelson listening to a man that looked like a shopkeeper.

"Samuel has hired a gunslinger to take you out and get Joe out of jail," the shopkeeper was saying.

Nelson nodded.

"They're down at Lily's restaurant having breakfast now," the shopkeeper said.

"Thank you," Nelson said. The shopkeeper turned, almost jumping out of his skin when he saw us. Alex tipped her hat and moved out of the way for the shopkeeper to leave. The shopkeeper hurried out of the office.

"What do you two want?" Nelson asked.

"Samuel Johnson is indeed down at Lily's having breakfast with a gunslinger," Alex said pulling out the paper, "This one." Alex showed it to Nelson.

"That just gives me a good reason to arrest them," Nelson said, "Besides rumours I've heard."

"And he'll let himself be hauled off by the sheriff he's hired to shoot?" Alex said sitting down.

"I'm sensing a better plan," Nelson said.

"We'll catch him and collect the bounty," Alex said, "No shooting, no deaths."

"You're gonna catch him without any shooting at all?" Nelson asked.

"Yes," Alex answered.

"Then go get him," Nelson said, "And I'll hold a cell for him."

"Good," Alex said as she stood up. We left the office.

"Now what?" I asked.

"Samuel always treats the gunslingers he hires the same way," Alex said, "He pays for them to eat at Lily's, he puts them up at the Sand Hotel and lets them drink for free at his saloon."

"Would't it be foolish to shoot the sheriff, then stay in town?" I asked.

"Yes, so if you're gonna have someone pay for everything while in town, what would you do?" Alex asked.

"Enjoy it for a while first," I answered.

"With any luck this gunslinger will do just that," Alex said. She started down the street.

"So, where are we going?" I asked.

"Samuel doesn't close his saloon," Alex answered. I followed her to the saloon. We went inside. There were a couple of drunks sleeping last night off, a few that were still drinking and a poker game in the back corner. Alex headed for the poker game and I followed. These four men hadn't been here all night, but they obviously had money. I guessed that at least three were professional gamblers. Alex was given an invitation to join them, but I just stepped back and watched them. Ever watched professional gamblers play? Alex fit right in with them.

It was close to noon when Samuel and the gunslinger came into the saloon. Samuel went upstairs to his office. The gunslinger went to the bar and ordered a drink. He spent the afternoon drinking. He never drank a lot, just sipped one drink until it was finished and then ordered another.

Evening came with many more people coming into the saloon. Even Samuel came down to join his customers for a while. In the middle of the evening the gunslinger left the saloon. Alex was deep in the game, so I followed him. He went to the Sand Hotel, just as Alex predicted. I stayed outside as he went in. Five minutes later I saw a light come on in the room on the second floor corner room. I saw him through the window. He looked like he was getting ready for bed. I went back to the saloon. Alex was still playing, but she excused herself when I went over. We left the saloon.

"So?" Alex said.

"He is at the Sand Hotel," I answered, "Second floor room."

"Then let's go pay him a visit," Alex said. We went to the hotel and went inside. The desk clerk was half asleep. He didn't stir as we went up the stairs. I pointed out the room to Alex. She tried the door, but it was locked. I headed back down to the desk. The clerk was asleep. I went behind the counter and took the second key from the hook. Back upstairs, I unlocked the door. Alex opened it and stepped inside. The gunslinger was fast asleep sitting in the chair. He was still dressed, and his gear was still packed. Alex went over and undid the gunslinger's gun belt. She slid it silently to the floor. Alex picked it up and handed it to me. I also grabbed the gunslingers gear.

"How much did he drink?" Alex asked as she did a gentle search for any other weapons.

"Six or seven," I answered, "Over the afternoon."

"Must've been something strong," Alex said. She pulled another gun out of the gunslinger's boot and a knife out of the other. She added them to what I was carrying. She continued searching. I put everything in to the bag and slung it over my shoulder.

"He's clean," Alex said. She took out her gun and checked the chambers. She pulled out the three bullets left.

"Do you ever reload?" I asked.

"Only when I remember," Alex said. She dug into her coat and pulled out something that looked like a bullet. She loaded it into her gun.

"What does that do?" I asked.

"Creates noise," Alex said, "But doesn't do any damage. Remind me to clean my gun after this." She pulled the trigger while pointing her gun at the floor. Something came out of the gun, but it just fell on the floor in small pieces without doing any damage. It sounded like a gunshot.

The gunslinger jumped to his feet and reached for his gun. But it wasn't there. Alex pointed hers at him. I pulled my gun out.

"You're gonna come with us," she told him. He looked at me.

"And where are we going?" the gunslinger asked.

"To collect the bounty on your head," Alex answered, "Now move."

"I can pay you more than I'm worth to the law," the gunslinger said without moving.

"Move," Alex said louder. The gunslinger slowly moved towards the door. I went out first the make sure he wasn't going to try to run.

We escorted the gunslinger to the sheriff's office. Nelson was sitting at his desk doing paperwork when we came in.

"And here I was waiting for the gun fire," Nelson said. I dropped the gunslinger's gear in the corner and watched as Alex and the sheriff took the gunslinger to the cell across from Joe. Once the door was locked, Alex put her gun away. They came back to the office where I had sat down. Alex sat in the other chair and had taken her gun back out.

"You did it," Nelson said, "Without any shooting."

Alex started to clean her gun.

"I wouldn't say 'no shooting'," Alex said, "Just no actual bullets. Samuel is gonna have to get another gunslinger."

"The trial for Joe is tomorrow," Nelson said, "Hopefully this will be all over by tomorrow night."

"Want us to stick around?" Alex asked.

"No, I think between you and Toby you've done enough," Nelson answered, "Besides you have four more to find and bring back."

"True," Alex said, "Do we have to wait until we bring in all five to get paid?"

"I was getting to that," Nelson said. He unlocked one drawer in his desk and pulled out an envelope. He placed it on his desk near Alex. She put her gun down. Picking up the money she counted it and then handed it to me. I put it away. Nelson sat back down at his desk. Alex finished cleaning her gun and put it away.

"You left your gear in the cell," Nelson said.

"Forgot about that," Alex said.

"You gonna sleep there again or are you gonna find a hotel room?" Nelson asked.

"Might as well sleep there," I answered, "Since we'll be leaving tomorrow morning anyway."

"Great," Nelson said. We all got up and once again Nelson locked us in the cell. The gunslinger was giving us funny looks. I lay down on the bottom bunk and Alex climbed on to the top one. I closed my eyes and drifted off to sleep.

I slowly became aware of the noises of the city through the walls of the prison. In here it seemed quiet. I opened my eyes and looked around. Joe was asleep, the gunslinger was just sitting in his cell and a man lay on the floor of the cell across from the one I was in. My guess, by the sounds from outside, was that it was close to sunrise. Suddenly there were sounds of a fight in the sheriff's office. I got up. The gunslinger looked that direction. Then Nelson and the deputy came through the doorway with a large man between them. The man was fighting as they dragged him to a cell. Finally they pushed him into a cell, quickly closed and locked it. The man rammed the door and tried to grab them. Nelson and the deputy stood back. The man kept trying to get out. The deputy went back to the office. Nelson stopped at our cell and unlocked the door. Alex jumped down from the bunk. And we both grabbed our gear and followed Nelson into his office.

"What's that all about?" Alex asked.

"A fight," Nelson said, "He was the only one standing, though we're pretty sure he didn't start it."

"Well, good luck," Alex said.

"Come back soon with those other four," Nelson said. We left the sheriff's office. Alex started for the stable and we were able to get our horses. Then we left the city.

"Where to next?" I asked.

"Forward," Alex answered, "Unless you know where we can find these men."

"No," I replied.

We rode until night fell and then we stopped to rest. We were there briefly and then we were moving again. Mid-afternoon the next day we rode into another town called Cactus Creek. This place had a saloon on one end of town and a church on the other end of town and a school near the church. There were several women around and better-dressed men. People stopped and looked at us before continuing on with their business. We stopped our horses in front of the general store. A boy came over as we got down.

"I'll take care of them for a dollar," the boy offered.

"We won't be here that long," Alex told the boy. The boy shrugged and turned away. Alex and I went into the general store. I picked up the supplies while she studied the bulletin board.

I had just paid for the supplies when a gunshot went off outside the store. I looked over to Alex, who was still standing near the bulletin board. She looked at me. I gathered up the supplies and followed her outside. There was a crowd gathered around a man lying on the ground. The sheriff was restraining a man on the other side of the street. I went to the horses and packed the supplies in the saddle bags. Alex had found something to lean against and watched.

"Is he dead?" the sheriff called. The crowd stepped back and a man that looked like a doctor stood up.

"Not yet, but he's close to it," the doctor called back. The doctor got two men to help him with the man, while the sheriff escorted his prisoner to the building marked Sheriff. Everyone else went about his own business, except for one man standing outside the saloon. Black pants and coat matched his hat, his shirt was white. His close cropped hair was black and his eyes were hazel. I might have thought him to be a professional gambler, but his clothes and gun belt was covered with dust that looked like he had been in a fight recently.

Alex stopped next to her horse and looked at the man.

"Gerald," Alex said as she got up into the saddle. I mounted as well.

"Who?" I asked.

"The gun is for show," Alex said, "The man who was arrested is his partner, Shane."

"Why is the gun for show?" I asked as we headed for the far edge of town from where we entered.

"He prefers his knives," Alex answered, "Good with them, too."

"Looks like they're in trouble," I said.

"Gerald will get Shane out of trouble," Alex said, "That's what he's there for."

"Gunslingers?" I asked.

"They take jobs like they are," Alex answered, "But never try to hire Gerald for his gun."

"Because he uses a knife?" I asked.

"Because he uses knives," Alex replied. We left town behind.

It was early evening when we stopped for a rest. I saw two riders on the horizon in the direction from which we had just come.

"Should we stop?" I asked. Alex looked at the riders that were just two dark shapes on the horizon.

"They'll catch up to us either way," Alex said, "And I'm tired."

We sat down and ate as the riders came closer. As we finished eating they were close enough that I could tell that the riders were Gerald and Shane. We didn't move as they rode up. Both men got off their horses. Shane was taller than Gerald, but thinner. He wore jeans, a blue shirt and a brown vest. His brown hair was too long and his blue eyes were bright with enthusiasm.

"That was fast," Alex commented.

"The man wasn't as dead as the doctor said he was," Gerald answered, "And willingly admitted to having tried to shoot Shane first."

"Does Jacob know you have a new partner?" Shane asked Alex.

"Yes," I answered.

"Uh oh, what happened this time?" Gerald asked.

"He decided to keep all the money for himself," Alex answered.

"So, what great adventure are you on now?" Shane asked sitting down.

"Tracking down fugitives for the law," Alex answered.

"Henry?" Gerald asked.

"Caught him," Alex answered, "These are new ones."

"Maybe you can help us," Gerald said.

"They're busy," Shane said, "That means we have to do this ourselves."

"What is it?" Alex asked.

"The biggest ranch near Greystone is run by a man named Maddock," Gerald said, "Has five children, all mostly grown, three girls and two boys. He and the boys were out one night and came home to find their guest had taken off with the girls. Maddock doesn't think the girls went willingly, based on the rearrangement of the furniture. And most of them have men who want their hands in marriage."

"And you've been asked to retrieve the girls," Alex said.

"Yes," Gerald replied, "The guest was a man named Eric Bradley. He has a place not far from here. Maddock is hoping that Eric hasn't done anything to the girls."

"And if he has?" Alex asked.

"We are to bring him back to be hung," Shane answered with a smile.

"Maddock just wants his daughters back unharmed," Gerald said.

"I suppose we could help," Alex said.

"Then we can help you with something," Shane said.

"We'll call it a favour owed," Alex said, "Right now we don't need any help."

"Fine," Gerald said. We all got back on our horses and rode a while. And Shane decided that he would talk. I tired quickly of it. Alex and Gerald seemed to be immune to it, but they didn't respond to anything he said.

We reached the edge of a field as the sun was setting.

"We camp here," Gerald said. Alex nodded. Each of us rolled out our bedroll and crawled into it. I must have been the first one to drop off.

The next morning we went across the field to a house. It was a large house, with fields of grain on every side and a narrow roadway that led away from it.

"Doesn't look like anyone is home," Alex commented. Gerald dismounted and handed the reins to Shane. Alex got down as well, but she just dropped the reins and her horse didn't move. They were almost to the house when we saw a man coming across the opposite field. We waited until he was within talking distance. The man was dressed in shirt, vest, jeans and chaps with a hat and a farmhand's squint.

"We're looking for Eric Bradley," Gerald said, "Are you him?"

"No," the man answered. The man looked like a farm hand. "Bradley hasn't been back here in a while."

"How long is a while?" Alex asked.

"Five, six months," the man answered.

"Mind if we check the house for him anyway?" Gerald asked.

"As long as you don't take anything," the man answered. Alex and Gerald went into the house. No one said anything as we waited for them. Ten minutes later they came back out.

"Sorry for imposing," Gerald said to the man. Alex and Gerald got back on their horses.

"Bradley might be in Greystone," the man said, "He has a ranch there."

"Thank you," Gerald said. We left by the road.

"Back to Greystone," Shane said once we were off the property, "You would think Maddock would've told us Bradley had a ranch in that area, rather than sending us on a four day hunt."

"He may not know," Alex replied, "Greystone has several large ranches around it as well as a few smaller ones."

"We'll find him either way," Gerald said. No one spoke for a while, then Shane went back to babbling.

We didn't stop to rest as we went back through the town. Shane even shut up during the time we rode through. However he went back to talking once we were on our way.

About noon, we could see people ahead. As we got closer I could see four people and a wagon. The wagon had a broken wheel and three men were trying to fix it. There was also another horse nearby. Even from this distance one of the men looked familiar; the square jaw, long hair and a scar that went across his right eye down to the corner of his mouth.

"I think we just came across a man from one of those wanted papers," I said to Alex. Alex pulled out the papers and looked though them.

"You have a very good memory," she said.

"What's he wanted for?" Shane asked.

"Highway robbery," Alex answered.

"Looks more like he is helping the poor travellers," Gerald said.

"Don't care," Alex said, "He is currently wanted." We got closer, just as they finished fixing the wheel. All the four men and the woman turned to look at us.

"Good day," Alex greeted them.

"Good day," the man looked like a settler. The woman looked as if she was his wife and the other unknown man shared a family resemblance with them. The man I recognized started toward his horse.

"Having problems?" Gerald asked.

"Just a broken wheel, but we managed thanks to this fellow's help," the man said. The wanted man got into the saddle. He didn't look happy; I think we spoiled his chance to rob the settlers.

"Glad everything is okay," Gerald said. The settlers got into their wagon and started in the opposite direction from us. The wanted man turned his horse around and started to ride away.

"West," Alex called. The wanted man turned around. The

settlers kept moving.

"What?" the wanted man asked.

"Since we happened upon you maybe you can help us with something," Alex said. The wanted man turned his horse around and came back towards us.

"And how do you know me?" he asked.

"Heard about you from a certain barmaid," Alex answered.

"She must have said some good things," West said, "Because you four don't look like you need anyone's help." The man stopped his horse just in front of ours.

"We're always glad for competent help," Gerald said.

“Then, perhaps, I can help," West said.

"This is as good a place as any to discuss the plan," I said after checking that the settlers were moving at a steady pace away from us. Alex nodded before dismounting. I dismounted as well, as did West. He joined Alex and me while we waited for Shane and Gerald to get down.

"What’s that?" Gerald asked pointing. West turned to look and Alex hit him on the back of the head with the handle of her gun. He collapsed. I bent down and checked his pulse.

"He's still alive," I said standing back up.

"Good," Alex said. She went over and grabbed the rope off West's saddle. I picked him up and dumped him over the saddle. Alex tied him on to his horse.

"I would never want to end up on one of the posters you get," Shane commented as we got back on our horses. Alex had the reins of West's horse.

"Then don't do anything stupid," Alex told him. We continued on.

When night came, we found some place to camp. West had woken up in the afternoon and after swearing for a few minutes had gone silent. Alex gave him some water, but otherwise we left him alone.

The next morning we packed up and went on. It was mid-morning when we arrived back at Red Alder.

"Civilization," Shane said, "A proper breakfast."

"Sounds good," Gerald said before turning to us, "We'll see you at the other side of town in about an hour."

"See you," Alex said. We continued down the street until we

reached the sheriff's office. No one came out to greet us this time. We tied the three horses to the hitching post. Alex untied West from his horse. He was ready to strike her until I pushed my cocked gun into his back.

"Let's go inside, quietly," I suggested. West complied and we entered the sheriff's office. Sheriff Nelson was sitting behind his desk working. He looked up at us. Without saying anything he pulled out his keys and headed for the cells. West and I followed. Alex sat down in the chair across from Nelson's instead. A large man sleeping was in the middle of the cell floor at the end of the left side, aside from that the cells were empty. Nelson opened the middle one on the right side, I pushed West in and Nelson locked the door behind him. I uncocked and holstered my gun before following Nelson back to the office. Nelson sat back down at his desk and pulled an envelope from a drawer.

"That's two," Nelson said placing the envelope in front of Alex. Alex picked it up and put it away.

"And three more to go," Alex replied.

"How'd the situation with Joe go?" I asked.

"Joe hung for murder," Nelson said, "Samuel is angry and has threatened to take me out. I'm not concerned."

"We'd offer to stick around, but we have other things to do," Alex said.

"I don't need you two sticking around to cause trouble," Nelson said, "Samuel won't try his luck against me directly right now, because the Millers will kill him. And he has sent for gunslingers."

"How long do you think this will last?" Alex asked.

"A month at least," Nelson answered, "After that he'll have to decide whether to hold a grudge or move on with life. Where're you two headed?"

"Greystone," Alex answered.

"Should I send the sheriff advance warning?" Nelson asked.

"No," Alex said, "We're just helping a couple of friends with a job."

"Good luck to them," Nelson said.

"We'll see you next time we're through with a fugitive," Alex said standing up.

"I'll be waiting," Nelson said. I stood up and we left the office. We mounted our horses and headed to meet Shane and Gerald.

They arrived ten minutes after we did.

"That was a short breakfast," Alex commented.

"Service was fast," Gerald replied, "You lost your cargo."

"Dropped him off with the sheriff," Alex said.

"Then I guess we can get on our way," Gerald said.

"You're the leader," Alex replied. Gerald prodded his horse into moving and the rest of us followed.

It took three days of travelling to get to Greystone. And Shane talked the whole way.

Greystone was surrounded by ranches, which we had to pass to get to the town. In town, the smell of the ranches still lingered. The town was mainly businesses establishments with only a few houses.

We stopped and tied our horses to the hitching post in front of the saloon. Alex, Shane and I went into the saloon. There were a few men sitting around drinking and a few bored dancing girls. We each bought a drink and sat down at a table. One of the girls sashayed over to our table. Her pink and cream dress matched the ribbons in her blonde hair.

"What're you boys doing in town?" the girl asked.

"Trying to finish a job," Shane answered.

"Must be pretty important to take all three of you," the girl said

"It is," Shane replied.

"How long are you in town?" the girl asked.

"Until we get the information we need to continue," Shane answered.

"And what information would that be?" the girl asked.

"The information he just got," Alex said pointing to Gerald who had entered the saloon.

"A job that takes four of you," the girl said, "Must be really big."

"Big enough," Gerald answered taking the fourth chair. The girl's back stiffened and then she sashayed back to the other girls.

"And?" Alex asked.

"I know where the ranch is, but no one knows if Eric Bradley is out there," Gerald answered.

"Shall we go find out?" Alex asked.

"The sooner this is over the better," Gerald answered. We stood up and left the saloon. Once we were all on our horses, Gerald led us out of town. We passed one ranch before we turned up the road to get to the next one. A house was on top of a small hill over looking the cattle pasture. No one came out to greet us and there didn't seem to be any ranch hands that I could see.

"Unless he's scared to come out, I'd say he isn't here," Alex said.

"Then we don't have to ask permission to search the house," Gerald said.

"You and Shane search the house, Toby and I will look around out here," Alex said. Gerald nodded and then he and Shane went into the house. I went one way around the building and Alex went the other. There wasn't much out here besides a stable for horses and the door to a root cellar. I looked in the stable, but there was no horse in there. I came out to see Alex come around the other side of the house.

"Anything?" I asked.

"No," Alex answered, "You?"

"Nothing in the stable, but I haven't checked the root cellar," I answered. I went over to the root cellar. There was a lock on the door. I went back to the stable and grabbed a shovel. I used the shovel to break the lock. Putting the shovel to one side I opened the doors. In the light that filtered down I could see three ladies. They looked scared and dirty, but otherwise unharmed.

"Alex," I called. Alex came over and looked inside. I stepped inside the root cellar and offered my hand to the closest woman. She hesitated a moment before taking it. I helped her out before offering my hand to the next one. She took my hand without hesitating and I helped her out. The third lady took my hand almost before I had stretched it out. Once they were all out, Alex and I escorted them around to the front of the house. We arrived there just as Gerald and Shane were coming out.

"You found them!" Shane said.

"You find anything?" Alex asked.

"No," Gerald said.

"Mr. Bradley locked us in there and then left," one of the ladies said, "We haven't heard him come or go since."

"We'll look for him later," Gerald said, "Let's get you home first."

"Thank you," the lady said.

"We'll wait and see if he shows up," Alex said, "You can take our horses."

"All right," Gerald said.

"But make sure you bring them back," Alex said.

"I will," Gerald said. We helped two of the ladies on to my horse and the other on to Alex's horse before Shane and Gerald mounted their horses. Then they rode away. Alex and I went inside and played poker.

It was getting late in the evening when Shane and Gerald showed up with our horses. We were waiting outside when they arrived.

"Did Bradley show up?" Gerald asked.

"No," Alex answered as she got on to her horse. I mounted mine.

"Then we need to figure out where he went," Gerald said.

"Do you still need our help for that?" Alex asked.

"You can go on to whatever you need to do," Gerald said, "The two of us shouldn't have any trouble."

“Then we'll leave tomorrow," Alex said. We rode the rest of the way to town without talking. Once there, Alex and I got rooms at the hotel. I immediately went up to my room and collapsed onto the bed.

Next thing I knew the sun was shining in my window. I got out of bed and washed up before going downstairs to the restaurant. Alex was already sitting at a table waiting for breakfast.

"Where’re we headed next?" I asked.

"I talked to the sheriff and the next wanted man we’re after came through here a couple weeks ago, which was two days before the wanted poster reached here," Alex said, "So, we'll go the direction he did an’ see if we can pick up his trail."

"Fine," I said. Two plates of food arrived and we started eating. We were just finishing when Gerald joined us.

"Got his direction?" Alex asked.

"According to the dancing girl Shane talked to, it’s six feet under," Gerald answered, "The barman confirmed that when I talked to him."

"But the person you asked before didn't know?" Alex asked.

"Apparently, Bradley took the ladies out to his place, dumped them in the root cellar and came back here for a game of poker,"

Gerald said, "He was caught cheating as the game was wrapping up and one of the other players shot him. The sheriff was called and the body put in the ground, but other than that no one cared enough to spread the word around."

"Doesn't sound like Bradley had a lot of friends," I said.

"The impression I've been getting around here is that he was a great person, as long as you only saw him for an hour or so every couple of weeks," Gerald said, "No one'll miss him."

"What'll you an' Shane do now?" Alex asked.

"We do have a job offer back at the city where we stopped for breakfast," Gerald said.

"Samuel Johnson?" Alex asked.

"Yes, why?" Gerald asked.

"You decide to take it and I'll shoot you," Alex said.

"What's the job?" Gerald asked.

"Shooting the sheriff for hanging Samuel's brother for murder," Alex answered.

"I think there might be a few jobs south of here that we could get," Gerald said, "That one doesn't sound like one we should take on."

"Wise choice," Alex said.

"I never want to see which one of us is better," Gerald said, "No matter what the pay. See you around."

"See you," Alex said. Gerald stood up and walked out of the restaurant. Alex and I headed out of the hotel. After getting our horses we rode out of town.

As we rode beyond the last ranch, we came across a man beating an Indian. Alex stopped her horse and pulled out her gun. She shot the man's hat off. The man whirled around to look at us.

"Leave the Nolawistep alone," Alex said.

"Why? He just an Indian," the man asked.

"Doesn't give you the right to beat him," Alex said.

"What do you care?" the man asked.

"You're beating another human being," Alex answered, "Why shouldn't I care?" The man turned back to his horse in frustration. The Indian got up and looked at Alex.

"Thank you, Chenarcor," the Indian said then walked off.

"Disgusting," the man said before riding past us and back into town. Alex and I continued on.

It was sunset when we stopped to camp. We slept until sunrise and started moving again.

In the two days it took to reach the next town, we met only a few people on the road. The rain started on the second day. Our rain slickers kept us fairly dry, but we didn't stop for the night or to rest very long. Reaching town was a relief.

We stopped at the stable first and then went to the hotel. After putting my gear in my room I went over to the saloon. There was a poker game going on in one corner. I was invited to join after one man left due to losing his stake.

It was late evening when Alex showed up in the saloon. She stood back and watched while I played two more hands before excusing myself. Alex and I went over to the bar.

"So, what did you find out?" I asked once the barman had poured our drinks and moved down the bar to serve someone else.

"He has been though here," Alex answered, "Stopped to pick up supplies. Stayed a couple days due to one of the girls next door. He still has a two week lead on us."

"We follow his trial until we catch him, I guess," I said, "Or until we see another one of the papers." Alex nodded. The barman came back down to refill our drinks.

"What does Chenarcor mean?" I asked Alex.

"Spirit talker," the barman answered before going off serve someone else.

"People think it means spirit talker," Alex said, "It actually means speaker for the dead."

"The title fits," I replied. Alex shrugged. We finished our drinks and went back to the hotel for the night.

It was still raining when we mounted on our horses the next morning and started riding. The rain continued for the week it took to get to the next town. We found a hotel room and Alex started looking for information. I slept.

When I got up and went to the restaurant for something to eat. Alex joined me. We were a week too late. Once we were finished eating we headed off after him again. The rain had lightened to a mist, which our rain slickers were little protection against.

We were on the road for another week. This time we stopped in one town for the night. The rain finally stopped, but everything was still damp.

It was the first day of the next week when we came across a campsite. There was one horse tied to a tree and it looked like someone was getting ready to prepare breakfast, but there was no one is sight. I looked at Alex; she shrugged in response. Alex got off her horse and started toward the campsite. A man stepped out of the trees with a pot of water. It was the man from the wanted poster. He was large with a double chin and potbelly. He was clean shaven on chin as well as head.

"What do you want?" he asked pulling out his gun.

"We saw your fire," Alex said, "And hoped that if you had warm food you would be willing to share. If not, we'll move on." The man studied us for a minute.

"I got enough to share," the man said. He put his gun away before coming over to the fire. I got down from my horse and tied mine and Alex's horses to a tree branch. The man started cooking food as Alex and I found places to sit down.

"Where're you two headed?" the man asked.

"Wherever the road takes us," I answered.

"Got money to do that?" the man asked.

"For now," Alex answered, "We'll find some way to get more when it runs out."

"Run out of supplies?" the man asked.

"Not yet," Alex answered, "But it's all cold food. If you hadn't been willing to share the only thing we would've had to warm us up was the bottle of whiskey."

"Whiskey?" the man asked.

"Sure," Alex said, "I'll bring it out." Alex got up and went to her horse. She pulled out the bottle of whiskey that Jacob had used to clean her wound. It had been refilled since then. She also brought over cups for me and her. I took the cups when she got back to the fire. She opened the bottle. The man offered his cup and she poured whiskey into it before turning to me and filling the others.

"This's good whiskey," the man said after taking a sip. Alex put the bottle down, sat down again and took her cup. I took a sip. It wasn't great whiskey, but it was drinkable.

"Bought it when we got our last batch of supplies," Alex said.

"Been a while since I had whiskey," the man said, "I've had to keep moving, so I'll get to my job."

"What kind of job?" Alex asked.

"Don't know," the man said, "A friend got it for me, even sent me money to get there." The man drained his cup and held it out. Alex poured him more. "He said it was good, honest work with not bad pay."

"Sounds good," I replied.

"I can't wait to start," the man said, "I only stop for rest when I eat other than that I've just been moving. Made good time so far."

We kept talking. He had one more cup of whiskey before the food was ready. Alex and I were still working on our first. No one said much as we ate. Alex and I each had a refill of whiskey as we continued to talk. The man drank the rest of the bottle.

He was starting to slur his speech when he decided to go to sleep. Alex started to clean up the camp. I helped her. Finally the only thing left of the camp was the fire and the man. Alex crept over and pulled out the man's gun. He didn't stir. So, she searched him for other weapons. He didn't so much as twitch as she took away his knife. Alex dropped them by the fire before grabbing the rope from his saddle. I picked him up and placed him over the saddle. Alex tied him to on the horse. Then we mounted and headed back the way we came.

"Two more after this," I said.

"And unless the bounty has changed on one of them I should have enough to enter the poker tournament," Alex said.

"So, we head to Riverside after this?" I asked.

"I thought that if we had enough time we could stop in at Cartwheel first," Alex answered, "I usually stop in and say hello to Nadine regularly."

"And while you're there Jacob comes up with a job?" I asked.

"I've been through without him even seeing me," Alex answered, "And sometimes I see him, but he doesn't have any jobs ready. Hopefully he won't have anything that will interrupt my plans to get to Riverside."

"Hopefully we won't see him," I said, "The last thing I want is another job where I don't get paid."

"I know," Alex said. We didn't say anything more for the moment.

Our burden didn't appreciate his situation when he woke up and let us know in the worst language I had heard in a long time. We ignored him and kept going.

We went around towns this time. When we needed supplies then one of us would go into town and the other would watch the prisoner. Into the second week of riding it started to rain again. The rain stopped when we went around the ranches.

By the time we rode back into the city, we had been gone at least a month. We stopped at the sheriff's office and tied our horses to the hitching post. A young man came out. His face still had baby fat on it and the gun on his hip looked new. But the brown eyes that studied us were those of someone that had seen the worst life had to offer.

"Sheriff Nelson in?" Alex asked.

"Yes," the young man answered.

"You his new deputy?" Alex asked. I noticed the star.

"Yes," the young man answered. Alex nodded. We brought our prisoner in, but kept his hands tied. The young man stepped aside and let us past. Sheriff Nelson was sitting at his desk same as last time. He looked up at us before taking his keys out. This time there no one in the cells. We untied the prisoner's hands before shoving him into the cell. Sheriff Nelson locked the door and we went back to his office. The young deputy wasn't there.

"I see you have a new deputy," Alex said.

"Had to," Nelson replied, "Samuel Johnson killed the last one."

"What happened there?" Alex asked.

"Samuel brought in a couple of gunslingers," Nelson answered, "I shot the gunslingers when they showed up to kill me. So when my deputy was doing his rounds, Samuel shot him. I don't have any proof of that of course, but everyone knows it. Samuel's father told him to go home and stay there. An uncle is now running the saloon and any other business in town. Haven't had a problem since."

"And the new kid?" Alex asked.

"He walked into town a week ago, half starved and looking for justice," Nelson answered, "I offered him a place to stay, food, a gun and a job with the understanding that he won't try anything stupid."

"Justice here in town?" Alex asked.

"He doesn't know where it is," Nelson answered, "He'll sort it out sooner or later, meanwhile he's a pretty good shot for not having shot a gun before. He also doesn't suffer from the feelings of power because he has a gun strapped to his hip."

"So a good deal for you," Alex said.

"Yes," Nelson said, "You going to bring in the other two?"

"Of course," Alex said, "Just thought we'd catch up on the local gossip."

"I'm sure there'll be more when you get back," Nelson said. Alex and I left the office and mounted our horses.

"Where to now?" I asked.

"The hotel," Alex answered, "To sleep and clean up before heading out again."

"Fine by me," I replied. We headed for the hotel. After checking in we went up to our rooms. Entering my room I dropped my gear in one corner, pulled my boots off and dropped on to the bed.

The sun was rising when I woke up. Getting up I found someplace to bath and get my clothes washed before going into the restaurant for breakfast. Soon Alex joined me.

"Well?" I asked.

"Don't know where the one is, but I know which way the other is heading," Alex answered, "We can head out tomorrow."

"Sounds good," I said.

When I was finished breakfast, I wandered to the edge of town and then turning around to walk to the other edge of town. I found a saloon that wasn't owned by the Johnsons or the Millers and joined the small group in the back that were playing poker.

About suppertime most of the other players went off to find something to eat. I stood up and looked around the saloon. There weren't that many people in here yet, there would be more soon. A man standing at the bar caught my attention. The man's face was thin and his clothes hung loosely off him as if he hadn't been eating properly. He looked familiar. But I wasn't sure where I had seen him. I shook my head and left the saloon. Going back to the hotel I went into the restaurant. Alex was already sitting there. I sat down in the chair across from her.

"Can I have a look at the papers?" I asked.

"Sure," Alex said as she pulled them out. I studied both faces before handing them back to her.

"You know what direction one of them is taking, which one?" I asked.

"This one," Alex answered showing me the paper.

"I know where the other one is," I said.

"Where?" Alex asked.

"He was having a drink in the saloon when I left," I answered, "I wasn't sure it was him until I checked the paper."

"Then we'll go back to the saloon after supper," Alex said. Food was brought for both of us.

After supper I led the way back to the saloon. The same man was leaning on the bar drinking, but there were a lot more people in the saloon now. I went over to the bar and waited for the barman to come over.

"I'll have a whiskey," I said. He put a glass on the bar and started pouring the drink. "And I'll buy my friend at the other end of the bar another of what he's having." The barman nodded and took the money I placed on the counter before going down the bar and stopping in front of the man. I picked up my glass. The barman pointed to me as he poured the man the drink. The man looked at me. I did a toast to him and drank the whiskey. I placed the glass back on the bar and went outside. Alex was already waiting out there. I stood on one side of the door and Alex took the other. A few minutes passed before the man stepped outside. He saw both us with our guns out. The man sighed but didn't move.

"Drop your gun belt," Alex told him. He did. "Let's go." Alex walked ahead of him and after picking up the gun belt, I followed.

"The wanted poster is all a misunderstanding," the man said, "I tried to help those people and someone thought I was the one that shot up the place instead."

"Don't know the story," Alex replied, "Just have the wanted poster and it doesn't have any information on it."

"Bounty hunters who only care about the money, just what I need," the man said, "Don't you care about justice?"

"Sure," Alex said, "But we also need the money."

"Anything for the money," the man said.

"We do plenty of things that don't pay us money," Alex said, "But those jobs cost a lot, so we need the ones that do pay."

"Then maybe you can find the real killer," the man said. Alex seemed to be fighting with herself. I knew she had the itch to hear the story and find justice. On the other hand she wanted to play the tournament in Riverside and this man was worth money towards it.

"Fine," Alex said, "We'll stop for a drink and you can tell us your story."

"Finally, someone who has some sense," the man said.

"But in exchange you have let us turn you over to the sheriff for the bounty," Alex said. The man thought this out.

"Fine," he said.

"Any attempt to escape, we will shoot you," Alex said. The man gulped and nodded. Alex led us into a building. It looked like a restaurant, but the only person inside was an older man standing behind a counter wiping it down. We sat down at the farthest table. The older man brought over a bottle and three glasses before going back to his cleaning. Alex poured the liquid into the glasses.

"Well?" Alex asked.

"I was heading home from guarding the gold train," the man started, "I had stopped in a certain place for lunch before moving on. I was sitting in the back corner with my back to everything. Suddenly everything went quiet. I didn't think anything about it until the gunfire started. I turned to see a man with a bandana over his mouth and his hat pulled down low. I went over to check on the proprietor and his wife when two men came in with their guns out. I recognized them as the men who were driving the stage that stopped just after I did. They were pointing their guns at me as I tried to explain that I had been eating. I took off first chance I could because they were talking about hanging me without the benefit of a judge.

"I can't go home. I have a wanted poster out for me. And as far as anyone is concerned I'm guilty when I was just trying to help. Haven't even been able to rest, until I came here. I thought I could lose myself in the city."

"What did this man look like?" Alex asked.

"Tall, thin, black hat, black bandana, jeans with chaps over them, a brown vest with a dark red shirt, white skin," the man said. Alex put her drink down rather than take a sip. The man turned to her. "What?"

"I know that man," Alex replied.

"Great then you can find him and people will stop looking for me," the man said.

"You must have been running a while," Alex said.

"Why?" the man asked.

"Because I shot him a few months back," Alex answered. The colour drained out of the man's face.

"He's dead?" the man asked.

"He went by Owen," Alex said, "He was into petty theft, amateur gunslinging and highway robbery. Was lousy at picking targets. I picked him up once, because he was wanted. He spent a couple of months in jail before they let him out. He shot first and I shot back, didn't recognize him until I looked at the body. But yes, he is dead."

"Then there's no hope," the man said.

"Tell the truth," Alex said, "Maybe the judge will believe you."

"My word against two witnesses?" the man asked, "I doubt it."

"We listened," Alex said. She placed the money for the bottle on the table. The man sighed, but stood up when we did. We left the building and headed back to the sheriff's office. Sheriff Nelson was standing at his desk looking at something. He put it down and picked up his keys when we entered. I stayed in the office with the deputy while Alex and Nelson walked the man to his cell. I sat down. Alex and Nelson came back into the office. Nelson pulled an envelope out of his desk and set it in front of Alex. After picking it up and putting it away Alex sat down in the chair across from his desk. Nelson didn't look happy, but sat down in his chair.

"You got your fill of gossip yesterday," Nelson said.

"What's the story behind this man's poster?" Alex asked.

"Why? Did he smell of injustice?" Nelson asked.

"There's nothing on the poster," Alex said pulling it out and setting it on the desk. Nelson picked it up and read it.

"I don't know what his story is," Nelson answered, "All I know is I'm supposed to send notice that he was caught and then keep him here until someone arrives to get him. Why?"

"He claims he didn't do it," Alex said.

"I've heard that excuse from a man that I watched kill another man," Nelson said, "I'm sure you've heard it."

"Yes, but why tell the bounty hunter?" Alex asked.

"Thought you might let him walk?" Nelson suggested.

"He told his sad story," Alex said.

"I hope he didn't have you crying," Nelson said.

"He claims Owen did it," Alex said, "But he described Owen, he didn't give us his name."

"So? Someone will pick Owen up and they will find out who really did it," Nelson said.

"Owen's dead," Alex said. Nelson stopped and looked at Alex.

"That piece of scum is dead?" Nelson asked, "He didn't just make it look like he died?"

"I know dead," Alex said, "Especially after I shoot them."

"You shot Owen?" Nelson asked.

"Yes," Alex answered, "Any chance that they can prove who did it without Owen talking?"

"I don't know," Nelson said, "But I'll pass the information on to the person that comes for him." Alex nodded. "Why'd you shoot Owen?"

"He shot first," Alex said standing up. I stood up as well.

"I guess that's one less piece of scum around," Nelson said.

"We'll see you when we bring the next person on the wanted posters back," Alex said. Then we left. We went back to the hotel. I packed up the clean clothes that were sitting on my bed before going to sleep.

The next morning we set out after the last wanted person. We stopped in towns to ask questions, gain information and resupply. I don't know how long we were on this man's trail, but when we finally caught the bastard I was almost ready to turn in my gun and go back to farming. Even Alex was getting tired, but she didn't let it show as much.

On the way back, every time we turned our backs he tried to escape. Alex finally offered to let him drag behind his horse, because it wasn't like we actually needed him alive. He was better behaved for a while until he figured that Alex may have been bluffing. It only took ten minutes being dragged behind his horse to convince him to behave.

We arrived back at the city and barely stopped to tie our horses up before dragging him inside the sheriff's office. Nelson led the way to the cells and locked the door behind the man. We went back to Nelson's office and sat down. Nelson pulled the envelope out of his desk and handed it over to Alex. Alex put it away.

"The man you brought in last time," Nelson said, "The one who said he didn't do it."

"I remember," Alex said.

"He really didn't do it," Nelson said, "He was supposed to the key witness in the case, but he ran before they could get him to testify. The wanted poster was to get him back in the hands of the law."

"What happened to him?" Alex asked.

"He was charged a fine for causing the law to go after him," Nelson answered, "Then they told him the suspected thief was the dead and took him home."

"He must've been relieved," Alex said.

"He was," Nelson said, "Got the amount you need for Riverside?"

"I do now," Alex answered.

"You have a month to get there," Nelson said.

"I have one more stop and then I'll hit the tournament," Alex said.

"I wish I was there to see it," Nelson said.

"You just want to be there to make sure I'm not cheating," Alex said.

"I've watched you play poker," Nelson said, "You don't need to cheat."

"Well, I have one fan at least," Alex said.

"You shouldn't have any problems even if the rest of the players are cheating," I commented. Nelson chuckled.

"Looks like you have two fans," Nelson said.

"I'll judge my poker skills after the tournament," Alex said.

"Need any more work?" Nelson asked.

"Probably another time," Alex said standing up.

"I'll keep an ear out to see how you did in the tournament," Nelson said. Alex nodded and then we left. We went to the hotel. This time I sent my clothes to the laundry and took a bath before falling into bed. In the morning my laundry was finished and waiting for me. I met Alex in the restaurant and after breakfast we left the city behind.

So six months after we left we arrived back in Cartwheel.

FREDERICK
CHAPTER 4

Toby

We rode into town and up the main street to the hotel. As we got closer I could see Jacob standing out front.

"Oh no," Alex said.

"He couldn't have known we were coming, maybe he's waiting for someone else," I suggested.

"And pigs have taken up soaring with the eagles," Alex said. We didn't say anything else as we got closer. We stopped the horses in front of the hotel.

"Just the two people I was hoping would ride into town," Jacob said smiling up at us. Alex got down first and tied her horse to the hitching post. I did the same.

"Hurry up with what you want, I want to check in," Alex said.

"Nadine has made up beds for both of you and would be extremely disappointed if you didn't show up for the supper she prepared just for you two," Jacob said.

"If I wanted that much horseshit I would have stayed at the farm," I replied.

"Lady Grace sent a message saying you two were headed back here and Nadine got ready for guests," Jacob said.

"Fine, we'll be her guests," Alex said. I looked at her, that didn't sound like Alex.

"But," Alex said, "If you so much as mention whatever job you have up your sleeve, I will leave and be half way across the country before tomorrow morning." That sounded better. Jacob's smile faltered a little, but he recovered quickly and his smile came back full force.

"Very well," Jacob answered. Alex and I got back on our horses.

"See you at supper," I said then we headed for Jacob's house. Arriving there, we went around to the back. We put our horses away in the barn before heading for the house.

"You think he'll listen?" I asked.

"He might just invite the person who is hiring for the job over for supper," Alex said, "In which case, I put my hat on and leave. He'll talk around to the job eventually. I just want to relax at least one night before then." I opened the kitchen door and Alex stepped inside, I followed her. Nadine was nowhere in sight.

"Something is cooking," I commented, sniffing the air. Someone moved upstairs.

"She's in the guest room," Alex said as she relaxed a bit.

"Shall we see if Jacob has something to drink around here and wait for her down here?" I suggested.

"Sure," Alex said. She headed for the cabinet. I put my hat on a hook and sat down. Alex set a bottle down and went looking for glasses. I pulled out the stopper and started pouring once Alex returned with the glasses. Alex took a drink. After setting her glass down she took off her hat and set it on the table.

"Lady Grace sent a message," Alex said, "Between her and Jacob we could die broke."

"Lady Grace isn't her husband, she doesn't realize how much gunslingers are worth," I said, "As for Jacob, he seems to be in the business for the danger and adventure."

"Then next time, if anyone shoots at us, we'll use him for cover," Alex said. We both finished our drinks and I poured more into the glasses. The footfalls came down the stairs and into the kitchen. Nadine looked the same as the last time I had seen her.

"Alex, Toby," Nadine said.

"You sound surprised to see us," Alex said.

"Jacob said you were coming, but I didn't think you would actually accept the offer to stay here," Nadine said.

"We said we'd stay as long as we're allowed to relax and he

doesn't mention a job," I said.

"Jacob said that Lady Grace sent a message," Alex said.

"She wrote a letter to us," Nadine said, "She thanked Jacob for that last job and said you two had left for parts unknown. Jacob jumped to the conclusion that you would come back here."

"When did this letter arrive?" Alex asked.

"Three months ago, I think," Nadine answered. Nadine went over and checked on the oven. Then she came back to the table. I poured myself a third glass.

"Got into Jacob's alcohol already, I see," Nadine said.

"He invited, we just accepted his hospitality," I replied, "And we'll leave if he doesn't hold his end."

"Yes, the job," Nadine said as she sat down.

"You know about this job?" Alex said.

"A man came to town a month ago and started flashing money around," Nadine answered, "Talks funny too. He came looking for Jacob two days after showing up. Said he had a job."

"Talks funny?" I asked.

"Like he's stuffy and rich, but it sounds fake," Nadine answered, "He isn't fake as far as being rich is concerned, but he wasn't raised stuffy."

"And the job?" Alex asked.

"Wouldn't talk about it in front of me," Nadine answered, "Said it wasn't for sensitive ears."

"Then maybe he shouldn't be saying it," Alex suggested.

"According to this man, a woman should stay in the kitchen and out of a man's world," Nadine said, "I just about took a swing at him the night Jacob invited him over for dinner. I told Jacob if that Frederick came over here again they would both be out on their butts."

"The man wants to be shot, right?" I asked.

"No, he wants revenge against a former partner," Nadine answered.

"I wonder how much the former partner would pay to have him shot," Alex said.

"I don't know that much detail," Nadine said, "But don't suggest killing off a client in front of Jacob."

"I know better," Alex said.

Nadine looked at Alex, "You're letting your hair grow out

again."

"I haven't bothered to cut it," Alex replied.

"You're gonna have to start braiding it soon," Nadine said.

"I know, but right now it's still too short," Alex said.

"Don't let Frederick know you're female," Nadine said, "He's likely to escort you back here and lecture you on the proper place for a woman."

"You can shoot someone without killing them," Alex said, "That is, if shooting at them and missing isn't good enough. Besides, when did Jacob start taking revenge jobs?"

"I don't know," Nadine said, "It must be one of those details he wouldn't mention in front of me."

"Will Jacob pay us for this one?" I asked.

"He didn't pay you for the last one?" Nadine asked.

"He tried not to," I answered, "He gambled away his thousand, but we had to steal our money from him before he gambled that away as well." Nadine stiffened up.

"He's gambling again?" Nadine asked Alex.

"And drinking," Alex answered, "After every job that ends in another town."

"The drinking explains his losing," Nadine said, "But that doesn't explain why he's doing either after he promised me he had quit."

"I don't know, but if he doesn't start paying for the jobs I help him with I'm not going to help him anymore," Alex said, "I've taken too many losses and had to steal back the money that he owes me."

"I think I will have a discussion with him over that," Nadine said. The front door opened and closed. Then Jacob came into the kitchen.

"I see you've made yourself at home," Jacob said seeing the half empty bottle on the table. I poured Alex and myself another drink.

"You invited us," Alex answered.

"Yes, I did," Jacob said. Nadine stood up and checked on what was in the oven.

"Supper is ready," Nadine said, "Move so I can set the table." Alex grabbed her glass and I picked up my glass and the bottle. Alex and Jacob moved to the other room. I set the bottle back in the cabinet, then helped Nadine set the table. Alex's and Jacob's voices drifted in from the other room.

"And what's wrong this time?" Jacob asked.

"Try not getting paid," Alex snapped, "Everyone I have worked for has been willing to pay, but you come up with a job and I never see the money. I don't do these jobs as a favour to anybody."

"I saved you from death and you can't do an old man a couple of favours," Jacob said.

"That was three years and a hundred jobs for you," Alex said, "If you need any more help you can hire people. Then when they beat your skull in I can drag you back here to Nadine. My life isn't worth it anymore."

"You wouldn't do that," Jacob said.

"You wanna watch me?" Alex asked. Jacob was silent. "Then make sure you pay me next time, before you start into your pleasures."

Nadine finished setting things on the table. Then she straightened her shoulders and went into the other room.

"Supper is served," Nadine said then came back into the kitchen. I sat down at the place where I had put my glass. Alex and Jacob came back into the kitchen. Everyone else sat down and supper started. Very few words were exchanged at we ate. After supper Alex helped Nadine with the dishes, while Jacob waited in the living room and I went outside.

I found somewhere to sit and relax. Alex joined me after the dishes were finished.

"I wouldn't recommend going into the house," Alex said as she closed her eyes.

"Jacob is in for a tongue lashing?" I asked.

"I didn't say anything to her while we were doing dishes, but I could tell she was getting angry with Jacob and she was headed for the living room as I went out back," Alex answered.

"Do you think we should've told her?" I asked.

"Yes," Alex answered, "Some times Jacob gets a little high headed and Nadine is just the person to put him straight."

"You don't think it'll do permanent damage to the relationship?"

"Never has before, and Nadine has dealt with all of these behaviours before."

We sat there in the quiet. About sunset Jacob came storming out of the house toward us.

"You lied," he said to Alex.

"And you expected differently?" Alex asked, "You would've done the same thing."

"Now Nadine wants to go on the next job to keep me in line," Jacob said.

"Doesn't sound like a bad idea," I commented.

"You stay out of this," Jacob told me.

"Why?" I asked, "I wasn't gonna get paid as well as Alex and that's wrong."

"I'm gonna lose the next job if Nadine demands to come," Jacob said.

"Yeah, Nadine said something about the idiot you've been dealing with," Alex said, "A man who doesn't think a lady should be anywhere but the kitchen."

"Doesn't sound like a man I'd want to deal with," I said.

"He has money," Jacob said.

"Is that what made you to break your no revenge rule? Money?" Alex asked, "That's pathetic."

"I have no part in the revenge part, I just guard him on his trip," Jacob said.

"For that amount of money the man is paying you for your gun, not as guard dog," I said.

"For someone new to this business you seem to think you know a lot," Jacob replied.

"That's because I'm willing to be hired out as a gun," Alex answered, "And Toby has been traveling with me. He's learned the difference in what the person wants by the price they're willing to pay."

"You hire yourself out as a gunhand?" Jacob asked.

"Good work, pays better than guard duty and is less tedious," Alex answered.

"And you die twice as fast," Jacob said.

"When I'm dead, I'm dead," Alex replied.

"I think it's time to go to bed," I commented as I stood up.

"Sounds good," Alex said. We left Jacob standing outside and went into the house. Nadine was sitting at the table, doing mending.

"You weren't gonna tell me?" Nadine asked once the door was closed.

"That's what I told Jacob," Alex answered.

"I'm glad you did anyway," Nadine said.

"Are you serious about going with him on this next job?" Alex asked.

"Someone has to keep Jacob in line," Nadine answered. Alex nodded. I went up stairs. I went into the guest room that I used last time. Alex came up a few minutes later and went into the other room. After undressing, I went to bed.

It was sunrise when I woke up. I dressed and went down stairs. Nadine was already working in the kitchen.

"Good morning Toby," Nadine said when she saw me.

"Good morning," I replied, "Need any help?" Nadine gave me a funny look. "At home the minute we were up we were expected to help with something. Now if I'm staying at someone's house, it makes me feel better to help."

"A form of payment," Nadine said.

"Yes," I replied.

"I guess there are a few things you could do," Nadine said. She listed off a few things and I started working.

By the time Jacob came down stairs breakfast was on the table and I was already eating. Nadine had eaten and was keeping the food warm. Jacob sat down and ate but didn't say anything. Alex came down just as I finished.

"Good morning, Alex," Nadine said.

"Good morning," Alex replied as she sat down. Nadine served her breakfast. Once Jacob was finished he left the house. Alex had eaten all she was going to by then. She once again helped Nadine wash dishes.

"With you two around cooking and cleaning gets easier," Nadine commented once the dishes were done.

"We were raised wrong," Alex replied.

"No, you both were raised right," Nadine said, "Jacob would never even think to ask if I needed help.

"You're welcome," I said. Jacob came back into the house.

"Willing to listen to what the job is yet?" Jacob asked Alex.

"Might as well," Alex replied, "If not now, then you'll keep asking."

"The man's name is Frederick Hall," Jacob said, "He needs

guards so that he can go from here to Georgetown because he needs to talk to a former colleague."

"Leaving when?" Alex asked.

"In the next few days," Jacob answered, "But he wants to meet his guards before hiring them."

"We might as well meet him now," Alex said. I stood up and we followed Jacob out. Jacob led us to a house and into the study. I guessed that this was where he had gone this morning, Frederick was sitting alone in the study. He wore a fancy suit and tried to sit like he'd been born with the money he had now. His hair was brown, his eyes blue and if you dressed him in everyday clothes you couldn't have picked him out of a field of labours.

"Mr. Hall," Jacob said.

"Mr. Wescott," the man acknowledged Jacob.

"These are the men I was talking about," Jacob said, "Alex and Toby."

"Ah," Frederick stood up to greet us, "Nice to meet you, Alexander and Tobias." He held his hand out. Alex paused for a second then shook it. Frederick turned to me. I considered breaking it and telling him not to call me that, but I refrained and simply shook his hand. "Then we can leave tomorrow."

"We'll be ready," Jacob said and turned to leave.

"I was hoping to ask Mr. Hall a question," Alex said. Jacob looked at Frederick; Frederick shrugged. Jacob left. Frederick sat down and signaled Alex to ask the question. Alex moved around and sat down on Frederick's desk, in front of the drawer he was about to open.

"So," Alex said, "We'll be traveling together." Frederick was silent; slowly he raised his eyes to hers.

"Yes," Frederick said.

"Then let's get one thing straight before we head out," Alex said. He didn't answer. "I am Alex and that is my partner Toby, we answer to nothing else. Understand?"

"And if I don't?" Frederick asked in a last attempt at defiance.

"That is why I have a gun and Toby has a gun and you don't," Alex answered.

"Jacob wouldn't like that," Frederick said.

"And Jacob can't save you if you're already dead," Alex replied, "And he likes us too much to hold a grudge for more than a couple days. By then we'll be a long way from here, enjoying the time without him." Frederick's face went another shade whiter.

"Who am I?" Alex asked.

"Alex," Frederick answered.

"And my partner is?" Alex asked.

"Toby," Frederick answered.

"Very good," Alex said, she got off the desk, "We'll be going now and I'm sure we'll see you tomorrow."

"Yes," Frederick said. We left the office.

"If you pulled out your gun, I think he would have shit his pants," I commented.

"All the more reason to not have taken it out," Alex said. We headed back to Jacob's house. Nadine was sitting in the parlour, mending, but Jacob was nowhere to be seen.

"When're we leaving?" Nadine asked.

"Tomorrow," Alex answered.

"Jacob believes that I can't go if I don't know the details," Nadine said.

"Someone needs to keep him in line," I said, "And you're the best person to do that from what Alex has said. Which means we need you along, even if he doesn't want you along."

"What did you think of Frederick?" Nadine asked.

"I almost shot him," Alex said, "But I just scared him instead."

"What did he do?" Nadine asked.

"He figured that we abbreviated our names and that anyone with money could extend them," I answered, "The only person I will let extend my name is my mother and she doesn't do that unless she has a very good reason."

"Still making friends all around," Nadine said.

"Jacob said Frederick was paying a lot of money for guards," Alex said, "Do you know approximately how much? I said something last time, so he isn't going to mention how much this time."

"It was close to seven hundred a person," Nadine said, "But I don't remember exactly how much."

"We'll just have to count it before he can spend any," Alex said.

"That doesn't sound like guard duty pay," I said.

"You think Frederick is hiring you for something other than guard duty?" Nadine asked.

"When was the last time you heard about a guard job that paid that much, with the exception of Lord Bennett?" Alex asked.

"Usually it's five dollars a day, plus expenses," Nadine said, "I never thought about that. Then what does he want?"

"A gunslinger gets paid by the job," Alex said, "The person buys the use of the gun and that isn't an unusual amount to be paid."

"Jacob doesn't take gunslinger jobs unless there aren't any others," Nadine said.

"I think Frederick is paying Jacob for the use of his gun," I said, "He'll make it so that the person he wants shot will pose some threat and as guard Jacob will shoot the person. Job done and Frederick finds some place 'safe.' Jacob takes the seven hundred dollars and never thinks about it again."

"But you two will be along," Nadine said.

"He assumed we would be similar to Jacob in that regard," Alex said. Nadine started to look nervous.

"It'll work out," I told her, "As you said, we'll be along." Nadine nodded.

"And we already know his game," Alex said, "Besides there's always the man he wants us to shoot."

"But you don't know anything about him," Nadine said, "He could be worse."

"Maybe," Alex said, "We'll see." Nadine nodded. Alex and I went into the kitchen. We sat there and played poker until it was time to make lunch, and then we broke off to make lunch. Nadine and Jacob joined us to eat. Then we did dishes and went back to our poker game.

When it was time to make supper we cleared out on Nadine's order. We went out back. I found the spot where I had sat the other night. Alex seemed restless and wandered.

"Something on your mind?" I asked.

"Not really," Alex said, "I just don't feel like I can sit still."

"Based on the last six months I would have to say that's normal," I said.

"I shouldn't be this bad until tomorrow," Alex said.

"Maybe you're nervous," I suggested, "Or you're just itching to shoot Frederick."

"I'm not going shoot Frederick until he has done something to deserve it," Alex said, "So far I've managed to straighten him out without shooting him."

"Yeah," I replied. Alex didn't say anything more and I left the quiet alone. When Nadine called us we went in for supper.

Supper was quiet with only a few words exchanged. Afterward I headed for the saloon and played poker for the evening.

I woke up at sunrise at the sound of someone going downstairs. I got up, packed everything, and I went downstairs. Nadine was busy making a quick breakfast.

"Good morning," Nadine said.

"Good morning," I replied.

"I left Jacob to sleep," Nadine said, "I wasn't sure when we're supposed to leave."

"Jacob will be up before we have to leave," Alex said as she came in the back door.

"When did you get up?" I asked, as Nadine recovered from her surprise.

"A couple hours ago," Alex answered, "I couldn't sleep." Nadine went back to making breakfast. "Frederick is getting ready."

"Should we be concerned?" I asked.

"No, he won't be looking for us for a least an hour," Alex answered, "But it looks like he'll be on horseback."

"That is good," Nadine said, "I was scared he would want a stage and then I would be forced to ride with him."

"According to Paige, it'll just be him and us. He's even giving his staff time off while he's gone," Alex said.

"Paige?" I asked.

"His cook," Alex answered, "Very talkative young lady."

"Why would he hire Paige as his cook?" Nadine asked.

"Because she had just lost her job cooking for the hotel and he won't cook for himself," Alex answered.

"And her parents allow this?" Nadine asked.

"She isn't giving them a choice by the sounds of it," Alex said, "They want her to marry a man who lives somewhere else and won't come here even to meet her. Her father wants to send her off to get married, but she doesn't want to leave Cartwheel."

"I doubt her parents will take no for very long," Nadine said.

"I'm not gonna get into that argument," Alex replied. Nadine served breakfast. Jacob came down the stairs and sat down. Nadine got up and served him breakfast.

After breakfast Alex and I did the dishes. Then we saddled our horses and set out for Frederick's house. Jacob went in and told Frederick we were ready. When they came out Frederick only looked briefly at each of us, so Jacob must have told him about Nadine accompanying us. Frederick retrieved his horse and then the five of us rode out of town.

Jacob and Frederick were in the lead, Nadine was behind them and Alex and I brought in the rear. It was a quiet morning, followed by a brief lunch.

In the middle of the afternoon Alex started to drop back. I caught up with, rode beside Nadine. Nadine looked at me and then turned to look at Alex. She looked at me again. I pretended not to notice. Nadine went back to looking forward. As the afternoon went on, Alex continued to drop back, until she was out of sight. The sun was setting when we came to a town.

Nadine, Jacob and Frederick got rooms at the hotel. I got permission to sleep in the stable. Alex hadn't caught up with us.

I was sitting outside the hotel with Nadine and Jacob when Alex rode up.

"Where did you go?" Nadine asked.

"I got bored with the conversation," Alex answered.

"You and Toby weren't talking," Nadine said.

"That would explain it," Alex said thoughtfully.

"Who's following us?" Jacob asked.

"No one," Alex answered, "But there is someone following Frederick."

"And you don't think that's a concern?" Jacob asked.

"He was watching Frederick back in Cartwheel, if he's going to do anything Frederick would already be dead," Alex answered.

"Why would someone just watch him?" Nadine asked.

"To see what he's going to do next," I suggested.

"And to keep him out of trouble," Alex said, "The man was hired by Frederick's former partner."

"The former partner must have money if he can hire someone to watch Frederick that much," Jacob said.

"It sounds like Frederick got the shorter end of the stick," Alex replied, "My guess is that he's out to get the rest of the stick."

"Did you tell that to the man following Frederick?" Jacob asked.

"I told him that we were headed for Georgetown," Alex said, "Since he just shrugged at that I don't think we have anything to worry about."

"You told him where we were headed?" Jacob said, "What were you thinking?"

"That guard duty is boring," Alex answered.

"You could get us all killed," Jacob said.

"Is that any worse than not getting paid?" Alex asked.

"You have more than enough money to survive," Jacob said.

"Is that how you justify it to yourself?" Alex asked, "Because I do other jobs I must have money. The fact that when I'm doing those other jobs I have to pay for all of my own expenses never came into your head? When I showed up for the last job I didn't have much for money. I got into the poker game on reputation alone."

"You had money to stay at the hotel rather than at my house," Jacob said.

"That's because staying with you gets me angry at you and I feel more like shooting you than working with you," Alex said, "You see me as owing you everything. I have paid you by working more than enough jobs for free and still you demand more. If it wasn't for visiting Nadine, I probably wouldn't stop in Cartwheel anymore."

"And this is a good reason to tell a man where we're headed?" Jacob asked.

"I didn't just stop and tell him where we were going," Alex said, "I spent the time talking to him. Learning things. Like the fact that Frederick's former partner isn't in Georgetown, he's in Riverside."

"Then we need to tell Frederick," Jacob said.

"No," Nadine said. Her voice was quiet but firm. Jacob stopped and stared at her.

"Frederick doesn't need to be told by us," Alex said.

"And who is supposed to tell him?" Jacob asked.

"Who ever he's meeting in Georgetown," Nadine said, "If you are only guarding him then you don't get into his business."

"And if he dies while I'm guarding him, that puts my reputation at risk," Jacob said.

"And that's why the person waited until after you were paid to kill Lord Bennett," Alex said, "Because he knew you wouldn't go after him once you were paid."

"Unfortunately for him, you were willing to take the job," Jacob said.

"It was part of the guard job," I said, "If you want repeat service you don't let the client die just because you have been paid. Being paid by Lady Grace just meant that our expenses were paid."

"Since your head is too thick I think it's time for bed," Alex said before turning and heading for the stable. I stood up and followed her. Once inside we climbed up to the loft. I lay down and went to sleep.

The sky was just beginning to lighten when I woke up. I listened for the sound that woke me up. Five minutes passed without any unusual sounds. I stood up and brushed myself off. Then a whimper came from farther along the loft. I walked over to where Alex was sleeping. Looked like she was having a nightmare again. Maybe it was just the time of the morning, or dealing with Jacob, but I felt like finding whoever caused those nightmares and beating them until they wouldn't be able to get up. Instead I bent down and shook Alex's shoulder.

"Alex," I said. Alex blinked up at me sleepily then slowly sat up.

"I was having a nightmare again," Alex said.

"Looked like it," I replied, "But it's getting close to time to get up anyway."

"Yeah," Alex said. I left her alone and went down the ladder. Finding some water I washed up. When Alex was ready, we headed over to the restaurant together. A number of men were eating before they had the go off to work. Nadine sat at a corner table. Alex and I went over to her.

"Good morning," I said.

"Good morning," Nadine replied as we sat down. Having acknowledged us she reverted to staring into the distance and sipping her tea. She didn't notice the food in front of her.

"Nadine," Alex said touching Nadine's hand. Nadine looked at Alex and then down at her plate. She started to eat.

I finished by the time that Alex had finished half her plate. She pushed it to one side.

"What's wrong?" Alex asked Nadine.

"Jacob is being stupid," Nadine answered, "And I don't understand why. Listening to him, it sounds like if Frederick asked him to, he would kill Frederick's old partner. I thought I knew Jacob, but this doesn't seem like him."

"Jacob seems to like Frederick," Alex said, "That makes him more willing to do Frederick a favour. But I doubt, no matter what he says, that Jacob would kill Frederick's old partner unless it's to protect Frederick."

"But," Nadine started.

"To prove I'm right," Alex interrupted, "We'll find out if we have switched directions. Because if Jacob has forgotten his oath to guard, not kill, he will tell Frederick that his partner isn't in Georgetown." Nadine thought about that for a minute.

"What if he has forgotten it?" Nadine asked.

"We knock him in the back of the head and drag him back to Cartwheel," Alex answered, "And then explain why when he wakes up."

"And Frederick?" Nadine asked.

"Frederick will have other problems," Alex answered.

"What do you mean?" Nadine asked, concern coming over her face.

"It won't kill him," Alex answered. Nadine looked at Alex wanting to hear what Alex knew, but just then Jacob came into the restaurant. Having seen us, he came over.

"Frederick should be down shortly," Jacob said, "Then we'll be on our way."

"You found a job that didn't involve getting up before sunrise, but the employer is a dunce," Alex said, "Can't you find any good jobs?"

"It pays well enough," Jacob answered.

"Money is only half the job," Alex said, "The better half usually, but still only half."

"And you don't ever come across jobs you shouldn't have taken in the first place?" Jacob asked.

"Sure, I have," Alex answered, "But I don't usually get paid for them."

"You would work for free?" Jacob asked.

"I end up doing it for you," Alex replied.

"Being a gun hand pays," Jacob said, "And you do that."

"Doesn't mean I always make money on it," Alex answered, "Too many times you pay for your own hotel, your own food and any other supplies you need. Then you break even, without so much as an extra dollar."

"Then why would you work for free?" Jacob asked.

"Which is better being rich or being right?" Alex asked.

"The right side can pay," Jacob said.

"Only if you're bounty hunting," Alex said.

"Lady Grace paid you," Jacob said.

"Lady Grace paid us enough to cover the cost of the hotel," I said, "If we wanted money to find the next job, we would have had to take another job in Dustcloud. Assuming that we found it before we went to bed for the night."

"I have one final thing to say on this topic this morning," Alex said, "In doing this job I'm looking for rich, because I don't think what is being done is right." Alex stood up and started toward the door. I followed her. We went to the stable and got our horses ready. Just as we started Nadine came in. She went to her horse. When the three of us had our horses ready we took them outside and waited for the other two.

"Frederick had just come in when I left," Nadine said. A short, solid man stepped out onto the hotel porch. There was no gun at his hip, even though he looked like there should be. I could swear he nodded at Alex, but I didn't see Alex respond in any way. He sat down with his cup of coffee to watch the traffic go past.

"Let's speed up this process," Alex said. She turned and went back into the stables. I took the reins of her horse and Nadine's, while Nadine followed Alex in. A few moments later they came out with Jacob and Frederick's horses. We mounted our own horses and led the two other around to the restaurant. We sat outside while we waited.

Ten minutes later Jacob and Frederick came out of the restaurant and mounted on their horses. Jacob and Frederick took the lead and we headed out of town.

Alex wouldn't talk to Jacob for the rest of the week it took to reach to Georgetown. Nadine, Alex and I would talk to each other, but we left Jacob and Frederick to themselves.

Georgetown was twice the size of Cartwheel. And it seemed to have three times the people. The noise was the first thing to hit you, and before you could recover the smell hit you. The source of the noise was obvious, but aside from the people and the horses the source of the smell was hard to identify.

We stopped in front of a hotel. Frederick and Jacob went inside.

"Why would anyone want to live here?" Nadine asked.

"There are jobs here," Alex answered, "And entertainment when they have money."

"There are jobs in places that don't smell this bad," Nadine said. Alex shrugged. Jacob came back out.

"There were only three rooms left. Frederick got one and I got the other two," Jacob said, "And they prefer that people don't sleep in the stables."

"And the problem is?" I asked. Jacob opened his mouth to say something.

"Toby and I have shared hotel rooms before," Alex interrupted him, "It just means we have to figure out who has to bring his bedroll up." Jacob handed me the key.

"The stable is just behind the hotel," Jacob said getting back on his horse and taking the reins of Frederick's horse. We followed him around back to the stable. Each of us dealt with our horse and we left Jacob to deal with Frederick's and went back to the hotel. Alex and I put our saddlebags in our room before going back downstairs.

Jacob was just coming in.

"How long are we here for?" Alex asked.

"Frederick said we'd be here three days," Jacob answered.

"All right," Alex said as we started to leave the hotel.

"Stay out of trouble," Jacob said.

"We will if you will," I replied. Then Alex and I left the hotel and headed over to the nearest saloon. Alex joined the poker game and I watched.

When the game ended, Alex and I went back to the hotel and up to our room. I rolled out my bedroll and lay down to sleep.

I woke up to the sounds of Alex tossing and turning in the bed. I sat up. It was still dark outside; perhaps it was two or three in the morning. I got up and went over to the bed.

"Alex," I said shaking her shoulder. She moved away from me, but didn't wake up.

"Alex," I repeated in a louder volume. She turned in her sleep. I could feel the panic rising, but I pushed it back. She said that she was a heavy sleeper when she went to sleep, which wasn't that long ago. So, what do you do for a heavy sleeper who is in the middle of a nightmare?

Alex whimpered. I sat down on the bed and took her in to my arms. She seemed to relax. Sitting there I felt my eyelids grow heavy.

The sun was shining when I opened them. Alex was sleeping soundly in my arms. I gently put her back on the bed and got up. I went over to the window and looked out. Based on the position of the sun and the amount of people about, I would have to say it was about noon.

There was a knock on the door. I went over and opened it. Nadine stood there looking worried.

"Good morning," I said.

"More like good afternoon," Nadine said, "I've been wondering where you two were." I could hear Alex moving behind me.

"Sleeping," I replied.

"It must have been a really long poker game for Alex to sleep this long," Nadine said.

"What time is it?" Alex asked from where she was sitting on the bed.

"Just about one o'clock," Nadine answered.

"Time to get up for lunch," Alex said standing up.

"I'll meet you in the restaurant," Nadine said, turning and going down the hall. Alex and I joined her for lunch in a few minutes.

"Where's Jacob?" Alex asked.

"He went off to look at something after I dragged him shopping," Nadine answered, "Frederick went off before Jacob woke up."

"Jacob said we would be here for three days," I said, "I assume he's going off to find the former partner."

"Jacob didn't think he should do it alone," Nadine said, "Apparently Frederick doesn't know someone is following him around. Jacob just about said something, but I stopped him."

"Frederick's former partner must've been the brains," Alex said, "He has Frederick followed and Frederick doesn't notice, he managed to give Frederick the short end of the stick and he didn't stay where Frederick would go looking for him. All Frederick seems to have done that was smart is hire Jacob."

"We'll see how this job goes," Nadine said, "What are your plans for this afternoon?"

"Poker," Alex answered.

"Same thing," I answered.

"Keep an eye out for Jacob," Nadine said, "I think I will spend the afternoon in the room." Alex nodded.

When we finished eating Alex and I left Nadine in the restaurant and went over to the saloon. Jacob was sitting at a table with a quarter of a bottle of whiskey left in front of him. He was singing something that I didn't recognize. Everyone else in the saloon would glare at him occasionally.

"He drinks fast," I commented in a low volume to Alex.

"I'm surprised there's any left," Alex replied in the same volume.

"Shall we take him back to Nadine?" I asked. Alex's eye glowed briefly with laughter.

"I think we should," Alex said. We went over to the table.

"Decided to stop by for a drink?" Jacob asked breaking off in the middle of a verse.

"Nadine is looking for you," Alex said.

"All she wants to do is shopping," Jacob said.

"Then how about we take you back to your hotel room and you can hide from her there?" I suggested. Jacob laughed.

"That might work," Jacob said trying to rise to his feet. He made it far enough to slide toward the floor. I grabbed one arm and Alex moved the chair out of the way before taking the other arm. Then we dragged him out of the saloon with applause following us. We dragged him back to the hotel. Once inside the clerk saw us.

"Room 209," the desk clerk said.

"Thank you," I said. We headed up the stairs. Stopping at 209 Alex knocked on the door. Nadine opened it a moment later. She took one look at Jacob and a flame came into her eyes.

"Can't hide here," Jacob said in a stage whisper.

"No more hiding," I replied.

"Put him on the bed," Nadine said. Alex and I dragged Jacob in to the room and dropped him on the bed before leaving the room again. Nadine closed the door behind her. We went back to the saloon. No one seemed to notice our presence. Alex joined the poker game and I watched.

Alex and I ended up playing in a mini poker tournament with the saloon owner and several local players, which lasted until midnight on the third day. Once the game was over we staggered back to our hotel room and collapsed. We had both ended up lying on the bed, but we were both asleep the minute we closed our eyes.

A knock came at the door causing me to wake up. Alex rolled off me and I got up. I opened the door. Jacob was standing there. He seemed a little haggard, but otherwise fine.

"Yes?" I asked.

"Frederick has determined that his former partner isn't here," Jacob said.

"Finally?" Alex asked, "It only took him three days."

"He's downstairs eating breakfast and believes that we should leave once he's done," Jacob said, "We're headed for Riverside."

"We'll be ready," I said before closing the door. I went over and washed up. Alex sat up and rubbed the sleep out of her eyes.

"Maybe two days of poker isn't a good idea," I said.

"I'm used to this much sleep," Alex said, "Besides now I have three thousand dollars and am headed for Riverside."

"Think Jacob will let you join the tournament when you're supposed to be doing a job?" I asked.

"Let him try to stop me," Alex answered. She got out of bed and washed up. Then we grabbed our gear and headed down to the stable. Nadine was already standing outside with her horse.

"Sleep in?" Nadine asked.

"According to Jacob," I said, "Could've slept longer if he hadn't interrupted."

"The poker game didn't end until two last night," Alex said, "But we're up now."

"I came down here when Frederick got up," Nadine said.

"We should probably get our horses before he and Jacob are done," Alex said. Alex and I went into the stable. We prepared our horses as well as Jacob and Frederick's horses. Then we led them out to where Nadine stood.

"So, Frederick couldn't find his former partner," Alex said.

"He spent three days with some old drinking buddies and came back with the news that his partner is in Riverside," Nadine said, "Sounds like he left his guards behind because he didn't want his friends to end up in the hands of the law."

"Nice friends," Alex commented.

"Thank you for bringing Jacob back," Nadine said.

"The other people in the saloon appreciated it," I said, "So, it was no problem."

"I can't believe he did that," Nadine said, "And he got a long lecture on that kind of behaviour, especially on a job. Frederick could have needed him during that time and he would have been too drunk to do anything."

"I hate to say it, but we told you what was going on," Alex said.

"I know," Nadine said, "But I didn't want to believe he broke his promise to me."

"He'll straighten up for while," Alex said, "Your lectures do that." Nadine nodded, but didn't look satisfied.

Frederick and Jacob came along and we headed out of Georgetown.

Another week of sleeping in stables and we arrived in Riverside.

Riverside is a city on the edge of a large river. It is also double in size. First there was the city of tents that surrounded the city on three sides of the city then we actually came to the city itself, which looked like it was ready to burst. Over it a large ship loomed at the end of the dock, sitting in the river.

We stopped at three hotels before we found one with rooms. In fact it had three rooms. A nice hotel in this city at this time and it has three hotel rooms available? It was a little strange. Then we had to find a stable for our horses. That was much harder, but we finally found a stable. It looked like it would fall down if one breathed on it wrong, but the owner slept in the loft so it couldn't have been as bad as it looked.

Alex and I dropped our gear in our room before going back downstairs. Alex asked the clerk a couple questions and then we left. Alex led the way down the sidewalk to the nearest saloon. It was empty, except for a man sitting at one of the tables with two gunslingers standing near him and a barman standing behind the bar. The two gunslingers stood up straighter when we entered. Alex ignored them and went over to the man at the table.

"I'm told you're the one I need to talk to about entering the poker tournament," Alex said.

"I am, but you're just about late," the man said.

"Problems on the road," Alex replied.

"I need two thousand dollars and your signature," the man said, placing a pen on the paper that was sitting in front of him. Alex pulled the money out of her pocket and placed it next to the paper before picking up the pen and signing her name.

"You'll be in the last qualifying round," the man said, "Which will take place here tomorrow afternoon. If you get in, you'd better be on the boat before nightfall." Alex nodded.

"And the two thousand doesn't cover the five hundred you'll need to get into the qualifying round," the man said.

"Fine," Alex said.

"Good luck," the man said. The gunslingers visibly relaxed as Alex and I headed for the door. We left the saloon and headed back to the hotel. Jacob and Nadine were sitting on the porch.

"Where did you two go?" Jacob asked.

"To talk to a man about a poker game," Alex answered.

"You entered the tournament?" Jacob asked.

"Unless Frederick needs us for anything, why shouldn't I?" Alex replied, "You're free and Toby can help if necessary."

"Where'd you get the two thousand?" Jacob asked.

"By taking well paying jobs," Alex answered, "Now are you finished questioning my actions? Because if you aren't I'm sure that we can discuss some of your recent actions."

"So, you'll be in the big game on the boat?" Nadine asked.

"Have to do a qualifying around first," Alex answered.

"You shouldn't have any trouble," I commented.

"We'll see," Alex said. Alex and I went inside. We found a table in the restaurant and started playing poker.

Jacob and Nadine joined us when we stopped for supper. We played a couple more hands after supper before putting the cards away and going up to our hotel room.

After breakfast the next morning, Alex and I headed out of the hotel. The man that had been sitting on the hotel porch at the beginning of our journey was leaning against the post near the door. Alex stopped.

"You shouldn't have brought Frederick into town," the man said.

"Not much choice in the matter, Jonathan." Alex replied, "Telling him he couldn't come here was admitting to knowing about your presence." Jacob came out of the hotel behind me.

"Jared is going to have a problem with this," Jonathan said.

"Where is Frederick anyway?" Alex asked.

"He found some new friends to drink with," Jonathan answered, "For a man who is trying to play the part of having money, he picks some scum to drink with."

"What do you think Mr. Pearson will do?" Alex asked.

"Don't know," Jonathan answered, "But I will have to tell him."

"Then tell him, so far Frederick hasn't done anything," Alex said.

"That's because Jared's house is a little ways out of town and to go out there Frederick would be seen," Jonathan said, "He'll wait until Jared comes into town."

"Then we have some time before we have to stop Frederick," Alex said.

"Not as much as you think," Jonathan said, "I have to go see if Frederick has been woken up from his drunken stupor." Jonathan straightened up and walked away.

"We have to stop this Jared Pearson before he can do anything to Frederick," Jacob said. Alex sighed.

"I'd be more worried about Frederick doing something to Mr. Pearson," she said.

"You're supposed to be working for Frederick, not Jared Pearson," Jacob said as he went down the stairs and headed for the stable.

"No, you're working for Frederick," Alex said following him, "I may or may not get paid depending on how you feel I am doing money wise."

"This Jared Pearson is likely out to kill Frederick," Jacob said.

"So far he hasn't killed any one," Alex commented, "And from what I've heard Jared Pearson can't be that bad."

"He's out to get Frederick," Jacob said, "I have to go confront him."

"Why?" Alex asked as she followed Jacob into the stable, "He hasn't done anything to threaten Frederick." I followed them inside. Jacob set his saddle on his horse.

"Because he'll be doing something soon," Jacob said.

"Only if Frederick does something stupid," Alex replied.

"You two stay here and take care of Nadine," Jacob said as he secured the saddle.

"You're going to get yourself killed, because Frederick is going to do something stupid," Alex said. Jacob turned to her.

"You complain about working with me and now you're complaining that I might die?" Jacob asked.

"Unlike you, I don't want to see Nadine hurt," Alex said.

"She knows there's always a risk," Jacob said and turned back to his horse. Alex took out her gun and hit Jacob on the back of the head with the handle. Jacob collapsed on his horse. Alex pulled him off and dragged him to a stall.

"Take care of his horse," Alex said. I went over and took the saddle off and led the horse back to its stall. By the time I got out Alex was in the saddle of her horse.

"Going to take his place?" I asked.

"I'll be back in time for the qualifying round of poker," Alex said.

"Good luck," I said.

"Make sure he doesn't come after me, even if you have to hit him again," Alex said. I nodded. Alex rode out of the stable.

* * * *

Jared Pearson

The sound of hoofs brought me on to the porch with my rifle. Few people visit me and most want something I'm not interesting in giving. I could see a single rider coming up the hill. On the short side, but had confidence to go with the gun on his hip.

The rider came just in shooting range and then stopped. He got off his horse and left the reins. The rider took off his hat and slicked the chin length hair back before putting his hat back on. Slowly he continued toward me. I pointed my rifle at him, but he continued forward and made no move for his gun.

"I was wondering if you had time to talk," the rider asked.

"You came all the way up here to talk?" I asked.

"Well, if I was going to shoot at you I could have done it from my horse," the rider said, "Besides I think we have a mutual acquaintance to discuss."

"Which one? I know a lot of people," I asked.

"Frederick," the rider answered.

"Let me guess, that piece of shit is back in town and wants what's coming to him," I said.

"Sounds about right," the rider said.

"So, why talk to me?" I asked, "Easier to just shoot him."

"I can't or I would," the rider answered. I stopped and studied at the rider. There was something strange about him, besides the fact the he hadn't pulled a gun out. I lowered the rifle.

"Why can't you shoot him?" I asked.

"I'm working for the man who Frederick hired to guard him," the rider answered.

"But you aren't here to shoot me?" I asked.

"Don't see how that would do anyone any good," the rider answered.

"Then why don't you come in and we can talk," I said, "I'm sure we can come up with something."

"We can talk out here," the rider said. He was cautious at the least. I sat down in one of the chairs on the porch. He came over and sat down in the other.

"I suppose Frederick is lying drunk somewhere waiting for me to show my face in town," I said.

"According to Jonathan," the rider replied.

"I'm glad to hear that Jonathan is still doing his job," I said.

"What happened that Frederick feels he deserves more?" the rider asked. The green eyes that looked back at me looked empty of emotion, except for a shadow of pain. Whoever had given the rider those scars had given more than just physical pain.

"We were drinking partners," I said, "We had gotten our hands on the worst rot-gut ever made. And since we had been kicked out of all the saloons in Georgetown we ended up wandering outside of town. Sitting down by a stream we drank until we passed out. I woke up to the sun glittering off the stream. Crawling over I put my head in and pulled it back out. I was studying my refection and how bad I looked when I noticed that the bottom of the stream was glittering in the sun. I woke Frederick and we went back into town. Coming back with a gold pan we started panning. I put more work in that day then I had since I left home and we came out with three pouches of gold dust and several nuggets.

"We kept quiet about it for a few days until we had gotten more out, then we went into town and bought a round for everyone at the saloon. After that everyone who could was out on the stream panning. We turned the gold in for cash, which we split evenly in half. Frederick used his to become the pompous ass that you have probably met."

The rider nodded. The eyes might have held some understanding but it was hard to tell.

"I invested mine," I said, "First, I bought the saloon and the hotel. Then I was conned into investing in a risky adventure that everyone said would fail. It didn't and I had three times as much money as I started with. Just after this Frederick came to me and suggested that we should partner up again. I could do the investing and he could reap the rewards. I told him what he could do with himself. He left town after that. I hired Jonathan to go after him and make sure he wasn't going to return to stab me in the back. Then I sold the hotel and the saloon and moved here. I now own most of the businesses in town and am one of the officials for the tournament."

"Sounds like Frederick needs a lesson on what is his and what isn't," the rider said.

"How much would it cost me to hire you away from your guard duty and shoot Frederick?" I asked.

"He is paying seven hundred a person for guard duty," the rider said.

"So, not likely?" I asked.

"I'll pass up the seven hundred and shoot Frederick," the rider said, "But you have to do me a favour."

"A favour?" I asked.

"I work for a man named Jacob Wescott," the rider said, "And he likes Frederick. He would do everything to stop me from shooting him. But I can't afford to have Jacob hurt."

"You want me to distract him, while you shoot Frederick?" I asked.

"There's one catch," the rider said, "I had to knock him out to stop him from coming up here and killing you. He knows where you live and your name."

Something flickered in those eyes. It was too fast for me to see what it was.

"I think I can do that," I said, "I have to go into town to watch the tournament. It should be the perfect time with everyone on the boat."

"Then I'll see you tonight at the game," the rider said standing up. He walked over to his horse and mounted. He turned back toward town. I watched him go. He took off his hat to push his hair back and put his hat back on.

I started to laugh. Frederick was going to by shot by a female gunslinger while I distracted his employer. No wonder there was something strange about the rider.

* * * *

Toby

It was just after lunch and Alex hadn't come back from her visit to Jared Pearson's house. I had checked on the time the poker game started and she had ten minutes before she was disqualified.

I was leaning against one of the posts outside the saloon. I could see Jacob and Nadine sitting on the porch outside the hotel. He would have wrung Alex's neck if he could've gotten hold of it, when he came around. Nadine heard the story and immediately gave him a piece of her mind. As far as she was concerned, shooting Jared Pearson was not part of the job until after he made a direct threat against Frederick.

With only two minutes until the game started Ale walked down the road. Jacob glared at her, Alex ignored him and kept walking.

"You just about didn't make it," I said when she was close enough.

"The time it took to travel was longer than I thought it would be," Alex replied.

"Did you solve anything?" I asked.

"I tell you later," Alex said. I followed her into the saloon. She sat down in the last empty chair. The man from the day before sat in the chair across from her in his position as dealer.

"Are we waiting for anything else?" he asked the group. No one spoke. "Good then we'll get this game under way. Everyone needs to exchange their five hundred dollars for chips."

The man went around the table and took the player's money and gave them chips. Once that was done he dealt the first hand.

By the time the game was over and Alex had qualified it was time to head to the boat. The man led the way. Alex and I followed him. One of the other players also followed. We were the last ones onto the boat. Alex and the man went into a room on the side of the main room. I went into the main room and found a place to stand next to Nadine and Jacob. They had a good view of the tables. The players were brought out. There were three tables of players. Each player was shown to a place to sit. Alex was seated on the far side of the table farthest from us.

It was midnight before those four games were over. Now there were four players left. Alex was one of the four. They picked the table closest to us and set it up for the final game. The players were seated, their chips had been moved for them, and the game started.

I could tell that the one player was cheating. A few other people seemed to realize this as well. Even the uniformed official that stood nearby and watched the game could see that the man was cheating. The only reason he wasn't removed from the game was because he was losing. Alex was making poker look like the easiest game there is and winning against the cheater.

It was two o'clock in the morning when the game was finally over. Alex was the tournament winner. Those who had rooms had gone off to them and a few people had just fallen asleep on the furniture. Jacob and Nadine had found a place to sit until the boat was back at the dock. I joined Alex who was still sitting at the table. I sat down. Alex picked up the cards and started to deal. We played poker until the boat docked.

The boat had docked, but Alex and I were still playing poker. Nadine had gotten up and wandered over to us.

"I would say that we should get back to the hotel, but Jacob fell asleep," Nadine said.

"We'll let him sleep for a while longer," Alex said, "There's no rush."

The official that I had seen earlier came over to our group. He looked like he had gotten some sleep. He was wearing a black suit, white shirt and a top hat. His face was rough from life, but his grin as infectious.

"I wanted to congratulate you on that amazing win," the official said.

"Thank you, Mr. Pearson," Alex said.

"I didn't think you would win when I noticed Mr. Eberhart was cheating," Mr. Pearson said.

"That's the only reason Alex didn't get bored," Nadine said.

"Mr. Pearson, this is Mrs. Nadine Wescott," Alex introduced, "And this is my partner Toby Lawton."

"I'm pleased to meet both of you," Mr. Pearson said with a smile.

"It is nice to meet you, too," Nadine said returning his smile. I nodded my acknowledgment.

"Do you have an interest in poker?" Mr. Pearson asked Nadine.

"Somewhat," Nadine answered, "My husband and I were here to watch Alex play. I've watched games, but I don't play."

"Your husband?" Mr. Pearson asked.

"He fell asleep on the chair over there," Nadine answered gesturing toward where Jacob was snoring away. They continued talking and were fully absorbed in the conversation. Alex stood up and left the room. Neither of them gave any indication they noticed. I got up and followed Alex.

I caught up with her as she was getting off the boat.

"That was Jared Pearson, wasn't it?" I asked.

"Yes," Alex said, "He's one of the officials for the poker tournament."

"Why introduce him to Nadine?" I asked.

"To give him a good excuse to watch Jacob," Alex said. The street was deserted, except for one man sitting on a chair in front of the general store. I recognized him as the man that was watching Frederick. Alex went over to him.

"Jared still on the boat?" Jonathan asked.

"Yes," Alex answered, "Why?"

"Frederick's drinking companions decided they wanted whatever money he had on him," Jonathan answered.

"Where's Frederick?" Alex asked. Jonathan stood up and

headed behind the general store. Alex and I followed him. Frederick was lying under the stairs that led to the second storey of the store. He looked like he could have been sleeping off the booze that permeated the air, except for the knife handle sticking out of his chest.

"Why not just steal the money?" Alex said examining the body, "He wouldn't have noticed."

"I wondered that myself until I noticed their pictures hanging on the bulletin board out front of the general store," Jonathan said.

"Then let's go after them," Alex said.

"Why?" Jonathan asked, "They'll get caught eventually."

"Because legally you're in trouble with the law for not reporting it," Alex said, "And we are supposed to be guarding him. Besides, if Frederick is dead then Jacob won't go after Mr. Pearson."

"They headed for a makeshift saloon just east of town," Jonathan said as he started to go east.

"First we report the death to the sheriff," Alex said. Jonathan stopped and then followed us as Alex led the way to the sheriff's office. Reaching it Alex went inside. We waited outside Five minutes later she came out followed by the sheriff. The sheriff went off toward the general store.

"Now we go after the men," Alex said.

"And if they aren't there?" Jonathan asked.

"Then we find out where they went," I answered. Jonathan led the way.

The makeshift saloon was a tent that had a bartender sitting on a crate beside other crates. Two men sleeping on the floor in the corner of the tent. Jonathan pointed to the men. The bartender on the crate looked up at us and then went back to the glasses he was polishing. We went over to the men. Alex searched them and took away a gun and a knife. I picked up one of the men and Jonathan picked up the other. Then we left the tent and headed back to the sheriff's office.

The sheriff was back and sitting at his desk when we entered.

"Are these the men that killed the other fellow, Frederick Hall?" the sheriff asked.

"Yes," Jonathan answered.

"Well, bring them back here," the sheriff said, leading the way to the cells. There were two empty cells. The sheriff unlocked the one on the left and held the door for us. I dropped the man I was carrying on the bunk. Jonathan went in and placed that man on the floor next to the bunk. The sheriff went in and looked the two over.

"Well, if it ain't those two drunks," the sheriff said. He stepped out of the cell and locked the door behind him. We all went back to his office. Alex was sitting in the chair across from the desk.

"I'll need your statement," the sheriff said pulling out some paper. Alex and I told him about our conversation with Jonathan. Jonathan gave a full account of Frederick's actions and what he saw. The sheriff asked about not reporting the murder, but let it go. Once that was over with we started towards the door.

"Aren't you forgetting something?" the sheriff asked holding up an envelope. Jonathan looked confused. Alex went over and took the envelope. Then we left.

"You want your share?" Alex asked Jonathan as we started back toward the boat.

"Share of what?" Jonathan asked.

"The reward money," Alex answered, "Those two were wanted men. That means you get money for turning them in."

"I don't need it," Jonathan said, "Jared will pay me for my work."

"All right," Alex said before tucking the envelope away. We went back to the boat. Nadine was still talking to Mr. Pearson. Alex and I sat down where we had been before. No one noticed. Jonathan found a seat some distance away. Alex dealt me a hand and we started playing poker.

It was an hour before the conversation started to wind down.

"You both play poker," Mr. Pearson said seeing the cards out.

"Prevents boredom," I answered. Something caught Mr. Pearson's eye and he looked over at Jonathan. Nadine glanced to where Mr. Pearson was looking.

"We wandered off for a little while," Alex said, "We chose not to disturb you two."

"Wandered off where?" Nadine asked.

"To talk to the sheriff," Alex answered, "Apparently, Frederick was killed by his latest set of drinking buddies. The sheriff has the two men in custody, sleeping off the alcohol they bought with the money they stole off the body."

"Frederick is dead?" Nadine asked.

"Unfortunately," I answered.

"I hope they find an appropriate dung pile to bury him under," Mr. Pearson said.

"Well, our job is done," Alex said.

"Jacob isn't going to like this," Nadine said, "Someone he was guarding was killed."

"It has happened before," Alex said, "He'll get over it." A man from the first day at the saloon came over to the table.

"The sheriff has said that he doesn't want a ceremony to end the tournament," he told Mr. Pearson.

"So?" Mr. Pearson said, "Just give the money to Alex and send everyone home."

"Yes, sir," the man said. He went off.

"What else is supposed to be done?" Mr. Pearson muttered. The man came back a moment later, this time he handed a bundle to Alex before going off again.

"Looks like enough to be able to came back again next year," Alex said as she put it away.

"You can do whatever you want with it," Mr. Pearson said, "But if you are coming back next year, bring less trouble with you."

"Then Jacob won't be coming," Alex said.

"But if you are coming back, you can bring Nadine," Mr. Pearson said.

"I'm sure that can be arranged," Nadine said with a smile.

START OF THE TOUR
CHAPTER 5

Toby

We headed back to Cartwheel three days later after everything was explained to Jacob and he got the twenty-one hundred dollars as payment for the job, which was divided three ways.

Arriving back in Cartwheel, we went straight to Nadine's house. We put our horses in the stable, and brought our bags in the house. It was suppertime. Alex paid for us to eat at the restaurant.

I woke to the sun shining in the window. I got up and went downstairs. Nadine was already cooking breakfast, but paused long enough to give me a few things I could help with.

Nadine and I were eating breakfast when Alex came down the stairs.

"Where're you two headed now?" Nadine asked.

"Don't know yet," Alex answered, "Nothing has pointed a direction yet."

"Don't wait around here too long or Jacob might find another job for you," Nadine said.

"I know," Alex replied. Footsteps came down the stairs and Jacob entered the kitchen and joined us. The conversation drifted to general subjects.

There was a knock at the door. Jacob answered it. Alex cleared off the table and I had started on the dishes when Jacob came back into the kitchen.

"It's a telegram for you two," Jacob said. Alex took it.

"Lady Grace wants to employ us," Alex said after reading it.

"For what?" I asked.

"Guard duty," Alex answered.

"We can go see what she needs guarding," I said.

"We don't have anything else to do at the moment," Alex said. Jacob headed out back and Nadine remained at the table. Alex and I did the dishes.

"When're you heading out?" Nadine asked.

"After we're finished washing dishes," Alex said. Nadine nodded.

When we were finished we went upstairs and packed our gear. Jacob was still outside when we came back down. Alex stopped in front of Nadine and pulled out the bundle that contained the money she won. Alex held it out to Nadine.

"You want me to keep it for you?" Nadine asked taking it.

"No," Alex answered as we headed for the door, "It's yours to keep." We went out the back door before Nadine could respond. At the stables we got our horses ready and we left Cartwheel.

We travelled at a leisurely pace. Except for a visit to Fitzgerald, the only reason we stopped was to rest the horses. While we were not in a hurry, neither of us felt like stopping anywhere.

A week after leaving Cartwheel Alex and I arrived in Dustcloud.

"Is Lady Grace still living at the hotel?" I asked as we rode into town.

"The address on the letter sent to Jacob was different from the hotel," Alex said.

"So, how are we supposed to find her?" I asked.

"I borrowed the envelope from Jacob," Alex answered, pulling it out of her coat pocket, "I figured he didn't need it."

"That should make this easier," I said. Alex looked at the address for a moment and then led the way.

Lady Grace's mansion was a couple streets off the main street, near similar estates. We sat on our horses outside the closed gate.

"She's doing well for herself," I commented.

"Lord Bennett didn't leave her penniless," Alex said. A man

came out of the front door and headed toward us. He was dressed formally, but the clothes were cheaper.

"A butler too," I said.

"I can't see Lady Grace taking a man in," Alex said, "Not unless she remarried."

"May I help you?" the man asked when he reached the other side of the gate.

"We're here to see Lady Grace," Alex said.

"And whom should I say is here?" the man asked.

"Alex and Toby," Alex answered. The man went back up the road and into the house.

"We don't even get escorted into the parlour to wait," I commented.

"They don't want us stealing the silverware while their backs are turned," Alex replied, "She probably only has three servants: a butler, a maid and a cook."

"Do you need anymore than that?" I asked.

"Some people have more," Alex answered. The man came back out, but this time he was followed by Lady Grace.

"It is wonderful to see you," Lady Grace said as the man opened the gate.

"You look like you're doing well," I commented as we entered. The man locked the gate behind us.

"I wish Patrick were still here to enjoy all this, but I can't let that stop me from living," Lady Grace said, "Life goes on and I don't want it to pass me by."

"Then what do you need us for?" Alex asked as we got off our horses. Lady Grace led the way.

"I was hoping to travel around and see old friends," Lady Grace said, "But my coach driver won't take me unless I have someone to guard me. According to him it isn't safe for a lady to travel alone. Don't worry, you will be paid for your time." We went around the house to a stable in the back.

"When were you thinking of leaving?" Alex asked.

"I was waiting for you to arrive," Lady Grace said, "So, tomorrow or the day after. I have lots of extra rooms so you don't have to worry about a place to stay."

"Whenever you're ready," I said. Lady Grace smiled before turning and entering the back door. Alex and I took our horses into the stables.

When we went into the house the butler showed us to our rooms. I dropped my saddlebag on the bed and washed up before leaving my room. Alex was already waiting in the hall.

"What do you think?" I asked.

"It shall be an interesting trip," Alex answered.

"How long do you think it'll take?" I asked.

"Don't make any plans for a couple months," Alex answered. We went downstairs and found Lady Grace in the parlour. We sat and talked until supper, which was served in the dining room. After supper we continued to talk until Lady Grace declared it was time to go to bed.

I woke to the sun shining on my pillow. I got up and went to the window. The city was just starting to wake up. The butler was opening the gate for a coach. I recognized the man as the driver of the coach when we guarded Lady Grace last time. I packed my saddlebag and headed downstairs.

Breakfast was waiting on the sideboard. I helped myself and sat down.

Soon Alex came into the dining room.

"Good morning," I said.

"Morning," Alex replied. I said not more until she had eaten. Then we began to play poker until Lady Grace entered the dining room.

"Good morning, Lady Grace," I said.

"Good morning, Toby," Lady Grace said, "Good morning Alex."

"Morning," Alex replied. Lady Grace watched us play while she ate.

"That is poker, isn't it?" Lady Grace asked.

"Yes," Alex answered.

"As a lady I'm not supposed to know that," Lady Grace said, "Nor have I seen it played. But it looks interesting to learn." Alex looked up at me; her eyes glittered. I suppressed my smile.

"It isn't exactly a ladies game," Alex said, "But ladies do play. Some even get into the tournaments."

"Really?" Lady Grace asked, "Perhaps you can teach me to play during the trip."

"Sure," I said.

"You have no qualms about teaching a lady to play poker?" Lady Grace asked.

"No," Alex answered, "Besides it's only when you play for money that people get their noses out of joint about it."

"And what is poker without betting?" Lady Grace asked.

"Poker," Alex answered, "But betting and playing for money can be two different things."

"We can teach you the game and the basics of betting," I said.

"Thank you," Lady Grace said, "We should be going."

"We were waiting for you," I said as Alex gathered up the cards. Lady Grace nodded before getting up. Alex and I went out to the stable for our horses. The butler and the driver loaded Lady Grace's bags. The driver climbed up into his seat. The butler helped Lady Grace into the coach. And we were on our way. Alex took up position beside the coach and I took up position behind it until we were out of Dustcloud then I moved up to ride on the other side of the coach.

We travelled without incident, stopped briefly at noon, and reached the next town by evening. After assisting Lady Grace into the hotel, Alex and I followed the coach around to the stables, and we took care of our horses. We went back to the hotel. Lady Grace was standing in the lobby.

"I rented each of you a room," Lady Grace said, holding out two keys.

"Thank you," I said as I took one key. Alex took the other.

"After supper you can show me how to play poker," Lady Grace said.

"Of course," Alex said. Lady Grace turned and went into the dining room. Alex and I headed upstairs. My room came first. I dropped my saddlebags on the bed and sat down beside them.

A few minutes later Alex stopped in the doorway and looked in.

"Tired?" Alex asked.

"A little bit," I answered, "Don't you ever get tired?"

"Sometimes," Alex shrugged. We both stayed quiet for a few minutes before meeting Lady Grace in the dining room.

When she finished eating, Lady Grace turned to us and said, "Now, you promised to teach me how to play poker. Shall we begin?"

So we began. We described the object of the game, the name of the cards, and various combinations, the method of play and strategy.

"No wonder they call it gambling," Lady Grace said. The server came past and took my plate.

"Let's try a hand, but open on the table so everyone can see the cards," Alex said.

"All right," Lady Grace said. Alex dealt out three hands on the table. Lady Grace got the ten of clubs, the ten of spades, the three of spades, the four of diamonds and the jack of clubs. I got the king of clubs, a joker, the six of spades, the king of spades and the king of diamonds. Alex got the three of diamonds, a joker, the nine of clubs, five of hearts and the jack of hearts.

"What do we have?" Alex asked.

"I have a pair," Lady Grace answered, "Toby has three of a kind. And you have nothing."

"Actually jokers count as wild cards," I said, "That means they can be any card in the deck that you need at that moment. So, I have four of a kind and Alex has a pair."

Lady Grace nodded, "What next?"

"You discard the ones you don't want and the dealer gives you enough cards to add up to five again," Alex said, "But you can't discard more than four cards."

"So, you discard anything that could hinder you from getting a hand," Lady Grace said taking the three and four out of her hand.

"Exactly," Alex said. I discarded the six and Alex discarded the three and the five. Alex dealt out cards to each of us. Lady Grace got the five of diamonds and the ace of clubs. I got the six of hearts. And Alex got the eight of clubs and the seven of diamonds.

"Now what do we have?" Alex asked.

"I have a pair of tens, Toby has four kings," Lady Grace answered, "And you have a straight."

"Good," Alex said, "Now we discard again." Lady Grace discarded the five of diamonds. I discarded the six of hearts. And Alex didn't discard. Alex dealt again. Lady Grace got the nine of diamonds and I got the ace of hearts.

"This is where we show our cards," Alex said, "And figure out who won. In this case Toby wins."

"And there is more to this?" Lady Grace asked.

"I figured we'd start with the basic game," Alex said, "Once you think you are ready we'll go through betting and then on to the other types of poker."

"Of course," Lady Grace said. I gathered up the cards. I shuffled them and dealt out the next round.

Lady Grace won with three queens. We continued to play for half an hour before Lady Grace felt she was ready to learn about betting. Alex explained the ante and the betting between you getting your cards and discarding.

We played another half an hour of that before Alex decided to explain about folding, bluffing and the more complicated aspects of poker.

When Lady Grace started to yawn we put the cards away and headed for our rooms. Alex stayed at the doorway to my room as Lady Grace went to her room.

"She isn't half bad," Alex said.

"With some time and practice we won't have to let her win," I said.

"Just don't let her hear any comments about letting her win," Alex said, "I don't think she'd appreciated it."

I nodded

“Good night,” Alex said before heading down the hallway.

In the morning, Lady Grace remarked,

"I thought poker was a lot harder then that. It always sounded harder."

"We'll teach you another variation tonight," Alex said.

"I can't wait," Lady Grace said. We exchanged a few a words as we ate, but otherwise we were quiet.

The day went by quietly. We stopped near a brook at noon to rest the horses. Lady Grace got out to eat and to stretch her legs.

It was late afternoon when we reached the next town. After dropping Lady Grace off at the hotel Alex and I followed the driver to the stables to care for our horses. When Alex and I arrived Lady Grace was talking to the clerk so we just stayed back.

When she was finished Lady Grace came over to where we were standing.

"I hope you don't mind sharing a room," Lady Grace said,

"There are only two available."

"That's fine," Alex said. Lady Grace handed Alex the key before going up the stairs. Our room was upstairs, the second on the left.

When I had finished laying out my bed, Alex and I went down to the dining room. Our food arrived the minute after we were seated. The server came and went so fast I suspected that she was scared of us. I gave Alex a puzzled look. She shrugged.

We were half way through our meal when a tall man with a gun on each hip entered the dining room. He looked around before coming over to our table.

"You two the gunslingers the sheriff sent for?" the man asked.

"No," Alex answered.

"Mind if I ask what you are doing in town?" the man asked.

"Only if you tell us who you are first," I replied.

"Deputy," the man answered opening his coat enough that we could see the silver star pinned to his vest.

"We have a job guarding a lady," Alex answered, "And this is where she plans to rest for the night."

"That all?" the deputy asked.

"That's all," I answered. The man nodded and then left the dining room. Lady Grace moved from the doorway, where she had observed the encounter.

"What was that about?" Lady Grace asked.

"He wanted to know what we were doing in town," I answered.

"How is it any of his business?" Lady Grace asked.

"I think we are a day behind some trouble," Alex answered.

"I hope we stay behind it then," Lady Grace said. The server brought Lady Grace's food. This time she moved much slower.

The conversation switched topics. After we had all finished eating, Alex started to explain draw poker.

I decided I was tired and went to bed while Alex was explaining seven-card stud. I woke briefly when Alex came into the room, but I just rolled over and went back to sleep.

I opened my eyes to a dark room. I lay with my senses alert for a moment. Then I heard Alex moving. I closed my eyes and rolled over.

The sound of a group of horses going past the hotel woke me up. I opened my eyes to find it light in the room. Sitting up I looked around. Alex was gone. I got up and packed up my bedroll. Once packed I washed up with the water that was left before taking my stuff and going downstairs.

Alex was sitting at a table in the dining room. I sat down in one of the chairs.

"How'd the rest of the lesson go?" I asked.

"Quite well," Alex answered, "I was thinking of seeing if I could give her a copy of Hoyle's rules, but I couldn't find one here."

"Maybe wherever we stay tonight," I said.

"I can look," Alex said. Two men entered the dining room and sat down at a table on the far side from ours. Each had a gun on his hip and the one had enough scars on his face to make you wonder how many of those fights he had actually won. They both were covered with road dust and smelled like they hadn't stopped to clean up before stopping for breakfast.

"Looks like the gunslingers the sheriff sent for have arrived," I said.

"They came in late last night," Alex said, "Lady Grace had to go to bed shortly after they came in or her tongue was going to start bleeding."

One of the men yelled something about the slowness of the service.

"It's better not to say anything," Alex said, "Unless you wish to challenge them to a shootout."

"I would guess that after winning you would have to help the sheriff with his problem," I said.

"Doubt it," Alex said, "They're old friends of the sheriff's, so you are more likely to end up being challenged by him."

"The deputy didn't know them?" I asked.

"Sounds like the deputy is new to this town," Alex said.

The server had not yet appeared so the men yelled about getting some food. A few more of the hotel's guests came into the dining room and sat down at tables.

"Have you heard why the sheriff needs his old friends?" I asked.

"Some kind of trouble," Alex shrugged, "Without asking the sheriff I couldn't find any specifics and I didn't want to get that involved."

I nodded.

The server appeared with two plates of food just as the man started to yell again. She placed one in front of each man and was back in the kitchen in less then a minute.

"Looks like breakfast is ready," I commented.

"Someone must have gotten eggs for the cook," Alex said.

I shrugged. The server brought out two more plates. She placed one in front of me and the other in front of Alex before going back to the kitchen. Alex and I didn't say much as we ate.

The two men left the dining room just before Lady Grace came in. She came over and sat down.

"Good morning," Lady Grace said.

"Good morning," I said. The server brought over another plateful of food. Lady Grace started to eat. When Alex and I were finished eating we went to the stables.

Lady Grace was waiting for us when Alex and I rode up to the hotel with the coach. The driver stowed the bags while Lady Grace got into the coach.

We were only about ten minutes out of town when I heard the sound of horses running behind us. I looked over my shoulder and saw five horses headed toward us. The driver saw them as well and moved over as much as he could. Alex slowed enough that she was riding behind the coach. The five riders went past us like a posse after a criminal, except there was no one being chased. They continued until they were out of sight. Alex shook her head as she went back to riding beside the coach.

Early evening we arrived in the next town. We stopped in front of the hotel. Lady Grace had opened the door and stepped out when a woman came over to greet her. They embraced and then started to talk. The woman wore similar styles of clothes as Lady Grace, but in red instead of blue. Her blonde hair was swept up in a style that much had required someone to help her. Alex and I couldn't hear anything they said. The driver, Alex and I sat waiting.

Lady Grace went inside the hotel. The lady waited outside. When Lady Grace returned a few minutes later, she talked to Alex briefly. Then she and her friend got into the coach. The driver started down the street. Alex stayed where she was so I didn't move.

"Lady Grace is going to stay with her friend for tonight and tomorrow," Alex said once the coach was gone, "She reserved us two rooms at the hotel and expects us to be ready to leave tomorrow morning."

"All right," I said as she handed me my room key. At the stable, the stablemaster accepted our money and told his helper to take the horses. Alex and I took our bags and went back to the hotel.

In the dining room, there was a poker game going at one of the tables. I sat down at a nearby table and the server brought my food. I watched the game as I ate.

Later one of the players ran out of money and I was invited join the game.

I hadn't seen Alex for a while. She arrived back as another player was leaving. The man, whose cards we were playing with, recognized her from the tournament and offered her the vacated seat.

We played through the night and most of the next day. We broke up the game for supper and afterward everyone dispersed.

When I came down the next morning, Alex was already in the dining room. I sat down in the chair across from her. Alex looked exhausted

"You gonna be okay?" I asked.

"I will be," Alex answered, "when this current bout of nightmares is over. But I can do what is required of me in the meantime."

"I know you can," I said.

We went to the stable and got our horses. Alex led the way to a house at the far end of town. The coach was already sitting out front. The driver was stowing the bags. He acknowledged us with a nod before climbing up to his seat. Alex climbed down from her horse and waited by the coach door.

Several minutes later Lady Grace came out of the house, saying farewell to her hostess. Alex opened the coach door for Lady Grace and handed her a book once she was inside. Then Alex closed the door and got back on her horse. Poker was going to be interesting tonight now that Lady Grace had a copy of Hoyle's rules. We started moving.

The next two weeks went by without much happening. We continued to guard Lady Grace and she continued to learn poker. We seldom had to let her win a game now.

Alex was on one side of the coach and I was on the other as we rode into town. There were two men leaning on a post outside the saloon. They watched us closely as if we might shoot at them. Both had fingers itching towards their guns. Neither Alex nor I looked straight at them.

The coach stopped in street in front of the hotel. Alex was off her horse and opening the coach door before the driver could move. She helped Lady Grace out of the coach. Lady Grace looked around as the driver got down her bags. Her eyes drifted to the men.

"Men and their pissing contests," Lady Grace muttered as she shook her head. Then she went into the hotel and the driver followed. I got down and went over to Alex.

"What do you think?" I asked.

"If they're a problem, you deal with it," Alex answered.

"Why? Because I have the right anatomy?" I asked.

"I was thinking because you're the faster on the draw, but that works too," Alex replied. The driver came back to the coach. Alex got back on her horse. I handed her the reins of mine and she followed the coach to the stables. Stepping up on the sidewalk, I walked towards the saloon. The men didn't move, but looked ready for the fight. Reaching the saloon I went inside and went to the bar. The men didn't follow me.

I ordered a whiskey and looked around. The place was quiet, a few men drinking, some bored dancing girls and a poker game going in one corner. The barman poured my drink.

"What's with the two itchy fingers?" I asked the barman. He studied me for a second. I poured the drink down my throat.

"They're trying to earn a reputation," the barman answered.

"By challenging everyone who rides into town with a gun?" I asked.

"Something like that," the barman answered, starting to move away.

"How many have they shot?" I asked.

"Seven dead, five injured and two disappeared after realizing they weren't fast enough on the draw," the barman said.

"Thanks," I said, placing money on the bar and drifting toward the poker game. The table was full, but I wasn't really thinking of joining. Watching and listening to the men I guessed that the tallest was the sheriff, the grey haired one was the judge, the one with the extra fancy tie was the mayor and the two that were losing were the deputies.

At five the poker game broke up and everyone but the sheriff left the saloon. The sheriff looked at me.

"Gambler?" he asked.

"Among other things," I answered.

"Gunslinger?" he asked.

"Occasionally," I answered.

"Why not challenge Charles and Edward?" he asked.

"Those the two that are standing outside with the itchy trigger fingers?" I asked. He nodded.

"I'd rather not," I answered, "There are faster ways to die and I ain't ready for any of them yet."

"You're smarter than most they come up against," the sheriff said.

"If they murder people shouldn't you be locking them up?" I asked.

"They claim self-defense and no witness will testify against them," the sheriff answered, "All I got is a dead body with bullet holes and them claiming self-defense."

"And you're never around when they shoot anyone?" I asked.

"They've been here six months, first killings they did when I was busy. I haven't had to do my job since that first month was over," the sheriff said, "Even the townspeople don't come looking for me."

Alex entered and the sheriff's eyes shifted to her.

"Two in a day?" the sheriff said.

"That's my partner," I said, "We're passing through with a lady."

"Who has found a friend she hasn't seen in a year," Alex said, "She'll see us in two days."

"Well, if you two are around for a while, I'd suggest you stay away from Charles and Edward," the sheriff said, getting up.

"And if we don't?" I asked.

"The doc will do you up nice and I'll say a few polite words before we bury the box," the sheriff answered before leaving.

"These men sound like they're good," Alex said.

"They are looking for a reputation," I replied.

"Never heard of them before we came to town," Alex said.

"Exactly," I said, "Shall we find a room?"

"Lady Grace got us rooms at the hotel before she headed out to her friend's house," Alex said.

"Headed out?" I started toward the saloon door.

"Remember the farm we passed on the way into town?" Alex asked.

"Sure," I said.

"That's where her friend lives," Alex said.

"So, we have two days," I said. We left the saloon and headed for the hotel. Charles and Edward were still standing there and they watched us, but they didn't move. We went into the hotel.

"Two days to do what?" Alex asked.

"According to the sheriff and the barman, those two have been killing every man who comes through town with a gun," I said.

"How many dead?" Alex asked.

"Seven," I answered.

"Any plan yet?" Alex asked.

"Other than that they need to be taken out, no," I answered, "But we need it to be self-defense."

"Scared the sheriff will lock you up?" Alex said.

"He'd do it to the other two if he could catch them," I answered, "And the town's people won't be too happy."

"They have to shoot first," Alex replied.

"Yes, but I'm not sure I want to rely on their inaccuracy," I said.

"Seven dead means they can hit something most of the time," Alex said, "Too often."

"So, what do we do?" I asked.

"See what happens," Alex answered before going into her room. We ate supper at the hotel before heading back over to the saloon. Charles and Edward were no longer standing outside. Entering we found them leaning on the bar. Alex headed for the poker table, where she was offered a seat. I went over to the bar and ordered a whiskey. The barman poured the whiskey and quickly moved on.

"He doesn't seem to like you," one of the men said. He was

about the same height as I am, but not as solid. His hair was greased back and his face held a smug look. The other man was slightly shorter with blonde hair and pale eyes. Looked like someone had used his face as a punching bag.

"Which are you, Charles or Edward?" I asked.

"Charles," the man stated.

"Good to meet you, Charles," I said offering my hand. He stared at me like he was confused. Then he shook my hand, firmly. Like that would scare me.

"You got a name, mister?" Edward said.

"Toby," I replied. I poured the whiskey down my throat. A gunshot went off behind me and both men pulled out their guns. I turned slowly to see Alex sitting at the poker table with her gun out and a man lying on his broken chair. Alex slowly put her gun away. Edward already had put his gun away and was helping the man up.

"What happened here?" Charles demanded.

"I was cheating," the man answered. He was trembling, but it didn't look like it was because of Alex.

"That's no reason to fire a gun," Charles said. He was looking at Alex, who was busy gathering up the cards.

"He didn't shoot anyone," the man to the right of Alex said, I realized that he was one of the deputies, "Durward did."

"He's right," the man that was helped up said, "I was pulling my gun out and it got caught and went off. Barely missed hitting my own foot." The two men looked at each person, and everyone looked back at him, except Alex. She was busy shuffling the cards. Durward gathered up his money.

"I'll be leaving now," Durward said and then scuttled out of the saloon. The barman took the chair away and brought a new one out.

"Either of you want to join the game?" Alex asked ready to deal.

"No," Charles answered as both of them retreated to the bar. The game continued. I turned around and ordered another whiskey. The barman quickly refilled my glass and then went back to the other end of the bar.

"So, what're you doing in town?" Edward asked.

"Resting," I answered, "Looked like a good place to stop."

"The man at the poker table, that who you came in with?" Charles started.

"My partner," I answered.

"Been together long?" Charles asked.

"A while," I answered.

"I suggest you keep him out of trouble," Edward said.

"And if I don't?" I asked.

"Then be prepared to look for another partner," Edward answered.

"You talk tough for two people that aren't the law," I said, "Maybe you should get elected sheriff before you start threatening out of town guests."

"This town doesn't need out of town guests like you two," Edward said.

"Like what? We're just travelers passing through," I said.

"With guns?" Charles asked.

"Need them if you're traveling. Even if you can't hit a damn thing, it still makes robbers think twice before they stop you," I answered, "You two don't get out a lot, do you."

"We've been around," Charles replied.

"When? The stone age was a long time ago," I said. The sheriff stepped into the saloon just as Charles threw the punch. I managed to avoid getting hit, but I tripped on the stool behind me and ended up on the floor anyway.

"No fighting in the saloon," the sheriff said.

"He started it," Charles shouted.

"Anyone see this man hit Charles?" the sheriff asked the room of people, a lot of head shaking. "Then, Charles, you started the fight by punching this man."

"I didn't even hit," Charles said.

"Looked like you did from where I was standing," the sheriff said, "You and Edward need to stay away from our guests during their stay. We don't need any more people turning up dead."

"Yes, sheriff," Charles said and then he and Edward left. The sheriff helped me to my feet. The others in the room resumed their activity.

"You want to give me a name for your tombstone and a reason for hitting the hornet's nest," the sheriff said, leaning against the bar. The barman came down and filled my glass for the third time.

This time he was much slower moving down the bar.

"Toby," I said, "And they started it. They warned me to keep Alex out of trouble. Alex hasn't even gotten into trouble yet."

"I heard that Durward was caught cheating and shot a hole in the floor," the sheriff said, "I heard the gunshot and Durward explained it to me when I bumped into him." I poured the whiskey down my throat.

"They assumed it was Alex who had done the shooting, so they gave me a warning," I said.

"Consider this your second warning of the night," the sheriff said, "Avoid Charles and Edward or you'll be dead. My word means nothing to those two."

"I came in here looking for a drink, not trouble," I replied.

"Well, you found it," the sheriff said as he straightened up. Then he headed for the door. The barman poured me a fourth whiskey. I sat down and sipped it as I watched Alex play poker.

A fifth glass of whiskey later Alex came over to where I was still sitting.

"Will you make it through the night?" Alex asked.

"As long as I can dodge the bullets," I answered.

"Should have stopped a couple of whiskey's ago then," Alex said.

"I'm fine," I said. I stood up, there was no feeling of drunkenness. We headed for the door; Alex stepped out first. The minute my feet touched the sidewalk someone called my name and if I hadn't continued forward the bullet would have gone into my chest. Instead it ended up in the door frame of the saloon. I looked at the direction it came from, but only caught a glimpse of a person, resembling Charles, running down the street. I watched him go, shaking my head.

"Walking with you is dangerous," Alex commented as we started down the sidewalk to the hotel. Someone peeked out of the saloon, but not seeing nothing went back inside.

"I'm gonna have to sleep with both eyes open," I replied.

"Cemetery here is the same as a cemetery anywhere else," Alex said.

"Sheriff will even know the proper name to put on the tombstone," I said, "That doesn't make it the place I want to die." We reached the hotel and went inside. "They'll probably go after you once I'm dead."

"Once you're dead, I'll go after them and explain to the sheriff afterward," Alex said.

"I'm allowed to have the tombstone, but you get the revenge, I'm not sure that's fair," I replied.

"Then don't die," Alex said. She went up to her room, leaving me shaking my head. Okay, maybe I should have stopped a couple whiskeys before, but I'm just buzzed, not drunk. I went up to my room. I carefully checked it over before slumping down in front of the door. Ironically I get a real bed for the night and I don't even get to use it. I pulled out my gun and held it in my lap. Closing my eyes, I let myself drift.

Ever been asleep, but awake? I was asleep, but I could hear myself snoring. It would wake me up, but the booze was keeping me asleep.

The window opened, slowly. I continued to snore. Someone stepped into the room and started toward me. He was standing over me as I jerked awake and shot him in the leg. He collapsed, swearing. I opened my eyes and grabbed the gun out of his hand. By the light of the moon I could see Charles clutching his leg.

A knock came at the door. I stood up and opened it. Alex stood there, dressed, and a lamp in one hand and her gun in the other.

"What happened?" she asked.

"Charles, here, decided to let me die in my sleep," I answered. The desk clerk came running up the stairs.

"What happened?" he gasped out.

"Charles's been shot. Go get the sheriff," Alex answered. The clerk didn't ask he just turned and ran back down the stairs. Charles glared at us, but didn't say anything as he sat there bleeding from the bullet wound. I lit the lamp in my room and sat down on the bed. I was still buzzed and Alex was quiet as she stood in the doorway watching Charles.

It took ten minutes before the sheriff showed up.

"What happened?" the sheriff asked.

"I was shot at coming out of the saloon and then Charles here tried to shoot me in my sleep," I said, "I don't have a problem with being shot at, but I'd rather it be in a proper fight. The last thing my reputation needs is the ending that I died in my sleep."

"Like you have much of a reputation," Charles said, "I never heard of you before you showed up here."

"I never heard of you until I showed up here, so we're even there," I replied, "But my mother would be most upset to hear that I didn't die honourably."

"You want me to arrest him or not?" the sheriff asked.

"Of course, that's why you were called instead of the doctor," I said, "You can charge him with attempted murder."

"Come on," the sheriff said pulling Charles to his feet and escorting him out of the room.

"Your mother?" Alex asked.

"You were right: I drank too much," I said.

"Go to sleep," Alex said. She shut the door behind her. I closed my eyes.

When I opened them again the lamp had gone out. I felt a slight banging in my head, but otherwise I was fine. Sitting up I saw the blood stain that confirmed that I had shot Charles. And by now I was sure that Edward had heard.

Downstairs, I met Alex for breakfast.

"Any word?" I asked.

"No," Alex answered. I nodded and continued eating. Then we headed for the sheriff's office.

Entering, we found the sheriff behind his desk and the judge sitting across from him. They looked up at us when we entered.

"You must be the ones that shot Charles," the judge said.

"I did," I answered.

"Been a long time since we've had a trial here," the judge said, "It's nice to be needed once in a while."

"We only have today and tomorrow," Alex said.

"We weren't planning on waiting until Edward breaks Charles out," the sheriff replied.

"Trial starts at one," the judge said.

"Has Edward been in?" I asked.

"Nope," the sheriff said, "But word is he's ready to shoot you the minute he sees you."

"Then I'll have to be careful," I replied, "How is Charles?"

"You can go back and see him," the sheriff said, "But don't stand too close to the bars." I nodded and went to where the cells were. Charles was lying on the cot in one cell. He jumped to his feet the minute he saw me. His left leg just about collapsed, but he managed to stay on his feet.

"Come to finish the job?" he snarled.

"I'm not stupid enough to shoot you while you're unarmed and in a cell with the sheriff a door away. You might do that, but I don't," I told him.

"You're gonna be dead before the end of the day," Charles said.

"This's where I hope that Edward is smart enough not to try to shoot me," I said.

"He doesn't shoot people unless they challenge him," Charles sneered.

"A knife man, is he?" Alex said, having come up behind me, "That's nice to know." Charles was silent, trying to figure out whether what he told us was going cause problems for Edward.

"Now he isn't gonna tell us anymore," I commented to Alex.

"Oh well," Alex said, "Edward will slip up, just like Charles. They got over confident without any serious opposition."

"We took out fourteen gunslingers," Charles said.

"You killed seven, injured five and run off two," I corrected him, "And I'm willing to bet that you didn't check if they were a gunslinger, you just shoot them because they were carrying guns." Charles was quiet. "That's what you were gonna do to us."

"Very bad idea," Alex said, "That means you end up taking out the men that aren't gunslingers and when one actually comes to town, you have problems."

"To get a reputation you need to find men with reputations and kill them, not sit and wait for them to come to you," I said. The sheriff came into the room.

"Can I leave yet, Sheriff?" Charles asked.

"You can leave only if you prove yourself innocent at your trial this afternoon," the sheriff answered, "Murder isn't something you can shrug off."

"But I didn't succeed," Charles said, "He's still alive and unhurt."

"We are civilized in this town," the sheriff replied, "Attempted murder is close enough to murder that it goes to trial."

"Let's go," Alex said, "I think we've said enough."

"Probably," I said. We turned to leave.

"I got Toby's name," the sheriff said, stopping us, "But what's yours?" Alex turned to him.

"Alex," she replied.

"Like Lawton and Turner?" the sheriff asked. I looked at Alex and she raised one eyebrow back at me. I turned back.

"Alex Turner and Toby Lawton," I replied.

"I've heard those names," the sheriff said.

"Someone has heard of them?" Charles asked.

"Shut up," the sheriff told Charles and then headed back to the other room. Alex and I followed. The sheriff started going through his desk.

"Had something here for you from a marshal that came through a month or so ago," the sheriff said.

"A marshal with a limp or just a usual marshal?" Alex asked.

"He had a limp," the sheriff said, pulling an envelope out and handing it to Alex. Alex opened it and looked the papers over. The sheriff watched her.

"You two work for the marshal?" the sheriff asked.

"Bounty work on occasion," Alex answered, handing me the papers. I looked them over. Two pages with sketches and names and the third page was from Thomas asking if we'd keep our eyes out for these two.

"Sounds like we should catch up with Thomas once Lady Grace is finished with touring," I said.

"Not knowing how long this tour is going to take, I'd say we can keep our eyes open for the men and contact the local law if we find them," Alex replied.

"Those warrants wouldn't happen to be for Charles and Edward?" the sheriff sounded hopeful.

"No such luck," I answered. Gun shots came from outside. The sheriff grabbed a rifle and headed out of his office. Alex and I followed him. Edward was standing in the middle of the street and a man in the middle of the far end of the street. The doctor came out of a building and over to where the man lay.

"You two," the doctor pointed to two men standing on the sidewalk, "Help me get this man to my office." The men came down and helped the doctor.

"Edward," the sheriff called. Edward turned to the sheriff and then pulled his gun back out.

"You shoot him and that's double murder," the sheriff said,

moving toward Edward. Edward looked like he was going to shoot me, then slowly put his gun away. "Now what happened here?"

"He challenged me," Edward answered, "He shot first."

"Fine," the sheriff said, "Stay out of trouble." Alex started down the sidewalk and I followed her. We headed for the doctor's office.

The two men had already left and the doctor was sitting in a chair having a drink.

"Is he dead?" Alex asked. The doctor looked up at us.

"What's it to you?" the doctor asked.

"They're gonna need the next two coffins if Edward and Charles get their way," the sheriff said coming in, "Is the man dead?"

"No," the doctor answered, "He just got clipped."

"And he fell because of that?" the sheriff asked.

"No," the doctor answered.

"He knows that Edward would have kept shooting," Alex said.

"Doesn't take much to figure that out," the doctor said.

"What's his name?" the sheriff asked.

"Don't know, you'd have to go and ask him," the doctor answered. The sheriff went into the other room.

"Come on," I said. Alex followed me outside.

"Don't want to know who he is?" Alex said.

"He walked into the middle of the street with Edward and shot first," I replied, "That means he isn't all that smart." We went back to the hotel. Taking up a table in the dining room we sat there and played poker.

A man came in just before lunch. He carried his jacket over one arm and had a bandage wrapped around the upper part of the other one. He was on the skinny side with a smooth face and a gun on his hip.

He noticed the cards and came over to the table.

"So, you're the man who got shot," Alex said before the man could open his mouth.

"James Lathrop," the man replied, "Professional gambler."

"Funny thing for a gambler to do," I said.

"I was walking across the street when the man told me to draw my gun and when I turned to face him, he shot me," James replied.

"Tell that to the sheriff?" I asked.

"Yes," James answered, "And there was a street full of witnesses."

"If that counts for anything," Alex said.

"How long have you two been in town?" James asked.

"Came in yesterday," I answered, "Already had to shoot one man because he decided he'd shoot me."

"This doesn't seem like a good place to stay," James said.

"Edward was the one that shot you, the one I shot, Charles, is Edward's partner," I said, "Other than those two, this town is safe."

"You two gunslingers?" James asked.

"Among other things," Alex answered.

"Other things?" James asked.

"Some gambling, some gunslingering, little bit of bounty hunting and some guard duty," Alex answered.

"Is that all?" James asked, wonder in his voice.

"Pretty much," Alex answered. A deputy came into the dining room and came over to our table.

"Sheriff requests you all at his office," the deputy said.

"All of us?" James asked.

"All three of you," the deputy answered. The cards went away and we followed the deputy. James was slower, but he followed.

The sheriff, the judge and the other deputy were sitting in the office when we arrived. James closed the door behind him. The deputy was sitting there was a towel to the back of his head.

"Charles escaped," the sheriff said, "Edward knocked Bill out and broke Charles out of the cell."

"They're still in town though," the deputy that brought us over said, "They've been seen."

"I know you aren't a gunman, Mr. Lathrop," the sheriff said, "Don't expect you to come, but I hope you will stay here with the judge."

"Certainly," James said.

"We believe that Edward and Charles are holed up in the house they have been staying in," the sheriff said, getting up. Alex pulled her gun out and checked that it was loaded.

"Ready when you are," Alex said as she holstered her gun.

"Let's go," the sheriff said. We left the office and followed the sheriff as he led the way to the house.

The house was a slapped together shack that was probably here from the early days of the town. It was hard to tell whether anyone was home or not. The sheriff and deputies found places with cover.

I followed their example. Alex walked right up to the door and knocked. There was movement in one window. Alex stepped to one side, then a shot gun blast went through the door. Alex stumbled back, but she hadn't been hit. Glass was broken out of a window and a gun fired at the rest of us. The sheriff and deputies fired back. I used the cover and started around back.

Charles was coming out the back door. I shot at him a couple times and he dove back inside. The door closed. I moved to a different spot. A hand came out the door and shot at where I had been. I shot the hand. It withdrew. I moved closer. The other hand came out and shot at me, I ducked. The hand withdrew. I moved closer. The hand came out again and shot in my direction, but missed. I ran the last few steps to the door and slammed the door on the arm before the hand could be withdrawn. I grabbed the gun and smacked the hand against the house. The hand let go of the gun and tried to withdraw. I opened the door wide and faced Charles. He turned around to run to the front of the house. I shot him. He fell and didn't move. I stepped over him and went to the front room. Edward was firing out the window at the sheriff and deputies. I went up behind him and hit him on the back of the head with Charles's gun. He collapsed. A gunshot went off behind me. I turned around Charles was sitting up with a gun in his hand and a second bloodstain growing on his chest. Alex put her gun away. Charles fell over.

"Should never turn your back on an enemy, especially when they have nothing to lose," Alex said.

"I took his gun away from him first," I said. The sheriff and deputies had stopped shooting so I slowly opened the door and stepped out. They came out of hiding and came over to the house.

"Both dead?" the sheriff asked.

"I think Edward might still be alive," I said. The sheriff went passed me and into the house. He saw the two bodies and Alex checking Edward's pulse.

"He's alive," Alex said.

"Why not just shoot both of them?" the sheriff asked me.

"The judge seemed anxious to have a trial," I answered, "Didn't want to disappoint him."

"Bill, go get the doctor," the sheriff said, "John, come help me escort Edward to his new cell." The deputies did as they were told.

Alex and I headed to the saloon.

When we got there it was still quiet. We each ordered a drink and sat down at the poker table. Once our drinks were delivered, we started to play.

James came in ten minutes later. He came over and sat down. Alex dealt him in.

"So, both of them are out of the picture," James said.

"Don't go thinking you can take over the town," Alex said, "I'm tired of shooting people today."

"I'm passing through town," James said, "Looking for the next big game."

"Those can be hard to find," Alex said.

"I suppose the two of you have done been gamblers and switched to something else," James said.

"Never done it exclusively," Alex said, "Never wanted to." The sheriff entered the saloon and came over to the table.

"Care to join us?" I asked.

"And lose? No thanks," the sheriff said.

"We'll let you win every third hand," Alex offered.

"And how are you gonna manage that?" James asked.

"When I stomp on your foot you fold," I answered. The sheriff laughed.

"Strangest gunslingers that have ever been through this town," the sheriff said, "I thought the marshal was out of his mind with some of the things he said, but he did nothing but speak the truth."

"Never quite got that reaction before," I commented.

"Well, I came in here to do two things," the sheriff said, "First I'll pay for all your drinks for today and second to tell you to stay out of trouble."

"Thank you," Alex said.

"We'll stay out of trouble as long as it doesn't come searching for us," I replied.

"Fair enough," the sheriff said, then went over and talked to the barman.

"And we still have a day before Lady Grace gets back here," I said.

"Too bad we couldn't have drawn the fight out a little longer," Alex commented, "Now we'll have to find something to do."

"You just won the last three hands," James said.

"Yeah, but all day poker games are only interesting for the middle part of the game when everyone still has money," Alex replied.

"I've got the money," James said.

"Then it will be a pleasure taking it from you," Alex replied.

We played poker until they tossed us out of the saloon because it was closing for the night, at which point we ended up at a table in the hotel dining room. We gave up the game shortly after lunch. I went to bed.

Lady Grace had arrived back at the hotel that evening.

The next morning Alex and I were waiting with the coach when Lady Grace stepped out of the hotel. Once she was inside, and her bags were stowed, we started out. The sheriff was standing on the sidewalk outside his office. He waved as we passed; we waved back. He looked relieved that we were leaving. Then we left the town behind.

ALEX'S PAST
CHAPTER 6

Toby

Three days later we entered another town. Alex seemed more alert this time. I was wondering whether she had been here before or she was just being extra watchful.

We stopped in front of the hotel. Lady Grace opened the door before any of us could react. She stepped on to the sidewalk. The driver followed her into the hotel with her bags. He came back out we went with him to the stables, then we headed to the hotel. Lady Grace was waiting in the lobby.

"Here you go," she handed Alex and me each a key, "I'm tired, so I will see you in the morning."

"Yes, ma'am," I answered. Lady Grace went upstairs. Alex and I headed up to our rooms. I put my stuff in the room before heading to the saloon, which was conveniently located in the hotel. Alex was already leaning on the bar with a drink in her hand. She was watching the three men playing poker. There were only three people in the bar besides the ones playing poker, Alex and me. Alex was watching the men playing poker. One was older with white hair, grey stubble and grey eyes.

"You look familiar," the old gentleman that was playing poker said to Alex, "I've seen you somewhere before."

"That is possible," Alex replied. The other two poker players looked her direction. The second player was a young fellow that was tall and thin with a square face; and the third man had dirty blonde hair, tanned skin and blue eyes. Out of the three I figured the last man was the one to watch.

"I know where I've seen you," the old man said, "You won the poker tournament, the one on the boat."

"That was a while ago," Alex said.

"I never entered, but I watched the whole thing. Best trip I ever took," the old man said, "You can join us if Marsden and Robert don't mind.

"His money is as good as anybody's," the tall man said.

"I accept your invitation," Alex said sitting down in the fourth chair. I went to the bar and ordered a whiskey. I watched from that distance, but no one noticed

An hour later Alex was obviously winning. The blonde man, who I had identified as Marsden, sat back.

"I don't know how, but you're cheating," Marsden said to Alex.

"And how do you figure that?" Alex asked, "Or is it just because I'm winning?"

"You're cheating," Marsden stated.

"I'm not cheating," Alex said, "I would say that I'm playing as straight as you are but that would be a lie."

"I don't cheat," Marsden said.

"No, you just shuffle the cards in your favour," Alex said. Alex took the deck that Marsden just shuffled. And called the card before turning it over. "All I do is counter your cheating with good poker playing." Marsden's hand started to toward his holster. I walked over and cocked my gun in his ear.

"Why don't you keep both hands on the table where everyone can see them?" I suggested. Marsden's hand came back onto the table.

"Let me introduce you to my partner, Toby," Alex said. I uncocked my gun and put it away. Then stepped back to the bar.

"Pardon me, but I think it’s time I called it a night," Marsden said as he stood up. He took his money and left the saloon. The old man gathered up the deck and started to shuffle them as he laughed.

"Same as the tournament," the old man said.

"Just deal," Alex said, but there was no hardness there.

When the saloon closed I stepped outside for a few minutes

before going to bed. Alex followed me out.

"Don't like Marsden?" I asked leaning against a post.

"He should have been hung a long time ago," Alex answered, "And if I wasn't a coward he would have been."

"As in, home sweet home?" I asked.

"Some thing like that," Alex answered.

"It'll work out," I told her.

"Why so sure?" Alex asked.

"It always seems to when we work together," I answered.

"Yeah," Alex said, her voice quiet, "Good night." She turned and went back inside the hotel. I stayed out there for a few more minutes before going in.

*   *   *   *

Lady Grace

The waiter had just placed my breakfast in front of me as Alex entered the restaurant.

"Good morning," he greeted me.

"Good morning," I answered signalling him to sit down. He sat. His hat stayed on, which is bad manners, but I knew better than to ask him to remove it. The server brought over a plate of breakfast for Alex.

"Where is Toby this morning?" I asked.

"Still sleeping," Alex answered.

"Will he be there all day?" I asked.

"He'll be up in time for lunch," Alex answered. I took another bite before addressing Alex again.

"He is missing a beautiful morning."

Alex nodded as he chewed. As he was rather uncommunicative, I refrained from saying any thing further. Alex had stopped eating long before I finished. When the waiter took both of our plates, I asked him to bring me some tea.

By the time he had returned with my tea, Alex seemed to have drifted off to sleep. Very ill-mannered, but I left him alone and drank my tea.

Half an hour had passed when the door to the restaurant opened and the daughter of my good friends the Turners, Simone, came in followed closely by a blonde stranger. Simone's brown hair was longer than the last time I had stopped here and her bright green eyes still held that streak of pain. I stood as they came over to the table.

"Lady Grace," Simone smiled before giving me a hug. I returned the hug.

"How are you?" I asked sitting back down.

"I'm fine," Simone said.

"And who is this?" I asked.

"This is my fiancé, Marsden," Simone answered. He did not look happy about some thing, nor did he make any attempt to greet me. He did shoot Alex a nasty look. Alex still seemed to be asleep.

"You're getting married?" I asked, "That is wonderful. When is the wedding?"

"Father would have us marry this month," Simone said, "But the minister keeps saying that he's busy."

"I will have to talk to your parents and see if I can get an invitation," I said.

"If you're in town when it happens, you're invited," Simone replied. I smiled at her.

"We have things to do," Marsden said taking a firm grip on Simone's arm and started pulling her away.

"I'll see you later, Lady Grace," Simone said still smiling.

"Good bye," I called. And then they were gone.

"There is one marriage that needs to be stopped," I said pouring myself another cup of tea.

"Couldn't agree with you more," Alex replied, her eyes open now.

"I thought you were asleep," I said.

"I was for a few minutes," Alex replied.

"From the looks he was tossing you direction, I would have to say you two have met before," I said.

"Last night, I showed his friends how he was cheating at poker," Alex said, "He wasn't happy about it."

"You have a knack for not making friends," I commented.

"I don't need his kind as friends," Alex replied. I finished my cup of tea.

"I think I will go see Simone's parents," I said as I stood up, "Perhaps I can stop this wedding before they make the worst mistake for their daughter."

"Good luck," Alex said. I left the restaurant.

*   *   *   *

Toby

I woke to someone poking my shoulder.

"You gonna get up today?" Alex's voice asked.

"I thought I locked the door," I muttered.

"Apparently not," Alex answered. I opened my eyes. She was sitting in a chair beside my bed, her boots resting on the bed beside me.

"You look well rested," I commented.

"You got more sleep that I did," Alex said, "I went to bed last night and kept waking up screaming every five minutes."

"Seeing Marsden was that bad?" I asked sitting up.

"He's the one who raped me and left me for dead," Alex said, "I don't think it gets worse." I wasn't sure how to respond to that, aside from tracking Marsden down and shooting him.

"What time is it?" I asked.

"Just about noon," Alex answered, "Lady Grace will be at the restaurant for lunch after she talks to Frank and Marsha Turner about letting their daughter Simone marry Marsden."

"Your sister?" I asked.

"My twin sister," Alex answered, "I wish her luck, but I doubt she'll change their mind."

"Didn't anyone ask why you disappeared?" I asked.

"I don't know," Alex said, "Haven't talked to anyone."

"Ask Lady Grace, she seems to know Simone, if she is trying to stop the marriage," I said.

"Yeah," Alex said getting up, "Get dressed, I'll see you down in the restaurant." She left the room and I got up. When I entered for the restaurant, Alex and Lady Grace were already sitting at a table. I took a chair.

"I cannot believe them," Lady Grace was saying, "They think he is perfect for their daughter. Once she is his nothing will prevent him from beating her."

"You're talking about Marsden?" I asked.

"Yes," Lady Grace said, "He is supposed to marry Simone." The server put a plate in front of each of us.

"Simone is?" I asked.

"I am sorry, I forgot," Lady Grace said, "I met the Turners on one of my previous visits. Frank Turner owns the bank here in town, his wife Marsha is a wonderful hostess and Simone is their daughter. One of their daughters, I have been told."

"What happened to the other one?" I asked.

"Alexandria Turner disappeared four years ago, I think," Lady Grace said, "She was never found and no one knows what happened to her. It hurts Simone a lot. But now Simone is to marry Marsden. What a horrible thing to happen."

"So, no luck on stopping the wedding?" Alex said.

"No, all I could do was convince them to let me take Simone on a brief month long tour of the surrounding towns," Lady Grace answered, "Maybe I can help her in other ways."

"When are we leaving?" Alex asked.

"Tomorrow," Lady Grace said, "I am sorry if this is inconvenient for you."

"We signed on without knowing how long this would take," I replied, "Another month doesn't matter."

"Wonderful," Lady Grace said. We finished eating then Lady Grace left.

"Well?" I asked.

"Doesn't sound like they searched very hard," Alex said.

"But it hurt one person," I said.

"Who would be out there searching if she hadn't been raised to be a proper lady," Alex said, "Which would be the same reason she's going through with the wedding."

"Well, you have a month to figure out how to stop this wedding," I said.

"True," Alex said.

The next morning we were sitting on our horses out in front of the hotel waiting on Lady Grace. Marsden leaned on a post just down the sidewalk from where we sat, watching us. He didn't look happy. A cart stopped on the other side of the street and Simone got out and crossed the street to the coach.

"Is Lady Grace ready?" Simone asked us.

"She should be coming," Alex answered. A man, Frank Turner I assumed, got out of the cart and came over dragging a trunk. He was going grey around the temples and there was a heaviness to his posture. The driver helped him put the trunk away. A staff brought Lady Grace's bags out. The driver placed them in and then held the door open for Simone. Simone got in, soon Lady Grace followed her.

"Make sure she is back in a month," Frank Turner called to Lady Grace.

"I will," Lady Grace answered, "I gave you my word and I always keep my word." Frank Turner went back to his cart and we started out of town.

Lady Grace played hostess to the world for Simone. Alex and I guarded them. And Simone wanted to see if we could find Alexandria. It would be a long month.

* * * *

Lady Grace

I sat at the table with Simone to my right. Alex came into the dining room and over to our table. I signalled him to sit. He took the chair across from me. This was our last stop before we returned Simone home.

"Where is Toby?" I asked.

"He found a poker game, said he'd eat later," Alex answered. The server brought Alex a plate of food.

"Well, tomorrow you will be back at home," I said to Simone.

"Yes," Simone's voice was quiet.

"I hope you enjoyed this month," I said.

"I did, but I keep thinking that my sister is out here somewhere," Simone said, "I really want to find her."

"I wish we could go searching," I said, "But we do not have the time, even if we knew which direction she went. Also it has been several years."

"But I want to find her so much," Simone said.

"We need to get you back," Alex said, "We should not to do anything that might delay your marriage." Alex pushed his plate away.

"I don't care about my marriage. I want to find my sister," Simone said. Tears threatened to spill down her cheeks.

"Calm down," I told her, "I will keep an eye out for Alexandria in my travels and bring her back to you when I find her. I promise." Simone calmed down, but I could feel that it would not last.

"If you'll excuse me, I'll go see how Toby is doing," Alex said, standing up.

"You've barely touched your food," I said.

"I'm not hungry," Alex answered.

"Then you may go," I said. Alex left the restaurant.

*　　　*　　　*　　　*

Toby

I collected my money and joined Alex at the bar.

"Where're the other two?" I asked.

"Probably in bed," Alex answered. She seemed to have had enough whiskey to depress her.

"You didn't stay with them?" I asked.

"Simone went off about finding her sister during supper and I couldn't stomach it," Alex answered.

"That the reason you got drunk?" I asked.

"No, that was more to do with hoping to sleep," Alex answered. She straightened up, but couldn't walk in a straight line as we headed for the stable.

"May you should tell her that Alexandria is fine," I suggested once we were in the stable.

"Probably," Alex said climbing up to the loft. She lay down, I lay down a little farther down. "Was supposed to marry the bastard before he raped me." I heard her muttered before her breathing evened out.

A noise below woke me up. It was dark, so I knew that it must be someone trying to steal a horse. Alex sat up, just as I did. I moved quietly to the edge and could see someone standing, looking at the horses. I headed for the ladder as Alex jumped knocking the person down. Once below I lit a lamp and took it to where Alex was holding the struggling person.

"Let go of me," Simone's voice said. Alex pulled her to her feet. Somehow Alex still had her hat on, but then she hadn't taken it off when she went to sleep.

"Simone," Alex's voice sounded tired.

"And what were you planning to do once you had stolen a horse?" I asked.

"You wouldn't understand," Simone said.

"If you were thinking about going after Alexandria, don't bother," Alex said as she let go of Simone.

"What?" Simone said turning to her.

"Go back to your room and get some sleep," Alex said. She looked like the hangover was already hitting.

"What do you know about Alexandria?" Simone asked. Alex didn't say anything. "Answer me."

"Another time," Alex said, "Now go back to bed." Simone looked like she wasn't going to move, but finally she left the stable. I put the lamp out and we climbed back up to the loft.

"Think she'll be here in the morning?" I asked.

"I hope so," Alex answered, "I don't want to have to going looking for her with this hangover." We went back to sleep.

The next morning Alex and I joined Lady Grace and Simone for breakfast. After breakfast we got ready to go and then headed out.

We reached town in early evening. We dropped Simone off at home before heading to the hotel. Lady Grace had rooms for us when Alex and I were finished dealing with our horses. Then she went off to find supper. Alex and I took our stuff up to our rooms before going into the saloon. Tonight the saloon held a larger crowd. Marsden was playing poker and I recognized Frank Turner as one of the spectators. The older man with the white hair and grey eyes was playing as well as a man with the silver star of the sheriff's office.

Alex and I ordered a drink each and watched from where we were. Between hands the old man looked around. He spotted Alex.

"Care to join us again?" he asked with a smile.

"Thank you for the offer, but there are only so many times you can play with a cheater before you've seen all their moves and get bored," Alex answered.

"He shouldn't be cheating tonight," the sheriff said.

"I've never seen that stop people before," Alex said, "And men like Marsden are as common as flies."

"Your deal," Marsden told the old man.

"So, Simone's back already," the old man said.

"Just as Lady Grace promised," Alex answered.

"If she hadn't felt the need to show Simone the world, she would have never had to make that promise," Marsden said.

"That doesn't sound like Simone wanted to come back," the old man said. He seemed to be the needle that was poking things to see what twitched.

"She is back more or less of her own choosing," Alex answered.

"What's that supposed to mean?" Marsden asked.

"She wanted to continue traveling," Alex answered, "She believes that she could find Alexandria."

"She's always had trouble letting Alexandria go," Frank Turner spoke up.

"No one knows where she went or why," the sheriff said, "Where would Simone start to search?"

"I'm not sure she knew, but she was going to try anyways," I answered.

"Then why bother trying?" Marsden asked.

"Hope," Alex answered.

"Waste of time," Marsden said.

"How so?" Alex asked, "From what everyone has said no one knows what happened to Alexandria. That means that she could still be out there."

"You travel," Marsden said, "What is the likelihood that you could find her?"

"I don't know," Alex answered, "But Lady Grace promised to find her and bring her back."

"More foolishness," Marsden said.

"Hope is foolish, or finding Alexandria is foolish?" the old man asked. Everyone looked at him as he played the winning hand. Marsden remained silent. "Or perhaps both."

"No one has found her yet," Marsden said, "And she hasn't come back on her own. Why would another search do any good?"

"Perhaps she stays away out of fear," the old man said.

"Fear of what?" Frank Turner asked, "She was happy before she disappeared. Simone didn't even think that Alexandria was scared of anything. She just went out to pick berries and never came back." Frank Turned suddenly turned to us. "Simone is stubborn, even Lady Grace promising to look would not have been enough. Simone would be out there searching if there wasn't something else." He looked like a man, who thought he had an answer.

"The promise of information," Alex answered.

"Information?" the sheriff said holding the deck.

"What information?" Marsden demanded.

"Why don't you tell us?" I said to Marsden.

"I have no idea what you are talking about," Marsden said. But the sheriff turned to Marsden.

"What are they talking about?" the sheriff asked Marsden.

"I don't know," Marsden answered, "Strangers come to town and start throwing wild accusations and now I'm a suspect. I was supposed to marry her at the time."

"And now you get Simone instead," Alex said, "Works out for you either way." The saloon was quiet and everyone was looking at Marsden.

"That's just the way it happened, I didn't plan it that way," Marsden said, "I didn't plan anything. These are just wild accusations."

"Unfortunately, Marsden is right," the sheriff said, "You two don't seem to have anything on him."

"We've talked with Alexandria," I said, "Marsden is the reason she won't come back."

"Yes, she is still alive," Alex told Marsden, "Doesn't go out much, but she is still alive."

"Where?" Frank Turner demanded as he stood up.

"We swore we wouldn't tell," I answered, "But she is safe from any more harm coming to her."

"And why does fear of Marsden keep her away?" the sheriff asked.

"Because he raped her," the old man answered, "Did the same to my daughter. That was why my Samantha took her own life. There are probably more out there, but they're too scared to come forward."

"Is this true?' the sheriff asked us.

"Took her a long time before she could talk about it, but yes, that is what she said happened," Alex answered. Frank Turner collapsed back on his chair. Marsden was starting to look for escape routes. The sheriff stood up and went around the table to stand behind Marsden.

"Stand up slowly," the sheriff said.

"No one has any proof," Marsden said, "These are wild accusations."

"Two strangers come to town and know more about Alexandria than the people living here. That tells me they aren't lying," the sheriff said, "Get up." Marsden got to his feet. The sheriff restrained him and started to walk him out of the saloon. Frank Turner stood up and followed them. Alex and I followed as well. Everyone else stayed where they were. Once outside we headed to the sheriff's office.

Suddenly Marsden pulled away from the sheriff and took off. The sheriff pulled out his gun, so did Alex and I. The sheriff shot first and Marsden kept running. Alex shot three times and I shot till my gun was empty and the sheriff emptied his. Somewhere in there Marsden collapsed. We went over to where he lay. The sheriff turned him over and we could all see that Marsden was dead.

"Well, he made that choice," the sheriff said.

"I'll get the doctor," Frank Turner said.

"Don't worry," the sheriff said, "We'll take the corpse to him." The sheriff took the feet and I took the arms and we carried him to the doctor's office. The doctor came down just as we put the body on the table.

"What happened?" the doctor asked looking at the six bullet holes in the body.

"He decided to run from the law," the sheriff answered, "I guess he's free now." I left. Frank Turner had gone home. Alex was standing outside the door.

"We stopped the wedding," I said as we started for the hotel.

"But no luck when it comes to watching him hang," Alex replied.

"Maybe it's better this way," I said, "A judge might have pardoned him for lack of evidence."

"True," Alex said. Lady Grace was standing out in front of the hotel when we got there.

"What happened?" Lady Grace asked.

"Marsden was shot," I answered.

"By you two?" Lady Grace asked.

"By the sheriff," Alex answered. Lady Grace nodded and then

went into the hotel. We followed her inside, but went up to our separate rooms.

END OF TOUR
CHAPTER 7

Toby

The next morning I stood waiting outside the hotel for Alex and Lady Grace. Two men rode into town. They seemed familiar, but I didn't think I have met them. They stopped up the street at the general store, tied their horses to the hitching post and went inside.

Alex came out of the hotel, followed by Lady Grace.

"What's up?" Alex asked.

"Remember the wanted posters Thomas left for us?" I asked.

"Sure," Alex pulled them out of her pocket. I glanced at each briefly.

"These two just rode into town," I said, "They're in the general store.

"More shooting?" Lady Grace asked.

"No, these men are wanted by the law, but they're wanted alive," Alex answered putting the hand bills back.

"I was hoping to stay and visit for a couple of days," Lady Grace said.

"We shouldn't be too long," Alex said. Lady Grace went down the street to the restaurant. Alex headed for the stables. I leaned against a post and kept an eye on the general store. Alex had just brought the horses around and had gotten off when the two men came out. They loaded up their supplies before getting on their horses. They headed the opposite direction from the way they had come into town. Alex and I waited until they were further down the street before getting on our horses and following them. The two men weren't going fast so it was easy to keep them in sight as we left town and went along the road.

We never let them out of our sight, but they didn't seem to notice that they were being followed. I figured that we could get them when they stopped for the night. Night fell and they didn't stop. Half the time I couldn't tell if they were ahead of us, but Alex seemed to know.

When the sun came up the two men were still the same distance ahead of us. We came to a town, but the two men went around. We followed them in going around the town.

"I think they know people are looking for them," I commented.

"Most people who're wanted know that," Alex said.

"So, how're we going to get them?" I asked, "They aren't gonna make it easy."

"We wait," Alex answered, "They'll give us our opportunity."

"Based on the amount of supplies they bought, they could be going for a while," I said, "We have only the basics for supplies. They can out last us."

"They'll stop at some point to sleep," Alex replied, "I can't see them sleeping as they ride."

"I hope so," I said.

They continued for the rest of the day with us following them. Night fell and again they didn't stop. The third day was the same, avoiding towns and not stopping.

The sky was getting lighter when they stopped. Getting off their horses the two men led their horse off the road and went into the trees.

"What do you think?" I asked Alex as we stopped.

"We wait," Alex answered. We had sat there for a while when I could smell beans cooking.

"I'd say they've stopped to rest," I said.

"They must've found, or known about, a cave," Alex said, "Because I don't see smoke."

"Shall we get closer?" I asked.

"Might as well," Alex said. We moved to the point where they went off the path. The smell was stronger and now I could hear the occasional pop of burning wood.

"Can't be very far off the path," Alex said quietly.

"Not a very good hiding spot," I replied in the same volume. We waited a while longer. The smell of food drifted away, but the sound of a fire didn't. Neither of us moved.

Finally Alex got off her horse and led it into the trees where the two men had entered. I got off my horse and followed her. A few feet into the trees the horses were tied to a tree branch. They didn't make a sound as Alex and I tied our horses near by. Alex pointed to something farther into the trees. I followed as she walked quietly over to it. It was a cave opening. There was the flicker of firelight on the walls, but the source was behind a bend. Alex stopped to listen. I couldn't hear anything besides the fire. I started forward. Alex didn't signal me to stop, so I kept going. I went around the bend in the cave. The two men were lying near the fire; both seemed to be sleeping. I went farther in. Neither moved. I could feel Alex follow me in. I went to the farthest man. He was unarmed as far as I could tell. Alex was checking the other man over.

Taking a rope that was lying nearby I tied the man up. Alex did the same, but the man woke up and she had to hit him when he started yelling. I had finished tying the man when he woke up because of the yelling. He figured things out quickly and opened his mouth to yell, but I stuffed his bandana in his mouth.

"Neither of these two have any weapons," I commented to Alex.

"The papers don't say why they're wanted," Alex said.

"I guess we won't know," I said, "Let's get these two to a sheriff who'll take them off our hands."

"Looking forward to some sleep?" Alex asked.

"And a hot meal," I answered, "With the possibility of a bath if there's time."

"I'm sure Lady Grace would appreciate it if we took the time," Alex said. I picked the man up and slung him over my shoulder. He continued to struggle. I carried the man and Alex dragged the other one out of the cave and back to the horses. We tied the men to their horses before getting on ours.

Once on to the road, we went back to the last town we passed. This time we went into town. We stopped at the sheriff's office. The door opened as we got off our horses. The sheriff was solid without it giving him extra size. Two guns were strapped to his hips and he rested the barrel of the eight-gauge on his shoulder. If it wasn't for the silver star that read sheriff I might have been worried about him. His grey eyes studied us, then our prisoners and back to us.

"You Alex and Toby?" the sheriff asked.

"Yes," Alex answered.

"Bring 'em inside," the sheriff said, "Thomas is here, too." Alex and I went over and took the men down off their horses. Then we took them inside. The cells were right in the sheriff's office. The sheriff was already standing with one door open. We put the men in the cell and the sheriff locked the door once we were out. Thomas was sitting in the chair facing the sheriff's desk.

"You got them?" Thomas said.

"You sent us after them," Alex said, "What did you expect?"

"I hadn't heard that you got my message," Thomas answered. Thomas reached into his coat and pulled out an envelope. Alex took it.

"Where're you going next?" Thomas asked.

"To find a hotel," Alex answered, "A bed, a hot meal and maybe a bath are all appealing right now."

"Ernie's hotel is the one you'll want then," the sheriff said, "The other two only provide the bed."

"Thank you," Alex said. We started for the door.

"And after that?" Thomas asked.

"We have a guard job waiting," I answered him. Thomas nodded. Alex and I left the sheriff's office. Getting on our horses we headed for Ernie's. We had stopped in front of the hotel when a young man came and took our horses to the stable that was in the back. Alex and I went into the hotel. I went up to my room and was asleep the moment my head touched the pillow.

I got up for breakfast the following day. After breakfast I took a bath. Once all the grime was gone I met up with Alex in the restaurant.

"Ready to go?" Alex asked.

"Nothing else that I have to do," I answered.

"I asked about our hotel bill," Alex said, "Apparently Thomas came by and paid it at some point."

"Why?" I asked.

"Based on his question while we were at the sheriff's office he has a job he needs done," Alex answered.

"I told him we were busy," I said.

"That's why he hasn't pushed it," Alex said, "Unlike Jacob, Thomas is willing to take busy as an answer. If he still needs it done the next time we see him, he might ask us." I nodded. Alex pushed her plate away.

"Shall we go?" I asked.

"Might as well," Alex answered. We got up and left the hotel. The young man had just brought our horses out front. I tipped him before taking the reins of my horse. Alex and I got on our horses and headed back to Alex's hometown.

It felt like a shorter journey going back than it did leaving. We went to the hotel, where our rooms were still waiting us. We left our gear there before inquiring about Lady Grace. The hotel clerk said that she was at the Turner residence. Alex led the way as we walked up the street. The house was a street off the main street, but from the looks of it the property had an orchard behind it. There were other houses around it, but this one stood out. It was painted white with a fence around the front yard and a road that went passed the house to a barn that was beyond it. There was a covered porch with a swing and a couple of chairs. The door to the house had a stained glass window in it.

"Nice house," I commented as we went up the walk.

"That's what happens when you own the bank," Alex replied. We went up the porch stairs. Alex knocked on the door. It took a moment before the door opened. The woman that stood there had eyes that were similar to Simone's except that they were blue. Her brown hair was up in a simple bun, but her dress was a little more elaborate than most women while not quite as expensive as Lady Grace's dresses. Her eyes lightened as if in recognition when she looked at Alex, but Alex missed it. She seemed to be a little shocked.

"Good day," Alex said. I took my hat off. "We're looking for Lady Grace."

"You're Alex and Toby, aren't you?" the lady said snapping out of the shock.

"Yes, Ma'am," I answered.

"I'm Simone's mother," the lady said, "Please come in. We're visiting in the parlour." Mrs. Turner opened the door to let us in. We stepped into the hall and Mrs. Turner closed the door behind us. The furniture and decorations in the hallway were simple.

"This way," Mrs. Turner said leading the way. We followed her. Lady Grace, Simone and Mr. Turner were all seated in the parlour, which continued the theme of simple decor.

"That was a long couple days," Lady Grace commented when she saw us.

"It happens," Alex replied, "I hope we didn't put you behind schedule."

"No," Lady Grace said, "I've been having a good visit."

"Have a seat," Mrs. Turner said, "Would either of you like some tea?" Mrs. Turner gestured to the teapot on the table.

"No, thank you," I replied sitting down in one chair.

"No," Alex said sitting down in the other unoccupied chair. Mrs. Turner sat down beside Mr. Turner.

"It's been a lot quieter since you left," Mr. Turner said, "Even the poker games haven't been as exciting."

"We're sorry for any inconvenience that was caused," Alex said.

"If you had any other story I would be upset," Mr. Turner replied, "But as it is, you're forgiven."

"Since I'm not getting married now I've been asking if I could travel with Lady Grace for a while," Simone said.

"And we have explained that you need to stay here," Mrs. Turner said.

"But Alexandria…" Simone started. Mrs. Turner shot her a look that stopped anything further.

"It looks like you will have good weather for your travels," Mr. Turner said.

"So far, we haven't had any trouble, " Lady Grace said, "I hope to be back home before the bad weather starts."

The conversation stayed on light topics. We were invited for supper and Lady Grace accepted the invitation for all of us. I left my hat in the parlour when we went into the dining room. Alex left hers on. Mrs. Turner noticed and gave a disapproving frown but no one said anything. After supper we all went back to the parlour, and visited a while.

After the conversation ran down Lady Grace, Alex and I got up.

Mr. Turner and Simone escorted us to the door.

"Good bye," Lady Grace said.

"It was nice to see you," Mr. Turner said. Lady Grace started down the path. Alex and I were going to follow her when Simone grabbed Alex's coat.

"What do you know about Alexandria?" Simone demanded.

"That she's fine," Alex answered.

"And safe," I added as Simone let go of Alex. Mr. Turner guided Simone inside as we turned and followed Lady Grace.

"Think she'll do anything foolish?" I asked.

"Only if they don't find something to channel that energy into," Alex answered.

"Well, finding Alexandria is a little problematic," I said, "Unless Nadine and Jacob feel like sharing."

"Jacob wouldn't, unless you come up with a very good reason," Alex said, "Nadine might be more likely to talk. But I doubt that Simone would get that far. Mr. And Mrs. Turner won't let her get that far without sending a search party."

I nodded. When we got back to the hotel I went up to my room for the night.

The next morning Alex and I rode on either side of Lady's Grace's coach as we left town. We were the only ones on the road all morning. Shortly after noon we turned onto another road. This one had more traffic. We came to a bustling city just before dark. Lady Grace got us rooms at the hotel. I ate supper with Lady Grace before going into the saloon. Alex had gone over earlier and was now playing poker. I watched her play while I had a drink. Then I went back to the hotel.

I woke up to gunshots. There were at least two guns involved and it sounded like it was coming from the street. I got up and looked out the window. Two men were standing in the street and firing at each other. Based on their uncoordinated movements, they were drunk. In the pre-dawn light I could see curtains in other buildings open and people look out. The drunks finally ran out of bullets without hitting each other or anyone else. Two men came out of the sheriff's office. The men escorted the drunks into the sheriff's office. Curtains closed as people either went back to bed or got dressed. I was about to turn from the window when I saw a man come out of the saloon. His hat was pulled low, his coat hung open revealing a gun on each hip and one holstered around his middle, his boots were dusty, and he had gloves on. The man grinned before going down the street toward the stable.

I turned from the window. I pulled on my clothes and going downstairs. I stepped outside the hotel in time to watch the man ride passed. The door opened and Alex stepped outside. She looked at the back of the rider.

"I see they woke you up as well," Alex said.

"Gunshots are hard to sleep through," I replied.

"He may have started it, but don't mess with him," Alex said before turning and going down the streets.

"What?" I asked as I started after her.

"Don't know his name," Alex said, "Don't even know what he does, but I've watched him take out five men in the amount of time it takes some of us to take out one. I've seen him a few times, but never dealt with him. I don't plan to start now."

"It doesn't bother you that he started the fight?" I asked, "Usually that bothers you."

"So far no one has gotten hurt," Alex answered, "Two drunks, that couldn't hit anything if they were nose to nose with it, firing at each other doesn't hurt anyone." We entered a restaurant that was open and half full of people. I followed Alex to a corner table that was empty.

We sat without talking until our food arrived. I finished all my food just as Alex finished half of hers. Alex paid for the food then we headed back to the hotel.

Lady Grace was sitting in the dining room eating breakfast when we arrived at the hotel. She saw us and signalled us to come and sit with her. Alex and I went over and sat down.

"Unless you had planned to stay, I thought that we could move on this morning," Lady Grace said.

"We don't have anything planned," Alex replied. Lady Grace waited for a moment to see if I would contradict Alex. I didn't.

"Then when I'm done, we can go," Lady Grace said.

"We'll get the horses ready," Alex said. Lady Grace nodded. Alex and I stood up and left the hotel. We went to the stables. The driver was still sleeping in the loft. He was snoring loud enough to shake to boards that made up the stable. I went up to the loft to where he was sleeping. I nudged him with my boot. He stopped snoring and looked up at me through half closed eyes.

"Lady Grace said we're leaving as soon as she has finished breakfast," I told him. He grimaced at me before sitting up. I went back down the ladder and to the stall where my horse was.

Alex was the first one ready, with me not far behind. We waited outside the stable for the coach driver. When he drove the coach out, Alex and I took up our positions. We stopped at the hotel to pick up Lady Grace and her luggage. The driver climbed back onto his seat and we started to move.

It was late afternoon when we reached the next town. The sheriff's office was the first building we passed as we came into town. The sheriff was sitting outside with a rifle across his lap. He stood up when he saw us. His eyes followed Alex. I glanced over at Alex. She gave the sheriff a mock salute. The left side of Alex's mouth turned up in an impish smile. Then it was gone, like it had just been a twitch of the muscles. Once we were passed the sheriff sat down again.

We stopped at the hotel to drop Lady Grace off before we went to the stables. Alex finished first and waited for me.

"The sheriff recognized you," I commented when I joined her.

"I've dealt with Sheriff Conners before," Alex replied as we started for the hotel.

"Is this something to worry about?" I asked.

"No," Alex answered, "He'll only bother us if we get into serious trouble or he needs our help."

"I'm not sure that's a relief," I said. Alex shrugged. We entered the hotel. Lady Grace was standing in the lobby talking to a woman that was about her age and she wore a similar style of clothes. A younger woman stood nearby, I assumed that they were mother and daughter based on their physical similarities. The younger woman looked bored until she saw Alex, then a predatory gleam came into her eyes. Alex didn't seem to notice.

Lady Grace paused in her conversation to hand each of us a key. Alex and I headed upstairs. I dropped my gear on the bed and then sat down on the edge.

A knock came at the door. I looked up to see Alex standing

there. She held up a deck of cards. I nodded and moved to the table. Alex sat down in the other chair. She shuffled and dealt out the cards.

We played until supper. Then we headed for the dining room. Lady Grace was sitting with the two women we had seen earlier in the lobby. Alex and I went over to the table.

"Finally," Lady Grace said when she saw us, "I want to introduce you to my friend." Lady Grace gestured to the older woman, "This is Mrs. Stacie Hunt, and her daughter, Tabitha Hunt." Lady Grace indicated the younger woman. I removed my hat.

"Very nice to meet you," I said. Alex nodded her acknowledgment.

"Stacie, these are Alex and Toby," Lady Grace said.

"It's nice to meet you," Mrs. Hunt said with a smile. Tabitha smiled up at Alex. Lady Grace signalled for us to sit. The waiter brought supper for the ladies. He was about to ask us if we were eating as well, when something distracted him. I turned enough to see that the sheriff had come into the room and was headed for our table. The waiter quickly slipped away. Lady Grace looked up at the sheriff.

"Is there something we can help you with, Sheriff?" Lady Grace asked.

"I need to borrow Alex and Toby," the sheriff answered, "If that's all right with you." Lady Grace looked as us. Alex shrugged.

"It's fine," Lady Grace replied. Alex and I followed the sheriff out of the hotel.

"What do you need?" Alex asked once we were standing on the sidewalk.

"A gang of about twenty men have been terrorizing this town for a couple years," the sheriff said, "They switch hideouts regularly so it's been difficult tracking them down. But someone has seen them at a farmhouse outside of town. This may be the only chance to get them and all I have are two deputies to help me."

"Do they have to be brought in alive?" Alex asked.

"No," the sheriff answered, "They would just be hung anyway."

"We'll get our horses," Alex said.

"My deputies are already out there watching," the sheriff said,

"I'll meet you at the end of this street." The sheriff pointed ahead of us. Alex nodded. Alex and I headed for the stables.

Once we were ready we headed for the meeting place. The sheriff was waiting. Alex and I followed him as he headed for the farmhouse. As we came in sight of the farmhouse, two men stepped onto the road. I saw the stars on their vests.

"What's happening?" the sheriff asked.

"They seem to be taking the night to rest and plan," one of the deputies answered, "They aren't going to go out tonight. And they don't have anyone keeping watch."

"Everyone find a place in a circle around the house," the sheriff said, "And hide there until I signal that everyone is ready." The sheriff, Alex and I tethered our horses by the deputies's horses. Then we surrounded for the house.

The sheriff whistled to let us know that everyone was in position and that we should be ready because gun fire was about to erupt. The farmhouse was quiet, as though they had heard. Men were peering out the windows.

A shot sounded from the other side of the house. There were several shots in return. Several men came out the back door. The sheriff fired first and the men fired back. I started firing.

In ten minutes the last shot was fired. The quiet was almost as loud as the shooting. I stepped out of the hiding spot. No one shot me. The sheriff stepped out as well.

"Looks like all of them," the sheriff commented. I nodded. A single shot came from the front of the house. The sheriff and I ran around the house to find Alex pointing her gun at the deputy.

"You shot the gun out of my hand," the deputy said to Alex. Alex slowly holstered her gun.

"Better than you putting another bullet into an already dead body," Alex replied.

"He wasn't dead yet," the deputy said.

"It was bad enough when you fired six times into the one man," Alex said, "The first bullet killed him." The deputy looked to the sheriff for support. The sheriff didn't so much as twitch.

"I do what is necessary," the deputy said.

"You wasted time and bullets," Alex replied, "Anyone with a brain could see that." The deputy walked over and picked up his gun and holstered it. The sheriff still hadn't moved. The deputy took a swing at Alex. Alex ducked and when she came up she delivered a right to the deputy's gut. He staggered a little before straightening up to take another swing. Alex hit him before he had a chance. He staggered backward and slipped. The deputy reached for something to steady himself and managed to grab Alex. She fell with him into a mud puddle. Alex rolled off him before kicking him and then getting up.

"Have you gotten Alex's lesson yet, Jake?" the sheriff asked, "Or do you need another ass kicking?" The deputy grunted before getting up. Both he and Alex were covered in mud.

"They're all dead," the second deputy reported.

"We'll send the mortician in the morning," the sheriff said, "In the meantime, we'll take Jake into town and let Miss. Margaret at him. Alex, there's a shower that way." The sheriff pointed toward a group of cliffs.

"Why not drag him to Miss Margaret's, too?" Jake asked.

"Because I don't want you to shoot me while I'm bathing," Alex replied.

"You want me to send someone back with soap and some clean clothes," the deputy asked.

"I can do that," I said. The five of us went back to our horses. Alex took the reins of hers and guided it back towards the cliffs. The rest of us rode into town.

When I found the waterfall Alex was sitting in the pool at the bottom of it. She was still dressed, but less muddy. I put the clean clothes on the rock with her gun and hat.

"So, the sheriff knows you're female," I commented going to the edge of the pool.

"There are some people you just can't hide things from," Alex replied. I tossed her the soap. She caught it.

"I'll go watch the pass," I said.

"Thank you," Alex replied. I turned and walked to the spot where the two cliffs created a pass. It was far enough from the pool that I couldn't see Alex, but close enough that I could hear if she needed help.

Soon Alex rode up leading my horse. She looked like nothing had happened except for the fact that the clothes that I had brought her were clean. We rode back into town. The sheriff was sitting on the porch of the hotel. He stood up when we stopped near him.

"Thought you might like to get paid," the sheriff said he pulled out a hundred dollars and held it out. Alex took the money.

"Thanks," Alex answered.

"How long are you planning to stay?" the sheriff asked.

"However long it takes for Lady Grace to visit with Stacie," Alex answered.

"Maybe you should talk to Lady Grace," the sheriff said. He turned and headed up the street towards his office.

"What does that mean?" I asked.

"He knows something we don't," Alex answered. We went into the hotel. Lady Grace was still at the table in the dining room with Stacie. Tabitha had gone up to her room. Alex and I went into the dining room to the table.

"It is nice to see you both back and unharmed," Lady Grace said when she saw us.

"There wasn't really a chance of us getting hurt," Alex answered.

"You seem to have cleaned up," Lady Grace said.

"Road dust was starting to get too much," Alex answered. Lady Grace raised one eyebrow. "Especially when you add mud on top of it," Alex finished. Lady Grace nodded.

"Stacie and Tabitha are coming to accompany us," Lady Grace said.

"When're we leaving then?" Alex asked.

"The day after tomorrow," Lady Grace answered.

"And tomorrow?" Alex asked.

"Stacie and I will be visiting a friend of ours here in town," Lady Grace answered, "Try to stay out of trouble."

"We won't get into trouble," Alex replied, "The sheriff will make sure of that." Lady Grace nodded.

"Good night, Lady Grace, Mrs. Hunt" I said.

"Good night," Lady Grace said.

"Good night," Stacie replied. Alex and I left the dining room.

"That would be what Conners meant," Alex said as we headed up the stairs.

"He must be good at his job," I replied.

"Let's keep on his good side," Alex said.

I was the first one up and in the dining room the next morning. Lady Grace joined me shortly after.

"Good morning," Lady Grace said as she sat down.

"Good morning," I replied. Alex entered the dining room, but it looked as if she had come from outside rather than from upstairs. She came over and sat down.

"Good morning," Lady Grace said.

"Morning," Alex replied. Alex smelled like she had slept in the stable. Lady Grace's eyebrow went up as if she hoping Alex would explain. Alex ignored the look.

"What do you plan to do for the day?" Lady Grace asked.

"Find a poker game," Alex answered.

"And that should keep you busy all day?" Lady Grace asked.

"It has before," I answered.

"Good," Lady Grace said, "But please remember that we are leaving tomorrow morning."

"We will," Alex replied. No one spoke until we finished eating and Lady Grace ordered her tea. Alex and I left the hotel and we wandered over to the saloon. It was quiet two men at the bar. There was no poker game in a back corner. Alex went over to the bar and asked the barman. The bar man answered. Alex walked back to where I was standing and we went outside.

"No poker game today," Alex said.

"Why?" I asked.

"Because the man who usual runs the game is recovering from a five day game," Alex answered.

"What now?" I asked.

"We'll find something," Alex answered.

"As long as we don't find trouble," I said. We went over and sat in the chairs in front of the hotel.

We went in to eat lunch and went back out to sit there. Shortly after a wagon loaded with furniture passed us and it turned on to the next street. Ten minutes later the driver walked down the sidewalk. He was short and stocky with a bit of a waddle when he walked.

"Excuse me," the driver said when he reached to us.

"Yes?" I asked.

"I don't suppose you two could help me," the driver said, "I finally brought my furniture to my house. Unfortunately the men I asked to help me move are busy. I was hoping that I could get your help moving into my house."

I looked at Alex; she shrugged.

"Sure, we can help you," I said.

"Thank you," the driver said. He turned and led us back down the street. The houses on the next street were private residences. We went to the house with the wagon in front. We helped him unload

By supper time, all of the furniture was moved into his house and placed in the correct rooms. He paid us five dollars each and we headed back to the hotel.

We entered the lobby and could see Lady Grace, Stacie and Tabitha in the dining room.

"I'm gonna get a drink," Alex said. She turned and left the hotel. I went into the dining room and over to the table.

"Good afternoon, Toby," Lady Grace said gesturing me to sit in the empty spot.

"Good afternoon," I replied.

"Where is Alex?" Lady Grace asked.

"Said something about a drink," I answered.

"I hoping he's staying out of trouble," Lady Grace said.

"He is," I said. Lady Grace returned to the discussion she and her friends were having.

Once I was finished, I excused myself and went over to the saloon. Alex was sitting at a table in the far corner. I got a drink and joined her.

"Not hungry?" I asked.

"I found something to eat," Alex answered.

"Problems with Tabitha?" I asked.

"Although I've never spoken with her," Alex said, "Yes."

"This job can't last forever," I said, "And when it's over Tabitha will stay with her mother."

"It's until then that I have a problem," Alex said, "So far avoiding her is working."

"We leave tomorrow," I said, "She can't bug you while traveling."

"There are times when it would be nice to just tell someone that I'm not a man," Alex's voice was quiet.

"Why not tell her?" I asked, "I'm sure she'll leave you alone then."

"Because Lady Grace might find out and then I'd be dragged back to Simone and my parents," Alex said.

"And you're not ready for that," I said.

"That's right," Alex said.

"Then you'll have to figure out what to do about Tabitha," I said.

"I know," Alex said. We finished our drinks and then went back to the hotel. It looked like Lady Grace, Stacie and Tabitha had already gone upstairs. I stopped at my room. Alex continued down the hallway to her room. She opened the door and looked inside. Then she closed the door and came back down the hallway.

"Something wrong?" I asked.

"Tabitha," Alex answered, "I'm going to sleep in the stable."

"See you in the morning," I said.

"Night," Alex said. I went into my room and went to bed.

The next morning after breakfast, I went to the stable. Alex had her horse ready. The driver was still snoring in the loft. I went to the stall to get my horse ready when the snoring stopped. The driver slowly came down from the loft. He started getting the coach ready. When we were all ready we headed over to the hotel, where we waited until Lady Grace came out with her bags. Stacie and Tabitha followed Lady Grace out and the driver stowed the bags. Tabitha smiled up at Alex, but Alex seemed to be studying something else. The ladies got into the coach and the driver climbed back up into this seat. Then we left town.

It was a quiet day of riding. Mid-afternoon it began to rain. Then it poured. The driver swore about his difficulty in seeing through in the rain, and the horses had trouble on the muddy road. It got darker as the evening wore on. We reached a town where we could spend the night. We stopped at the hotel. Lady Grace, Stacie and Tabitha got out and went inside while the rest of us dealt with the horses.

When we had finished putting the horses in their stalls Alex and I headed back to the hotel. The clerk was just about to turn us away when Lady Grace came down to make sure we got our rooms. Once in my room I stripped down, hanging my clothes up, before lying down and going to sleep.

In the morning I got up and dressed in some clean, dry clothes and went downstairs. Alex was already sitting at a table in the hotel dining room. I sat down in the seat beside her.

"No problems last night?" I asked.

"Mrs. Hunt and her daughter are staying in the same room," Alex answered, "As long as we are staying here I doubt I'll have that problem. Since it rained all night and it hasn't stopped this morning, I would have to say that we will be here at least another day."

"A day stuck in a hotel," I said.

"Mr. Walton, the owner of this hotel, holds a poker game here in the dining room on days like this," Alex said, "He saw me and asked if I cared to join."

"You said yes," I said.

"I said that unless Lady Grace wishes to continue our journey today I was available," Alex said. Lady Grace came into the dining room. She saw us and came over to the table.

"Good morning," Lady Grace said.

"Good morning," I replied.

"It does not appear that we can continue today," Lady Grace said, "I hope we can move along tomorrow. I was hoping to get home before the worst of the storms hit. But I cannot go back on my word to escort Stacie and Tabitha to their destination."

"We should be able to continue in a day or two," Alex said, "The real storm season doesn't usually come for another month."

"I hope so," Lady Grace said. The waiter brought our food. We didn't say much as we ate. We were just finishing when Stacie and Tabitha came into the dining room.

"Good morning," Lady Grace greeted them.

"Good morning," Stacie replied.

"Good morning," Tabitha said her eyes on Alex.

"We aren't continuing today, are we?" Stacie asked.

"No," Lady Grace answered, "We will continue when the rain has stopped or when it isn't quite so severe. The only problem I foresee is what to do."

"There'll be a poker game here after breakfast is over," Alex said.

"They would hold a poker game in the hotel dining room?"

Stacie asked, "I'm surprised."

"The hotel owner allows it when the guests have no where else to go," Alex answered, "He uses it as a form of entertainment."

"It shall be interesting to watch," Lady Grace said. They ate breakfast before moving to the lobby, where they waited until the game table was set up.

Slowly people came back in to the dining room to watch the game. The players took their seats. Alex sat on the far side of the table from us. Each of the six players ante up. The one man took out a deck of cards. Judging by the cost of his white and green striped suit I guessed him to Mr. Walton. He opened the pack and shuffled the cards.

The first hand was dealt. Three of the men seemed to be professional players. Mr. Walton knew what he was doing, but a muscle near his mouth twitched when he had a good hand. The fifth man also showed tick when he had a good hand.

The man sitting in front of us was the first to run out of money. The audience applauded his efforts. The man to Alex's right was the next to go. Mr. Walton ran out of money but continued to be dealer.

At noon there was a call for a break. After everyone had eaten the game resumed. It didn't take long for another player to lose. A round of applause came as he stood up and left the game. Now there were just two players left in the game, Alex was one of them.

Over the afternoon they seemed to be winning and losing the same amount. As it went on, it seemed to me that the man was winning more. Alex's pile of money was going down, but slowly.

When it was time to break for supper Alex 's money was all gone. There was applause as Alex stood up. She held out her hand and the man shook it, then she stepped back. Mr. Walton congratulated the man and then announced that if everyone would step out into the lobby the hotel staff set up the dining room. I stood when the ladies did and we all went back out to the lobby where Alex joined us.

"You lost," Lady Grace said.

"There's the chance of that happening every time you play," Alex said with a shrug.

"You lost a couple hundred dollars," Stacie said, "And you just shrug it off?"

"I just lost my five hundred as well as any money I earned from the first part of the game," Alex said, "That's the price you pay for playing. If I didn't want to lose it, I shouldn't have played."

Stacie stared at Alex for a minute before shaking her head in disbelief.

After supper, Lady Grace and Stacie insisted Tabitha come for a short walk with them now that it had stopped raining. Alex and I played comet.

Some time later Mr. Walton sat down in the chair across the table.

"It was a good game this afternoon," Mr. Walton said.

"And if you ever deal that crooked again you are going to get shot," Alex replied.

"No one really noticed," Mr. Walton said, "Only the people I warned before hand."

"I hope everything works out for George Quintin," Alex said, "Because if that was a scam, he will be hunted down."

"I checked out his story," Mr. Walton replied, "And he let me. You aren't the only one who would be angry if that was a scam."

"George Quintin?" I asked.

"He was the man who won," Alex explained, "He needs money to rescue his wife and son. So, Frank offered to have him win today's poker game."

"We'll know tomorrow morning whether George's wife and son are freed," Mr. Walton said.

"And if they aren't?" I asked.

"Then we see what the law can do about the situation," Mr. Walton answered.

"I'm for hoping it all works out," Alex said.

"I'm hoping for that as well," Mr. Walton said as he stood up, "Good night."

"Good night," Alex replied. Mr. Walton walked away. Alex and I continued to play for a few more minutes before putting the cards away and going upstairs. Only after she closed the door to her room did I go into mine.

In the morning, I met Alex in the dining room.

"Have you heard what happened with George Quintin?" I asked.

"Not yet," Alex said, "But if word doesn't come back soon then

I may not know. It hasn't rained since yesterday, so I expect the Lady Grace will want to continue on today."

"Probably," I said.

Stacie and Tabitha came down first for breakfast and Lady Grace followed soon after.

"I see the rain has not started again," Lady Grace said.

"I hope the weather stays clear for the rest of the way," Stacie said. Mr. Walton brought Lady Grace's food to her. Today his expensive suit had yellow and white stripes.

"What happened?" Alex asked him before anyone could say anything.

"It all went well," Mr. Walton answered, "Mr. Quintin and family are headed for home."

"Good," Alex said. Mr. Walton went back to the kitchen.

"What was that about?" Lady Grace asked.

"The last word on someone who needed a favour," Alex answered, "If you'll excuse us, we'll go wake the coach driver."

"You are excused," Lady Grace said. Alex and I went to the stables. The driver readied the coach. Alex and I got our own horses ready. Once everyone was ready we headed for the hotel and picked up the ladies. We headed out of town.

The road was busier today. We passed some people and a few passed us, but there was always some travelers in sight. Late in the afternoon it started raining. It was light, but enough to make me feel damp all the way through my clothes to my skin. We reached the next town about suppertime.

After supper I went to my room. I had just laid down and thinking about sleep when there was a knock at my door. I opened it. Alex was standing there.

"Something wrong?" I asked.

"Tabitha," Alex answered. I stepped out of the way and Alex entered my room. I went and sat on the bed. Alex sat down in the chair.

"She and her mother aren't sharing a room this time?" I asked.

"Apparently not," Alex said," Though I think even as a man I would be turned off when I found someone else in my bed."

"Depends on the man and depends on the situation," I replied.

"I'm trying to figure out where I'm going to sleep tonight," Alex said, "She isn't in a deep enough sleep for me to get my stuff so I can't go out to the stable."

"You can sleep on the floor in here," I offered.

"Thanks," Alex said.

"Just don't wake me when you bring in your bag," I replied.

"I'll try not to," Alex said. I lay down again. I closed my eyes and let myself drift off.

When I woke up it was dark in the room. I heard the door shut. I rolled over and went back to sleep.

It was morning when I woke up again. Alex was in her bedroll on the floor. She was still asleep. I was about to get up when I saw her toss in her sleep and the pained look cross her face. I got up and went over to her. Squatting down, I shook her shoulder until she woke. Alex opened her eyes and slowly sat up.

"You were having a nightmare," I said straightening up.

"Thanks," Alex said. Alex stretched and rubbed the sleep out of her eyes. I packed up everything. We went downstairs. Lady Grace was already sitting at a table in the hotel dining room.

"Good morning," I said as Alex and I sat down.

"Good morning," Lady Grace replied, "It stopped raining so we will continue."

"Where do Mrs. Hunt and her daughter plan to stop?" Alex asked.

"The next town," Lady Grace answered, "They live at a ranch just outside of town. It will take us most of the day to get there." The waiter brought our food.

"So, tomorrow we'll just be guarding you," Alex said.

"As far as I know," Lady Grace said, "Though I am sure Tabitha would not mind if you decided to stay at the ranch." Lady Grace smiled.

"I hope her mother would see that as a problem," Alex replied.

"Her father would have more of a problem," Lady Grace said, "Stacie said that he has already arranged a match for Tabitha."

"Good," Alex said, "That goes along with my plan of not staying there." Just then Stacie and Tabitha entered the dining room.

"I hope it doesn't rain today," Stacie said, "It will make the whole trip easier."

"Storm season has come early this year," Lady Grace said. Alex and I excused ourselves and headed for the stable.

The road was busy again and the sky stayed clear. It was supper hour when we rode through town. We took a road to the right. It led right to the ranch house. Mr. Hunt came out to meet us. Stacie greeted him warmly. He invited all of us to stay for supper. Lady Grace went into the house with Stacie and Tabitha. Mr. Hunt directed us to the stable, where we tied up the horses. The ranch foreman showed us where we could wash up.

Then we went in the kitchen door. The driver, Alex and I ate with the servants. And when supper was over we went back to the horses. We took the coach and horse where the three of us sat and waited.

It was a while before Lady Grace came out. Her friends said goodbye as she got into the coach. We headed back to the hotel in town. In my room I pulled my boots off, dropped my hat on my saddlebags and then laid down on the bed.

There was a knock at my door. I opened my eyes to find the sun had risen. I got up and went to the door. I opened it. Alex was standing there.

"You coming?" Alex asked, "Because the rest of us have already eaten."

"I'm coming," I answered, "Just give me a few minutes." I closed the door. I washed up before pulling my boots back on, grabbing my hat and saddlebags. I left the room in a hurry and went outside to where everyone else was waiting.

Today the road wasn't as busy. It rained a little now and then. In all it was a quiet day. We travelled through territory sparsely inhabited. We hadn't reached any civilization before night fell and found it abandoned, so we travled through the night. We rested the horses at a pond about sunrise before continuing on.

Mid-afternoon we came to Red Alder, Nelson is the sheriff. Alex pointed out a hotel to the driver. We stopped in front of it and helped Lady Grace with her bags. Once we had put our horse in their stall Alex and I went back to the hotel. I put my stuff in my room before heading back downstairs. Alex joined me as we exited the hotel. Sheriff Nelson was standing outside.

"Have we done something wrong already?" Alex asked.

"No, I saw you enter town," Nelson answered, "I need help with something."

"How long?" Alex asked.

"A day, maybe two," Nelson answered.

"We have to check with our current employer," Alex said.

"If it's a yes, come to my office," Nelson said.

"We will," I said. Alex and I went back into the hotel. Lady Grace was sitting in the dining room having tea. She looked up at us when we stopped by the table.

"Yes?" Lady Grace asked.

"The sheriff asked for our help," Alex answered, "He said it might take a day or two."

"I suppose I can wait a day or two before continuing," Lady Grace said, "I think my friend Catherine lives in town. I will see if I can find her. Be careful."

"Usually are," Alex said. The imp twitch showed itself. Then Alex and I left.

Upon entering the office we found Nelson sitting behind his desk, Thomas sitting in the chair across from him and the deputy sitting on his bunk in the corner.

"Good, you're here," Thomas said.

"What do you need?" Alex asked sitting down on the chair beside the stove. I leaned against the wall next to the door.

"Help dealing with Terrill Lambert," Thomas answered.

"Who is he?" I asked.

"You may have seen him around," Nelson said, "He is good with a gun, but he seems to prefer starting fights so that people kill each other off."

"I think I know who you're talking about," Alex said, "We saw him not that long ago. He had two drunks who couldn't hit anything shooting at each other first thing in the morning."

"Sounds about right," Nelson said.

"He wiped out a group of men who were travelling because they wouldn't share their supplies with him," Thomas said, "Three of those men were law enforcement officers."

"And how do you plan to capture him?" Alex asked, "I've seen him shoot, he'd kill us all before we could draw our guns."

"He can't be that good," the deputy said.

"If I could get more people that could shoot I would," Thomas said, "He's here in town and I need him either dead or captured."

"Do you have a plan?" Alex asked.

"At sunset we call him out and shoot him," Thomas answered.

"Let's put a few more details into that plan before we try it," Nelson said, "Calling him out works, but we need to make sure that no innocent bystander is going to get hurt. And we need to be strategically placed so he can't just shoot us all down in a minute."

"I have an idea," I said.

"Let's hear it," Nelson said. I explained it to them.

"It should work," Thomas said.

"Or at least give us half a chance before we get shot," Nelson said.

"Shall we go now?" Thomas asked.

"You in a rush to die?" Alex asked, "Tomorrow is soon enough."

"I would rather get him before he leaves," Thomas said.

"He won't be leaving for another couple days," Nelson said, "He has paid for his hotel for two days and has hired a girl from the hotel's saloon for those days. He isn't going to be leaving yet."

"Tomorrow will work better, because we'll all have had time to prepare," Alex said.

"Fine, we'll do it tomorrow," Thomas said.

"Then we'll go for supper," Alex said standing up. Alex and I left the office.

After supper we found a saloon. I had a drink while Alex played several hands of poker. She was still playing when I went back to the hotel and up to my room.

The next morning Lady Grace was sitting in the dining room. I went over and she signalled that I should join her.

"Good morning," Lady Grace said.

"Good morning," I replied.

"Is the job done?" Lady Grace asked.

"No," I answered, "It'll take place this evening."

"I found my friend," Lady Grace said, "We're going to spend today shopping and tomorrow we're going to spend the day together. I was thinking we could leave the day after that."

"That will suit us just fine," I said.

"Good," Lady Grace said. We ate without talking about much.

After Lady Grace went out shopping Alex came down for

breakfast. Alex and I played poker until after lunch. Then we went over to the sheriff's office. Nelson was sitting behind his desk. The deputy was sitting on the chair by the stove. There was no sign of Thomas.

"Are we early?" Alex asked sitting down in the chair across from Nelson.

"Thomas is out watching Mr. Lambert," Nelson answered, "Hopefully he'll be back soon."

"Hopefully he doesn't tip Mr. Lambert off," Alex said.

"You've worked with Thomas before?" Nelson asked.

"We chased the same bank robbers for six months because every time we got close, he did something to screw it up," Alex said, "And having a man on crutches following you everywhere is a big tip off."

"We'll give Thomas some more time, but then we may have to go after him," Nelson said. Soon Thomas showed up. Then we discussed the plan.

After supper all five of us waited until dusk before going over to the saloon where Terrill Lambert was drinking.

Nelson and his deputy quietly cleared the street. Thomas found a barrel across the street from the saloon that he could sit and fire from. Alex and I found places in the shadows on either side of the saloon. The deputy found a spot farther down the street but still in range. We all drew our guns as Nelson went into the saloon. I saw Alex check to make sure her gun was loaded.

A few minutes went by. Terrill Lambert stepped out of the saloon with Nelson right behind him. They stepped off the sidewalk. Terrill pulled his gun, went down into a crouch and spun to shoot Nelson. But Nelson hadn't gone forward when Terrill stepped off the sidewalk, instead he had stepped backwards to give Alex and me clear shots. Terrill managed to hit Nelson in the lower leg. I shot several times and could hear other guns doing the same. Pain shot through my thigh, but I kept firing until I was out of bullets. Terrill Lambert was on his knees with several bullet holes through him, but he was still trying to reach for his other gun. Nelson limped down and pulled it out of his grasp. The hand continued to search for a weapon. Nelson put his gun away and took the gun he had taken away from Terrill Lambert with his dominate hand. He aimed and fired. Terrill Lambert slumped over with a hole between his eyes.

I started to slide down the wall of the saloon towards the sidewalk. Alex helped me to my feet and provided support. Thomas used his crutches to move over to the body. Thomas didn't look as if he had been injured. The deputy came over as well. He had a hand on his stomach trying to stop the flow of blood from his wound.

The doctor came down the street as well as the mortician. The mortician and his helpers dealt with the body. The doctor directed the rest of us to his office. It was halfway down the street. Every step on the way there caused pain to go through my leg. When we arrived Alex helped me to a chair until the doctor could attend to me. I noticed something wet on my hand. I turned it over and saw the blood and looked up at Alex. She was pressing her hand into the bullet wound in her shoulder.

The doctor began with the deputy and the bullet in his stomach. Nelson helped out in any way he could. Once he was finished there he dealt with the bullet in my thigh. After my thigh was bandaged up he turned to Alex, who was sitting on the floor by the door. She looked half asleep and pale.

"Let's get you up on the table," the doctor said. Alex didn't respond.

"Alex," Nelson called loudly.

"Yes," Alex looked up at him.

"We need to get you up on the table," the doctor repeated. Alex slowly got to her feet and walked over to sit on the examining table. Slowly she removed her coat. There were two growing blood spots on her shirt, both in her shoulder. The doctor cut the shirt around the area and started dealing with the bullets.

If Nelson noticed anything unusual about Alex he never showed it.

Finally the doctor finished with Alex. She put the jacket back on and got off the table. Nelson was next. The bullet went through his ankle, so the doctor's job was easier.

The deputy was put in one bed, I was given the next one, Nelson left the minute the doctor was finished with him, and Alex took off back to the hotel even though the doctor tried to talk her out of it.

I laid there in pain for a long time before drifting off to sleep.

The next morning the doctor brought breakfast for me and the deputy. After breakfast I taught the deputy the basics of poker and we played until lunch. Nelson brought us lunch and told us that Terrill Lambert had been buried. And that Thomas had moved on to wherever he was needed next. Alex showed up and played poker with us for the afternoon. For supper I went with Alex to find a restaurant. I was limping and in pain, but it wasn't too bad. After supper I went back to the doctor's office, where he insisted that I stay there for another night.

In the morning I went back to the hotel for breakfast. Alex came down after the waitress had brought my food. Alex sat down across from me.

"Have you seen Lady Grace this morning?" Alex asked.

"Not yet, but since she said she wanted to leave today she'll probably be down," I answered.

"I haven't seen her since yesterday morning," Alex said, "She said something about a day out with her friend. She left after having tea."

"If she isn't down soon we can look for her," I said. Alex nodded.

When we were finished eating, we played poker. Lady Grace still hadn't come down for breakfast. Alex went upstairs to check Lady Grace's room. I waited in the lobby. Alex came down a few minutes later.

"She isn't there and it looks like she hadn't sleep there," Alex said. I walked over to the clerk.

"Have you seen Lady Grace?" I asked.

"Not since yesterday when she went off in the carriage with another lady," the clerk answered.

"Did you recognize the other lady?" I asked.

"I might have seen her around town, but I don't know her personally," the clerk answered.

"Do you know where they went?" I asked.

"No, Lady Grace hasn't spoken with me since she received her room key," the clerk answered.

"Thank you," I said before going back to Alex, "No answers there."

"Did she say who her friend was?" Alex asked.

"Catherine," I answered.

"Let's go find Nelson," Alex said. We left the hotel. Alex slowed down a bit so that I was limping with her rather than behind her. Getting to the sheriff's office, we went inside. Nelson was working at his desk. He looked up as we entered. I sat down.

"Something wrong?" Nelson asked.

"We're missing our employer," Alex answered, "We were planned to leave today, but we can't find her. And no one has seen her since yesterday morning when she left the hotel in a carriage with her friend Catherine."

"Do you wouldn't know Catherine's last name?" Nelson asked, "It might help in the search."

"Lady Grace never told us Catherine's last name," Alex replied.

"That makes things difficult," Nelson said.

"Has anyone else gone missing?" I asked.

"Not today and none yesterday," Nelson answered. The door to the office opened and a man stepped inside. He looked like he belonged behind the counter at a general store with his black pants and the white shirt with the sleeves pinned at his elbows. He hesitated when he saw us.

"What can I do for you, Mr. Berd?" Nelson asked.

"My wife is missing," Mr. Berd answered.

"Catherine?" Nelson guessed.

"Yes, she took the carriage, "Mr. Berd replied, "Lady Grace was in town and they were going to ride out and have a picnic. I had to work half the night at the store, so I didn't get home until this morning. Now she's missing."

"So is Lady Grace," Alex said.

"What could have happened to them?" Mr. Berd asked.

"Did your wife tell you where they planned to go?" Nelson asked.

"A place just south of the Miller property," Mr. Berd answered, "We go there occasionally on Sunday afternoons."

"Good. You can show us where it is," Nelson said standing up, "Alex and Toby, go get your horses."

Alex and I left the office and headed for the stable. We saddled our horses and rode back to the sheriff's office. Riding was painful, but I didn't say anything. Nelson and Mr. Berd were sitting on horses waiting. They led the way out of the city. Once out of the city Mr. Berd led the way. We came to a shaded bank of a creek. Alex and Nelson got down. They looked over the area.

"Looks like the carriage stopped here," Nelson said, "And went that way." Nelson pointed farther south.

"Let's follow the trail," Alex said getting back on her horse. Nelson got back on his and we continued along the trail. We rode for an hour before we came to a wooden structure that might have been a house at one point, now it looked like it was at the point of collapsing. The carriage and horses were tethered to a pole that was sticking out of the ground along with four other horses.

"Shall we assume that there are enough horses to go around?" Alex asked.

"Don't assume anything," Nelson answered.

"There doesn't seem to be any movement from inside," I commented, "And if I saw four men on horse back standing outside my hideout, I would be busy preparing to shoot them."

"They have to be in there," Nelson said, "No one abandons horses like that."

"Then let's check it out," Alex said as she got off her horse. Nelson and I got off ours. Mr. Berd sat there as if he didn't know what to do.

"Mr. Berd," Nelson said turning to him, "You wait out here and look after the horses."

"Certainly, Sheriff," Mr. Berd replied getting off his horse and taking the reins of the other ones. I handed him the reins of my horse and followed the other two to the door of the structure. Alex and I went to either side of the door. Nelson kicked the door and it crashed inward. The three of us entered with our guns drawn.

Four men who were sleeping on the floor were groping for their guns. We took their guns away from them. Alex and Nelson dealt with the four men while I went over and untied Lady Grace and Catherine. Both ladies were dishevelled and a little dirty but otherwise fine.

"Thank you, Toby," Lady Grace said once she was free, "I'm so glad to see you!"

"This's our job," I replied, "Though it's easier to do when we know where you are."

"Next time you will," Lady Grace said. We started to leave with me limping behind them.

"Are you wounded?" Lady Grace asked me when she noticed.

"I'll be fine," I replied.

"What happened?" Lady Grace asked.

"I was shot," I answered. When we got outside Nelson and Alex had two horses ready to go with two men on each. The other two horses were left to roam free. Mr. Berd was sitting on the driver's seat of the carriage.

"Walter," Catherine said running over to her husband. Mr. Berd climbed down and wrapped her in his arms.

"Let's go home," Mr. Berd said when he finally let go to Catherine.

"Sounds good to me," Nelson replied. Mr. Berd helped Catherine into the carriage and then helped Lady Grace before climbing up to the driver's seat. I got up on my horse. Mr. Berd led with his horse as well as the other two tied to the back of the carriage. Nelson, Alex and I followed them.

In town we stopped at the sheriff's office to drop off the prisoners and the two horses. The rest of us went to the hotel where Lady Grace was dropped off. Then Alex and I stabled our horses. Alex and I ended up in my room playing poker.

Later there was a knock on the door. I got up and opened it. Lady Grace was standing there.

"Come in," I sat standing out of the way.

"Thank you," Lady Grace said as she stepped into the room. I closed the door and went back to my chair. Lady Grace sat down on the third chair.

"I'm sorry for not telling you where I was going," Lady Grace said, "Catherine had been to the place many times and never had anything like that happen. "

"Most attacks are unexpected," Alex replied, "We're just glad that there was enough of a trail to find you."

"Tomorrow morning we will head back to Dustcloud," Lady Grace said.

"If you have more visiting to do, you can still do it," I said, "Just tell us where you're going first."

"No, there isn't any place I want to stop between here and there," Lady Grace replied. We sat quietly for a few minutes. Lady Grace watched us play.

"You seem so good at this game," Lady Grace said.

"Practice," Alex replied.

"Would you like to be dealt in?" I asked.

"Certainly," Lady Grace answered. Alex dealt her in and we spend the rest of the afternoon playing poker.

The next morning we left Red Alder. The road was quiet. We might have passed only two people. It was quiet all the way to Dustcloud. That night it rained and we helped pull the stagecoach out of the mud, was the most eventful thing that happened.

The afternoon was sunny and bright when the coach stopped in front of Lady Grace's mansion. Lady Grace went inside and came back out in a few minutes. She paid the coach driver, who took the money and left with the coach. Lady Grace handed Alex our pay.

"Where are you off to now?" Lady Grace asked.

"Probably a hotel," Alex answered, "For about a week."

"Why?" Lady Grace asked.

"To rest and recover," I answered.

"Oh, yes, you were shot," Lady Grace said.

"We both were," I said.

"Anytime you need a place to stay, you are welcome to stay here," Lady Grace said.

"Thank you," Alex said, "That's very kind of you. I think we'll stay here for the week."

"You know where the stable is," Lady Grace said before went back inside. Alex and I went around the house.

After putting our horses in their stalls we left our things in the rooms had we stayed in before we spent the rest of the day playing poker. We went shopping for supplies the next day. We found a poker game the day after. And the rest of the week was spent joining in poker games at one of the saloons in town.

On the last day of the week, Alex and I were thinking about entering a small poker tournament, when a letter from Jacob arrived. He was asking for help with a job, the name of place and the date that we were expected. So Alex and I packed up and headed for the town.

BRIGHTEN
CHAPTER 8

Toby

Alex stepped out of the hotel and on to the sidewalk. She walked to where I was resting against a post.

"Civilization my butt," Alex said.

"The stable doesn't take guests," I told her.

"The hotel only takes guests that can pay the two hundred a night," Alex replied, "Which is robbery. There isn't any other place to stay in the whole bloody town."

"Why did Jacob pick this town?" I asked.

"Because every stage that comes through stops here," Alex answered, "Apparently that means the hotel can charge extreme rates."

"Poker game?" I asked.

"Next town," Alex answered, "We don't want to disturb the honest citizens with a rough crowd; they might sleep through church rather than attend."

"Gamblers can be as honest as anyone else out there," I said.

"Preaching to the choir doesn't help," Alex said.

"So, what do we do for sleeping arrangements until Jacob gets here?" I asked.

"We could skip sleeping and make noise all night until they give us a room for free," Alex suggested.

"Why not turn yourself over to the sheriff now and save

yourself the trouble?" I asked.

"Because Jacob would let me rot in there," Alex answered. We were silent a while. A young lady came out of the hotel and walked down the street passed us. Her skirt was green with a white shirt and a shawl that matched her skirt. The young lady has blonde hair pulled back in a fancy updo and her eyes were deep blue. Her face was heart shaped and the pale of not spending time outside. She entered a dress shop farther down the street. Alex's eyes followed her.

"Looking for a date?" I asked.

"Not my type," Alex answered, "But she might have money."

"You're going to steal money from the lady?" I asked.

"She has gone in and out of the hotel a couple times since we arrived into town, always alone," Alex said.

"Maybe her husband is bed ridden or just an old cripple," I suggested.

"A lady who looks like that doesn't have an old cripple for husband," Alex said.

"How do you know?"

"She isn't married, nothing reflected off her left hand, so no ring. But she is staying at the hotel, so she has money from somewhere."

"And what do you plan to do?"

"Get her to share?"

"Maybe, if you date her, she'll pay for your hotel room."

"I told you she isn't my type, but that would work for you."

"And if I say no?"

"Where would you like to sleep tonight?"

I was silent. All the possibilities went through my head, none of them worked for this town.

"And you think I know anything about dating a woman?" I asked finally.

"You'll do fine," Alex said, "As least she won't shoot you if you fail."

"Not comforting," I answered.

"I'm going to check the stagecoach schedule," Alex said before she headed across the street. I stood there for a few minutes pondering my situation when the lady came out of the dress shop carrying a large box. I walked over.

"Pardon me Miss, but you look like you need help with that," I said.

"If you could," the lady responded. I took the box from her.

"Thank you," she said.

"Not a problem," I answered. The box weighed a ton, what do they make dresses out of these days? I followed her as she headed back to the hotel. A man coming out held the door for us as we entered. The lady stopped at the desk to get her key. She and the desk clerk exchanged greetings, then she started up the stairs; I followed. She stopped at her room and unlocked the door. I followed her in with the box.

"Just put it there on the bed," she said. I placed it on the bed and turned to go.

"I didn't catch your name," she said.

"Toby Lawton," I answered, turning back to her.

"I'm Elizabeth Brighten," she said, "I want to thank you for your help."

"It was no problem," I said tipping my hat and heading for the door again.

"Let me buy you supper," Elizabeth said. I stopped and turned back.

"It's hardly necessary," I replied.

"Please," Elizabeth said, "It would be wonderful to have a meal with someone to talk to. Until my stagecoach arrives, I have no one here to talk to."

"It's hardly appropriate," I started.

"Please, Mr. Lawton," Elizabeth pleaded, her blue eyes begging.

"Very well, Miss. Brighten," I replied, "I will join you for dinner."

"Meet me in the hotel dining room in an hour," Elizabeth smiled.

"I'll see you then," I answered, and then left the room, closing the door behind me.

Alex was waiting for me when I came out of the hotel.

"Well?" Alex asked.

"I have a supper date with Miss. Elizabeth Brighten," I answered, "And you're not invited."

"I didn't expect to be," Alex replied, "Jacob's stage arrives in three days."

"Three days?" This was not good.

"If I had known it was going to take this long I would have entered the poker tournament," Alex said, "Then Jacob would be the one paying for our to stay at the hotel."

"That would've been more interesting than eating supper with Miss. Brighten," I said.

"It'll all work out, I'm sure," Alex said.

"Next time, you can play the gentleman," I told her.

"Thanks, but it doesn't work quite the same way for me," Alex said before walking away. I sighed, then went and found a place where I could wash up.

I was back at the hotel within the hour. Elizabeth hadn't come down yet, so I waited for her in the lobby.

When Elizabeth came down for supper she was wearing a much fancier dress. I escorted her into the dining room and to the table the host showed us.

I played the part of the gentleman, even gave her some hope of the romance she seemed to be looking for. As supper came to a close she seemed to be a little nervous about me leaving. But she finally suggested that I could escort her on her walk, which I did.

When we arrived back at the hotel she stopped at the door and kept asking questions. She finally got to the important one and asked where I was staying for the night. I answered with the truth, well half of it anyway. She immediately went into the hotel and got me a room on her bill. She gave me the key. I tried to refuse at first, being a gentleman. Her eyes did the puppy dog look and I took the key. She made me promise to have breakfast with her before she disappeared up to her room.

I went in search of Alex. She was sitting in the shade of a tree near the edge of town.

"How was supper?" Alex asked.

"I got a room at the hotel," I answered, "And the start of three awful days."

"She's good-looking and she is rich, what more could you ask?" Alex asked.

"Substance," I answered, "Miss. Brighten appears to lack in brain power what she makes up for in looks."

"Then hopefully she won't notice that you have no interest in her," Alex said as she stood up. We walked back to the hotel.

Taking our belongings we went up to the room. Alex took her bedroll out and made herself a bed on the floor. I lay down on the bed.

I could hear Alex's breathing even out before I even closed my eyes and it took a while for me to fall asleep.

As I predicted the next three days were tedious with Elizabeth clamouring for my attention. Alex managed to stay out of sight the whole time.

The stage arrived the evening of the third day. Jacob was riding up with the driver and no passengers got off when the stage stopped. In fact it went straight to the stables, not even dropping Jacob off.

"This looks bad," Alex commented as she watched the stable doors close.

"You mean it looks like we'll be guarding the stage and its passengers," I said.

"Take it one step worse," Alex said, "The only person in town waiting for a stage is Miss. Brighten."

"Damn."

"Sorry, if I had realized that before, I would've never suggested using her to get a room," Alex said.

"It's done," I replied, "As long as Miss. Brighten isn't going home to her father to tell him she has met the man of her dreams."

"Anyone with that much money doesn't want his daughter to marry a gunslinger," Alex said.

"He lets her travel alone," I said.

"I'm sure you can come up with some reason that you can't marry Miss. Brighten," Alex said before turning and going into the hotel. I followed her after a moment. She was already in her bedroll when I entered the room. I fell into bed.

The next morning we went to the stable. Jacob was helping the driver get the stage ready.

"Good to see you two," Jacob greeted us. I wanted to shoot him for his cheerfulness.

"Next time you get to wait for us," Alex said.

"Why?" Jacob asked. He actually looked truly confused.

"Because the hotel is a little beyond our price limit, especially when you cut into our poker time," Alex answered.

"Did you lose it all?" Jacob asked, "Last time I stayed there it was five dollars a day."

"They upped it by a hundred and ninety-five," I replied. Jacob looked shocked.

"And people pay to stay there?" Jacob asked.

"Only place in town," the driver answered

"Well, then we should get going," Jacob said, "I don't want to have to stay here another night."

Alex and I got our horses ready.

"What's the job this time?" Alex asked once we were all waiting outside the stagecoach office.

"To guard a friend's daughter on her journey home," Jacob answered, "Just means that we watch the stage."

"Brighten?" I asked.

"Yes, how did you know?" Jacob asked. Elizabeth came out of the hotel, with two of the hotel staff following her. The men had three bags each. She hurried over to the stagecoach. The men followed at a slower pace.

"Good morning, Mr. Wescott," Elizabeth greeted Jacob.

"Good morning, Elizabeth," Jacob said.

"My father sent you again, didn't he?" Elizabeth asked.

"He's concerned," Jacob replied, "These are my men. Alex Turner." Elizabeth smiled at Alex; Alex barely nodded her acknowledgment.

"And Mr. Lawton," Elizabeth said her smile widening. I tipped my hat.

"You've met Toby?" Jacob asked.

"Yes," Elizabeth answered.

"Time to get moving," the driver called.

"Of course," Jacob said, helping Elizabeth into the stagecoach; the driver stowed the bags. Once they were ready, Jacob and the driver got on to the driver's seat and we headed out of town. Alex and I were on either side of the stagecoach.

We arrived in the next town with enough time to drop Elizabeth off at the hotel and get to the stable before it closed. Jacob and the driver went back to the hotel, while Alex and I stayed at the stable. We slept in the loft.

The next morning Alex and I had our horses ready before Jacob and the driver arrived at the stables.

"Elizabeth seemed to enjoy her visit with you," Jacob told me as they readied the stagecoach, "But for both of you staying in the same hotel, she doesn't remember Alex."

"We needed some place to stay and you didn't tell us what the job was," Alex said.

"And Alex wasn't interested in Elizabeth," I added.

"How can you not be interested in Miss. Brighten?" the driver asked, "Not to mean any disrespect, but she is a good lookin' woman."

"With fluff for brains," I commented.

"Better she got fluff for brains than to be ugly," the driver said.

No one answered him. Once ready, we headed for the hotel, where Elizabeth was standing outside waiting.

"Good morning, Mr. Lawton," Elizabeth said, "And Mr. Turner." I tipped my hat and smiled. Alex once again nodded. Jacob helped Elizabeth into the stagecoach, while the driver got her bags. And we were off again.

The next five days were pretty much the same. Shortly after noon we reached our destination. The stagecoach rolled up to a house that was slightly larger than some hotels. A servant came out first to take the bags and the driver unloaded them. Then a well-dressed man came out as Jacob helped Elizabeth out of the stagecoach.

"Father," Elizabeth said hugging the man.

"Welcome home, child," Mr. Brighten said, "I see you brought all of this season's fashions with you." A second servant had come out to help with the bags.

"Only the ones I liked," Elizabeth replied letting go of her father and going inside. Mr. Brighten turned to Jacob.

"Thank you," Mr. Brighten said.

"Anytime," Jacob replied.

"You and your men are invited to supper," Brighten said.

"We'll be there," Jacob said. Mr. Brighten went back inside. We headed for town and stopped at the stable before going to the hotel, where each of us got a room.

"Remember we have a supper invitation," Jacob said before going up the stairs. Alex let him get out of sight before following him. I followed her up. Once on second floor there I went to my room. Dropping my stuff on the bed I left. Alex was already headed back down. I caught up with her and we went into the saloon together. I went to the bar and ordered a drink. Alex went over to the poker game and was immediately invited to join.

When the time came to meet with Jacob, I paid for my drink and left the saloon. Jacob was waiting out front of the hotel.

"Where's Alex?" Jacob asked.

"Involved in a poker game," I answered.

"I told both of you to be ready for supper," Jacob said.

"And how do you intend to explain why she won't take off her hat?" I asked.

"I guess she can be left alone," Jacob replied. We headed back to the Brighten residence.

A servant was waiting with the door open when we arrived. We were quickly ushered into the parlour. Mr. Brighten and Elizabeth were already seated. They looked up as we came into the room. Mr. Brighten was probably in his sixties, but in good shape for his age. His manner and dress suggested that at some point he had been in the military.

"Where's your third man?" Mr. Brighten asked as we sat down.

"Playing poker," Jacob answered, "Once Alex starts playing it's difficult to pull him away."

"He will miss the special dinner Cook has made," Elizabeth said.

The servant that showed us in appeared at the other doorway.

"Supper is ready," the servant announced.

"Thank you," Mr. Brighten said as he stood up. Elizabeth stood up and Mr. Brighten escorted her through the door. Jacob and I followed them into the dining room. Elizabeth was seated; then the rest of us sat down.

As we ate Jacob and Mr. Brighten talked with only a few comments from Elizabeth and me.

Once supper was finished Elizabeth excused herself. Mr. Brighten invited us into his study for a drink.

"Any work lined up?" Mr. Brighten asked when we were comfortable.

"A few possible jobs, but nothing for sure yet," Jacob answered.

"I have a job offer," Mr. Brighten said, "But it could take a while."

"What kind of job?" I asked.

"Guard job," Mr. Brighten answered, "Five dollars a day, plus room and meals."

"Sounds like a good deal," Jacob commented.

"Guarding what?" I asked.

"I have a mine not far from here. The city sort of grew up close to it," Mr. Brighten answered, "A man by the name of Mr. Howard built the city. He owns the hotel, the saloon and the general store. I didn't have a problem with him until a couple of months ago. Since, my miners have been beaten up, equipment has been damaged and I've had to have all my supplies shipped in. I couldn't figure out what was going on until a week ago when Mr. Howard and his right hand man showed up. They were polite about it, but they tried to intimidate me into selling the mine to him. Maybe with you three guarding the mine he'll stop messing with things."

"Room and meals?" I asked. Jacob looked like he wanted to just accept the job and get all this information later.

"There's a bunk house out by the mine," Mr. Brighten answered, "My cook and a couple of helpers go out there and make lunch for the miners. She can bring you breakfast and leave you lunch leftovers for supper."

"Starting when?" I asked.

"Tomorrow, unless you need some time," Mr. Brighten answered.

"We can start tomorrow," Jacob said. Mr. Brighten looked at me for confirmation; I nodded.

"Good," Mr. Brighten said, "After you come for breakfast, I'll show you around up there."

"Sounds good," Jacob said. Then he and Mr. Brighten switched topics.

Shortly after I excused myself and headed for the saloon.

Alex was still playing poker. I went to the bar and ordered a drink. Sipping it, I looked around the room. Most of the patrons were miners. Three people besides myself were wearing a gun; Alex, a man watching the poker game who wore a silver star that said deputy, and a man sitting at a table on the other end of the bar. The man at the table was sitting with a well-dressed man. Looked like a gunslinger and his employer.

Alex got up, letting the deputy have her seat in the game and came over to where I was standing.

"How was supper?" Alex asked.

"Fine," I answered, "It was the job offer after that was interesting." I set the empty glass on the bar.

"What is it?" Alex asked.

"I'll tell you as we walk," I answered. Alex nodded and we left the saloon. As it was evening, only a few people out.

"So, what's this job?" Alex asked.

"Guarding Mr. Brighten's mine," I answered.

"The other players at the game made some comment about Mr. Brighten and Mr. Howard not getting along," Alex said.

"According to Mr. Brighten, Mr. Howard started it," I said, "But we're supposed to guard the mine. Make sure nothing gets damaged and the miners don't get beaten up."

"Pay?" Alex asked.

"Five dollars a day, plus meals and sleeping space," I answered.

"No poker after the first day, probably," Alex said, "Because Mr. Howard owns the saloon."

"Probably," I replied.

"Should be a good deal anyways," Alex said, "As long as we actually get paid."

"If Jacob tries not to pay us, he can ride home tied to his saddle," I replied.

"When does the job start?" Alex asked.

"Tomorrow after breakfast," I answered.

"Probably should be there," Alex said.

"Jacob won't be too happy if you aren't," I said.

"Nothing I do will make Jacob happy," Alex said, "Unless I started to actually listen to him. And I would, but I like eating."

"We aren't getting paid for escorting Elizabeth, are we?" I asked.

"Wasn't a job," Alex answered, "It was a favour between friends, otherwise Mr. Brighten would have paid Jacob once Elizabeth was inside. We got our room paid for and that was it."

"Now I feel a little less guilty about that," I said. The imp twitch showed up briefly on the side of her mouth.

"How early is breakfast?" Alex asked.

"Mr. Brighten didn't say," I answered.

"Then we should be up early," Alex said. We headed back to the hotel.

In the morning I met up with Jacob outside the hotel. We waited another ten minutes before Jacob decided that Alex wasn't coming. After stopping at the stables we headed for the Brighten residence.

The servant showed us in to the dining room, where Mr. Brighten was already eating. We served ourselves from the sideboard and sat down.

"You're missing your third man again," Mr. Brighten commented.

"Alex didn't show up this morning," Jacob said, "I don't know where he is."

"Not the first man to get waylaid in town," Mr. Brighten said, "As long as he's dependable for the job."

"Alex will be here," I said. The conversation continued on another topic. Just as we were finishing Elizabeth came into the dining room. Mr. Brighten and I returned her greeting. Then Mr. Brighten, Jacob and I got up and left the house. Alex was just coming up the roadway.

"You're late," Jacob told Alex when she had stopped in front of us.

"I was given a breakfast invitation I couldn't refuse," Alex said, "And I did try."

"Miss. Greenaway?" Mr. Brighten asked.

"Yes," Alex answered. Mr. Brighten chuckled.

"She's impossible to refuse," Mr. Brighten said, "But you seem to have made it out of there in good time."

"Good time?" Alex asked.

"I've seen men get stuck having breakfast, still there at lunch time," Mr. Brighten said. The imp twitched. A servant brought Mr. Brighten's horse. We mounted. Mr. Brighten took the lead with Jacob right on his tail. Alex and I gave them some space before following them.

"A lady waylaid you?" I asked in a quiet voice, glancing sideways at her.

"Miss. Greenaway is at least eighty and lonely," Alex responded in the same volume, "She'll do just about anything for some companionship." I nodded and we didn't say anything else on the trip up to the mine.

The mine looked like a hole in a hill with several buildings scattered around it. Mr. Brighten pointed out the office, the stable, the bunkhouse and the cookhouse. Miners were already working hard.

The first stop was the stable to leave the horses there, and then we went to the bunkhouse. The bunkhouse had ten bunks double-decked. Alex and I took the set closest to the door on the right side. Jacob took the bottom bunk on the far wall. We left our stuff there. Then Mr. Brighten introduced us to the Underlooker, who showed us around further while explaining what we needed to know. He was average size and height was a nervous temperament. When Mr. Brighten was sure that we were settled he headed back into town.

Based on what the Underlooker said about the attacks and the damage Jacob set out three routes that we could walk without getting in the way of the miners. So, we started our rounds.

I finished my round in time to join the first group of men for lunch. The only problem I had had to deal with was two miners who got into a fight over a woman. I broke up the fight and suggested they could continue it in town later when they didn't have as much to do.

Just as I was about to leave the cookhouse Alex came in.

"Anything?" I asked.

"No," Alex answered.

"Broke up a fight, but otherwise no," I replied.

"Hopefully it will continue like this," Alex said. I nodded. She went to get her lunch and I went back to my route.

I went around twice before the workday for the mine was over. When I got back Alex was standing there watching the miners leave. I sat down and waited.

As the last of the miners left the gate, the Underlooker came out and locked the office door behind him. He headed for the stables. Ten minutes later he came out driving a wagon. He had the horses stop next to the door of the cookhouse. The cook came out with a bag. The Underlooker helped her up to sit beside him. The two helpers came out and climbed into the back. Jacob came out and walked over to Alex.

"You should go down with them," Alex told Jacob.

"Why?" Jacob asked, "We're supposed to guard the mine."

"Because I sense that something is going to happen," Alex answered.

"Fine," Jacob said and headed to the stables. The Underlooker, having heard the exchange, waited until Jacob came up on his horse before starting the wagon toward the gate.

Once they were through the gate, I went over to where Alex was standing.

"You sensed that something was going to happen?" I asked.

"Yeah, I was going to kick his ass," Alex answered, "And after his lecture on missing supper and breakfast he deserves it."

"Right," I said, "I suppose our supper is waiting for us in the cookhouse."

"Unless Jacob ate it," Alex replied. The wagon went into the trees and left our sight. I turned and headed for the cookhouse; Alex followed. There were two plates of food sitting at the table closest to the door. I sat down on one side and Alex sat down on the other. We didn't say anything as we ate.

Once we were finished we went back out. We found a flat place, but with a view of the road and started a poker game.

It was getting dark by the time that Jacob came riding back. While he was in the stable caring with his horse, Alex and I went to the bunkhouse. Alex took the top bunk and I laid down on the bottom. Jacob came in a few minutes later.

"Nothing happened," he announced.

"Good thing you went with them then," I answered, "Probably scared whoever it was off."

"Good night," Alex said. Jacob went over to his bunk. He jerked off his boots and dropped his hat on them before lying down. I closed my eyes and went to sleep.

It was dark when I opened my eyes. Something had woken me up. Jacob was snoring loud enough to be a train. I didn't move as I listened for any other sounds. Then I heard the whimper from above me. Alex was having nightmares again. I got up and shook her shoulder.

"Yeah?" Alex asked, her voice thin with sleep.

"You were having a nightmare," I answered.

"Thanks," Alex said sitting up.

"You able to get back to sleep?" I asked.

"Probably not," Alex answered.

"How 'bout a poker game?" I asked.

"Don't let me keep you from getting enough sleep," Alex replied.

"You're not," I said.

"Then sure," Alex said. I went over a lit a lantern. Then Alex and I left the bunkhouse and went over to the cookhouse. Sitting down at the closest table, we started to play poker.

About dawn we put the cards away and went outside. Alex took up her lookout spot and I went down to the gate.

The sun had been up for an hour when I heard a door open up at the mine. I could see Jacob standing outside the bunkhouse and stretching. I turned back to the road and saw the wagon with the Underlooker, the cook and the two helpers come out of the trees. The wagon stopped beside me.

"How were things last night?' the Underlooker asked.

"Quiet," I answered.

"Here's your breakfast," the cook said, handing down a pastry, "I'll start the coffee once I get to the cookhouse."

"Thank you ma'am," I took the pastry, "I'll get some when I'm up there."

"You're welcome," the cook said with a smile. The Underlooker started the horses moving again. As I ate the pastry, the miners started coming out of the trees. I stayed there until all the miners had arrived. Then I headed back up to the mine. I stopped at the cookhouse. Stepping inside, I could smell the coffee. Alex was sitting at the table closest to the kitchen. The cook handed me a cup of coffee through the window between the kitchen and eating areas.

"Thank you," I said.

"You're welcome," the cook said. I went and sat with Alex.

"Where's Jacob?' I asked then took a sip of coffee.

"Off doing his rounds," Alex answered, "I told him we would get to ours after breakfast. He muttered something about breakfast being over."

"Whatever he wants to do," I said, "I doubt anything will happen in the next ten minutes."

"Mr. Howard heard that you were here," the cook said,

"Someone told him last night. Apparently he laughed it off that Mr. Brighten had someone guarding the mine."

"He can laugh," Alex said, "But since he gets the first one, we'll probably get the last one."

"Depends on whether his gunslinger is faster than we are," I said.

"He won't send the gunslinger up here," Alex said, "The gunslinger is his protection."

"But he can do damage in town," the cook said.

"Yes, he can," Alex replied, "But unless Mr. Brighten is going to hire more gunslingers for protection in town, there isn't anything we can do. Hopefully the sheriff can stop too much from happening."

"He has stopped some, but far from all," the cook said.

"I don't think anyone can stop all of it," I said.

"We will guard the mine and deal with what comes our way," Alex said.

"I hope Mr. Howard stops all this nonsense before someone gets killed," the cook said. Alex stood up and gave her empty cup back to the cook.

"That would be easiest," Alex said, "Thanks for the coffee."

"Just part of my job," the cook replied taking the cup. Alex left. I drank the rest of my coffee in quiet. I gave the cup back to the cook and left the cookhouse. I started my first round of the day.

I did two rounds before I joined the first group of miners for lunch. Again I was leaving as Alex came in. She shrugged to say she didn't have anything to report. I shook my head to say the same thing. I went back out and did three rounds before the workday was over. Then Alex and I watched the miners leave while Jacob ate supper. Then Alex and I ate after Jacob escorted the Underlooker and the cook into town.

Alex and I played poker until he got back.

The rest of the week held little variety from that first day. Alex continued to have nightmares, so we got up in the middle of the night to play poker. Then I watched the miners arrive, talked with Alex and the cook over a cup of coffee, did some rounds, had lunch, did some more rounds, had supper, then played poker until it was time to go to bed.

Friday, I was coming back from my second round before lunch when I saw four large men beating on two others. The four didn't look like miners, but the others were. When I heard that Mr. Howard had miners beaten up, I thought he did it in town. I walked until I was close enough to be seen, heard, and to shoot without getting hurt.

"Hey! Leave those two men alone," I called. The four men looked up at me. The one man sneered.

"We were told that Brighten hired some guards," the man said, "But I only see one. Where's your backup?"

"Don't need any," I replied, "Got six bullets and there are only four of you. So, this is your chance to go home before you have to be taken away in a casket."

"Your gun makes you tough now," the man said, "By you can't keep it on you all the time."

"Are you leaving or do I have to shoot you?" I asked.

"We're leaving," another man said. They walked away from the miners, who were slowly getting up, and started toward the fence on the property line. I followed from a distance. They climbed the fence and headed for town. I waited there for five minutes after they were out of sight before turning and going back to where the miners were.

"Thank you," one of the miners said. He had a split lip, an eye swollen shut, and possibly a broken arm. The other miner was unsteady on his feet with his arms cradled around his middle.

"Just doing my job," I replied, "Now let's get you back to the office." The one miner and I helped the other miner back to the office. We were spotted coming in and the Underlooker was waiting when we arrived.

"What happened?" the Underlooker asked.

"Just some thugs doing what their boss told them to," I answered, "These two need to see a doctor." I saw Jacob pushing through the crowd of miners that had gathered.

"I can't spare anyone," the Underlooker said.

"That's okay," I said, "I'm sure Jacob here won't mind taking them into town." Jacob was about to protest, but stopped quickly.

"Of course," Jacob said, "Won't be a problem. I just need to borrow the wagon."

"It's in the stables," the Underlooker said, "I'll get it ready for you." The Underlooker went off to the stables and Jacob followed him. A few minutes later they came out with Jacob driving the wagon. The one miner got up into the back of the wagon and helped me get the other into the back. Once they were settled Jacob headed for town. The crowd dissipated. Alex came up to me.

"Mr. Howard's men?' she asked.

"I assume so," I answered, "They didn't say why they were here or who they worked for. Just that they had heard there were guards up here. They backed off when I suggested that I could shoot them, but they didn't leave without threatening to come back when I didn't have my gun with me."

"Probably at night," Alex said, "People assume that you can't sleep wearing your gun."

"Just means that I can shoot them at night when my backup is nearby to help," I replied.

"Hopefully we've seen the last of them," Alex said.

"I'm going to eat and then go back to my rounds," I said.

"I just got back from my last round," Alex said, "I saw the crowd and heard some muttering about miners being beaten up." I headed for the cookhouse and Alex followed me. The group of miners had already changed from the ones I usually ate with. I got in line with the rest and was quickly moved to the front of the line. Alex was given the same treatment. Then people gave us space at a table without even asking. I looked at Alex she raised one eyebrow back, I shrugged and then we started eating.

After eating I went back to my rounds. I was trying to figure out whether the scene in the cookhouse was fear or respect when a miner tipped his hat with a smile. I replied in kind and kept going.

Jacob came back as I finished that round. I saw him put the wagon away in the stables. He saw me waiting and came over.

"Doctor said they'll be fine," Jacob said, "Mr. Brighten and the sheriff were there to make sure both men were okay and safe. But I doubt that the men will go after them again."

"No, they'll be after me for spoiling their fun," I said, "But I know they won't strike again today. I won't worry about it until after the mine is closed for the night." Jacob nodded. I headed off for my next round leaving Jacob to do the same.

Two more rounds later the workday was over and the miners

were headed home. Alex watched them leave as usual. I waited nearby. When the Underlooker and the cook headed back to town Jacob went with them. They seemed nervous when it appeared he was going to stay here, but they relaxed when he headed for the stable to get his horse.

Alex and I watched them until they were out of sight. Then we went into the cookhouse. We brought our supper back outside tonight.

We were on edge and every sound seemed twice as loud tonight as we sat there playing poker.

"Some times I would rather have a fight than this waiting to see what the other person is gonna do," Alex commented as she gathered up the cards again.

"It's nice to just get it over with," I replied.

Jacob came back just as it was getting dark. We all headed for the bunkhouse. Alex lay down. I sat down on the bottom bunk. Jacob lay down on his bunk and went to sleep. He was soon snoring. I pulled out my gun and checked that it was loaded. I heard Alex do the same.

Half an hour went by and it got dark in the bunkhouse. An hour later Alex's breathing had evened out to be similar to Jacob's snoring. She was asleep, but she would wake up if there was trouble. Two hours later I still sat there listening to Jacob and Alex sleep. I'm pretty sure that midnight came and went without anything happening.

I jerked awake to find dawn lightening the sky. Alex and Jacob were still asleep. Apparently Alex was over her nightmares for a while. I got up and stretched. It didn't disturb either of them. I left the bunkhouse and took a walk around. Nothing had been touched or damaged overnight. By the time I was back to the bunkhouse, Alex was awake and standing outside.

"Anything?" Alex asked.

"Nothing," I answered.

"Probably letting you sweat," Alex said, "Too many nights worrying about when they might strike could slow you down."

"I had the same amount of sleep last night that I've had the every night we've been here," I said.

"Yes, but they don't know that," Alex said.

"Then they'll be in for a surprise," I said, "If that's their plan."

"Act normal," Alex said, "If you appear jumpy, people will know the threat got to you."

"So far, so good," I said. I turned and headed for the gate. Alex went to her lookout spot.

I was standing at the gate when the Underlooker and cook came through. They stopped to give me my breakfast. When I finished the miners started showing up. One man out of the first group came over to me.

"Eric," he said holding out his hand.

"Toby," I replied shaking his hand.

"My brother was one of the men attacked yesterday," Eric said.

"How's he doing?" I asked.

"Doctor said he broke some ribs, but once those heal he'll be back to work," Eric answered, "He said you managed to fend off those bullies without even drawing your gun."

"It was unnecessary to draw my gun," I said, "They just needed a bigger threat than they were."

"Word is Mr. Howard has told his men that they can use whatever force they need to, to get rid of you and the other two," Eric said, "Until now his men have only been allowed to injure people."

"Thanks for the warning," I said, "But I'm not worried about Mr. Howard's thugs."

"That's about what Mr. Brighten said when someone told him about all this," Eric said.

"He hired us for that reason," I said. Eric nodded.

"Good luck," Eric said before heading up the mine. I continued to watch the miners arrive.

When all had arrived I went up to the cookhouse for my cup of coffee. Alex was already sitting there with a cup. The cook handed me my cup.

"They're calling you a hero," the cook said, "For helping those men."

"I'm not a hero," I said, "Just doing the job I was paid to do."

"That doesn't matter to these men," the cook said, "What matters is that two of their own aren't as badly beaten as they could have been."

"Mr. Brighten said this had only been happening for a couple of months," I said.

"Try close to a year," the cook said, "He just hadn't heard about it until a couple months ago. The damage wasn't bad enough."

"Men are being beaten up and that isn't bad enough to tell the mine owner?" Alex asked.

"No one wanted to bother him with it because he has been a good boss," the cook said, "They didn't want anything to change with him."

"Did anything change?" I asked.

"No," the cook said, "Nothing changed until you showed up."

"Maybe next time there won't be as long a time difference between bad things happening and telling the boss," Alex said.

"Maybe," the cook said. The door opened and Mr. Brighten stepped inside.

"Good to see you," Mr. Brighten said as he came over to us.

"Good morning," I said.

"I hear that things are changing around here," Mr. Brighten said.

"It was only one incident," Alex said, "It's far from over."

"But it's good to know you are on the job," Mr. Brighten said. The deputy entered the cookhouse and came over to our table. He was carrying a metal box.

"Something wrong in town?" I asked.

"No," Mr. Brighten said, "The deputy accompanies me when I come up here to pay my men."

"The sheriff believes it's best," the deputy said.

"He's right," Alex said.

"This all brings us to the other reason it is good to see you," Mr. Brighten said. The deputy put the box down on the table and Mr. Brighten unlocked it. Then he pulled out a piece of paper and writing utensils. Mr. Brighten studied the paper for a moment before pulling out sixty dollars and separating them into two equal piles.

"Sign here to say that you've been paid," Mr. Brighten said turning the paper towards us and pointing at the last two lines. Alex signed first and then I did. Mr. Brighten handed us each one of the piles.

"I will give Jacob his when I see him," Mr. Brighten said.

"It's nice to know we're appreciated," I commented as I put the money away.

"I told you I would pay you," Mr. Brighten said.

"Most times that we work with Jacob, the employer pays Jacob," Alex said, "And Jacob doesn't always remember to pay us."

"And you still work with him?" Mr. Brighten asked.

"It's complicated," Alex answered. Mr. Brighten nodded.

"Well, I have to go see about the rest of my business," Mr. Brighten said, "See you."

"See you," I said. Mr. Brighten left, followed by the deputy carrying the metal box. Alex and I stood up and gave the cups back to the cook before headed out to do our rounds.

It was a quiet for the two rounds I did before lunch. At lunch the men were busy as usual, except around me. Coming out of the cookhouse, I saw Jacob talking to the Underlooker. Jacob had an eye that was swelling shut. I went over.

"What happened to you?" I asked interrupting the dressing down that Jacob was giving the Underlooker.

"I was hit by one of the miners," Jacob said.

"You really shouldn't annoy them," I said, "Just because they're getting beaten up doesn't mean that they can't fight back."

"I was trying to break up a fight," Jacob said.

"Jacob, you should know better than to get between two combatants," I said, "You stop the fight without getting in the middle. And you don't take you anger out on the Underlooker, who can't do anything about it anyways."

"I got hit," Jacob said.

"Over your own foolishness," I replied, "Be a man and take responsibility for your own actions. Even Alex can take a hit without this much complaining. Excuse me, but I have to get back to work." I walked away and went on to my rounds.

When I went passed the office next Jacob was gone. I did two more rounds before the workday was over. The evening was the same as always with Alex watching everyone going home and Jacob escorting the Underlooker and the cook back into town. Alex and I ate, played poker and then went to bed when Jacob got back. Nothing more was said about Jacob's swollen eye.

Saturday was the same as the rest of the week, but Sunday was quiet with the cook making one trip up just after lunch. Monday, Tuesday and Wednesday went as usual.

The workday on Thursday went as normal, so when Jacob came back from town we went to bed. Jacob had just fallen asleep when I heard a sound coming from outside. I sat up. I heard another sound.

"We have visitors," Alex said in a whisper.

"Then let's go greet them," I replied quietly. I got up. Alex climbed down from the bunk. Opening the door a little I looked out. The four men from the other day were taking clubs to a piece of machinery. I stepped outside and Alex followed me. We got close enough to the men so that we didn't have to yell, but far enough that we could shoot anyone before they could reach us. The men hadn't noticed us.

"I thought I told you to go home," I said, "Or I do have to send you home in a casket?" The men stopped and turned to us.

"You brought your backup this time," the main man laughed.

"That's because you were making too much noise for me just to sneak out and deal with you," I replied, "Now, you can leave or you can be shot."

"What if we don't like either option?" the man asked.

I shot at the man on his right. The man collapsed. Another went over and checked for a pulse.

"Conrad is dead," the other men said standing back up.

"And the rest of you can join him if you don't leave immediately," I said.

"Let's go, Fergus," the other man said. The three men started toward the gate.

"Why don't you take Conrad with you?" Alex suggested, "Then we don't have to worry about the wrong person getting the body." The main men went back and picked up the body of Conrad before following the others out the gate. They had just disappeared from sight when Jacob came out of the bunkhouse.

"I heard a gunshot," Jacob said.

"And missed all the action," I replied, "Time to go back to bed." Alex and I headed back to the bunkhouse.

"Will they be back tonight?" Jacob asked.

"I doubt it," Alex answered. Jacob followed us.

At dawn Alex and I looked at the damage. It didn't look serious, but I don't know a lot about mining equipment. Our attention switched to the gate when we heard a horse coming. Then the Underlooker came out of the trees riding fast towards the mine.

"Some thing is wrong in town," Alex said. The Underlooker came through the gate and up to us. Jacob came out of the bunkhouse and came over to us as the Underlooker brought the horse to a stop.

"What happened?" Jacob asked.

"Mr. Howard kidnapped Mr. Brighten," the Underlooker gasped out. Jacob turned to head for the stable before Alex grabbed his arm to stop him.

"What happened exactly?" Alex asked. Jacob stopped and turned back. Alex let him go.

"Mr. Brighten was taking his daughter out to breakfast. He climbed down from the carriage first and was dragged off by three men before he could help his daughter down. His daughter came to me and said that Mr. Howard had her father and that I was to ride up here and get the three of you. I started to come up here in panic, but I had to go around the roadblock to get up here," the Underlooker said.

"Roadblock?' I asked.

"Mr. Howard has several men blocking the road so that none of the miners can get to work," the Underlooker said.

"And any help can't get back into town," Jacob said.

"Jacob, take him back into town and make sure that everyone is safe," Alex said nodding toward the Underlooker, "And try to avoid the roadblock."

"What about you and Toby?" Jacob asked.

"We'll head for town once you're on your way," Alex answered. Jacob nodded and then headed for his horse. The Underlooker headed for the gate. Before they were out of sight Alex had turned back to the bunkhouse.

"And what're we doing?" I asked following her.

"Making sure we have enough ammo before taking out a roadblock," Alex said, "Then I thought we should pay a visit to Mr. Howard."

"Sounds good," I said. We went into the bunkhouse and gathered ammo. Then we headed for the stable to get our horses.

"I wonder where the sheriff is in all this," I said as we started to ride toward the gate.
"We'll find out," Alex replied.

We slowed down as we came out of the trees close to town. There were five men standing across the road. They were facing the town but one turned as we approached. He said something and the rest turned as well.
"Halt," the man said. We stopped.
"Under whose authority are you blocking this road?" Alex demanded.
"Mr. Howard's," the man answered.
"This is not Mr. Howard's property to block," Alex said.
"Not yet, but it will be," the man said.
"And until we have orders that say it is, you have to move," Alex said. The man laughed.
"We ain't moving," the man said. Then the shot rang out and he collapsed forward. Alex's gun was out. The other four men charged at us. I pulled out my gun and shoot two of them. Alex hit the other two.
"The roadblock is gone," Alex said, "Now on to the saloon." We reloaded and rode passed the bodies.
We rode into town. It appeared to be deserted. We stopped in front of the sheriff's office. I got down and tied the reins to the hitching post; Alex did so as well. The sheriff came out of his office.
"We heard that Mr. Howard has Mr. Brighten," Alex said.
"That's true," the sheriff said, "Elizabeth came to my office after she sent the Underlooker up to the mine. But I thought there were three of you up there."
"Jacob came down with the Underlooker. He should be busy making sure everyone is safe," Alex said, "What can you tell us?"
"Mr. Brighten is being held at the saloon until he signs the mine over to Mr. Howard," the sheriff said, "I would have gone over there, but my deputy seems to have disappeared. Walking in there alone is suicide."
"What was your deputy doing before he disappeared?" I asked.
"Keeping an eye on Mr. Brighten after Mr. Howard threatened to do whatever was necessary to get the mine," the sheriff said.

"Then let's go see if Mr. Howard has him," Alex said. Alex and I started toward the saloon with the sheriff close behind us. Curtains twitched as the occupants of buildings watched us, but no one came outside. I was the first to the saloon. I stepped inside the swinging doors; Alex followed me. The barman stood behind the bar wiping it down with a rag and a group of about seven men sat around a table. I recognized three of them as the men that had been causing problems.

"What do you want?" the barman asked.

"We're looking for Mr. Brighten," Alex announced as we both took another step inside and the sheriff followed.

"He isn't here," the barman said, "Mr. Brighten doesn't come in here."

"Then bring Mr. Howard down," Alex said, "So that we can ask him if he's seen Mr. Brighten."

"Mr. Howard is busy," Fergus said coming over.

"We'll disturb him if you don't," I told Fergus. A door opened in the second floor and footsteps could be heard. The gunslinger I had seen near Mr. Howard the first night came into view at the top of the stairs. A smile came over Fergus's face

"Mr. Howard said he'll be down in a minute," the gunslinger announced. The smile fell from Fergus's face and he turned his head to look at the gunslinger.

"Mr. Brighten wouldn't be up there talking to Mr. Howard, would he?" the sheriff asked. The gunslinger was silent. The door on the second floor opened and closed. The footsteps were louder this time. Then Mr. Howard came into view at the top of the stairs. He stopped to survey the scene before starting down the stairs. . Mr. Howard looked like a labourer stuffed into expensive clothes. His leathery skin and overstylized hair emphasized this. The gunslinger followed him down.

"I don't believe I've met you two before," Mr. Howard said looking at us, "But I'd gladly buy you a drink. I'm Mr. Howard, I own this town."

"Alex," Alex said moving farther into the saloon. Mr. Howard stopped at the bottom of the stairs.

"Toby," I supplied, following Alex's lead. The gunslinger looked surprised, but quickly forced his face back to a neutral expression. The sheriff stayed at the door; he looked like he was trying to figure out exactly how this was going to play out.

"What would you like to drink?" Mr. Howard asked starting toward the bar.

"Nothing," Alex answered, "We're looking for Mr. Brighten and your men were seen dragging him off."

"Your witness must be confused," Mr. Howard said leaning against the bar, "Mr. Brighten isn't here and my men have been here all morning." Mr. Howard gestured toward the seven men at the table.

"Including the five men who claimed they were blocking the road to the mine on your orders?" I asked, "Which, by the way, are no longer blocking the road."

"If I was pressuring Mr. Brighten to sell the mine through a road block, why would I bother to kidnap him?" Mr. Howard asked.

"Where's the deputy?" Alex asked.

"What deputy?" Mr. Howard asked, looking actually confused.

"My deputy," the sheriff answered, "He was watching Mr. Brighten and now both of them are gone."

"Perhaps we should ask Fergus here," I suggested, "where the deputy is." Fergus looked like a man searching for an escape route.

"I told you my men were here this morning," Mr. Howard said. There was a crash from upstairs. Everyone froze. I started toward the stairs; no one moved to stop me.

"I wonder what that was," Alex said.

"I was dealing with some business when you interrupted me," Mr. Howard said, "My guest probably just knocked something over. I'll figure out what it was and make him pay for it later." I reached the top of the stairs and saw that there was only one door and that it was at the far end of the hallway.

"Perhaps we should invite him down for a drink," Alex said.

"I already offered him one and he declined," Mr. Howard said, "I have told you Mr. Brighten isn't here. Perhaps you should be looking some place else." I started toward the door. I could hear scratching sounds from the room. I opened the door to find Mr. Brighten tied to a chair that was lying on its side. I stepped into the room and used a knife from the desk to cut the rope. Mr. Brighten sat up. He was a little bruised, but otherwise fine. He opened his mouth to say something when I shook my head. I withdrew from the room and went back to the stairs. No one was moving. I started down the stairs.

"How is Mr. Howard's guest?" Alex asked.

"Fine," I answered. Mr. Howard moved fast. He reached under the bar and grabbed the shotgun that was there and turned toward Alex. I could feel Mr. Brighten stop next to me. Mr. Howard looked like he was about to shoot when Alex's gun went off and Mr. Howard dropped the shotgun to clutch his chest. It was slow motion as he slid to the floor. Fergus was suddenly in motion and launched himself at Alex. I shot him and he fell to the ground before he reached her.

The sheriff had his gun out, daring the rest of the six men to move. None of them did. The gunslinger bent down and checked Mr. Howard's pulse.

"He's dead," the gunslinger said standing back up.

"I guess that leaves you with a choice," Alex said.

"Not really," the gunslinger replied. He turned and went out the back door of the saloon.

"You're just going to let him go?" the sheriff asked.

"It's Mr. Howard's men that you want," I said coming down the stairs, "Not him."

"Toby is right," Mr. Brighten said, "Even when Mr. Howard was trying to get me to sign over the mine to him that man didn't participate."

"Then let's all go quietly," the sheriff said to the men. The men did what they were told as the sheriff, Alex, and I escorted them to the jail. Mr. Brighten followed us. But he stayed outside while we helped the sheriff lock the men in the cells. We came back out as Jacob came down the street with Elizabeth and the Underlooker following him.

"Father," Elizabeth cried wrapping her arms around Mr. Brighten. Mr. Brighten hugged her back.

"I'm all right," Mr. Brighten said.

"Where are the men who were blocking the road?" the sheriff asked me and Alex.

"On the road that they were blocking," Alex answered. The sheriff nodded and then headed that direction.

"What happened?" Jacob asked.

"Alex and Toby dealt with Mr. Howard," Mr. Brighten

answered, "And the mine can go back to operation without further incidents."

"I'll spread the word," the Underlooker said before going off.

"If you three come with me to my house I will pay you what I owe you," Mr. Brighten said.

"After you," Alex said before Jacob could finish opening his mouth. Mr. Brighten and Elizabeth started for home. Jacob, Alex and I followed them.

Mr. Brighten paid us. Then he and Jacob got talking. Alex and I went back into town for our horses. We rode back up to the mine. After getting our things from the bunkhouse we started back down.

All the way down we kept meeting groups of miners coming up to work. All of them greeted us warmly. We returned their greetings and stopped to answer the occasional question. When we finally reached town we stopped at the restaurant for breakfast. Then we mounted our horses.

"Which way?" I asked.

"I don't know," Alex answered, "You pick." I thought about it for a minute before starting off. Alex followed my lead and we left town.

THE LAWTON FARM
CHAPTER 9

Toby

The trees and shrubs slowly gave way to grassland. And the weather warmed up. It was the type of day that you know you had better harvest today because snow could hit one day soon, usually when your back was turned.

We had been travelling for two weeks when we arrived in Golden. It hadn't changed since I left. The wagon ruts in the road might deeper. Mr. Newton's store still had the paint peeling. The sheriff's office needed painting and a proper hitching post. Mr. Alger was sitting outside the hotel smoking cigarettes that had a sweet smell.

I stopped in front of Mr. Newton's store. Alex stopped her horse bedside mine. We tied the reins to the hitching post, and went inside. I ignored the general store end and went to the café side. As usual, for mid-afternoon the place was empty, except for Mrs. Newton standing behind the counter. She looked at us.

"Afternoon, ma'am," I said.

"Toby Lawton!" Mrs. Newton said, "What're you doing back?"

"Just stopping in for a visit," I answered.

"Well, have a seat. I'll bring you some of my fruit bars and coffee," Mrs. Newton said. We took a seat at a table near the counter. Mrs. Newton set a coffee and piece of fruit bar in front of each of us.

"I'm sorry," Mrs. Newton said, "I forgot to introduce myself. I am Joyce Newton." Mrs. Newton held out her hand to Alex.

"Alex Turner," Alex replied shaking the offered hand.

"Very nice to meet you," Mrs. Newton said.

"Nice to meet you as well," Alex replied.

"So, what've you been up to?" Mrs. Newton asked me.

"Travelling," I answered, "With Alex."

"You seem to be doing well for yourself," Mrs. Newton said. The door opened and Kane Radford stepped inside. Mrs. Newton went back around the counter. Kane's eyes swept the store before coming rest on me.

"Good afternoon, Sheriff Radford," Mrs. Newton said. Kane turned towards us and I could see the silver star on his chest.

"Afternoon, Mrs. Newton," Kane replied. He came over to the café area.

"I thought I saw trouble ride into town," Kane said to me, "But I didn't expect it to be you. How are you, Toby?"

"Doing well," I answered, "Kane, this is my partner, Alex Turner. Alex, this is Kane Radford."

"Nice to meet you," Alex said.

"Same here," Kane replied.

"Would you like something?" Mrs. Newton asked Kane.

"No, thank you," Kane answered, "If I eat anything I might not be hungry for supper and then Sadie would be upset."

"You got married?" I asked.

"I got trapped," Kane answered.

"You were trapped before I left," I replied.

"What've you been up to?" Kane asked.

"Travelling," I answered.

"Last time I heard that kind of answer, you were trying to explain to your father where we found the mud puddle," Kane said.

"Been doing odd jobs and playing poker," I said.

"What kind of odd jobs?" Kane asked.

"Some guard duty, a little bit of bounty hunting," I answered.

"Bounty hunting?" Kane asked, amusement seeping into his voice.

"Why not?" Alex asked, "He has the memory for it."

Kane looked surprised.

"How did you end up with the job of sheriff?" I asked.

"After you left, Mertick took me aside and told me if I didn't smarten up I was going to end up dead," Kane said, "So, I took the job as his deputy. When he died a couple months ago I got his job. Something about the government not wanting to send someone else to an out of the way farming town."

"You got stuck with a job and a woman," I said, "After all that dreaming about the places you would visit."

"You'll have to stop by some night and tell me about your adventures so I know what I'm missing," Kane said.

"I'll try, but I haven't been out to the farm yet," I said.

"See you," Kane said. He turned and left the store. Alex and I finished our coffee and fruits bars without talking. I put the money on the table to pay for our food as we stood up.

"Delicious as ever," I told Mrs. Newton.

"You're welcome," Mrs. Newton said. Alex and I left the store. I led the way out of town.

We rode along the road for a few miles before turning on that led to the road to the farmhouse. In a far field I could see my father, brother and brother-in-law working. As we got closer I could see my two sisters, Jessica and Vicky, and my sister-in-law, Diane, out in the yard doing laundry. When they saw us, Vicky ran into the house and came out with my mother. Everyone stood waiting to greet us.

"You can tell them I'm female if you want," Alex said. Her voice barely carried to me. I nodded.

"Toby!" Vicky yelled when she realized who I was, "It is Toby!" Vicky was bouncing all over the place. I smiled and saw the imp twitch.

"Settle down, Vicky," my mother said, "That isn't the way a proper young lady should act."

"But Toby is home," Vicky said.

"I can see that, but it isn't reason to jump around," mother replied. Vicky didn't stop. We reached them. I jumped off my horse. Vicky ran the short distance to me and I lifted her up in a hug.

"You're home!" Vicky said.

"Yes, I am," I replied before putting her back on the ground. Jessica walked over to get her hug before I could turn to my mother and give her a hug.

"It's good to see you," mother said.

"I thought I should visit," I said. Diane came over for a hug.

"And who is this?" mother asked. Alex had gotten down and was standing beside me.

"This is my partner, Alex Turner," I said, "Alex, this is my family. My little sister, Vicky; my oldest sister, Jessica; my sister-in-law, Diane and my mother, Alice."

"Nice to meet you all," Alex said.

"It's wonderful to meet you," mother said, "How long will you be here?"

"We haven't discussed that," I answered.

"It would be helpful if you could stay until the end of the harvest," mother said.

"How 'bout a month?" I asked.

"There's no rush to get back," Alex replied.

"A month leaves plenty of time to help with the harvest and still get back before the snow falls," I said.

"I guess that will have to be good enough," mother said.

"What happened to your throat?" Vicky asked Alex.

"Someone tried to kill me," Alex answered.

"Why?" Vicky asked.

"Victoria," my mother said, "That is not a polite question."

"That's all right, I don't mind," Alex said.

"That doesn't mean she should be asking," mother said, "Come into the house."

The sound of crying came from the house.

"Caleb," Diane said turning to the house and hurrying inside.

"My nephew?" I asked.

"Two months old," mother said, "Looks like Richard when he was a baby."

Alex and I led our horses and we all walked toward the house.

"I can put your horses away," Vicky said.

"Are you sure?" I asked.

"I do it for father all the time," Vicky said.

"All right," I said. I handed my reins over to Vicky; Alex did the same. Vicky led them off around the house to the barn.

"How did you two meet up?" mother asked.

"We both were employed as guards by the same man," Alex answered.

"Was it an accident?" mother asked.

"No," I answered, "He was looking for three guards."

"Did it go well?" mother asked.

"He was shot," Alex answered, "And we were the only ones willing and able to bring the killer to justice."

"What about the sheriff?" mother asked.

"We turned the killer over to the sheriff after we caught him," I answered. We entered the house. Jessica went back to the laundry. Mother led the way to the kitchen where she had been baking. Alex and I sat down.

"Not much has happened around here," mother said.

"I already saw Kane," I said, "He invited me over some evening."

"He and Sadie look good together," mother said, "He'll complain he got trapped but from the looks of the situation, he wouldn't change any of it."

We continued to catch up. Alex occasionally added her comments. Diane brought Caleb down and introduced me to my nephew. When mother started supper Alex and I went out to the barn to see what was taking Vicky so long. Vicky had finished my horse and was still working on Alex's. Alex helped her. They had finished and Vicky had gone back out front when father, Richard and Tracey came around the house in the wagon.

"I thought I saw guests for supper," father commented seeing me, “Welcome home.”

"Gonna stay longer than that," I replied.

"Good, we could use a few extra hands out in the field," father said. They got down and started unhitch the horses.

"Who’s this with you?" father asked.

"This’s my partner, Alex Turner," I answered, "Alex, this is my father, John; my brother, Richard and my-brother-in-law, Tracey."

"Nice to meet you," father said holding out his dirty hand. Alex shook it.

"Same here," Alex replied.

"What do you need a partner for?" Richard asked, "I thought you could get into enough trouble on your own."

"That would be why he needs the partner," Tracey said, "To get him out of trouble."

Richard and Tracey laughed as they took the horses into the

barn. Vicky came up to us.

"Mother says everyone needs to wash up for supper," Vicky said before going back into the house. Alex followed.

"Hurry up in there," father yelled into the barn, "Or you'll be late for supper."

I started to walk toward the house. Father walked beside me.

"Alex doesn't smile much," father commented.

"She's out of practice," I replied, "You just need to know what to look for."

Father fell behind a step before catching up to me.

"She?" father asked. We reached the step and stopped to wash up. I didn't respond. We went inside. Everyone sat down in their place at the table and a chair was found for Alex. Like the rest of us Alex had taken off her hat, but she must have had some thing to hold her hair in place because the braid didn't fall down her back. She received a few puzzled looks during the meal as the family began figured out that she was female, but no one said anything.

After supper the table was cleared quickly and everyone, except Alex and I, was given a job. Alex went outside and I followed. She went over to the coral. She climbed the fence and sat on the top rail while I just leaned on the top rail.

"You have an interesting family," Alex said.

"Is that a compliment?" I asked.

"An observation," Alex answered. Alex's horse came over to Alex, Alex reached out and stroked the horse's neck. Vicky climbed up next to Alex.

"What's her name?" Vicky asked.

"Nightingale," Alex answered.

"A nightingale is a bird," Vicky said.

"Nightingale was the name the breeder gave her," Alex said, "You don't mind being named after a bird, do you?" Alex directed the question to the horse. The horse shook her head. Vicky laughed.

"Grampa used to talk to horses all the time," Vicky said.

"Sometimes, especially when a horse is your only companion, it helps to talk to your horse," Alex said, "After one conversation you will either be closer to your horse or you'll need to buy another one."

"How could you afford a horse as beautiful as Nightingale?"

Vicky asked, "Father says that buying horses from breeders are expensive."

"I didn't buy Nightingale," Alex answered, "She was a gift."

"A breeder gave you a horse?" Vicky asked.

"Yes. After I save a herd of them from horse rustlers," Alex answered, "And brought the man who killed his son to justice."

"Is that really true?" Vicky asked me.

"I wasn't there," I answered, "But based on what else I've seen it's very likely to be true."

"You must be a hero where you live," Vicky said.

"No," Alex replied, "Just another person looking for gun work."

"Just one of the better known people," I said.

"For certain things," Alex said.

Vicky opened her mouth to ask another question when mother called to her from the house. Vicky climbed down and walked to the house.

"No one has said anything," Alex said.

"Give it time," I replied, "They might have to get over the shock." The imp twitched.

When the sky started to darken we went inside. I was given my old room, while Alex was given the guest room.

It was still dark when I woke up to the sounds of people moving in the house. Downstairs. Father, Richard, Tracey, Mother and Vicky were sitting in the kitchen eating breakfast.

"Good morning," father said.

"Morning," I replied. I got a plate and served myself before sitting down.

"You gonna be helping out in the fields today?" father asked.

"That was the plan," I answered.

"Good," Father said.

"What's Alex going to do?" Vicky asked.

"She's going help us here at the house," mother answered. Everyone continued to talk while I sat there eating and enjoying it. Outside there was a slight chill in the air to let you know that winter was coming, but the sun was rising. Alex was riding her horse toward the barn. I walked over.

"I see the family is up," Alex said.

"Nightmares?" I asked.

"Yes," Alex answered, "I decided come out here and clear my head. I didn't want to wake anyone."

"I'm going out to work in the field today," I said, "Mother said you will stay at the house and help."

"Fine," Alex said. Father, Richard and Tracy came out of the house. Alex went to put her horse way. I helped get the wagon ready. Once we were ready father climbed up on the driver's seat and the three of us climbed into the back.

"She's up early for a city person," father commented.

"Alex has trouble sleeping," I replied.

"Have anything to do with those scars on her neck?" father asked.

"Yes," I answered.

"Do you know what did it?" father asked.

"I know who did it," I answered, "I also know he's dead."

"And she still can't put it behind her?" father asked.

"She's working on that," I answered. Richard changed the subject and we talked about something else the rest of the way out to the field.

We worked out in the field all day. We stopped twice, once for lunch and once in the middle of the afternoon. About time for supper we went back to the house.

Father drove the wagon into the barn before stopping it and getting down. Richard, Tracey and I climbed down. I saw Alex and Vicky sitting on hay bales farther down the barn playing cards. Richard and Tracey were getting the horses ready to go in their stalls. I watched the card game. After a few minutes I realized that they were playing go-fish. Mother shouted that it was time for supper. I turned and went to the house. I stopped and washed up before entering the house. Father, Jessica and Diane were already sitting at the table. Richard and Tracey came in after I had sat down. Mother finished setting the food on the table and sat down.

"Where are Vicky and Alex?" Father asked.

"They were out in the barn," Tracey said. Alex came inside and Vicky followed her.

"Sorry," Alex said as she sat down. We started to eat.

After supper everyone was given a job to do. Once I was finished I went out to the coral. Alex joined me a few minutes later.

"What do you think so far?" I asked.

"That city life and farm life might be different, but they're not that different," Alex answered.

"What happened?" I asked.

"Your mother gave me some jobs that anyone could do. I finished those this morning," Alex answered, "But she couldn't find anything more for me because I wouldn't know how to do most of the jobs that were left. And of course you couldn't make a female guest do any kind of hard labour. Vicky snuck away for the afternoon and I ended up playing cards with her."

"Sounds like you were bored," I said.

"What it comes down to is that your sister is interesting to spend time with, but your mother needs to readjust her thinking," Alex replied.

"I'll talk to her if she hasn't figured out by the end of the week that you're willing to help," I said.

"Why did you leave?" Alex asked.

"Boredom," I answered.

"You seem to be enjoying your time here," Alex said.

"I will this week and maybe next week," I replied, "But the week after I'll be ready to leave."

"And the week after?" Alex asked.

"I'll be on my way out of here," I answered. The imp twitched.

We stood there talking until the sky darkened.

The next week continued as the first day had. I went with Father, Richard and Tracey to the fields, while Alex stayed at the house and tried to help out. In the evenings we would go out and watch the horses. Various other guests joined us each night.

Saturday evening we came back in. When we arrived home, Alex and Vicky were standing in the coral with Alex's horse. Alex was wearing a dress, which looked similar to the ones Simone wore and fancier than the ones my mother and sisters wore.

"She's going to get it all dirty," father commented.

"Clothes wash," I replied. I helped put the wagon away. When we came out of the barn we heard a horse coming.

"Dolph is coming for supper," Tracey muttered before go into the house. Mr. Dolph Langdon came around the corner on his horse. He was dressed in expensive clothes, as usual, and had a stiff, almost aristocratic air about him. When I left the farm it might have impressed me, now I could see through it. Apparently he still came over for supper on Saturdays.

"Good evening," Mr. Langdon greeted.

"Good evening," father replied.

"How is the harvest going?" Mr. Langdon asked.

"Well," father answered.

"That is good," Mr. Langdon said, "Hopefully this good weather will hold." Mr. Langdon dismounted his horse. Richard took the reins and put the horse in the barn. I turned to get away from Mr. Langdon before he started spouting stuff like he was a farmer. You aren't a real farmer unless you actually work the land yourself. I wasn't sure how he could make so much money farming.

I saw Alex and Vicky coming from the coral. Vicky was trying to direct Alex away from Mr. Langdon. Unfortunately Mr. Langdon saw Alex.

"And who is this guest?" Mr. Langdon asked. Alex came over.

"Alex, this's Dolph Langdon," I said, "Mr. Langdon, this's Alex."

"Very nice to meet you," Mr. Langdon said taking her hand and kissing the back of it.

"Thank you," Alex said. She gave him a tentative smile. The smile cautious the kind you give strange people who get too close.

"Shall we go inside?" father asked starting toward the house. Mr. Langdon stuck close to Alex asking her all kinds of questions. Alex politely answered them. Richard kept glancing back at them and then at me like I was supposed to have a problem with the situation. I ignored him and kept going.

When we were all inside Mr. Langdon pulled out the chair for Alex and made sure he got the seat next to her. Mother saw them and glanced at me. I ignored it.

All through supper Mr. Langdon didn't seem to notice anyone but Alex. Alex, however, was including everyone in the conversation.

After supper I did my assigned chores in the house before going out to the coral. Mr. Langdon was still talking to Alex, though it looked like Alex and father were trying to get him to go home. After Mr. Langdon was finally gone Alex came over. Vicky was already sitting on the top rail of the fence.

"How can you stand him?" Vicky asked.

"By being polite and hoping he'll go away soon," Alex answered climbing up to sit beside her.

"I don't like him," Vicky said.

"He does leave one with a feeling of uneasiness," Alex said, "He kept saying he was a farmer, but I doubt his hands have touched dirt in a very long time."

"He owns the next farm," I replied, "He believes that owning a farm makes him a farmer."

"He has men to do all the work for him," Vicky said, "We were in town to get supplies one day when his men were in town. They were scary."

"How were they scary?" Alex asked.

"They didn't talk," Vicky said, "They knew what they were doing, but they didn't talk to each other. And only the foreman talked to anyone else. And their eyes looked empty. Except for the boy. Mother said he was a half-breed. They pushed him around, but he just accepted it."

"If he is a half-breed it would not be unusual for him to be abused," Alex said.

"He was the only one that looked normal," Vicky said.

"It happens," Alex replied, "People have always declared themselves superior to another person, even though we're all equal."

"It that why you dress like a man?" Vicky asked.

"That wasn't the original reason, but it has worked out that way at times," Alex answered. Mother called Vicky.

"Good night," Vicky said as she climbed down.

"Night," Alex replied.

"The man Vicky was talking about is actually Mr. Langdon's son," I said, "He kidnapped and raped a Nolawistep woman. She ended up having his son. Last I heard, he treats the boy pretty badly."

"Sounds like he still treats him badly," Alex said, "What happened to his mother?"

"No one knows," I answered, "Most people figure he killed her. He claims that she got away and that she left the child because she didn't want him."

"I guessing the sheriff didn't do anything about this," Alex said.

"The sheriff at the time was a good man, except when it came to the Nolawistep," I answered, "Rumours were that there was a half-breed in his family somewhere, which made him less interested if anything bad happened."

"What about Kane?" Alex asked.

"I'm guessing that unless someone brings him proof of any wrong doing, he won't touch it," I answered.

"Understandable," Alex said, "Why stir up the wasps nest if you don't have to."

"You're going to stir it up, aren't you?" I asked.

"There doesn't seem to be much else for me to do," Alex answered, "I get bored a lot faster than you do."

"Yes, but I have work that I'm doing," I said, "Be careful you don't get stung."

"I will," Alex said.

"And if you need help, ask," I said. The imp twitched.

"Of course," Alex said. She got down and we headed inside for the night.

Sunday morning we all went into town to attend the church service. Alex wore a dress rather than explain anything to people. After church we went back to the farm for lunch and then spent the afternoon working.

Mr. Langdon stopped by to talk to Alex. She told me later that he asked her to come for lunch on Monday. My mother refused to let a lady visit a man without an escort, so it was decided that I would go with them. Mr. Langdon apparently was not happy about this, but accepted it.

Monday morning while father, Richard and Tracey headed for the field I remained at the house. Alex, Vicky and I played go-fish until it was time for Alex and me to leave. We took the carriage as Alex was wearing a dress and she had no interest in borrowing a side saddle.

When we arrived, Mr. Langdon's men were getting ready to head back out to the field. A boy about sixteen was walking toward the wagon with his head bowed. He looked up when he heard the carriage. This was obviously Mr. Langdon's son. He froze on the spot when he saw us.

"Chenarcor," he cried, falling to his knees. One of the other men hit him on the side of the head and told him to get up. I stopped the carriage in front of the house. Mr. Langdon was already standing outside waiting.

"He may have other problems but he can still tell beautiful," Mr. Langdon commented offering his hand to help Alex down. Alex smiled a fake smile and let him help her down. I tied the horses to the hitching post before following them into the house.

Mr. Langdon ignored me entirely during the whole meal. He gave all his attention to Alex. Alex smiled where appropriate and answered his questions, usually with vague answers. I wandered the house a little bit and spent a lot of time admiring the house. If Alex needed me she would ask. Like me, she probably had her gun on her somewhere not visible.

Finally Alex said that we had to go. Mr. Langdon invited her back for tomorrow's lunch, but Alex declined because I was needed at the farm. Mr. Langdon accepted that, but I figured he would probably show up at the farm instead. Mr. Langdon escorted us out of the house. He helped Alex up into the carriage as I untied the horses and climbed up to the driver's seat. As Mr. Langdon said his last goodbyes I started to drive away. Once we were far enough away Alex climbed up to sit next me on the seat.

"What do you think he's up to?" Alex asked.

"Hard to tell," I answered, "But his son knew who you were."

"Yes, that was unexpected," Alex said, "Hopefully Mr. Langdon never learns what it means."

"Even if he finds out I doubt he'll believe it," I said, "Many people laugh at Nolawistep traditions, especially people like Mr. Langdon."

"He may not believe it, but it might make him more suspicious," Alex said, "Like the old man, who was told that the sky was going to fall on him tomorrow. He laughed, but he always checked out the window to make sure the sky was still where it should be before going outside."

"I see your point," I said, "Hopefully he never asks the kid what that means."

"I think the kid's mother is dead," Alex said.

"Why?" I asked.

"Because he was half-expecting me," Alex answered, "That was his cry for help. As speaker for the dead, I should be here to avenge his mother."

"And are you going to?" I asked.

"I'm going to have to find something else beside speculation," Alex answered, "Otherwise it'll look unprovoked."

"You'll find something," I said. We rode the rest of the way without talking. Back at the farm, Alex helped me with the horses. We were just finished when Vicky came in.

"What was Mr. Langdon's place like?" Vicky asked.

"Bigger than this one," Alex answered, "Expensive furniture and decorations. Otherwise normal."

"No ghosts or dead bodies?" Vicky asked.

"Not in plain sight," Alex answered.

"Who has been saying Mr. Langdon has ghosts and dead bodies at his house?" I asked.

"Joshua," Vicky answered, "He bugs me after church."

"Has Joshua ever seen Mr. Langdon's place?" I asked.

"He was there when his father stopped there," Vicky answered.

"Well, he wasn't telling you the truth," I said.

"What was Joshua's father doing there?" Alex asked.

"I don't know," Vicky said, "Joshua said that his father stops there weekly to pick up crates of stuff. Why? Is the stuff in the crates bad?"

"I don't know what's in the crates, so I don't whether it's bad," Alex answered, "Without the proper information it's better not to make judgments."

"You're going to look for the proper information, aren't you?" Vicky asked, "That's why you went there for lunch. Just like your stories."

"Vicky," I said, "Alex knows what she's doing. You need to stay out of anything involving Mr. Langdon. You can hear the whole story when there is a story."

"I know, but I want to help," Vicky said.

"I thank you for the offer, but Toby is right, you need to stay out of this," Alex said.

"I guess," Vicky said. She sounded disappointed.

"But I'm sure the story will be interesting," Alex said, "But there isn't anything more we can do about that today. How 'bout a card game?"

"Sure," Vicky said. I took out my set of cards and we all found spots to sit on hay bales.

We played comet until father, Richard and Tracey came back then we went in for supper.

The next morning I went out to the fields to work. Alex told me that evening that Mr. Langdon invited himself over for lunch. Nothing had happened, except that Alex was sure that he hadn't asked his son what chenarcor meant.

Wednesday father sent me into town. Mother and Diane needed for few things so they came with me. Vicky begged to join us until mother let her. And Alex, dressed in her usual clothes, rode in with us. When we arrived in town Diane took Caleb and went to her parent's house. Mother went into the general store to purchase everything that was needed. Alex and Vicky went into the café in the general store. I went across the street to the sheriff's office.

Kane and I talked for an hour at least, before I figured I had to meet mother and the others. I arranged with Kane to come back to visit him after taking everyone back to the farm. I went back to the general store. Alex was helping mother load the wagon. I helped with the last few items. Mother and Vicky got into the wagon and I drove back to the farm. Alex got on her horse.

Once back at the farm I helped unload everything. Alex and I put the horses away. Then I saddled my horse and went back into town.

Kane and I spent the afternoon talking. When suppertime arrived we went to Kane's house and Sadie served supper. After supper we continued to talk.

It was almost time for me to head back when we heard a commotion coming from the street. Kane and I went outside to see what was going.

Jared Herge and his son, Joshua, were up on his wagon trying to stop Mr. Barrett from pulling a crate off it. There were three crates already lying smashed on the street. Mr. Herge was shouting for Mr. Barrett to stop and Mr. Barrett just pulled harder. Kane shot his gun in the air. Both men stopped and looked over at him.

"What's going on?" Kane demanded.

"I'm trying to get my stuff back," Mr. Barrett answered.

"Why are you going through Jared's belongings?" Kane asked.

"Everyone knows that Jared sells whatever Langdon's gang steals," Mr. Barrett answered, "And it was them who stole my property."

"Let's put everything back in the wagon," Kane said.

"Finally some common sense," Mr. Herge muttered.

"And then the wagon can go to the stable behind my office," Kane said, "There it will stay until this has all been sorted out. You can both come by my office tomorrow morning."

Mr. Herge didn't look happy. But he and Joshua got down and helped Mr. Barrett put the three crates and their contents back in to the wagon. Once it was all back in the wagon Mr. Herge drove the wagon to the stable behind the sheriff's office. Kane and I followed him. When we go there Kane opened the door for Mr. Herge. Mr. Herge climbed down and left. Kane unhooked the horses and led them each to a stall.

"Now I'll have to sit in here all night," Kane said coming back.

"What's all this about Mr. Langdon having a gang?" I asked.

"Mr. Langdon's men ride north regularly, even during harvest, and hold up anyone who uses the road," Kane said, "He has a few men here in town who take the stolen goods and sell them in the town south of here."

"And you can't arrest him for it because?" I asked.

"So far there hasn't been enough evidence to put Mr. Langdon behind bars," Kane answered, "I've been trying."

"This sounds complicated," I said.

"Sheriff Mertick was willing to turn his back to all of Langdon's activities, especially the murder of the Indian woman," Kane said, "Now I'm trying to stop it. Mr. Langdon has avoided giving me any evidence that I could use. And I'm getting frustrated with it all. Especially since I don't have a deputy to help me with things, like watching these crates so no one steals them overnight."

"I can watch them tonight," I said, "I'm used to sleeping odd hours and I have a gun."

"Are you sure?" Kane asked.

"This is the kind of work I've been telling you all evening that I've been doing," I answered, "You need the rest to deal with Mr. Herge and Mr. Barrett tomorrow. This's no problem for me."

"If you're sure," Kane said.

"I am," I replied.

"I'm grateful," Kane said, "But I can't pay you for this."

"Don't worry about paying me," I said, "Go home and get some sleep."

Kane left the stable. I lit a lantern before closing the door and getting into the back of the wagon. I sat down on one of the crates and leaned on another.

I sat that way all night, keeping watch.

Sunlight was filtering through the cracks in the wall and I had blown out the lantern a couple hours ago, when the door to the stable opened. I put my hand on the handle of my gun until I saw that it was Sadie. She was carrying a tray with food on it.

"Toby," she called as she looked around. I stood up and hopped down off the wagon.

"Good morning," I said.

"I brought you breakfast," Sadie said.

"Thank you," I replied taking the tray.

"Actually, thank you," Sadie said, "This town has farmers and merchants but no one willing to help the sheriff enforce the laws. Since Mertick died, Kane has been struggling to fill his shoes. And no one has ever offered to help."

"It's the least I can do for my best friend," I said, "He got me out of more than enough trouble when we were kids."

Sadie smiled before leaving. I sat down and ate the breakfast.

I had just finished when Kane came in. But Mr. Barrett arrived before we could talk. Mr. Herge arrived a few minutes later.

Kane had Mr. Barrett describe the stolen objects first of all. Then Kane, Mr. Barrett and Mr. Herge went through the crates. It took most of the morning, but they did find the items that had been stolen from Mr. Barrett. Mr. Barrett took his them and went home. Kane gave Mr. Herge a warning about doing business with Mr. Langdon before letting him have his horses and wagon full of crates back.

Kane came over and sat down beside me.

"Not going to charge him with anything?" I asked.

"No point," Kane answered, "Unless I can find the people the rest of the stuff belongs to and they're willing to testify that it was stolen from them. Mr. Barrett is appeased because he got his things back, otherwise I could charge Mr. Herge."

"Mr. Langdon will mess up somewhere and you'll be there to help him fall," I said.

"I hope so," Kane replied. We stood up. I picked up the tray and we walked to Kane's house. Sadie was busy making lunch. I returned the tray, but she insisted that I stay for lunch. So Kane and I sat on the porch talking until lunch.

After lunch I went back to the farm. Alex and Vicky were out in the barn playing cards. I thought about joining them, but mother had seen me ride up and had several jobs that needed to be done. Which meant that I was kept busy until suppertime.

After supper I went out to the coral. Alex joined me.

"Where were you last night?" Alex asked.

"Guarding a wagon loaded with stolen property for Kane," I answered.

"Stolen property?" Alex asked.

"Mr. Langdon's men are highwaymen," I answered, "They stop travellers on a road north of here. They bring the loot back to the farm, where it is packed into crates. Joshua's father is one of the men that pick up these crates and take them to a town south of here to sell the stuff."

"Sounds like something needs to be done about Mr. Langdon," Alex said.

"Kane is trying but between Mr. Langdon's activities and lack of help, he's having trouble," I said.

"Then we'll just have to help out while we're here," Alex said.

"Since we already started to do that," I said.

"Any word on what actually happened to the Nolawistep woman?" Alex asked.

"According to Kane, Mr. Langdon killed her," I answered.

"Which goes with the kid's cry for help," Alex said.

"That's all I found out," I said, "Now I have got to sleep before someone wants something done before the day is over."

"See you in the morning," Alex said. I went back into the house and up to my room. I laid down on the bed and was out before the thought of taking my boots off fully registered.

The next two days I worked out in the fields. Alex spent the time at the house. Mr. Langdon visited but only long enough to invite Alex to supper Sunday night. Mother once again would not let Alex accept unless I went along. Mr. Langdon agreed to that.

Sunday morning we went to church. Sunday afternoon I worked in the field until it was close to time to leave.

Alex helped me with getting the carriage ready. Then we were on our way to Mr. Langdon's farm.

"Do you have a plan yet?" I asked.

"Not quite yet," Alex answered, "I have an idea on how to kill him and make it seem provoked, but his men are going to be a problem."

"Maybe we can get Kane to arrest them," I suggested, "He's already looking for a reason. Then when Mr. Langdon is alone you can enact your plan."

"We'll have to come up with a good reason for Kane to arrest them," Alex said, "But it could work."

"While you keep Mr. Langdon busy I'll poke around," I said.

"Sure," Alex said. We rode the rest of the way in silence. We passed the field where Mr. Langdon's men were working. They didn't even glance up at us. I noticed that Mr. Langdon's son wasn't with them.

Mr. Langdon came out to greet us again. He helped Alex down and went into the house. I took my time tying the reins to the hitching post. I looked around as I did so. There was no one around, but I could hear someone moving around behind the house. I went over to the barn being aware of the person. He looked to be the cook and he was busy. I slipped into the barn. There were few horses but no people. I looked around but there didn't seem to be any evidence visible. I turned to leave when I heard a groaning coming from one of the far stalls. I went to look. It took looking in a few empty stalls before I found the right one. Mr. Langdon's son was lying on the floor of the stall. He looked like the men had kicked him around a few times. He was alive, but obviously he had been hauled in here and dumped.

I didn't even stop to think before I was helping him out of the stall, out of the barn and over to the carriage. I put in him on to the floor of the carriage where I threw a blanket over him. No one had noticed.

Then I went into the house after Alex and Mr. Langdon. Mr. Langdon acknowledged me when I sat down.

Shortly after supper was served. And we stayed there for a

while after supper until Alex felt that it was polite enough for us to leave. Mr. Langdon invited Alex back for Wednesday's supper and I agreed to come with her. Mr. Langdon helped Alex back into the carriage, but didn't notice the blanket. I untied the horses and then climbed up on the driver's seat. We left Mr. Langdon's farm.

Alex waited until we were far enough away before pulling the blanket off the kid.

"What the hell did they do to him?" Alex asked.

"I don't know," I answered, "But I figured we should get him out of there before he died."

"Is there a doctor in town?" Alex asked.

"Sadie's father is the town doctor," I answered.

"Then let's take him there," Alex said. I had the horses speed up a little to get us there faster but not enough to bounce the kid around too much.

"Chenarcor," the voice was faint.

"My name is Alex," Alex said, "And you're gonna be all right."

"There's nothing for me if I live," the kid said.

"We'll help you find something," Alex told him. The kid didn't respond.

We reached town I went a street over from the main street. The Butterworth house had lights on. I stopped in front of it and got down. Reaching the door I knocked. It was a few moments before the door opened. Mrs. Butterworth stood there.

"Toby, what are you doing here?" Mrs. Butterworth asked.

"Is Dr. Butterworth home?" I asked, "I need his help."

"Certainly," Mr. Butterworth answered, "I'll go get him." She went back down the hall. A moment later Dr. Butterworth and Kane came to the door.

"What do you need?" Dr. Butterworth asked.

"Medical help," I answered pointing to the carriage. Alex was getting down. Dr. Butterworth went over and looked into the carriage and saw the kid. Kane followed him.

"What happened?" Kane asked.

"Toby can answer that in a minute," Dr. Butterworth said, "Right now we need to get this kid into my office." Kane and I carried the kid from the carriage to the building next to the house. Dr. Butterworth went ahead of us and lit a lamp. Alex followed us. Once we had set the kid on the bed. Kane and I went back to the waiting area, where Alex had stayed. Dr. Butterworth closed the door so that he could examine the patient in private.

"What happened?" Kane asked.

"I found him in Mr. Langdon's barn," I answered, "And decided to help him."

"What were you doing in Mr. Langdon's barn?" Kane asked.

"Looking around," I answered.

"I know you volunteered to help me the other night, but this is a bad idea," Kane said.

"Someone needs to deal with Mr. Langdon," Alex said, "And if you're having problems then you need some help. We also have the advantage that he doesn't suspect us."

"We do this all the time," I told Kane.

"This isn't a good idea," Kane said.

"We may have just brought a witness to the crimes of Mr. Langdon's men," Alex said.

"If he's willing to testify," Kane replied, "And getting Mr. Langdon's men doesn't mean any of this will stop."

"You get Mr. Langdon's men out of the way and we'll get Mr. Langdon," I said.

"What're you gonna do to him?" Kane asked.

"Make sure that what you charge him with will not only stick, but make sure he can never do anything like this again," Alex answered.

"If you can do it," Kane said, "But if you get caught I'll disavow all knowledge of this plan or my involvement."

"That would be usual," Alex said. Dr. Butterworth came out and closed the door behind him.

"The patient is going to be fine," Dr. Butterworth said, "But he needs to rest."

"Can I talk to him tomorrow?" Alex asked.

"Tomorrow, yes," Dr. Butterworth answered. Alex nodded. We all left the office. Dr. Butterworth and Kane went back to the house. Alex and I went back to the carriage. This time Alex climbed on to the driver's seat with me.

"I'm glad the kid will be fine," Alex said as we started back toward the farm.

"I'm hoping you can talk him into testifying against Mr. Langdon's men," I said.

"I'll try," Alex said. We didn't say anything more. Alex ended up leaning against me and falling asleep.

When we arrived back to the farm a lamp was still on in the kitchen. Alex woke up and helped me put the horses in their stalls. We went into the house. Mother was sitting at the table.

"What happened?" mother asked, her voice hushed, "You've been gone all evening."

"We had to stop in town before we could come back," I answered, also keeping my voice quiet, "We found Mr. Langdon's son beaten and took him to Dr. Butterworth."

"Is he going to be alright?" mother asked.

"Yes," Alex answered, "Tomorrow I'm going to town to check on him."

"Take Vicky and the carriage," mother said, "Diane is probably ready to come back. You can pick her up, since you will be there."

"I will," Alex said. We all went upstairs to our rooms for the night.

The next morning I went out to the fields as usual. Alex was getting ready to go to town when I left. Vicky was excited because she could to go with Alex.

Father, Richard, Tracey and I worked all day on the second to last field. At suppertime we went back to the house.

When I had finished mine chores, I went over to the coral and leaned against the fence. Alex came over and climbed up to sit on the top rail.

"The kid is willing to testify," Alex said, "And the judge showed up this morning."

"So, everything is set?" I asked.

"Kane is still trying to convince the judge to accept the kid as a witness," Alex answered, "The judge doesn't really want to charge anyone on the testimony of a half-breed."

"The half-breed is the only witness who is willing to testify," I said.

"Kane is also talking to Joshua Herge," Alex said, "He's in the care of Mrs. Newton while his father goes off to sell the stolen property."

"Jared Herge left his son in the care of Mrs. Newton?" I asked.

"No," Alex answered, "He was left to care of his mother, but

Mrs. Newton volunteered to take Joshua in after Dr. Butterworth was called to care for Joshua's mother."

"I've never seen or heard anything of Mrs. Herge," I said.

"Apparently she's been sick for years," Alex said, "And she died this afternoon. Which's unfortunate and Joshua is taking it hard. Kane is trying to talk him into testifying, but it's going to take a few days. Mrs. Newton is trying to help as well."

"Joshua is willing to turn on his father?" I asked.

"Kane has promised to drop Joshua's father's charges," Alex answered.

"When will everything be ready?" I asked.

"Probably by Wednesday," Alex answered.

"That works out," I said. We switched subjects and talked until the sky grew dark.

Tuesday everything went as usual I was out in the field and Alex in the house. We were coming from the field when Kane was approaching the house.

"Afternoon," father greeted him.

"Good afternoon," Kane replied.

"What brings you out this far?" father asked.

"I need to talk to Toby and Alex," Kane said.

"The three of you aren't getting into trouble, are you?" father asked.

"Not yet," Kane answered. Kane rode with us back to the house.

"Good afternoon," mother greeted when she came outside to see who the guest was.

"Good afternoon," Kane replied.

"Shall I set another plate for supper?" mother asked.

"Please," Kane answered.

"Where's Sadie?" father asked.

"At her mother's." Kane answered, "I warned her I was coming out here so she decided to go over to her mother's for supper."

"As long as you aren't here because you're having a fight," mother said starting to go back into the house.

"The only fight we might have is if I don't get back tonight," Kane replied. Everyone laughed, but I sensed something else behind his words. The horses were put away and we all headed inside for supper.

After supper Kane, Alex and I went out to the coral.

"What is it?" I asked.

"The judge is willing to listen to Mr. Langdon's son and let the charges stand based on his testimony," Kane answered, "Joshua has also agreed to testify as to what he knows about Mr. Langdon's operation. And the marshal who's traveling with the judge has offered his help in bringing Mr. Langdon's men in."

"Sounds like everything is ready," Alex said.

"We'll go out tomorrow morning," Kane said.

"And tomorrow night we'll do our part," I said.

"I'll go out as well," Kane said, "I'll probably arrive after you do. In case you need help bringing Mr. Langdon in."

"It'll be about suppertime," Alex said.

"All right," Kane said. Mother called for Alex from the house. Alex climbed down and went to the house.

"What's that about?" Kane asked.

"I don't know," I answered, "So, what's going on? I mean besides this plan to take down Mr. Langdon."

Kane smiled. He looked the happiest I had seen him in a long time.

"Sadie is pregnant," Kane said.

"Congratulations," I said.

"Thanks," Kane said, "She doesn't want too many people to know yet."

"I won't tell anyone," I said, "I think you got the better deal by staying here."

"What about you and Alex?" Kane asked.

"We're partners," I answered, "Despite what everyone thinks it looks like, we're just partners."

"You'll find someone, somewhere," Kane said.

"In the meantime, it's been fun traveling," I said.

"I have to get back," Kane said.

"See you tomorrow," I said. Kane headed back to town. I went inside. Richard, Jessica and Vicky were sitting at the table playing comet. Vicky invited me to play, so I joined their game. When the game was over we all went to our rooms.

Sunrise on Wednesday found me and the rest of the men headed for the harvest last field. We were near enough to the road today that in mid-morning I saw Kane ride passed with another man. An hour later they rode back toward town with all of Mr. Langdon's men in the back of a wagon.

Mid-afternoon I went back to the house to get washed up. Once Alex and I were ready, I hooked the horses to the carriage. Alex and I drove to Mr. Langdon's farm.

When we arrived, Mr. Langdon was waiting outside waiting.

"Here is the best part of my day," Mr. Langdon said helping Alex down.

"What happened to the rest of it?" Alex asked.

"Something I have to deal with tomorrow," Mr. Langdon answered, "Nothing I want to think about tonight." Alex smiled as they headed for the house. I climbed down and tied the reins to the hitching post. I was about to head inside the house when I saw Kane coming down the road. I remained where I was and waited for him.

"How is it?" Kane asked when he had stopped.

"So far so good," I answered. Kane got down and tied his horse to the hitching post.

"Then I guess I should stay out of sight until you're ready," Kane said. Before I could respond a gunshot came from the house. Both Kane and I ran for the house. We found Alex standing in the parlour with her gun in her hand and the front of her dress ripped. Mr. Langdon was lying on the floor with blood coming out of the hole in his chest. He was still alive but he wouldn't be for long. I put my gun back in its holster before entering the room. Kane followed. Alex looked at us.

"I guess that's the end of Mr. Langdon," Kane said, "But I was hoping he would get to trial."

"I'm sorry," Alex said.

"That's all right," Kane said, "But we need to get him back to town. The judge will want to know what happened."

Mr. Langdon was dead now. We wrapped him up in a blanket we found and put him on the floor of the carriage. Before getting up on the driver's seat I gave my jacket to Alex. She put it on before climbing up beside me. Kane mounted on his horse and we all headed for town.

We stopped at the sheriff's office. The judge and his marshal were sitting on the porch.

"Where is he?" the judge asked Kane, "What happened?"

"He's dead," Kane answered. The judge stood up.

"You weren't supposed to kill him, you were supposed to bring him in for trial," the judge said.

"I'm the one who shot him," Alex said.

"Why would you," the judge stopped after he looked up at Alex. He could see the ripped dress under my jacket. "I guess we bury him and just have a trial for his men."

"I'm gonna go see Dr. Butterworth," Alex told me before she left the carriage. She went in the direction of the doctor's office. Kane and I headed for the mortician's house.

We left the body with him. Kane went home and I went to the doctor's office. Dr. Butterworth was sitting at his desk.

"Alex went in to see the kid," the doctor said.

"I'll wait out here." I sat down in one of the chairs.

"Did Kane arrest Dolph Langdon?" the doctor asked.

"No," I answered, "We just dropped the body off at the mortician's."

"Well, Mr. Langdon can't get out and cause trouble again," the doctor said.

"Yeah," I said. Alex came out of the room.

"He's sleeping now," Alex told Dr. Butterworth.

"Good," Dr. Butterworth said. I stood up. Alex and I started for the door.

"See you another time," Dr. Butterworth said.

"See you," I replied. Alex and I left. We climbed up on the driver's seat and started the carriage toward the farm. We travelled in silence for a while.

"You gonna be all right?" I asked Alex.

"I had a plan," Alex said, "But I just ended up reacting."

"And he got what he deserved," I said, "You know plans go wrong. Nothing goes as smoothly as we hope. As least this time you could stop him before anything more happened."

"I guess learning how to use a gun helped somewhat," Alex said.

"Alex, you don't need pants and a hat to have confidence," I said, "Your usual 'I don't care what you think' attitude works whether you're wearing a dress or not."

"Some days are just harder than others," Alex said.

"You've been doing better," I said.

"We still have a week and a half before we can leave," Alex said.

"The harvest should been done by the end of the week," I said, "We can probably leave then."

"I hope so," Alex said, "Because if I'm stuck without something to do for a week, you can find me at Nadine's house when you're ready."

We talked about other things the rest of the way back. It was dark when we arrived back so once the carriage and horses were back where they belonged we quietly entered the house. Mother was sitting at the kitchen table with a lamp beside her.

She saw Alex's dress.

"What happened?" mother asked with a look of concern.

"It's fine," Alex answered quietly, "There's nothing to worry about."

"Are you sure?" mother asked.

"Yes," Alex answered.

"It looks like it needs repairs," mother said.

"I can do that tomorrow," Alex said.

"It's all right," I told my mother, "Neither of us are hurt and the dress is repairable. So, let's go to bed."

"All right," there was reluctance in mother's voice. We all went up stairs to our own rooms. I closed my eyes, sleep came.

I helped finished the harvest, while Alex repaired her dress and helped at the house.

Mother called us for supper as we were just finish with the horses. Richard led us to the house and Tracey followed me.

After supper I went to the coral. Alex joined me a few minutes later.

"We're finished," I told her.

"So we can leave?" Alex asked.

"When would you like to leave?" I asked.

"Tomorrow," Alex answered.

"Then we'll do that," I said. Alex looked like she was going to say something else when I saw Kane come around the house on his horse. Alex turned and saw Kane too. Father came out to greet him. Kane talked to him for a minute, before coming over to us.

"Good evening," I said.

"It is," Kane replied, "I thought you might like to know what's been happening in town."

"The trial is over already?" Alex asked.

"The judge needs to move on quickly," Kane answered.

"So, what was his decision?" I asked.

"All the men were guilty and they all got ten years in prison," Kane answered, "The judge and his marshal are taking them there."

"What about the kid?" Alex asked.

"The judge dealt with Mr. Langdon's property while he was here," Kane said, "The kid got whatever money Langdon had and the amount the land is worth. The marshal also escorted the kid to the nearest Nolawistep tribe, where apparently he was welcomed when they found out who his mother was."

"He'll be fine then," Alex said.

"What about Mr. Langdon's land?" I asked.

"The judge said that your father and the neighbour on the other side have the option of harvesting the grain," Kane said, "But other than that it'll remain empty until it can be sold to someone."

"Sounds like everything has been wrapped up nicely," I said.

"Does that mean you're leaving?" Kane asked.

"Tomorrow," Alex answered.

"Good luck then," Kane said.

"You too," I said. We shook hands, then he offered his hand to Alex. She shook it. We watched Kane ride off.

"Time to go," Alex said.

"Yes," I replied. We stayed out there until it was dark, but we left the comfortable silence alone.

The next morning I woke to the sounds of people moving about. I looked outside to see the sun hadn't risen yet. I rolled over and went back to sleep.

The second time I woke up it was because the sun was shining in the window. I got up and got ready to leave. I found Alex sitting at the kitchen table eating the breakfast my mother set out. I sat down and ate some of it while I wrote a note for them. Then Alex and I went out to the barn. We got our horses ready and then started back down the road to the farm. We rode back through town and back the way we came three weeks ago.

"Where're we headed?" I asked Alex once we were through the town.

"I figured we could go visit Nadine," Alex answered.

"And if Jacob has a job?" I asked.

"Depends on the job," Alex answered, "We did get paid for the last couple."

"Maybe he's figured out that not paying us is a bad idea," I said.

"More likely he'll pay us until he figures we've forgotten about the last time," Alex said, "Then he'll try it again."

"Does he ever learn from past mistakes?" I asked.

"Only if it hurts bad enough," Alex answered.

"Then next time we might have to go with pain," I said. The imp stayed longer than just a twitch, but it still disappeared too fast.

"We'll see what the next adventure brings," Alex said.

RESCUING SHANE & GERALD
CHAPTER 10

Toby

We had been riding for five days when Alex stopped her horse and stared down at something. I caught up to her and looked down. A man lay at the edge of the road with a knife sticking out of his right eye. He was dead. Alex climbed off her horse and bent down. She pulled the knife out of the man's eyes, wiped it off on the man's shirt and then climbed back on her horse.

"What is it?" I asked.

"I recognize the knife," Alex said holding it up, "Shane and Gerald have been through here."

"One of Gerald's?" I asked.

"Yup," Alex said, tucking it away. Going around the body we continued along the road.

An hour later we reached a town. It had one very muddy street from the recent heavy rain. There was one hotel and one general store, but several saloons and a couple whorehouses. And the only ladies that I could see in the town were probably from one or the other of the whorehouses. There were plenty of men though. There was one passed out drunk in the middle of the street. A few people glanced in our direction, but no one seemed to care.

Alex led the way around the bigger puddles in the street to stop in front of the saloon which did not have anyone leaning against a post out front. It also looked much better then the rest. We tied our horses to the hitching post and went inside. The place was cleaner than I thought it would be; it was half full of men sitting at tables drinking. The noisiest table in the saloon was at the back where there was a poker game in progress. Everyone else just talked quietly.

Alex started toward a table, but stopped when a man came into view at the top of the stairs. He signalled her to come up. Alex headed up the stairs and I followed. The man disappeared from sight until we reached the top. Then we saw him enter a room at the far end of the hallway. We followed him into the room. Alex shut the door behind us. The man had sat down behind the desk. Alex and I sat down in the two chairs in front of it. The man was dressed in black pants and a black vest of a white shirt. His brown hair looked like he had a nervous habit of running his hand through it, his hazel eyes had a slight chill to them and there was a scar above his left eye.

"Shane and Gerald are in town," the man said, "But don't go asking around about them."

"What happened?" Alex asked.

"They killed a group of men who worked for one of the more powerful men in town," the man said, "He owns more than half of this town. The men who're now dead were his gunhands. He sent the rest of the gunhands after Shane and Gerald. They caught them and are now holding them."

"And what's he planning to do with them?" Alex asked.

"From what I've been hearing, he hasn't decided yet," the man answered.

"What would happen if they disappeared?" Alex asked.

"He would go searching for them," the man answered, "There's supposed to be a marshal coming through here in the next couple days. The marshal is in the man's pocket and will do whatever he's told."

"The marshal should ask that they stand trial," Alex said.

"And the other half of the gunhands will stand there and say it was murder," the man said.

"There a judge in town?" Alex asked.

"No," the man answered.

"Any chance of one coming through?" Alex asked.

"No," the man answered.

"Then we hope the marshal has to take Shane and Gerald with him to find one," Alex said, "Even if he has to take the other half of the gunhands with him to testify, there still might be a chance to get them out of the situation."

"And if he decides to hang them here?" the man asked.

"We'll have to think of something else," Alex answered, "Until they decide what's happening we can't plan anything. We'll need someplace to stay until the marshal gets here."

"I lost a girl a couple months ago and haven't been able to replace her," the man said, "So, I have one room free. But it ain't exactly the best place to sleep."

"It'll have to do," Alex said.

"All right then," the man said standing up. Alex and I stood up and followed him from the room. He went down the hallway and stopped at the last door. He took out a key and unlocked the door. I followed Alex inside.

I just about gagged from the smell of perfume. I blinked back the water in my eyes and looked around. The blanket was pink and white lace, the curtains were pink and white lace, and the pile of clothes covering the floor were pink and white with lace. If it was possible for something to be pink it was.

"As I said it ain't exactly the best place to sleep," the man said.

"Hopefully it won't be for long," Alex said. She went over and opened the window.

"I have to check on something," the man started to turn away.

"Before you go," Alex said, "Where's the best place to leave our horses?"

"I have a stable out back," the man said, "I can have someone take them back there."

"We can do it," Alex said.

"Whatever you want," the man shrugged before leaving.

"I wonder if the stable has a loft," I commented.

"If it did Danny would have offered it before he offered us this room," Alex replied, "He wouldn't want this room occupied in case he got a new whore."

"You've been through here before?" I asked.

"I recognized the saloon from Danny's description," Alex answered, "I'd been asked to ride the stage coach carrying a payroll, but they didn't want anyone riding shotgun. They felt it was more likely to get robbed that way. Danny was one of the passengers on the stagecoach. And it was a long and boring trip."

"And Shane and Gerald were there, too?" I asked.

"No," Alex answered, "I was being paid for a round trip and Danny was also on a round trip. Shane and Gerald were in the town looking for a job. Danny and I ended up playing poker the evening we got to our destination and Shane and Gerald joined us. It made for an interesting evening. Danny ended up hiring Shane and Gerald for a job."

"We should put our horses away," I said starting to leave the room. Alex followed. We went downstairs and outside. My horse was still tied to the hitching post, but Alex's horse wasn't. I spotted it farther down the street with a man riding it.

Alex whistled. The horse stopped moving. The man tried to get it moving again, but the horse refused to move. Alex stepped over the sidewalk and whistled again. The horse turned around and walked to Alex bringing the man on its back. The man was still trying to get the horse to obey him. The horse stopped in front of Alex. Alex reached up to pat it on the nose before fixing a look on the man.

"I'm pretty sure stealing a horse is against the law, even in this town," Alex said, "So, you can get off and never try it again, or I can kick your ass."

"I'm going," the man said sliding off Alex's horse. Then he walked away glowering over his shoulder every few steps. Alex didn't move until he was out of sight. I untied the reigns of my horse and Alex and I walked our horses around to the back of the saloon. The stable was a building across the alley from the back door of the saloon. We took our horses inside and found them stalls.

When I was finished I waited for Alex just outside the stable. She came out a few minutes later.

"Now what?" I asked.

"Now we see what information we can gather without asking direct questions," Alex answered.

I nodded and we headed back to the street. When we reached it, Alex went off to one saloon and I headed for another.

I spent the rest of the afternoon sitting and listening. I found somewhere else to have supper and switched saloons again to spend the evening.

When I was finally tired, I went back to the saloon where Alex and I were staying. Entering the room, I found Alex curled up in her bedroll on the floor. I closed the door. Dumping the clothing off the chair, I dragged it over to the window. I sat down and leaned my head against the window frame. The fresh air felt good.

There was shouting in the street. I straightened up to peer out. There was a large fight going in the middle of the street. The combatants did not appear to have any guns. Alex was still sleeping curled up in her bedroll. I leaned my head against the window frame and closed my eyes.

There was a gunshot. I opened my eyes and looked out. A man in an expensive suit was shouting at the combatants with a gun pointed up at the sky. It looked like he was trying to stop the fight. Alex rolled over in her sleep, but didn't wake up. Again I leaned my head against the window frame. Closing my eyes, I drifted back to sleep.

I woke up to the sound of movement. Without opening my eyes I knew that the sun was coming into the room. It sounded like Alex was the person moving around the room. I opened my eyes. She was standing with her back to me. She was wearing her jeans, but she didn't have a shirt on. The two scars that I could see didn't stand out against the whiter skin. I closed my eyes again and pretended I hadn't woken up yet.

Alex moved around a little more, before everything was still. After a moment I opened my eyes. Alex was dressed and sitting on the bed brushing out her hair.

I stood up and stretched.

"Did you find out anything last night?" Alex asked.

"There isn't an honest poker player in town," I answered, "What did you find out?"

"Shane and Gerald killed the gunhands of a man named Joseph Kistler," Alex answered, "And Danny wasn't exaggerating about what Mr. Kistler is worth."

"Any more information?" I asked.

"He bought the town off the man who owned it before," Alex

said, "A couple hours before he shot him. That was about a month ago."

"This sounds like Mr. Kistler is scum like Frederick Hall," I said.

"I haven't seen him or talked with him myself so I don't know," Alex said, "But the man that owned this town before him would kill if you gave him half a reason."

"Hear anything about how Shane and Gerald got into this situation?" I asked.

"Depends who you're talking to," Alex answered, "Most tell it as though Shane and Gerald are at fault."

"We know that Gerald did kill one man," I said, "How likely is it that it was their fault?" Alex started to braid her hair.

"Shane has been known to let his mouth get him into gunfights, but they're usually one on one fights," Alex said, "And Gerald stays back and waits to figure out how much trouble he has to get Shane out of."

"So to get the real story we have to ask them," I said.

"If we can figure out where they are," Alex said. She put her hair up and put her hat on.

"Then I guess that will be the information we look for today," I said.

"And anything else that might be helpful," Alex replied as she stood up.

We left the room and went downstairs to the main room. There weren't any customers except two men passed out at a table in the corner, but Danny was sitting at one table eating breakfast. When he saw us he signalled that we should join him. We sat down. Danny took a drink to help swallow his mouthful of food.

"I hope the fight last night didn't bother your sleep much," Danny said through the crumbs that were still in his mouth.

"Who was the man trying to stop it?" I asked.

"Probably Joseph Kistler," Danny answered, "It's usually his man, Wylie Cawthorne, who starts the trouble and Joseph Kistler who has to finish it."

"Would that hold true for what happened to Shane and Gerald?" Alex asked.

"I don't know," Danny answered, "Whatever happened didn't occur here in town. But it's better to stay away from Wylie

Cawthorne."

"Do you know where Shane and Gerald are being held?" Alex asked.

"Probably Joseph Kistler's barn," Danny answered, "This isn't a good time to try and free them.

"The information helps with the planning," Alex replied, "One more question. Where's a good place to find breakfast?"

"Go outside, turn left and you'll come to a building that has three prices listed on the board outside," Danny said, "If there's no one there it's because the owner is passed out drunk somewhere, in which case you have to come up with your own breakfast."

"This town doesn't seem to be a good place to live," I commented.

"It is a great place to live if you make money on vices," Danny said, "Everyone else moves on after they've left all their money here."

"Yet another reason to leave," Alex said as she stood up. I stood up as well. We left the saloon. Turning left once outside we went down the sidewalk until we reached a building with a board outside. The board read breakfast $3, lunch $5, supper $10. We went inside. There were two tables that had people at them. Alex and I sat down at an empty table.

A man came out of the back with two plates. He put one in front of Alex and one in front of me before heading back to the kitchen. The smell of rotgut liquor lingered in the air a moment after he left.

I tried a small bite of the food. It was edible so I started to eat. Alex waited a moment after watching me before starting her own breakfast.

When we were finished both of us put three dollars on the table before leaving. Once outside I followed Alex to the alley behind the restaurant. It was empty, but then the whole town was quiet this morning. We walked down passed Danny's stable. Finally Alex stopped behind the biggest saloon in town. The building behind it was half the size of a barn and smelled like one.

Alex pulled on the door and it opened with a small squeak. She signalled that I should stay and keep watch before coming inside. After a moment I heard Alex whistle. I stepped inside. She was standing at the far end. I joined her. She opened the stall door in front of her. Shane and Gerald were bound and gagged sitting on the floor. Alex stepped into the stall. I held the stall door and kept watch on the barn door. Shane tried to say something through his gag. Alex bent down and removed Gerald's gag.

"What're you doing here?" Gerald asked.

"Making sure you're still alive," Alex answered. Shane asked a question through his gag.

"We can't just let you go, without causing more trouble," Alex answered him.

"Then you want to avoid Wylie Cawthorne," Gerald said, "It's his fault we're in this situation."

"What happened?" Alex asked.

"It was dark so we stopped and set up camp for the night," Gerald answered, "We had just finished eating when a group of men showed up out of the dark. Wylie appeared to be the leader. They were coming back from somewhere and could smell food, which made them hungry and they hoped we would share, according to Wylie. Shane mouthed off. I told him to shut up and then explained to Wylie that we had just eaten the last of our food and were hoping to restock at the next town. Wylie got angry and ordered the men to attack us. We killed about half of them before I was knocked out."

Shane said something I didn't understand.

"When I came to, we were tied up in a wagon on its way here," Gerald said, "We arrived, they dragged us into this stall and we haven't seen anyone since except the boy who brings us food."

"Wylie's boss is waiting on a marshal to arrive so he can charge you with murder," Alex said.

Shane tried to talk again.

"It doesn't matter whether Wylie started it, his boss is going to finish it," Alex said, "We're hoping the marshal does things properly and takes you to see a judge because that'll make things easier. But either way, be ready."

"We will," Gerald said. Alex put the gag back and stood up. She exited the stall and I let the door close. We went back to the barn door. I looked out. There was no one in the alley. Alex and I left the barn and I closed the door. Then we went back down the alley to Danny's stable. We went inside. It was empty aside from six horses.

"I figured we could spend the afternoon at Mr. Kistler's saloon,"

Alex said as we sat down, "See what Mr. Kistler is like and what Wylie looks like."

"Any ideas yet on how to get Shane and Gerald free?" I asked as I took out a deck of cards.

"Hope the marshal takes them to a judge and then waylay them along the road," Alex answered. I shuffled the cards.

"Sounds good," I said dealing out the cards. We spent the rest of the morning playing comet.

At lunch time we went back to the restaurant where we had breakfast. This time there were many more customers. There were still empty tables. Alex and I sat down at one. The man that had served us breakfast came around with a tray. He stopped at tables where people were sitting without food and put a plate in front of them before moving on to the next person. Alex and I were the last two he served before he had to back to the kitchen to get more plates. Alex and I didn't say much as we ate.

When we were finished we left our money on the table and headed for Mr. Kistler's saloon. It was only half full of people and most of them looked like they were just starting to drink for the day. I ordered a bottle of whiskey and then joined Alex at the table in the back of the room.

Most people went about their business without bothering us, even when we started playing poker, except a man that stood at the bar. He had a shiny revolver on his left hip while he used his right hand to sip his drink. His hat seemed to be trying to hide his eyes but failed. If I had been asked I couldn't say what colour his eyes were, they just looked soulless. His face gave the impression that he would be laughing as he filled you with lead. He noticed us the moment we walked in and he kept watching us.

About the middle of the afternoon a man came in, got a drink, saw that we were playing poker, he came over, introduced himself as Thorpe and asked if he could join in. Alex and I let him join.

A few minutes later the man at the bar signalled someone to him. He gave the man some instructions then the person came over and asked to join the poker game. We let him.

It was getting close to suppertime and the man was getting frustrated because he kept losing. Since he wasn't a good player, without throwing the good cards he got, there wasn't much anyone could do for him. Thorpe was a good player and won enough to keep playing.

I noticed a man come in the back door. He stopped and surveyed the room. From his outfit I figured him to be Joseph Kistler. He didn't look like scum. Instead he had that tired look that I've seen comes into Alex's eyes when it's the middle of a long job and she thinks no one is looking.

Alex won another hand. The man stood up fast shoving the table away from him. It hit me in the stomach.

"You're cheating," the man yelled to get everyone's attention. Mr. Kistler didn't move, but Wylie moved from his place at the bar over to out table.

"What's going on here?" Wylie demanded.

"They're cheating," the man pointed to me and Alex. The crowded saloon was quiet, everyone's attention was on us.

"No, we just happen to be winning," Alex said.

"Stand up," Wylie told us. Neither Alex nor I moved.

"We don't like cheaters in this saloon," Wylie said pulling out his gun, "Now stand up." His eyes dared us to make him shoot. Alex gathered the cards up. Thorpe handed over his cards before getting out of firing range.

"I told you to get up," Wylie said.

"You offered to shoot us too," Alex said, "I'm just wondering how you intend to explain to everyone watching how it was self-defense when the people you just shot still had their guns in their holsters."

Wylie looked like he was going to say something, but a voice from behind him stopped him.

"Wylie, get back to your place at the bar," Mr., Kistler said. I don't remember seeing him move, but Mr. Kistler was standing right there.

"Yes, Mr. Kistler," Wylie said slinking back to the bar. Mr. Kistler turned to the man.

"How much did you enter the game with?" Mr. Kistler asked.

"A hundred dollars," the man answered.

"It was fifty," Thorpe said, "He counted it in front of us during the first hand."

Alex counted out fifty dollars from her winnings and offered it to Mr. Kistler. Mr. Kistler took the money and handed it to the man.

"Go muck out the barn," Mr. Kistler told the man.

"It's suppertime," the man said.

"I expect the barn to be clean enough to eat off of the floor before you have supper," Mr. Kistler said. The man was upset but went out the back door. Mr. Kistler turned to Alex, Thorpe and me.

"If you want to keep playing poker you'll have to do it some place else," Mr. Kistler said.

"Yes, sir," Alex said. We took our winnings and left the saloon. Thorpe was not far behind us, but he went the other way down the sidewalk.

The marshal rode into town. He saw us and tipped his hat to Alex. We watched him stop in front of Kistler's saloon and go inside.

Alex and I found a saloon that served supper for less than ten dollars. After supper we headed back to Danny's saloon. Danny saw us enter and started up to his office. Alex and I followed. When we were all inside I closed the door.

"The marshal has arrived in town," Danny said.

"We saw him," Alex said, "Any word on finding a judge?"

"I'll know in a couple of hours," Danny answered.

"Well, there isn't much we can do 'til then," Alex said. Danny nodded and then left the office.

"The marshal knew you," I said once the door was closed.

"Thomas and I passed through his territory once," Alex said, "He gave us a place to stay and anything else we needed. And he wouldn't take any money for it."

"Sounds like a good person," I said.

"I think Mr. Kistler is trying to do things by the law," Alex said, "That's why he asked the marshal to come for Shane and Gerald. I doubt Mr. Kistler pays Marshal Brady."

"Based on what I've seen of Mr. Kistler I don't think he would," I said.

"All this could work in our favour," Alex said, "I know Marshal Brady will take Shane and Gerald to a judge. So, the problem there is going to be the men who will be there to guard them and to testify against them."

"You're still thinking ambush?" I asked.

"Yes," Alex answered, "It'll get the men away from town and anyone that might help them."

"We'll have to get ahead of them," I said.

"If we leave about dawn we should have a couple hours lead on them," Alex said.

"I hope this works," I said. Alex nodded and pulled out a deck of cards. We started playing comet.

An hour later Danny came back into the office.

"I just received the word. The marshal is going to take Shane and Gerald to a judge. Six men are going with them, but Wylie isn't going anywhere. They're supposed to be leaving after breakfast tomorrow morning," Danny said.

"We'll be leaving at dawn then," Alex said as she gathered up the cards to put them away, "If the plan changes, we need to know."

"I'll let you know," Danny said.

Alex and I left the office and went down the hall to the room. Once inside Alex laid down in her bedroll and closed her eyes. I sat down in the chair, put my feet up and closed my eyes.

Someone shook my shoulder. I opened my eyes. There was a lamp lit and Alex was getting her belongings together. Standing up, I stretched then picked up my stuff. The rest of the building was silent as we left the room. Going downstairs, we went out the back door. Once inside the stable, we got our horses ready and we headed out of town. The sun was just shining its first rays over the town. Except for a couple drunks passed out in the middle of the street, it looked deserted.

It was close to noon when we approached four buildings; two on one side of the road and two on the other. There appeared to be a saloon, a blacksmith's shop, general store and a private residence. There was noise coming from the blacksmith's shop, but other than that all was quiet.

We stopped in front of the saloon and tied our horses to the hitching post before going inside. There were six men in the saloon. Four playing poker, one slumped over drunk, and the barman. The five glanced up at us as we entered and then the four poker players went back to their game.

"We have food and any kind of drink you want," the barman said.

"Food and whiskey," I said.

"Five dollars," the barman said. I handed him the money before Alex and I sat down at a table. The barman came over with two glasses and a bottle. He set the glasses down, poured whiskey in each and took the bottle back behind the bar. As I took a sip of the whiskey, he said something to the person in the back room.

Ten minutes later a lady came out of the back room carrying a tray. She set two plates on our table and went back into the kitchen. Once Alex and I finished eating we went outside. I leaned against one of the posts and Alex sat down on the bench. We waited

It was an hour later when Marshal Brady, Shane and Gerald, and six of Mr. Kistler's men rode into town. They stopped in front of the general store where there was a water trough for their horses.

"How do you want to do this?" I asked Alex as she stood up.

"Wound only if necessary," Alex answered.

Everyone but Shane and Gerald dismounted. Shane and Gerald were still bound and gagged. Marshal Brady saw us and recognized Alex, but didn't say anything to the rest of the riders. The six men didn't recognize us. Alex and I stepped off the porch and started across the road towards them. Marshal Brady left the group and met us half-way.

"Whatever you're going to do isn't a good idea," he said.

"Shane and Gerald are innocent," Alex said.

"I know that but it's a judge who needs to say it before they can be let free," Marshal Brady said.

"Not likely to happen with you dragging the evidence around with you," Alex said.

"I don't have a choice," Marshal Brady said.

"Then let me give you one," Alex said, "Get out of our way or get hurt." Marshal Brady didn't move, he just stared at Alex.

"Your gun," Alex said pulling out her own. Brady gently took out his gun with his thumb and index finger and handed it to Alex.

"Thank you," Alex said taking it from him. Brady stepped out of the way, the rest of the riders were now paying attention to what was going on.

"If you do as you're told no one has to get hurt," I announced after taking my gun out.

"We don't take orders from anyone," the man closest to Alex said pulling out his gun. Alex shot it out of his hand. The man swore and held his hand. The man nearest to the horses had pulled out his gun. Alex shot that gun out of reach as well.

"Drop your gunbelts," I said. They all undid and dropped their gunbelts.

"Gather them up," Alex told Brady as she put her gun away. Brady did as he was told. Alex pulled out Gerald's knife and used it to cut Gerald loose before returning the knife to Gerald. Gerald used it to cut Shane loose. Alex went back into the saloon.

We all stood there and waited until she came out. The barman stepped out onto the porch and looked at us. Alex stopped near me.

"There's food and drink waiting for you in the saloon," Alex told the six riders, "The barman will let you head home in four hours and no sooner." I put my gun away.

The riders looked surprised, but headed for the saloon without asking any questions. Brady nodded and stuffed the gunbelts into his saddlebags. Alex handed Brady his gun back.

"We still have some business with Wylie," Gerald said.

"I know," Alex said. Alex and I went back to our horses and mounted. Brady mounted his and the five of us headed back.

It was early evening when we stopped at the edge of town. Everything looked normal.

"Alex," Gerald said.

"Yes," Alex replied.

"Did you ever name your gun?" Gerald asked.

"No, why?" Alex asked.

"I lost Vanessa a while back," Gerald answered, "And the last time I tried to use Cindy, she jammed on me even though Shane claimed he had just cleaned her."

"That's what you get for naming them after jilted lovers," Alex said as she undid her gunbelt. She handed it to Gerald. Gerald got off his horse, put the gunbelt on and headed down the street.

"Are you sure this's a good idea?" Brady asked.

"Gerald is good with a gun," Shane said.

"And once Wylie is gone Mr. Kistler will have a lot less trouble," Alex said.

"Mr. Kistler will be glad of that," Brady said, "Part of the deal for the property included keeping Wylie on."

Gerald stopped in the middle of the street out front of Mr. Kistler's saloon.

"Wylie Cawthorne," Gerald shouted, "Come out here you son of a whore or I'll come in for you."

Moments went passed. People stopped to watch, there were faces in every window and even a few coming out to look. Finally Wylie stepped out of the saloon. I could see Mr. Kistler looking out one of the windows in the second storey. Wylie grinned as he moved to his position. He stood in the middle of the street about ten feet from Gerald. They held themselves motionless and alert there waiting for the other person to draw. Even the horses seemed to feel the tension.

Wylie drew first. Gerald drew and shot six bullets into Wylie before he had cleared the holster. There was another moment of silence before everyone went back to his own business.

Brady headed for Mr. Kistler's saloon to talk to Mr. Kistler and give him the gunbelts. Gerald walked back to us. He took off the gunbelt and handed it back to Alex before mounting his horse. Alex put her gunbelt back on and reloaded her gun. Then the four of us left town.

When we reached the next town, Gerald and Shane continued on their own.

This was a good-sized town with multiple streets, a few hotels, a couple of saloons, a church, a school, and stores of various kinds. Alex and I found a hotel that advertised a restaurant, baths and laundry while still being affordable. Alex had been close to swearing because both sets of clothes had gotten extremely muddy.

We got rooms. Mine was the second one on the left at the top of the stairs. I dropped my bags on the bed and washed up before going back down stairs. There were a few people in the dining room. I sat down at an empty table.

I took out a deck of cards and started to play solitaire. Half an hour later Alex sat down in the empty chair across from me. She was wearing her dress with her hair properly done up.

"The sooner the laundry finishes with my clothes the better," Alex muttered. I gathered up the cards, shuffled them and dealt out two poker hands.

We stopped the poker game for supper and started again after we had finished. A gentleman asked if he could join in. He turned out to be a professional gambler, so we took turns winning.

In the middle of the evening another man asked to join. After the first hand I figured that he was trying to cheat and excused myself from the game.

I left the dining room and went outside to get some fresh air. There were benches out front. I sat down in the one farthest part from the lamp.

It was quiet out here. The only lamps were the ones on either side of the hotel entrance and some out front of the saloon down the street. The wind blew passed moving a couple of signs and bringing the faint smell of horses. It was nice to just sit here and relax.

I was starting to think about going in, when I saw a couple come out of the hotel. I remember they had been a few tables over from Alex and me. They had been talking to another couple.

The lady was laughing at something the man said. They didn't see me as they went passed. They went as far as the alley between the buildings. I saw them freeze and the laughter died.

I stood up and quickly went around to the other end of the alley. There were two men with guns demanding valuables. I moved down the alley as quietly as I could. The couple were so focused on the bandits they didn't notice me.

Pulling my gun out I used the handle to knock the first bandit on the back of the head. He went down. I moved aside quickly. The other bandit turned and fired at where I had been. So the bullet ended up in the wall. I managed to get close enough to grab the bandit's gun hand. The bandit was still trying to aim the gun at shoot me. I slammed him into the wall. I hit his hand into the wall hard enough that he dropped the gun. Then I punched him several times in the stomach, which caused him to double over. I picked up his gun and then walked over and picked up his partner's gun.

The hotel clerk arrived with a lantern and followed by another employee of the hotel.

"I heard a shot!" the hotel clerk said, "What's happening?"

"They tried to rob us," the man said pointing at the bandits, "And he stopped them." He guided the lady to the bench and she sat down.

"Leo," the clerk turned to the man following him, "Go get the sheriff." The man nodded and hurried off.

"Got rope?" I asked the clerk.

"I'll get it," the clerk said, setting the lantern on the bench. He went back inside and came out a moment later. I traded the guns for the rope to tie up the bandits. The man was trying to calm the lady down. From the way his hands were trembling he was just putting on a brave face.

"Can you watch them?" I asked the clerk.

"Sure, but what're you planning to do?" the clerk asked.

"Escort this couple home before coming back to talk to the sheriff," I answered. The man looked up at me, there was gratitude in his eyes.

"Yes, sir," the clerk said. The man helped the lady to stand and we started off toward their house. It was a few streets over. They jumped at every noise and didn't like any area that was dark. They relaxed a little when we reached their house.

Once they were inside and the door was locked I headed back to the hotel. I had just turned on to the street when I heard something behind me. Before I could turn to check it out something smashed into the back of my head. Everything went black.

When I came to I was tied up and on a moving horse. The two bandits were riding on either side of me. My head was echoing the hit making it hard to think straight.

The pain had dimmed a little, when we rounded a corner. I could see a figure ahead. As we got closer I could tell the figure was female and she was standing in the middle of the road. And she was aiming a shotgun at us. Then I recognized Alex.

"Stop!" Alex's voice yelled once the horses were within range. The bandits stopped their horses and the reins on mine were pulled to stop the horse.

"If you shoot us you could hit your friend," the man to my right said, "Especially a young lady like you using a gun like that."

I heard the gun cock.

"I guess I'll have to take that chance," Alex replied, "But I would rather that you all dropped your gunbelts."

"I'm calling your bluff," the man on my left said, "You wouldn't do anything to wound your friend."

"If you're dead and he's only wounded, I win," Alex said, "However if you insist I will shoot you."

"She's serious," I said.

"Shut up," the man on my right said. I heard a second gun cock, but neither bandit had his gun out and they didn't seem to have heard it. I slid to my right a second before Alex pulled the trigger. The bandit on my left jerked a couple of times before his horse took off with him falling to one side. The horse dragged him until his foot slipped out of the stirrup. The man to my right managed to get his horse under control quickly. He slid off to be less of a target if Alex fired again. And I barely hit the ground before the horse that I was on panicked. The horse barely avoided hitting me as it ran off.

The bandit pulled out his gun and pointed it at me.

"I will kill him," the bandit said. There was a shot and the bandit's gun dropped to the ground. I moved so that I could grab it. The bandit was clutching his gun hand.

"Unfortunately for you Eric Harrison was a rifleman in the army," Alex told him. The gambler from the hotel stepped out of the trees onto the roadway.

"Fortunately for you, the sheriff demanded that we bring one bandit back alive," Alex finished. The bandit looked around for his gun only to see me pointing it at him. He put his hands up. Alex and Eric came over.

"That didn't take long," I said as the gambler cut the ropes that were around my wrists.

"There was a witness," Alex said, "Who was able to point us in the right direction. The sheriff would have come, but he had to deal with a bar fight that had gotten out of control." Alex used a piece of rope that she had to tie the bandit's hands behind his back. I stood up and retrieved my gunbelt off the bandit's saddle. Alex told the bandit get back on his horse.

"What happened to the hotel clerk?" I asked as we mounted. We started back towards town.

"The doctor was tending to him as we left," Alex said, "He apologized to the sheriff for letting the bandits get away."

"I shouldn't have left him alone with them," I said.

"Mistakes happen," the gambler said.

"What happened to the cheater?" I asked.

"We took all his money and then escorted him to the front door of the hotel once we found out he wasn't a guest," Alex answered, "That was when we found the clerk. As he was explaining what happened, the sheriff showed up. The sheriff heard the situation and then the person who had seen you captured spoke up. He knew which direction the bandits would head, but before he could do anything, his deputy showed up with news of the fight. I borrowed his shotgun and went after you. Eric wouldn't let me go alone."

"Though apparently she can handle herself," Eric said.

"Just as well that you were there," I said.

The sheriff's office was our first stop when we arrived back in town. The sheriff was just locking up two men from the bar fight. He locked the bandit in a cell and took back his shotgun. He also told me that I must to stay in town for a few days. Then Alex, Eric and I went back to the hotel. Eric went off to his room. Leo was behind the front desk.

"How is he?" I asked Leo.

"Doc says he'll be back in a couple days, but his arm will take longer to heal," Leo answered. I nodded.

"You all right?" Alex asked me.

"I have a headache, but I'll be fine," I answered.

"Better see the doc for the headache," Leo said, "I had an uncle that was hit hard and he didn't wake up the next morning."

"Where's the doctor's office?" I asked.

"Street over and mid way down," Leo answered.

"You need company?" Alex asked.

"Unless there're more bandits in alleys knocking people out I should be all right," I answered.

"Then I'll see you in the morning," Alex said. She went upstairs. I left the hotel and headed in the direction Leo had pointed. The doctor's office was the only building on the street that had a light on. I went and knocked on the door. The door was opened by the doctor. He invited me in.

"What do you need?" the doctor asked.

"I got knocked on the back of the head," I answered.

"You the man who helped the couple from being robbed?" the doctor asked as he indicated that I should sit on the examining table. I sat down.

"Yes," I answered, "How's the clerk?"

"A few cuts, a few bruises and a broken arm, but otherwise he's fine," the doctor said as he examined the back of my head.

"That's good," I said. The doctor poked at something that hurt. He studied the back of my head for a while longer before going into the back room. He closed the door behind him. Five minutes later he came out with a cloth filled with something.

"Press this against the lump for a while," the doctor said, "It doesn't look too serious, but come back and see me tomorrow." He handed me the cloth. It had ice in it. Where he got the ice I don't know but I gratefully pressed it to the place that hurt. The doctor let me out of his office. I went back to the hotel and went up to my room. Going inside I found my hat sitting on the bed. I moved it to the bedpost knowing that I wouldn't be wearing it for a few days. I sat there with the ice pressed to the back of my head until it had melted. After that I lay down and went to sleep.

In the morning I stopped in at the doctor's and was told that everything appeared to be fine. That didn't stop the headache, but it didn't hurt as bad as it had last night. After that I stopped in at the sheriff's office and was informed that I was to be at the courthouse at one. I went back to the hotel and played poker with Alex and Eric until then. The clerk at the front desk gave me directions to the courthouse.

I arrived a minute to one and took a seat. The entire case was put in front of the judge, including my story. The judge reserved judgment until later in the day. I went back to the hotel for the rest of the day.

The sheriff came by the hotel after supper to tell me that the bandit had been found guilty and was going to spend the next twenty years in prison. He also said that I was free to leave.

The next morning Alex and I left town. It took us a few more days to reach Cartwheel.

Cartwheel did not appear to have changed since we were here last. This was one town that didn't have any visible industry, but didn't grow or die off.

Rather than stopping at the hotel we went straight to the stable behind Nadine's house.

"Are you sure 'bout staying here?" I asked.

"No," Alex answered, "But we're here." Jacob's horse was gone, but Nadine's was in its stall. We put our horses in their stalls before leaving the stable and heading for the house.

"Nadine hasn't put her garden in yet," Alex commented.

"Maybe the rain has been too bad," I said.

"Could be," Alex replied. Reaching the kitchen door Alex opened it and I followed her inside.

There was a pot simmering on the stove but no one was in the kitchen.

"Hello?" Alex called.

"Alex?" Nadine's voice came from upstairs.

"And Toby," Alex called back.

"I'll be down in a minute," Nadine replied. I put my stuff on one chair and sat down in another. Alex did the same. She took out a deck of cards and we played a couple hands of poker while we waited.

Twenty minutes later Nadine came downstairs.

"Sorry about the wait," Nadine said, "What're you doing back?"

"Thought we would stop in and visit," Alex answered.

"There's nowhere you need to be?" Nadine asked.

"Not that we know of," I answered.

"How are you doing?" Alex asked.

"I've been trying to keep busy," Nadine answered, "Jacob was home for a month. Then he received a telegram and was off to wherever."

"I noticed you haven't put your garden in this year," Alex said.

"Not because I didn't want to," Nadine said, "But the weather hasn't been the best for it until this last week. I was thinking I should get it in tomorrow or the next day. How long do you plan on visiting?"

"Don't know yet," Alex answered.

"Is this another case of you going out the back door as Jacob is coming in the front?" Nadine asked.

"Not necessarily," Alex answered, "Depends on Jacob's attitude."

"So you'll stay until you figure out his attitude," Nadine said, "And then decide."

"He keeps volunteering us for jobs," I said, "Even ones that don't pay."

"Or he decides to take the pay all for himself," Alex said, "The last job we did with him the employer paid us each directly because he knew that otherwise Jacob might not share. And the worst part is that he doesn't see the problem with this behaviour."

"I keep hoping he has changed that behaviour," Nadine said.

"Until I see evidence that he has changed I feel better avoiding him," Alex said.

"Can you try to stand him if he shows up?" Nadine asked, "You'll be off soon enough anyway."

"I can try," Alex said.

"Thank you," Nadine said. Nadine went over and took the pot off the heat. Alex dealt out another hand of poker while Nadine started supper.

It was a quiet next couple of days. Alex volunteered to put in Nadine's garden, so Nadine found her an old dress that she could wear to work in. I did some jobs that Nadine had been hoping that Jacob would get around to soon.

It was the middle of the afternoon on the third day when Jacob showed up. He had a man I didn't know with him. I could tell that Alex and Nadine didn't recognize the man either. Nadine was trying to figure out what to do with the strange man because Jacob seemed to assume that the he could stay at the house. I offered to sleep in the loft. Nadine took me up on the offer and prepared while I moved my stuff. The loft was a cramped space that had barely enough room to stretch out in. Alex and I went to the hotel for supper and a poker game that evening.

There was a light in the kitchen when we got back, so rather than going straight to the stable, I followed Alex inside. Jacob was sitting at the kitchen table playing solitaire. Alex went to stand across the table from Jacob and crossed her arms over her chest.

"Albert needs help," Jacob said.

"Really, I thought you just brought him to annoy Nadine," Alex said.

"He knows you're female," Jacob said, "It's Toby's help I need." Alex looked at me.

"And how much does this job pay?' I asked.

"It doesn't, but I'm sure you're used to those working with

Alex," Jacob said.

"Yeah, but I wouldn't be working with Alex for this one," I said, "I'd be working for you. Different rules. What would Albert have to say if I asked him what the job paid?" Jacob was silent.

"Since you haven't figured it out on your own, I'll explain it to you," Alex said, "Jerk people around too many times and being helpful loses its appeal."

"And I don't owe you anything," I said, "Because you haven't helped me with anything, except maybe teaching me how to rip someone off."

"It pays a hundred dollars," Jacob said, "Total."

"That makes fifty for you and fifty for me," I said, "What about expenses? And length?"

"It will take how ever long it takes," Jacob said.

"Then what about expenses?" I asked, "I'm not exactly so flush with money that I can pay for a month of hotel rooms or a whole lot of supplies."

"I have to pay for my own expenses," Jacob said.

"But you're hiring me after someone has already hired you," I said, "But I'm sure you know plenty of people you can get to help you who can afford it. Good night." I opened the kitchen door and went outside closing the door behind me. I walked to the stable and climbed up to the loft. I sat down on a bale of hay.

It was fifteen minutes before I heard someone enter the stable. Standing up I looked over the rail and saw that it was Alex. She climbed up and stopped next to me, leaning on the rail. I had forgotten to put out the lamp that was below us, so I could see her clearly.

"Jacob angry?" I asked.

"Once the shock wore off," Alex said, "I told him he was only getting what he deserved."

"Think he'll change his mind and pay?" I asked.

"It's likely," Alex answered, "He thinks he needs help and no one is willing to work with him more than a couple of times. It's your choice whether you take the job or not."

"What are you gonna do?" I asked.

"The necessary work to put in Nadine's garden," Alex shrugged.

"Then I just have to figure out whether I can spend that much time with Jacob without killing him," I said. In the light I saw the laughter come into Alex's eyes. The rest of her face stayed neutral.

"Don't kill him in any way that doesn't look like an accident," Alex said.

"Just means somewhere that doesn't have any innocent bystanders or witnesses," I said. Alex smiled.

"As long as you remember you would have to lie to Nadine," Alex said.

"That would be the hard part," I said, "But I'm sure I could figure out something that would sound heroic."

"Don't make him sound too good," Alex said, "Or Nadine won't believe you."

"That's always the problem with stories, they have to be believable," I said. Alex laughed. An impulse came into my head and I acted on it before I thought about it. I kissed Alex. She pulled away, mumbled good night and was gone. I slumped down on the bale of hay.

How could I be such an idiot? I should know better. Alex might be female, but she's still Alex. Maybe this job with Jacob is a good idea. I closed my eyes and tried not to think about anything.

When I entered the kitchen the next morning. Nadine was starting breakfast. I helped her. Albert came down downstairs next. He looked like he hadn't slept well. Alex came down as we started to eat. She was wearing the old dress so that she could go back to the garden when breakfast was over.

Jacob came down after everyone else had finished and Alex had gone outside. Albert had gone out front to sit on the porch. Nadine set some breakfast in front of Jacob before going upstairs.

"Expenses will be paid," Jacob said without looking up from his breakfast. His voice suggested that he really didn't want to do that.

"Fine, I'll help with the job," I said, "When're we leaving?"

"Tomorrow," Jacob said.

"Fine," I said and went off to finish a job that I had started yesterday.

The rest of the day went by quickly. Jacob and Albert went out somewhere. Alex worked in the garden, Nadine had her own work and I finished the list of jobs Nadine had given me. I spent the evening in the loft, playing solitaire until it was time to go to sleep.

SIMONE'S WEDDING
CHAPTER 11

Lady Grace

Having finished my evening meal, I decided to walk over and visit Nadine. I had heard that Jacob and Toby had taken a job causing them to be gone for several weeks. I thought she might like some company, and I wanted to hear what Alex was up to.

I had turned the corner and saw a woman working in the garden. She stopped and watched as I approached. The woman was too young to be Nadine, but the dress was an older one. Her height and the brown braid brought Simone to mind. But Simone was busy, even if she did know Jacob and Nadine. Alexandria! Had Jacob and Nadine found her? Did they know she was missing?

She hadn't moved as I came through the gate. Nadine poked her head out of the door.

"Alex?" Nadine started, then she noticed me. She stepped outside, "Lady Grace, what a pleasant surprise."

The green eyes were Alex's, so was the half smile that Toby called the imp twitch. If I was anything other than the lady that I am I might have shown my surprise. Instead I turned to Nadine.

"I was in town and thought I might stop by for a visit."

"It's nice to see you. Come in," Nadine said.

"Thank you," I replied going up the steps. Once inside Nadine took my hat and shawl and we sat down in the parlour. We talked about how she was doing, where Jacob and Toby were, and the weather when the door opened and closed.

"Alex?" Nadine called.

"Yes?" Alex came to stand in the doorway. She was trying to rub dirt off her cheek, but was merely smearing it around.

"Are you finished?" Nadine asked.

"Not quite, but tomorrow I will finish it," Alex said. The dress and the hair, even the shoes, might be female, but the voice sounded male. That was what had tripped me up, the thing that stopped me from realizing that Alex was Alexandria.

"What're you going to do now?" Nadine asked.

"I'm going to clean up and meet Jacob and Toby," Alex answered.

"They're coming in tonight?" I asked.

"They're supposed to," Alex answered.

"That's good," I replied. Alex turned to go. "I have something for you and Toby." Alex turned back. I extended the letter to her. Alex took it and opened it.

"Simone is getting married," Alex said.

"I received an invitation for myself as well as your invitation," I told her, "I am on my way there."

"I'll talk to Toby," Alex said before leaving the room. Nadine shook her head and we continued out conversation about the weather.

When Alex came back into the room she looked like she was male once again.

"Such a change," I commented looking at her.

"Born out of necessity," Alex replied, her tone was cold; her face expressionless.

"Excuse me," Nadine said standing up, "I have to check the other guestroom. Perhaps you can take Lady Grace back to the hotel, Alex."

"Certainly," Alex said. Nadine left the room.

"This explains how you know so much about Alexandria," I said as I stood up.

"And the fewer who know the better," Alex said. We walked to the front door.

"I will not tell anyone," I promised, "But you should tell Simone." Alex held the door for me and then we went down the steps.

"One day," Alex replied, as we left the yard.

"Come for the wedding and tell her then."

The sigh was quiet, but seemed to have years of emotions behind it.

"Maybe," the voice was louder. There was so much to say and so much to ask, but from her demeanour it did not seem like a good idea. We stopped in front of the hotel. I was about to say good night when I heard hoof beats. Turning toward the sound I saw four horses with riders coming down the street. As they stopped at the hotel I recognized Jacob and Toby.

"A welcoming party," Jacob said as he got off his horse, "Good evening, Lady Grace. To what do we owe the honour of your presence?"

"I'm passing through on my way to attend Simone's wedding," I answered.

"Who's she marrying?" Toby asked.

"Sheldon Kendall, according to the invitation," I answered, "But I haven't met the man."

"Hopefully, he's a better man than Marsden," Alex said.

"I still don't understand why Marsden was shot," I said. Each one stiffened a little.

"He was running from the sheriff," Alex answered, "After the sheriff found out what he had done."

"Which was?" I asked.

"Raping Alexandria," Alex answered as Toby opened his mouth. No wonder Alex did not want to talk about it.

"I should see if there're still rooms available," Toby said.

"Nadine prepared the other guestroom for you," Alex said.

"Good," Toby said.

"I must go to bed," I said, "So, good-night. And if you are going to the wedding, I will be leaving the day after tomorrow."

"Good night," Jacob said.

"I hope you sleep well," Toby said. Then the three of them headed for Jacob's house. Jacob and Toby leading their horses. I went up to my room.

*   *   *   *

Toby

Alex seemed quiet, barely nodding at what Jacob was saying. He was rehashing the job as if Alex had had the option of going and chose not to.

Nadine was waiting on the porch. Alex took the reins and we walked the horses around to the stable, while Jacob went to greet Nadine. We didn't say anything as we dealt with the horses.

Once I was finished I watched her.

"The wedding?" I asked.

"Simone sent Lady Grace two invitations," Alex answered, "One for her and one addressed to us."

"She isn't worried that we'll wreck this one?" I asked.

"Apparently not," Alex answered, not even cracking a smile. She closed the stall door and came over to where I was standing.

"What happened?" I asked remembering the conversation with Lady Grace.

"Lady Grace believes I should tell Simone I'm Alexandria," Alex answered. Her eyes drifted to the sunset.

"You'll tell her someday," I said, "You've been waiting for the right time. If you had told her last time she would have tried to convince you to stay. Maybe the right time will come up during the wedding festivities."

"You wanna go to the wedding?" Alex asked. The light was visible through the muddiness of those green eyes.

"Of course," I told her, "We have to go and make sure she's marrying the right man this time." The imp twitch started. After a moment she gave in and let the smile come out.

I pulled her into my arms and kissed her. This time she kissed me back.

We came up for breath and Alex stepped back. I let her go.

"So, Lady Grace has figured out that you're female," I said as we started for the house.

"I was gardening when she decided to stop by for a visit earlier," Alex replied, "And she connected things from there."

"Will she tell Simone before you get a chance?"

"She said she wouldn't tell anyone." We went in the back door and up the stairs.

"Good night," Alex said.

"Good night," I replied. And we went into our separate bedrooms.

I undressed and crawled into the freshly made bed. It felt good to be in a real bed. I closed my eyes and tried to sleep.

As soon as I started to relive the kiss I opened my eyes and sat up. I grabbed the deck of cards and played solitaire until I couldn't keep my eyes open.

When I came down stairs, Alex and Nadine were sitting at the table, eating breakfast.

"Good morning," Nadine greeted me.

"Good morning," I replied, as I dished up some breakfast for myself. I sat down. Alex was wearing the old dress, so I figured she was planning to work in the garden.

"Jacob left early this morning," Nadine said, "He muttered something about collecting payment for the job."

"I'll talk to him when he gets back then," I said. I finished breakfast and went out to the barn.

I started cleaning the barn.

Jacob showed up with my money just before noon. I went inside when Nadine called me for lunch. After lunch I went back to work. I worked until supper.

After supper I stopped in and visited Lady Grace. She was still in the dining room. I took the seat across from her.

"Good evening," Lady Grace greeted me.

"Good evening," I responded, "You said you're leaving for the wedding tomorrow?"

"Yes, I was thinking of leaving in the morning," Lady Grace answered, "Then we'll get there with time to settle in before nightfall." I nodded.

"Do you think Alex will tell her sister?" Lady Grace asked.

"If she finds the right time," I answered.

"I promised Simone that I would find her sister and take her home," Lady Grace said.

"And you did. Alex faced Marsden and has been seen by Simone," I replied, "Now it's Alex's turn."

"It just doesn't feel right," Lady Grace said.

"It would feel worse if you told Simone the truth before Alex is ready," I said, "Alex knows her sister well enough to know the right time."

"I guess you're right," Lady Grace said.

"Then I will see you in the morning," I said as I stood up, "Have a good night."

"Good night," Lady Grace said.

I left the hotel and went back to Jacob's house. Alex was sitting at the kitchen table playing solitaire. I watched over her shoulder until she turned and glared at me. I shrugged and backed off.

"Lady Grace wants to leave tomorrow morning," I said.

"Fine," Alex said without looking up.

"Something wrong?" I asked.

"Some self-doubt about whether I really want to go to this wedding," Alex answered.

"Maybe the right time to tell Simone won't come up," I suggested.

"Then I have to listen to Lady Grace pressuring me into telling Simone," Alex said.

"Or maybe the right words will come when the right time does."

"I hope so." Alex gathered up the cards. She shuffled them and started another game. Lots of words went through my mind, but none of them seemed like the right ones.

"I'll see you in the morning," was all I said. Alex nodded. And I went upstairs to the guestroom.

The sun was just coming up when I woke up. I got dressed and went downstairs. Alex had fallen asleep at the table and Nadine was starting breakfast.

"She must've been awake half the night playing solitaire," Nadine commented, "She was playing when Jacob and I came home. We went to bed and thought she was going to do the same."

"If she sleeps through breakfast, I'll have to wake her," I said.

"Going somewhere?" Nadine asked.

"We're traveling to Simone's wedding with Lady Grace," I answered.

"Try to keep Lady Grace from pressuring Alex into revealing herself to her sister," Nadine said, "Alex has been through enough when it comes to her past."

"I only know what she told me," I said.

"She's been better since Marsden died," Nadine said, "But I think she still has nightmares. Putting pressure on her to do the 'right' thing will cause more problems." I nodded. Nadine finished making breakfast and we both ate. Jacob came down just as I finished.

"She's still there?" Jacob asked as he sat down. Nadine got him some breakfast.

"Like this is a shock," Alex said lifting her head. She rubbed the sleep out of her eyes. Nadine got Alex some breakfast while she was still up. Alex and Jacob ate while Nadine finished hers. I started washing the dishes. When everyone was finished Alex helped me with the dishes. Then we collected our belongings. And soon we were sitting on our horses out in front of the hotel beside Lady Grace's coach.

"After this, we need to find a real job," Alex commented.

"Running out of money?" I asked.

"My last hundred," Alex answered.

"No poker games?" I asked.

"My poker money is kept separate," Alex answered, "I'm not foolish enough to leave myself without poker money. I just don't like dipping into it to pay other expenses."

"Your poker money must be quite a lot by now," I commented.

"I don't keep all the money I win at poker as poker money," Alex said, "Just enough."

Lady Grace came out of the hotel; she nodded to us before getting into the stage. And we started out of town.

Lady Grace estimated our time right and we arrived there in the early evening. We stopped at the hotel and Lady Grace got out. The driver took her bags in for her. Alex and I were just about to go around to the stables when Simone came down the street with a man following her. She waved at us. We waved back. The man was an ordinary height and size with black hair.

"Alex and Toby, I'm so glad you could come," Simone said once she was close enough.

"We're hardly going to refuse such an invitation," I answered.

"This is my fiancé, Sheldon," Simone said, "Sheldon, this's Alex and that's Toby."

"Good evening," the man said with a nod. I think he would have removed his hat if he had been wearing one.

"Nice to meet you," Alex said.

"Two weeks until the wedding," Simone said, "So many people

are already here."

"Lady Grace just went into the hotel," I said.

"Where're you two staying?" Simone asked.

"Don't know yet," I answered.

"Mother and Father will let you stay in the barn," Simone said, "I'm sure they won't mind." Alex looked at me; I shrugged.

"Fine by us," Alex said.

"Wonderful," Simone said. She grabbed Sheldon's hand and headed towards the Turner house.

The driver came out.

"Lady Grace says that there aren't any more rooms," the driver said.

"That's fine," I told him, "We've had another offer." The driver nodded and climbed up to his seat and started for the stables. We turned out horses around and followed after Simone and Sheldon.

"I don't get it," I said.

"What?" Alex asked.

"Your parents don't have much for land and definitely no farm," I said, "Why do they have a barn behind their house?"

"Something to do with the previous owners," Alex said, "Probably bought up a farm and then sold parts to people as the town was being built."

"Why not take the barn down?"

"A place to keep their horses," Alex shrugged. Simone was waiting outside when we arrived.

"Mother and Father said it's fine for you to stay in the barn," Simone said.

"Thank you," I said.

"Mother said that if you're hungry there are still some leftovers," Simone said.

"Tell her thank you, but we already ate," Alex said. Simone nodded and then went into the house. We headed for the barn.

"They'll want us to come in for every meal, won't they?" I asked.

"We are their guests," Alex answered, "Anything else would be rude."

"And leaving your hat on?" I asked.

"Is going to be a problem," Alex answered.

"You could cut your hair," I suggested. Not that I thought she should.

"No," Alex said, "I'll figure something out." We went inside the barn with our horses and headed for the house.

Mrs. Turner opened the kitchen door when we got there.

"Good evening," I said.

"Good evening," Mrs. Turner answered, "Please come in." We entered the house. I took my hat off.

"Simone said you had already eaten," Mrs. Turner said.

"We did," Alex said. Mrs. Turner led us into the parlour where Mr. Turner, Simone and Sheldon were sitting.

"Wonderful to see you two again," Mr. Turner said.

"Hopefully there won't be any shooting this time," Alex said. We sat down.

"That was one piece of scum that the world is better without," Mr. Turner said.

"Frank," Mrs. Turner said, her tone was the warning tone that my parents used with each other.

We switched to a different topic and we learned a lot more about Sheldon. He was a carpenter that had moved to town shortly after we left the last time. Simone was in love with him and the only thing missing in her happiness was her sister. But even then she seemed too busy with Sheldon to worry much about that. Sheldon occasionally gave us a suspicious look when Simone went off on how great we were. I don't think stopping a wedding by shooting the groom-to-be was all that great. Maybe it takes seeing it from the bride-to-be's perspective.

After night fell, Sheldon went home, the family went to bed and Alex and I went out to the barn.

"So?" I asked.

"It's been a long day," Alex said, "And I'm not going to judge Sheldon tonight."

"He seemed to be concerned over Simone's hero worship of us," I said.

"As far as he can tell, we're two unattached men that Simone likes," Alex said, "What isn't there to be concerned about when you're supposed to be getting married in two weeks and have heard a few stories about the last man?"

"We'll have to talk to him," I said.

"Another time," Alex said. We went into the barn and up to the loft. Alex lay down and was soon asleep. I laid down a little ways away and went to sleep.

Something woke me, but I couldn't figure out what. The night was silent, then a whimpering came from where Alex lay. I got up and went over to her. She was still asleep. I tried to wake her, but she was in a deep sleep. I picked her up and wrapped her in my arms before lying back down. She was quiet after a while and I fell back asleep.

I woke up slowly. Alex was still in my arms, but I could tell she was just waking up as well. Another yell came from outside.

"You have noisy neighbours," I commented.

"I think that was the call for breakfast," Alex answered. I opened my eyes, the sun was streaming through the cracks. Alex shifted and sat up.

"Looks like it," I said. I sat up and then stood up. I dusted myself off before grabbing my hat. Alex shook her braid out and started brushing her hair.

"I'll be in when I'm finished," Alex said.

"All right," I said, then went down the ladder. I left the barn and headed for the house. Mrs. Turner let me in the kitchen door. I put my hat on a hook and sat down at the dining room table where everyone else was waiting to eat.

"Where's Alex?" Mrs. Turner asked.

"Coming," I answered.

"Then we'll start and he can join us when he gets here," Mr. Turner said. Mrs. Turner brought the food into the dining room and we started to eat. Alex came in ten minutes later, she didn't bother to take her hat off, and sat down. No one said anything.

Alex and I were finished about the same time, but we sat and talked while everyone else finished. Once breakfast was over we headed over to the hotel, Simone came with us.

We found Lady Grace still sitting in the restaurant.

"I wondered where you two went," Lady Grace said once she had greeted Simone.

"We were offered all the comforts of home," I said, "Hardly something you can turn down."

"It’s good that you are comfortable," Lady Grace said, "The

hotel seems to be full."

"People are already showing up for the wedding," Simone said, "Father's family had to travel a ways to get here."

"What are all these people doing while they're here?" Lady Grace asked.

"Mr. Peterson hired a lot of them to pick apples," Simone answered, "He needs his orchard cleared by the end of the week or he won't be able to sell them."

"Perhaps he needs a few more hands," Lady Grace suggested looking at us.

"Didn't come here to be paid two dollars a day to pick apples," Alex answered.

"You've already talked to him?" Lady Grace asked.

"No," Alex answered, "Two dollars is the going rate for fruit pickers."

"Then what do you plan on doing for the next two weeks?" Lady Grace asked.

"Don't know, but we'll find something," I answered.

"Try to find something that isn't violent," Lady Grace suggested.

"Not everything we do involves violence," Alex said.

"How is the wedding coming along?" Lady Grace asked Simone. Simone started to tell Lady Grace all that had been done and what all needed to be done.

Alex and I got bored and left after about half an hour. We had only stepped out the door, when we came on someone in need of help.

The week went by with Alex and I finding various jobs to do for the town folks. We managed to stay out of trouble and without it finding us. Even Lady Grace was surprised.

Sunday Alex slept while everyone else, including me, went to church. She joined us for lunch, to which Lady Grace was invited to as well. After lunch Alex and I sat on the porch watching the world go passed. A while later Sheldon came up the steps.

"Good afternoon," he greeted us; his eyes were still suspicious of us.

"Afternoon," I replied.

"Simone went for a walk with Lady Grace," Alex said. Sheldon nodded.

"You both seem to have a history with Simone," Sheldon said.

"Something to do with shooting the last man she was supposed to marry," Alex said. Sheldon nodded.

"Marsden was a marriage arranged by her parents," I explained, "When they found out he had raped Simone's sister, the wedding was called off and the sheriff arrested him. We were along to make sure the sheriff got Marsden to the jail."

"He tried to escape and between the three of us he died," Alex finished.

"Simone talks about her sister occasionally," Sheldon said, "She seems to think you know her."

"We do," I answered.

"Do you think she'll show up for the wedding?" Sheldon asked.

"Maybe," Alex said, "But she's been gone a long time. Even Simone hasn't seen her since she left." Sheldon nodded.

Lady Grace and Simone were now coming down the street. No one said anything as we watched them come.

"Well, this has been a pleasant afternoon," Lady Grace said when they reached us. Simone hugged Sheldon and he hugged her back.

"So far," Alex answered.

"Have you two done anything today?" Simone asked.

"Six days to work, one day to rest," Alex answered.

"You're starting to sound like an honest citizen," Lady Grace commented. The sound of gunshots came from down the street.

"I thought grass was starting to grow," Alex said as she stood up. I stood up and followed her toward the gunshots. Sheldon ushered Simone and Lady Grace inside.

As we got closer I could see a man that appeared to be drunk standing in the middle of the street waving a gun around. The sheriff and a small group of men were on the far side of him from us. The man's back was turned to us, but every time one of the group tried to move toward him he shot at them. He missed but the group wasn't taking chances that he would continue to do so.

Alex walked up behind the man and knocked him on the back of this head with her gun. He collapsed to the ground as she put her gun away. Then she knelt down and made sure he was alive. The sheriff came over as I reached her.

"Who is he?" Alex asked.

"Marsden's father, Cyrus" the sheriff answered, "Heard that the lady Marsden was supposed to marry was getting married to someone else and decided to show up and ruin the wedding."

"We can't have that happen," I said.

"We can take him to the jail and he can dry out there," the sheriff said.

"I have a different idea," Alex said, "If you don't mind."

"You gonna shoot him?" the sheriff asked.

"No, just talk to him," Alex said, "If it doesn't work, we'll do it your way."

"Fine," the sheriff said.

"Thank you," Alex said, "Now we just need a horse." There were two tied up outside the general store. The sheriff looked at the group of men.

"Robert," the sheriff called. Robert came out of the crowd, I recognized him from the poker game the first time we were in town.

"Can they borrow a horse?" the sheriff asked.

"We'll bring it back tonight or tomorrow morning," Alex said.

"Fine," Robert said. He went over and untied of one the horses and brought it back. Alex and I lifted Cyrus on to the horse and we walked the horse down the street. Once out of town we went to the woods. Far enough in we stopped and tied the horse to a tree. I pulled Cyrus off the horse and laid him down a short distance away. I sat down beside Alex and we waited.

Alex had fallen asleep on my shoulder and night had fallen before Cyrus started to stir. I twitched my shoulder and Alex woke up.

"I think he might be waking up," I said.

"Finally," Alex said, rubbing the sleep out of her eyes. Cyrus sat up blinking at us. He felt for his gun, but we had left it with the sheriff.

"Who the hell are you?" Cyrus asked. Alex stood up.

"I'm the one who hit you over the head and stopped you from ruining a wedding," Alex said.

"The wedding shouldn't happen," Cyrus said, "She should still be mourning Marsden."

"She never married Marsden, because Marsden raped her

sister," Alex said, "He ran from the sheriff rather than face that charge."

"My son is dead," Cyrus said, "Someone has to mourn him."

"Maybe you should have taught him better values," I suggested, "Then he wouldn't be doing things that could get him hung."

"You should be the one mourning him," Alex said, "You're his father and he was your legacy; a very sad one."

"What do you expect of a drunk?" Cyrus demanded.

"To get dry and find your place in this world just like everyone else has," Alex said, "You have no more problems than the rest of and we live without drowning them in alcohol." Cyrus was quiet.

"And what do you think I should do?" Cyrus said.

"There's a man in Cartwheel who hires anyone for different kinds of work," Alex said, "His name is Richard Kelp, he'll keep your money for you until you think you can handle it. He'll even give you a second chance if you end up drunk again."

"Richard Kelp in Cartwheel," Cyrus said.

"Yes," Alex said. Cyrus nodded and then stood up.

"No warnings to stay out of town?" Cyrus asked.

"We aren't the law, but if you go back, you'll end up dealing with the sheriff," Alex said. Cyrus nodded and then walked away, in the direction of Cartwheel. I stood up. Taking the reins of the horse I started back to town with Alex.

We stopped long enough to return the horse and then continued on to the barn. Everyone in the house was asleep. I opened the door to the barn and we found Sheldon sleeping sitting on a bale of hay.

"Should we wake him, hear what he has to say and send him home?" I asked.

"Probably should," Alex said. I got a container of water and poured a little on his face. He woke up fast.

"Far as we know you have your own house," Alex said, the imp twitch was there, watching Sheldon sputter.

"It's a large building, so we'll share if we have to," I said.

"Did you kill him?" Sheldon asked when he had finished sputtering.

"Is that all?" Alex asked, "Personally I thought it might be more interesting."

"The sheriff said he was here to ruin the wedding," Sheldon

said.

"He was, but he won't," Alex said.

"Did you kill him?" Sheldon asked.

"What's it to you? He won't bother the wedding," Alex said.

"I was warned once that a death at the time of a wedding is bad luck," Sheldon replied.

"The two aren't connected," Alex said, "Why don't you just go home?" Sheldon stood up and left the barn. I exchanged questioning looks with Alex then we went up to the loft and went to sleep.

The next morning, when we went to the house our breakfast was sitting on the kitchen table.

"Sheldon's parents are here," Alex said as we started eating.

"And apparently they have a no hat policy," I said.

"Removing your hat is polite," Alex said.

We had just finished and were just about to leave when Mrs. Turner came into the kitchen.

"Good morning," she said.

"Good morning," I replied, "Thank you for breakfast."

"You're welcome," Mrs. Turner said. Simone came in carrying dishes. She smiled when she saw us.

"Good morning," Simone said.

"Good morning," I replied.

"What did you do with Marsden's father?" Simone asked, "Did you kill him?"

"Very morbid out today," Alex commented. A lady came into the kitchen. Her posture was straight, even her expression seemed unbending. Simone put the dishes on the kitchen table and then hurried back into the dining room.

"I didn't realize you had a farm out back," the lady said.

"We don't," Mrs. Turner said, "Alex and Toby are guests, staying out in the barn." The lady set the dishes down on the table.

"I can see why you have them staying out in the barn," the lady said.

"Nice to meet you too, Ma'am," I said removing my hat. Alex opened the door and we left.

"And here, with the exception of last night, I thought Sheldon was normal," I said. Alex burst out laughing.

"Mrs. Kendall is just…" Alex tried to say between fits of laughter.

"Stuffy," I suggested, smiling.

"Proper," Alex finished.

Alex still hadn't quite stopped laughing when we started down the street. We were half way down when the sheriff stopped us.

"So, where'd he go?" the sheriff asked.

"For a long walk," Alex answered, the laughter gone now.

"We sent him to a man who could give him some work and try to keep him dry," I answered.

"I hope he succeeds," the sheriff said.

"So do we," Alex said. The sheriff went on his way. Someone else came up to us with a job. We accepted.

It was suppertime when we headed back to the Turner house.

"You know honest work is tiring," I said.

"Not to mention dirty," Alex said.

"How about the rest of the week off?" I suggested.

"Sounds good, but we might get accused of looking for trouble," Alex said.

"The only time someone has been shooting in town, we dealt with it, not started it," I said. Mr. Turner was standing on the porch and waved us over when he saw us.

"Good evening," I said.

"The sheriff said you dealt with Marsden's father after he tried to shoot up the town," Mr. Turner said.

"We did," Alex answered.

"Did you kill him?" Mr. Turner asked.

"That seems to be the question of the day," Alex said.

"He did try to ruin my daughter's wedding," Mr. Turner said. Mrs. Turner came out.

"Supper is ready," She told Mr. Turner.

"I'll be in there in a minute," Mr. Turner said.

"Yours is on the kitchen table," Mrs. Turner told us.

"Thank you, Ma'am," I said.

"Did you?" Mr. Turner asked.

"No," Alex answered.

"Then where is he?" Mr. Turner asked.

"He took a long walk," Alex answered, "He won't be back."

Alex and I headed around the back of the house.

"Good thing our supper is in the kitchen," I commented, "I would hate to drag this much dirt too far into the house."

"If I could find a safe place to bath I would," Alex said. We went in the kitchen door and sat down at the table.

We had finished eating when we heard people coming into the kitchen. We left before they could see us.

"That may have been rude," Alex said, "But it's better than hearing from Mrs. Kendall again."

"She might have worse things to say about the dirt," I said. We went out to the barn and washed up the best we could. Then we sat outside to enjoy the evening.

Simone and Sheldon came out and over to us when they saw us.

"How are you?" Simone asked.

"Doing well," Alex answered.

"A little sore," I answered.

"What are you planning to do tomorrow?" Simone asked.

"Nothing," Alex answered.

"You haven't planned anything?" Sheldon asked.

"No, we plan to do nothing," I replied. Simone giggled. Alex's imp twitched.

"How're the wedding details going?" Alex asked.

"I get to try on my dress tomorrow," Simone said, "Mother had to send for the lace, but I haven't been allowed to see it yet. And Sheldon's parents are here, so there are only a few guests who still haven't shown up."

"Yes, we met Sheldon's mother this morning," I said.

"That would explain what she was upset about," Sheldon said, "She said something about improper men."

"Confusing us with farm hands was being proper?" Alex asked, "Then I would rather be improper."

"She didn't know," Simone said.

"Your mother doesn't think we are proper guests either," Alex said, "Otherwise we would have to refuse to eat in the dining room."

"She just realized how Sheldon's mother is and figured it would be better," Simone said.

"And she's right," I said.

"Well, I was able to refrain from saying anything this morning,"

Alex said.

"I was brought up to be a proper farmer, what was I supposed to say?" I asked. Alex's bowed her head in laughter.

"What did you say?" Simone asked.

"Perhaps it's better left unsaid this morning," Sheldon said. The kitchen door opened and Mrs. Kendall stood there. Sheldon looked and then sighed.

"I'll be back," Sheldon said then headed for the kitchen.

"She always does that," Simone sighed, "I met her last night and I already don't like her."

"Once the wedding is over then she'll go home and you can have Sheldon all to yourself," I said.

"But it isn't coming soon enough," Simone said.

"I agree," Alex said, "Four days of doing nothing is going to get boring."

"You just want more than a hundred dollars in your pocket," I said.

"I have a hundred and fifty now," Alex said.

"Have you heard any more from Alexandria?" Simone asked. Alex sighed. "I'm sorry, I must sound like a child, but…"

"It isn't that," Alex said.

"Then what is it?" Simone asked concerned. Alex pushed her hat up a little bit as if trying to figure out what to say.

"And you figured this would be easy," Alex told me.

"I didn't say it quite that way," I said.

"What?" Simone asked.

"I am Alexandria," Alex said. Simone was silent, shock slowly coming over her face. "I didn't want anyone to know. First because of Marsden and now because people would expect me to stop doing what I do."

"But why didn't you tell me? I wouldn't have told anyone," Simone said.

"I know, but I wasn't ready," Alex said. Simone shook her head and looked like she might cry. "It wasn't you. And I'm telling you now."

Simone took a deep breath and slowly let it out.

"You don't want me to tell Mother and Father, do you?" Simone asked.

"Please don't," Alex said.

"When will you tell them?" Simone asked.

"Before the wedding," Alex answered.

"I wondered how you were going to get away with wearing your hat in the church," I said.

"Why do you wear it all the time?" Simone asked. Alex pulled her hat off and the braid quickly fell out of the bun and down her back. "Why don't you cut it?"

"I do sometimes, but then I let it grow until it doesn't fit under my hat anymore," Alex answered putting her hat back on without putting her hair back under it.

"When I saw you sitting with Lady Grace in the restaurant I thought there was something familiar about you, but you sound so different and you've changed," Simone said.

"Presents from Marsden before he left me for dead," Alex replied, "But he's dead now."

"You got to shoot him," Simone said.

"With half the satisfaction of watching him hang," Alex said, "Shooting him means there are stories, but no one is sure. With a trial everyone would know what he did."

"I'm supposed to be too much of a lady to even say I'm happy he's dead," Simone said.

"No one stops you from feeling glad," Alex said, "That's more important than being able to say it."

"But to have the freedom to say it," Simone said.

"Even dressed up as a man doesn't mean I can say everything I think," Alex said, "Like with Mrs. Kendall, there're still certain expectations."

"If you told her walking on your hands was proper, she'd find someway to do it and expect you to do it too," Simone said.

"She'll leave after the wedding," I said.

"So will you two," Simone said.

"I'm sure we can find time to stop in any time we're close by," I said.

"I should go see if I can save Sheldon," Simone said. She headed for the house. Alex leaned back and closed her eyes.

"One down, two to go," I said.

"Yeah," Alex said, "Makes me glad that Sheldon's parents are staying here."

"Why?" I asked.

"Is a barn a proper place for a lady to stay?" Alex asked.

"Sure," I answered, "Of course your parents probably see things differently."

"Usually," Alex said. I didn't say anything else and we sat there in quiet.

After the sunset, we went into the barn and went to sleep.

The next morning I woke up to find that Alex was gone. As I left the barn, I found Alex was sitting outside, eating an apple.

"You're up early," I commented.

"Didn't sleep much," Alex said.

"Coming for breakfast?" I asked.

"Already ate," Alex said, holding up the apple.

"How many of those?" I asked.

"This is my second, but the third one is in my pocket," Alex said.

"From Peterson's orchard?" I asked.

"Not many other places to get apples around here," Alex answered, "Besides he grows the best apples."

"You've been eating apples all last week," I said.

"Same apples," Alex said, "But I only have one left. And I can't take anymore because they all got picked."

"I'm going to eat breakfast," I said.

"Go ahead," Alex said, "Be careful of Sheldon's mother." I went into the house and my breakfast was on the table. I could hear the voices of everyone else in the dining room. I ate. Just as I was finishing, Simone came into the kitchen carrying out the breakfast dishes.

"Where's Alex?" Simone asked.

"Out back eating apples," I answered.

"She's still stealing apples?" Simone said.

"Apparently certain habits don't change," I said.

"The dress maker is supposed to be here with my dress this morning. I know she doesn't want anyone to know, but I was hoping she could be there since you hadn't planned on doing anything else." Mrs. Turner came into the kitchen.

"I'll tell her," I said, "Good morning. Mrs. Turner."

"Good morning," Mrs. Turner said. I went outside. Alex was still sitting by the barn.

"Simone invites you to see her wedding dress this morning," I said. She looked up at me.

"That'll look good to Sheldon's mother," Alex said, "A gunslinger who sleeps out in the barn is invited to see the wedding dress before the wedding."

"I want to see her face when she hears that," I said.

"Then come with me," Alex said.

"I thought that was bad luck," I said.

"Only if the groom sees it before the wedding and you aren't taking Sheldon's place," Alex said.

"Is that an order or a fact?" I asked.

"A fact," Alex said, "If you had any interest in my sister I would know about it by now." Alex got up and we wandered around to the front of the house and sat on the porch. We said good morning to Mr. Turner when he went off to work, and to Mr. Kendall when he went out and we let the dressmaker in when she arrived. We also followed her inside. Mrs. Turner stayed with us as Simone and the dressmaker went into the bedroom. Mrs. Kendall seemed to have disappeared. Ten minutes later the dressmaker came back out.

"I need her to move as little as possible but she wishes to show it off," the woman said. Mrs. Kendall appeared from the kitchen.

"It's bad luck to show it off," Mrs. Kendall said.

"This's Simone's choice," Mrs. Turner said. Alex and I stood up and went into the bedroom while they continued to talk about it. Simone was standing in front of a mirror in a beautiful white lace gown.

"What do you think?" Simone asked, smiling.

"Beautiful," I said then stood back.

"Close, but something is missing," Alex said.

"The veil and train are too much to put on for today," Simone said. Alex took her hat off and put it on Simone's head.

"There that looks better," Alex said. Simone smiled at her reflection of the white dress with the black, dirty hat. Alex let the imp twitch turn into a smile.

"What do you think?" Alex asked me.

"Needs cleaning, then it would be perfect," I replied.

"I think it looks good," Simone said, "But that doesn't mean I'm going to exchange my veil for it."

"No, I'll need my hat back before then," Alex said. They were giggling like girls when Mrs. Turner came into the room. She did the double take and then shook her head in amusement.

"Good thing, Anna decided to stay out there," Mrs. Turner said, "She would have a fit."

"She's no fun," Simone said.

"But I don't believe the hat works with the dress," Mrs. Turner said.

"Then I'll take it back," Alex said taking it off Simone's head. She coiled her hair up before putting her hat back on.

"Do you have a dress for the wedding?" Mrs. Turner asked.

"Yes," Alex answered.

"Is it suitable for a wedding?" Mrs. Turner asked.

"I may've spent the last four years dressed as a man, but I still know how to dress like a lady," Alex said.

"Then we need to get Simone out of the dress so the dressmaker can put the finishing touches on it," Mrs. Turner said. Mrs. Turner led the way as Alex and I left the room. The dressmaker went back into the bedroom to help Simone out of the dress. We sat down in the parlour.

"What are you going to do for the rest of the week?" Mrs. Turner asked.

"Nothing," Alex answered.

"Good then maybe I can get your help with some of the wedding preparations," Mrs. Turner said.

"I suppose so," Alex said.

"Excellent," Mrs. Turner said then left the room. She came back with a list and gave us jobs off it for each of the next three days and one for this afternoon.

Simone came out and the dressmaker left.

"I wish it was Saturday already," Simone said.

"Be careful what you wish for," Alex said.

"Why? Because it might come true?" Simone asked.

"Because when it comes true it will be twisted in a way you don't like," Alex said.

"I thought you didn't believe in all that stuff," Simone said.

"I don't, but I don't wish for things either," Alex said. Simone made a face at Alex; Alex stuck her tongue out in return.

"Stop it," Mrs. Turner said. A knock came at the door. Mrs. Turner went and answered it. A moment later she and Lady Grace entered the parlour.

"I was wondering where everyone was," Lady Grace said.

"We were invited to see the wedding dress," Alex replied.

"And is it beautiful?" Lady Grace asked.

"Not quite perfect, but close," I answered.

"Not quite?" Lady Grace asked.

"She didn't try on the veil," Mrs. Turner replied.

"We found a good replacement," Alex said.

"She'll wear the veil to the wedding," Mrs. Turner said.

"And what was this alternative?" Lady Grace asked.

"Alex's hat," Simone answered.

"Where's Mrs. Kendall?" Alex asked.

"In the guestroom doing some work on her dress," Mrs. Turner said, "The door is closed."

"I haven't met her, what is she like?" Lady Grace asked.

"Very proper," Mrs. Turner said.

"Extremely proper," Simone said.

"She mistook me and Toby for farm hands," Alex said.

"Some days that isn't hard," Lady Grace said.

"This was shortly after breakfast," I said, "We hadn't even started rolling in the dirt for the day. But we were wearing our guns."

"Strange," Lady Grace said.

"I don't think she's sympathetic," Alex said.

"Doesn't seem that way," I replied, "If you'll excuse us then." I said standing up. Alex stood up as well.

"You're excused," Mrs. Turner said. We went into the kitchen.

"So, what now?" Alex asked.

"We're going to make lunch," I said.

"Fine," Alex said.

We got started.

No one disturbed us, but we could hear them talking in the parlour. It was half an hour to twelve when someone in the parlour realized what time it was. Mrs. Turner rushed into the kitchen, came to a dead stop. She stared at us. The food was cooking and we had a hand of poker going.

"Yes?" Alex asked.

"Lunch?" Mrs. Turner asked.

"Is cooking," Alex said. Mrs. Turner sighed.

"I got so busy talking…" Mrs. Turner said.

"We thought we would pay for the rent on the barn by making lunch," I said.

"Thank you," Mrs. Turner said.

"You can go back to talking if you like," Alex said as she placed her cards down to win the hand.

"I think I will," Mrs. Turner said before turning around and leaving the kitchen. I gathered up the cards and shuffled.

Mrs. Turner came back into the kitchen about the time lunch was ready; Simone followed her.

"Frank is home," Mrs. Turner said.

"Along with Mr. Kendall," Simone added.

"It's all ready to go on the table," I said. Mrs. Turner and Simone picked up the dishes and went into the dining room. Alex sat back down at the table. I sat down as well and we started to eat.

"Shall we start on the wedding project after lunch?" I asked.

"I have something I want to do first," Alex said, "But after that, sure."

"I'll help with the dishes then," I said.

Once she was finished eating, Alex left.

*   *   *   *

Mr. Peterson

I had just stepped out on my porch when I could see someone coming up the road to my house. That Alexandria girl, what did she want? She stopped before the steps.

"So, what does the apple thief want?" I asked.

"To pay for the apples," Alexandria answered.

"To pay for the apples," I repeated, "You travel the world dressed as man and now you want to pay for the apples."

"I can keep my money, if you don't want me to pay for them," Alexandria offered.

"How about a different deal?" I asked.

"As in what?" Alexandria asked.

"I'm getting old. I've got five more years in this orchard, maybe," I said, "You're young. I'll sell you the orchard and you can eat all the apples you want."

"I'm not sure I'm ready to give up traveling and buy land,"

Alexandria said.

"And I'm not ready to give up my orchard, but the time for both is coming fast," I said, "You buy it now, I work it until I die and then you take it over."

"And what about your children, Mr. Peterson?" Alexandria asked, "Wouldn't they want the land?"

"My son, Thayer, wouldn't know what to do with it," I said, "He's so busy with city life. Never understood that without the farmer and growers there is no city life. He'd probably sell the land to someone who will chop the trees down and expand the town in this direction. No, it's better in the hands of someone who cares what happens to it."

"And you think I'm that person?" Alexandria asked.

"Wouldn't make this offer if I didn't," I answered, "Besides if you marry that farmer boy who's your partner, he'll be comfortable here."

"I only have a hundred and fifty dollars," Alex said.

"Done," I said, "I don't need the money. I already have the money from this year's harvest."

"And you'll have the money from next year's harvest until you die," Alexandria said.

"Exactly," I said. Alexandria took out some bills and handed them up to me. I took them. "I'll go to town tomorrow and get the paperwork cleaned up."

"I'll see the lawyer tomorrow evening then," Alexandria said.

"A pleasure doing business with someone who understands," I said.

"Why turn down a deal that can't be beat?" Alexandria said, then headed back to town. I smiled; she would be the perfect owner. Thayer had hated the taste of apples since he took a bite of one for the first time. An orchard owner who didn't eat what they grew was as bad as a gambler that couldn't hold cards.

* * * *

Toby

I had finished the dishes and was sitting on the porch when Alex finally showed up.

"Finished whatever it was?" I asked.

"Pretty much," Alex said.

"Then shall we deal with the wedding project?" I asked.

"Well, since we've been talked into it, sure," Alex said. I stood up and we headed off to do the job.

The next three days were spent avoiding Mrs. Kendall, doing jobs related to the wedding and giving Alex and Simone some sister time. Alex was still having nightmares, but she was much happier. And I pretty sure I'm falling for my partner.

Friday night we were sitting outside the barn watching the sunset.

"After tomorrow Simone will be married," Alex said, "She wished it would come faster. I think she might've gotten that wish."

"You were kept busy, time went faster," I said. Rather than just the imp twitch Alex smiled.

"Four years ago it could have been me and Marsden," Alex said. The smile disappeared.

"But it wasn't," I said.

"True, but sometimes it doesn't seem like four years," Alex said, "And sometimes it feels like centuries ago."

"Would you give anything for things to be different?" I asked.

"No," Alex said, "Too many good things have happened during those years. Simone told Sheldon that I was her sister. Apparently he just about went into shock. But he was happy to hear it."

"He no longer needs to be suspicious of you," I said.

"There's no point being suspicious of you either, but I suppose he has to figure that out on his own," Alex said.

"After tomorrow he shouldn't be worried about anyone," I said.

"Think that'll stop him?" Alex asked.

"No, he sees Simone as the most beautiful woman in the world and is scared that every other man sees the same thing," I said, "Some of the rest of us don't see her in the same light."

"You ever think about marrying?" Alex asked.

"Maybe someday," I answered. The last of the light disappeared. "In the meantime I'm tired." I stood up and went into the barn. I was climbing the ladder when Alex came in and shut the door. She followed me up and we lay down in our separate spots.

And I went to sleep.

It didn't feel like I had been asleep very long when I woke up to Alex whimpering. I went over and took her in my arms. She woke enough to bury her face in my shirt and start crying. I held her close. She finally fell back asleep. I sat there with her in my arms for a long time, just watching her sleep.

The sun was shining into the barn when I woke up. Alex was still sleeping. I didn't move and let her sleep.

Someone called out that breakfast was ready. Alex moved, rolled off me and sat up. I sat up.

"I'm gonna be a few minutes," Alex said.

"All right," I said as I stood up. I dusted myself off and headed for the house. Breakfast was sitting at the kitchen table as usual. Alex came in five minutes later.

We had just finished when Mrs. Turner brought the dishes from the dining room. Mrs. Kendall came in with dishes as well. She looked us over as if we were covered from head to toe in mud.

"I hope you plan to clean up if you're coming to the wedding," Mrs. Kendall said. Alex smelled her sleeve and gave me a shrug.

"I didn't think that was necessary," Alex said.

"I don't know," I replied, "I was thinking of falling into some water at some point. Might as well go in clothes and all, then I don't have to get laundry done for another month." Mrs. Kendall looked horrified and she hurried back into the dining room.

"Don't torture the guests," Mrs. Turner said.

"She asked for it," Alex said.

"Even if they ask for it," Mrs. Turner added.

"With all these orders you're starting to sound like my mother," Alex said.

"Good," Mrs. Turner said.

"We'll be at the hotel until just before the ceremony," I told her before she went back into the dining room. We left through the kitchen door and headed for the hotel. Lady Grace was coming down the stairs as we entered.

"There you two are," she said.

"With orders to clean up," Alex said.

"Orders from whom?" Lady Grace asked as she led us back up the stairs.

"Mrs. Kendall," I answered.

"That lady needs surgery to remove the rod her parents shoved up her butt," Lady Grace said.

"Lady Grace! Your language," Alex said.

"That's as polite as I can put it," Lady Grace said, "She doesn't even have a sense of humour." Lady Grace handed me a key and pointed me at a door before going down the hall with Alex. I unlocked the door and went inside. A tub with pipes was in one part of the room and a clean set of clothes was laid out on the bed, just as Lady Grace agreed to do.

It was half an hour until the ceremony and I was still waiting for Alex and Lady Grace to come down. Sitting in the lobby I had seen other guests already leave, but the ladies were taking their time.

Lady Grace came down. She was wearing a fancy dress that would probably top any other guest's, if not in looks then in cost to make.

"Has Alex come down?" Lady Grace asked.

"Not yet," I answered.

"I'll go check on her then," Lady Grace said. She was just about to start up when Alex came into view. Her hair was up in a way that I had seen other fashionable women do theirs and her dress would not have looked so beautiful on any other woman. In my opinion she out shone every other woman in the world. She glided down the stairs. Lady Grace stood back.

"Shall we go then?" I asked.

"Yes," Lady Grace said. Lady Grace started for the door. I offered Alex my arm, she wrapped hers around it and we followed. We took the stage rather than walking distance to the church because Lady Grace didn't want us to get dirty before the wedding.

Going into the church we were shown to a pew near the front. Lady Grace saw someone she wanted to talk to and went over to her.

"You looked like you were having trouble closing your mouth for a minute," Alex said softly, "But you recovered fairly quickly."

"When I agreed to come I didn't think I would be escorting the most beautiful lady here," I replied in the same volume. She smiled, but I could see a bit of the blush creeping up her neck.

Mr. and Mrs. Kendall were shown in and seated a couple pews

in front of us. Mrs. Kendall turned around to see who was here. She looked at us. I nodded my acknowledgment. She did a double take and then her mouth fell open. She stared like a landed fish for a minute before her husband poked her. She turned back around. Alex giggled behind her hand.

"I almost thought she wasn't going to recognize us for a second there," I said.

"She was looking for two farm hands, remember," Alex said. Lady Grace sat down with us.

"Looks like it will be a full church," Lady Grace said.

"Well, we made quite the impression on one guest," I said.

"Who?" Lady Grace asked.

"Mrs. Kendall forgot her manners about staring until her husband elbowed her," Alex said, "It's almost like she didn't expect us to clean up after she gave us the order to."

"I can imagine," Lady Grace said.

"It doesn't take much to imagine," I said, "If you've ever seen a landed fish." Lady Grace took a deep breath and tried to keep a straight face. She barely succeeded.

The rest of the church filled and the last person had been seated when the organ started. The preacher moved to his place, then the groom came in and took his place. Another minute of music and everyone stood up. We stood as well and then Simone went passed us with Mr. Turner escorting her. He took her to Sheldon, handed her over and as he sat down, so did the rest of us. The preacher gave a sappy, but boring miniature sermon on marriage. Then he asked the important questions of Simone and Sheldon, who answered appropriately and were then told that Sheldon could kiss the bride. Which he did with applauds from the crowd. Then Simone and Sheldon went back up the aisle, where I knew they would be taken away for a photograph and meet the guests back at the hotel lobby for the reception.

The guests slowly made their way out of the church. Alex and I stayed seated with Lady Grace until most of the crowd had cleared. Then we walked back to the hotel.

There was food, drinks, a band and lots of people. A good time seemed to be had by all, especially the bride and groom. They couldn't stop and talk to anyone for more than a minute before they had to move on. They did take some time to dance though.

I spent the evening in Alex's company. We talked to people, ate and danced some. About the usual supper hour the clouds came in and it started pouring rain. As the party began to wind down I stepped out onto the covered sidewalk. Sheldon and Simone had been given the use of Lady Grace's stage to get home and everyone else was slowly leaving as well.

It felt good to be out in the fresh air. Alex and I were to help clean up, but I needed a break first. Alex came out and watched the rain with me. I wrapped my arms around her and we stood there for a long time. Finally she started to get chilly so we went inside and helped clean up. By the time all cleaned up, most much everyone had left Alex and I went up and changed back into our clothes we had worn this morning. We left the fancy clothes with Lady Grace and walked back to the barn. We were soaking wet when we got there.

"If you were serious about falling into water so you wouldn't have to do laundry, the weather certainly provided the water," Alex said.

"I wasn't serious," I said, "Laundry isn't that hard to do." Alex went up to the loft and I stayed below. I stripped off my wet clothes and put some dry ones on. Then I found some place to hang them to dry. Alex hung her wet clothes up too. Then she lay down and went to sleep. I went up to the loft and lay down in my usual spot. It seemed like forever before I went to sleep.

I woke up to the sound of Alex moving around. She was down below grooming with her horse. It was still raining outside. I got up and went below.

"Good morning," Alex said.

"Morning," I said.

"The clothes we hung out to dry smell like barn," Alex said.

"We'll wear them outside and let the rain wash them again," I said.

"Shall we go to breakfast wearing them as well?" Alex asked.

"No, we'll spare your parents that much," I said. She had finished with her horse. We put our coats on and headed for the house. We found Mrs. Turner still busy in the kitchen trying to get breakfast ready.

"Good morning," Alex said. Mrs. Turner just about jumped out of her skin.

"I didn't hear you," Mrs. Turner said. We hung up our coats on the hook by the door.

"You seemed preoccupied," I said. Mrs. Turner went back to her cooking.

"When are you leaving?" Mrs. Turner asked.

"After breakfast," Alex answered.

"Already?" Mrs. Turner asked.

"Have to," I answered, "Otherwise we might start to grow roots."

"Would that be a bad thing?" Mrs. Turner asked.

"Sure," I said, "We don't have any money left to pay for the expenses those roots cause."

"Considering your lifestyle would you ever have the money to settle down?" Mrs. Turner asked.

"Hopefully, when we get that far," I answered.

"There isn't a place for us here right at the moment," Alex said, "You don't need two bored gunslingers in town. It'd bring all kinds of trouble that no one wants to deal with."

"Perhaps if you put your guns away," Mrs. Turner started.

"And do what?" I asked, "The skills we have lend themselves to gunslinger. Sure, I could do the work of a farmer, but it's the wrong type of soil around here. It wouldn't work."

"But your work is dangerous," Mrs. Turner said.

"So are a lot of other things," Alex said. Mrs. Turner nodded. She served us breakfast and then took the rest to the dining room. We ate, then went back to the barn. We changed back into the clothes from yesterday. We mounted our horses and started toward the edge of town.

We passed Lady Grace on her way to breakfast. She waved and we waved goodbye back.

"Should we say good bye to Simone as well?" I asked.

"Probably should," Alex said.

"But will we?" I asked.

"Remember the conversation with my mother?" Alex asked, "Simone may be mad anyway but I think it best if we leave her alone." And few people watched us ride by. When we reached the edge of town we continued on to whatever adventure awaited us next.

VULTURE
CHAPTER 12

Toby

A week later, we had begun to leave behind the trees and get into cactus country. We had stopped for lunch when Alex spotted the vulture. It was circling above something, but it hadn't landed. After we were finished lunch we headed in the direction of the vulture.

As we got close, we could see a man lying on the sand underneath the circling vulture.

"Waiting for the man to die," Alex said.

"Doesn't look like a long wait," I said pointing to the trial of dried blood in the sand. The man had been moving forward while still bleeding. We followed the blood trail to where he lay. I got off my horse and bent over him. He was still breathing, and his wound had started to close, but he was seemed have no water, not to mention any equipment. I opened my canteen and poured a little down his throat. He gulped it.

"No gun, no gear and lying out in the desert," Alex said, "With a wound that bad, it sounds like a dump job." I gave the man a little more water. He swallowed and then coughed.

"Who…you?" the man asked.

"I'm Toby and that's my partner, Alex," I answered him then gave him more water. I slowly gave him most of my canteen before he could talk properly.

"Name's Harry Porter," the man said, "My brother-in-law, Robert Stewart, said he had a job for me. Said I just had to accompany some of his men and bring back something he sent them to get. Said he'd pay off my debts. Then my wife and I could live in peace. I found the map. I took it and started after the treasure myself. He followed me and shot me down. He thought he found the map and left. I tried to get back to town, but I'm dying. Bullet wound is still bleeding."

"We need to get him back to town," I told Alex, "At least he can see his wife before he dies."

"Sounds like a good idea," Alex said. Harry started coughing, this time he coughed up blood and spit it out on to the sand. "But we should hurry."

"You two really gonna take me back to Mary?" Harry asked.

"The least we can do," Alex answered. Harry dug into his pants and pulled out a packet of papers.

"Even the thought matters more than the world to me," Harry said, "Robert is going to be back for me when he finds out he doesn't have the map, but you treated me well. It only caused me trouble anyway." Harry handed me the packet. I took it and gave it to Alex. I helped Harry up on to my horse and tied him in position so that he wouldn't fall off. I took the reins and got up behind Alex. We started in the direction that Harry had been headed.

It took a day before we saw any buildings. Once we saw them I got off Alex's horse and started to walk mine. Harry was still alive, but he was coughing up more blood than ever and was bent over the neck of my horse.

We stopped at a well just outside town. A woman was there drawing some water.

"Where's the doctor?" I asked her.

"There's a sign over his office," the woman said, "On the first big building."

"Thank you," I said and we continued and found it just as she said there was a sign over the door that said doctor's office. The doctor came out as we were untying Harry.

"What happened?" the doctor asked.

"He was shot and then ran out of water," I answered as Alex and I carried him up onto the sidewalk.

"Harry?" the doctor said, when he saw who we were holding.

Several heads turned our direction and a woman dropped her parcels to run over.

"Harry!" she cried, she tried to take him from us, crying all the time.

"Mary," the doctor said gently, "Let these two men bring him into my office and we'll see what I can do to save him." The woman withdrew enough for us to get inside. We laid him down where the doctor indicated.

"Harry," Mary sobbed.

"Mary," Harry's voice was quiet.

"I'm here, Harry," Mary said taking his hand.

"I love you," Harry managed to say. Then the doctor took over, but I could see that Harry was pretty much gone now. We had brought him back in time to say good-bye to his wife. Alex and I left the doctor's office. A man wearing a fancy suit was standing outside.

"I'm grateful to you for bringing my sister's husband back," the man said, "I would be willing to give you something for your troubles."

"You're Robert Stewart?" Alex asked.

"Yes," the man answered.

"Save your money," Alex said. I went over and picked up the rope and put it away.

"I'm surprised," Robert said, "Most people are willing to take something for a good deed." Mary came out of the doctor's office, tears streaming down her face. She turned to us.

"Thank you for bringing him back, even if it's only to be buried," Mary said. Then she broke down completely. Robert looked pained then patted Mary's shoulder as if he wasn't sure how to comfort a woman. I have sisters too, but I learned early on how to handle it when they got upset. I caught Alex's nod toward the horses.

"We're sorry to be the bearers of the bad news, and for your loss," I said. Then Alex and I got on to our horses. We rode through town and back out into the open on the other side.

"She's going to worse off for all of this," Alex said.

"Seeing how her brother was dealing with her, I agree with you," I said, "Her husband is dead, his debt is still unpaid and now her family isn't going to help her."

"Do you think what Harry said was true?" Alex said taking out the packet.

"About the treasure map?" I asked.

"Yes," Alex said.

"You have the packet," I replied. Alex opened it slowly and looked inside. She pulled out a piece of paper and put the packet away. Alex unfolded it and studied it. After a moment she handed it to me. I looked it over. It was a map. Everything was labelled and a there was a spot marked where treasure was supposed to be buried.

"Looks like a treasure map to me," I said as I handed it back, "The one Robert was willing to shoot his brother-in-law over."

"You want to go back and give it to Robert?" Alex asked.

"No," I said, "It just means we'll have to be extra careful."

"We'll have to give some to Mary Porter," Alex said.

"That I agree with," I said. Alex studied the map for a while as we rode.

"He was headed the wrong direction," Alex said, "Either that or he knew about a short cut."

"Why?" I asked.

"According to this map and our position, we're headed in the right direction," Alex said, "But we found Harry on the other side of town."

"I don't know," I replied.

"Maybe we'll find out, maybe we won't," Alex said putting the map away.

We started across the desert, stopping whenever we could get food and water and traveling at night as much as possible. We tried to avoid meeting up with any of Robert's men, but they picked up our trail. However, we lost them three days later and never saw them again.

Part way through the second week, we reached a mountain range. Alex led us to the mountain pass opening and along the trail.

"Looks like others travel this road," Alex commented.

"Good, then if there's trouble, help shouldn't be too far away," I said.

"Or we could be farther from help because those who cause the trouble use the trail," Alex said, "We need to keep on alert."

Late in the afternoon I could see something on the trail a head of us. As we got closer, I realized that it was a man lying there. He looked like he hadn't seen civilization in months, let alone water. When we stopped by him, I took my gun out and kept watch as Alex turned him over. He was dead from a bullet that went through his heart.

"Blood is still fresh," Alex said, "And I don't see any horses around."

"Or any gear," I commented, "Another dump?"

"Maybe," Alex said getting back on her horse, "But we should stay alert."

"Definitely," I said as we started forward.

A while later we heard the sound of a cart ahead of us. Going around the next bend we could see a wagon with four passed out men and a dozen boxes in the back and one lone driver. Most of the men were dirty and would have matched the corpse. As we started to catch up to the wagon the driver noticed us. He seemed slightly wary of our presence. Alex took the lead and we started to go single file beside the wagon. I could smell booze from the men in the back.

"Long way from anywhere, aren't you?" the driver said once we were along side of him.

"But the only way to our destination," I replied.

"Not much in the way of destinations ahead," the driver said.

"Every road leads somewhere," I said, "By the way I think you lost a passenger a ways back on the trail. He must have been really drunk for him to fall off the wagon." The driver looked over his shoulder at his passengers, he seemed to count them.

"Well, I guess I must have lost one," the driver said, "I'm sure he'll wake up and find his own way. It isn't far."

"Good luck then," I said as we passed the wagon and went a head. We had gotten a little ways a head when the first gunshot rang out. I ducked and the bullet missed me by just a little. The second and third shots came immediately afterward, both missed.

"That just isn't nice," I commented and we both pulled out our guns. I shot back at the man, but I missed. Alex shot and the driver was quiet for a moment then started swearing.

"I think I hit him," Alex said.

"Better shooting than him," I said, "Unfortunately, also better than me."

"Shall we go back and ask why he decided to shoot at us?" Alex asked.

"Because he was too nervous to do the smart thing and leave us alone," I answered as we started back to the wagon. The driver was holding his bleeding hand. His gun was lying on the ground next to the wagon.

"We were just trying to be helpful," I told him, "Hardly a reason to start firing shots at us." The drunks in the back of the wagon were still out. They were going to have a hell of a headache in the morning. The driver continued to swear at us. Alex slowly raised her gun to his eye level; he shut his mouth.

"We would have just gone on our way without minding your business," Alex said, "But now that you have our attention, I think we'll stick our noses in." I dismounted from my horse, picked up the driver's gun and got into the back of the wagon. I stepped over the drunks to the boxes. I opened the first one I came to. It was full of gold coins. I picked one out and looked at it.

"From the robbery of what's-his-face from up north who was trying to run the town like he was a king," I commented.

"How can you tell?" Alex asked.

"He had his face stamped on the coins," I said, "People are still willing to take them, but only for the amount of gold they're worth. A couple have been showing up here and there since the robbery a couple months ago." I dropped the coin back into the box.

"How much was stolen?" Alex asked.

"Probably the first two of these boxes," I said as I opened the next one. It held the same gold coins. I opened the third box, inside were gold bars. I took one out and looked it over. It was unmarked. I put it back and closed all the boxes before looking in the other nine. They were gold bars, all unmarked.

"Looks like they were all stocked for the winter," I said getting out of the wagon with a length of rope that was back there. I tied the driver's hands behind his back. I made him to move to the back of the wagon and then tied his feet. I shoved a piece of cloth in his mouth before sitting in the driver's seat. Alex had grabbed my horse's reins and we started off again, with Alex leading the way.

Night fell without any place to camp. We stopped anyway. We

used the rope to tie up the drunks and removed their weapons. We also checked the driver's ropes. Then we took turns on watch. In the morning we checked the ropes and then started on our way. The drunks slowly woke up as the morning wore on. I could tell by the moaning without have to look back and checking on them. When we stopped for lunch we gave each some water. We did the same when we stopped for the night as well.

About mid-morning of the next day we left the mountain pass. By afternoon we could see a town ahead. It was small, with mostly mud buildings, but a few that were made of wood. Everyone stared at us, but no one stopped. People looked like honest, hard-working people, so this wasn't likely to be the robber's final destination. We stopped in front of a building that looked to be the general store, it was one of the three wooden buildings. There was a bulletin board next to the door to the general store. There were six pictures there. Five of them matched the men hogtied in the back of the wagon. And the sixth one looked like the man that was rotting along the mountain pass. Rewards were listed under each name.

And man stepped out of the building next to the general store. I would have taken him for a gunslinger, but he had a silver star pinned on his chest. Alex tied our horses to the hitching post. The sheriff walked to the back of the wagon to see what we had in there. Then he stopped and looked at us. Another man came down the street. This one was wearing a suit. My guess was that he was mayor.

"May I enquire where you found these men?" the sheriff asked.

"The mountain pass," I answered.

"And what were you planning to do with them?" the sheriff asked. The mayor stopped close by, he was buzzing with energy.

"Don't know," Alex answered, "If you have a use for them you can have them." The sheriff's eyebrows went up.

"You tied them up and dragged them this far without planning what to do anything with them?" the sheriff asked.

"The driver shot at us while the others were passed out drunk," I said, "We don't have any use for them, we just didn't want to have them try to shoot us again."

"Perhaps you can help me put them into cells in the jail," the sheriff indicated the building he had come out of, "And then you won't even have to worry about them escaping."

"Sounds good," Alex said. We got down and the three of us moved the men to cells in the jail. Once we were finished the mayor congratulated us on such a capture and the sheriff gave us the reward money. Then Alex and I headed next door to the general store, where people were either helpful or stayed out of our way. We purchased our supplies and went back out to where we left the horses. We made one last stop to fill our water containers before we left town. I was still driving the wagon and Alex was leading both horses.

"For a job we didn't expect to take on, this has been very profitable," I commented once we had left the town, "Gold from robbers, reward money from turning in the robbers and then the treasure we started out looking for in the first place."

"What are you gonna do with your half?" Alex asked.

"Find someplace to keep it until I need it," I answered, "I don't exactly have a lot to spend it on. What about you?"

"I don't know," Alex answered, "I have pretty much everything I want."

"And not that long ago you were complaining you were broke," I said.

"Yes, but that's the life of a gunslinger," Alex said.

"Not for us anymore," I said.

"Does that mean you want to give up the life of a gunslinger?" Alex asked.

"Not yet," I answered, "Having money shouldn't change everything." Alex nodded, but didn't respond.

A week later we came upon another set of mountains. This time we followed the map to the entrance of a mine instead of going through the mountains.

"I wonder how they found this place," I said as we stepped into the mine entrance having secured the horses.

"It looks like someone put a whole lot of work into it," Alex said.

"Maybe Robert dug it out and then couldn't come back for the rest of it," I suggested.

"Theory seems real, except that Robert didn't dig this," Alex said, "He didn't know which direction to send his men to come after us, so he has never been here before. Second, I can't see the man getting his hands dirty for anything and getting men out this far would be difficult."

I could see the tunnel going straight back for ten feet and then there was a bend in it. After that I couldn't see anything.

"You think he stole the map?" I asked.

"Or found it some how," Alex answered. We went down the tunnel. We reached the bend in the tunnel and turned. The light wasn't as strong but I could see that the tunnel was filled with crates blocking anyone from going any farther.

"That's strange," I commented.

"Let's see what's in them," Alex said, "but be careful."

"Definitely," I said. We each pulled a crate into the light. I pried the lid off. The minute the light hit the contents it glittered back. The crate was filled with gold bricks. The bricks looked a little rough, like the person making them used whatever tools they had on hand. Alex's crate held the same thing.

"Looks like we found the treasure," I said.

"Now we need to get it back to civilization," Alex said.

"How about taking it to Dustcloud and keeping it there," I suggested, "And we can change most of the gold into cash as we need it."

"Sounds fine," Alex said, "We'll head there first and exchange a few before going back to visit Mary Porter."

"Agreed," I said. I went and got the wagon. I had the horse back up into the tunnel so that we could load the wagon and drive out when we were finished. Alex and I started to stack the crates in the wagon along with the boxes that were already in there. Once we had filled the wagon, we put the piece of canvas from the bottom of the wagon over the contents and tied it down. Then we rested for the night.

The next morning we started the journey back. We stopped again in the town to get more supplies and water. The sheriff watched us and I could tell he was wondering where we had gone. Then we went on our way. It took us four days to make it through the mountain pass. Once on the other side we headed for Dustcloud.

A month later we rolled into town. We stopped at the mansion Lady Grace calls home when she isn't traveling around. She wasn't home yet from the wedding, but the butler let us in and gave us permission to use the shed on the grounds. We put moved all the crates from the wagon into the shed. The butler watched us, but didn't help. Then Alex took the wagon back into town, while I looked after our horses. The butler and housekeeper made up our usual rooms for us. When Alex got back we split the money from the sale of the wagon and then rested for the night.

The next morning when I came down for breakfast I found Lady Grace sitting in the dining room. She looked up at me. Alex came into the room behind me.

"I was told I had guests," Lady Grace said, "But I didn't quite think it would be you two."

"We were passing through and needed a place for the night," Alex said.

"Well, you are welcome here," Lady Grace said, "Some days it hardly seems worth it to have a house when I don't stay here much."

"But you do have some place to call home," Alex said.

"That's why I keep it," Lady Grace replied. We sat down and the butler brought breakfast out.

"How is Simone?" Alex asked.

"So busy trying to be a wife to Sheldon that she almost didn't notice that you had left without saying goodbye," Lady Grace said.

"I'm glad she's happy," Alex said.

"And what kind of trouble have you been up to?" Lady Grace asked.

"This and that," Alex answered.

"Why do I feel like I should be worried?" Lady Grace asked.

"Because you never trust us when it comes to what we do on our own time," I answered.

"That's true," Lady Grace said, "You have also given me every reason not to trust anything you do on your own time."

"Maybe you can try this time," Alex suggested. Lady Grace didn't respond so we finished breakfast without speaking. Once breakfast was over Alex and I got our horses and bag of gold bars before leaving.

"Think we should have told her?" I asked.

"If she gets curious she can look for herself," Alex answered, "And the fewer people who know the better." I nodded.

We stopped and exchanged the gold bars for money. Alex divided it into three piles, she took one, I got the second and the third was put away. Leaving town we headed back to where Mary Porter lived. It took us two weeks to get there.

TAKING THE TOWN
CHAPTER 13

Toby

We rode back into town in early evening. After finding a place for our horses we found a room at the hotel. After supper, we headed over to the saloon. Alex was able to join the game of poker while I watched it. I saw Robert Stewart and a few of his men briefly when they came in and went upstairs with the saloon owner. The man next to me at the bar noticed as I watched Robert and then went back to watching the poker game.

"I hope you aren't looking for trouble," the man said without turning from his drink.

"Not usually," I answered.

"Robert Stewart owns this town," the man said, "Or at least he owns every inch of land the town is built on and half of the actual buildings. People don't mess with him."

"Just because he owns the town?" I asked.

"Because he'll kill anyone that gets in his way or he thinks is causing him problems," the man said, "He may be charging outrageous amounts for people to use his land, but at least the town stays peaceful."

"As in there are a lot of corpses out in the desert somewhere," I said, "And no one goes out to claim them unless it's to bury them where they fell."

"I like the peace," the man said, "Beats a lot of other towns."

"Didn't come to cause trouble," I said, "Did come to talk to Mary Porter though."

"There's trouble," the man said, "Since Harry died she's been shooting at anyone who comes near the hovel that she and Harry called home. Even Robert, her brother, couldn't get within rifle range of the place. Someone must get passed because she has food. Harry's creditors have been trying to squeeze money out of her since Harry isn't here to pay them anymore."

"Sounds like everyone else has a problem and she's just trying to survive," I said.

"If that's the way you want to see it," the man said. Alex quit the game, gathered up her money and came over to where I was sitting at the bar. Someone else sat down in the vacant spot.

"Game not going well?" I asked. Alex looked over at the man next to me, he quickly went back to his drink.

"Something like that," Alex said. I finished my drink. Then we left the saloon. Night had fallen, so people had gone in leaving the street deserted.

"I saw Robert Stewart going up to visit the owner of the saloon," I said.

"This town seems to be full of people I wouldn't associate with," Alex said, "Especially if that poker game was any indication of the people in this town."

"My guess from what I've seen is there are two groups of people in town," I said, "The scoundrels, of which Robert is leader, and the peaceful folks, who won't do anything to that could cause trouble."

"Let's just deal with Mary Porter and get out of here," Alex said.

"There might be a small problem there," I replied.

"And what's that?" Alex asked.

"According to the fellow in the bar, she has barricaded herself in her house and is shooting at anyone who comes within rifle range," I answered.

"That's a problem," Alex said. We walked passed the hotel and continued down the street. When we reached a cross street we went along it to the next street and continued down to the end. We stopped when we could see Mary Porter's house. It was slightly more than a shack. The window beside the door had been broken, but otherwise it looked like someone had cared for it.

A movement caught my eye, I took Alex's arm and pulled her into the shadows. Someone came down the street, being watchful of his surroundings. The moon moved from behind a cloud and I could see that it was the doctor. He had a bundle with him. Going up to Mary's door he knocked and was let in. Alex started back down the street. I followed her. We went back to the main street and then along it to the doctor's office. Alex tried the door and it opened. She entered first and I followed her inside. There was no one in the main area, in the living quarters, or the surgery.

I sat down the doctor's chair and Alex sat down on the bed. We left the lights off and sat there and waited. Half an hour later the door opened and the doctor stepped inside. He lit the lantern near the door and just about dropped it when he turned and saw us.

"May I help you?" the doctor asked.

"Maybe," Alex said, "Or maybe we could help you." The doctor looked scared and confused.

"We're the men who brought Harry into town about two months ago now," I said. The doctor looked relieved.

"If you two hadn't done that Mary would have never known what happen to Harry," the doctor said, "Not that she had any money to bury him."

"What happened to the body then?" Alex asked.

"I dug the grave, put in the body and covered it up," the doctor said, "No ones else was going to do it and I can't have a body sitting in my office rotting away."

"And her brother didn't bother to help her out?" I asked.

"Robert is the one who shot Porter," the doctor said.

"We know," Alex said, "But he offered us money as a reward for bringing the body back. Using the same logic, why wouldn't he pay a little money to put the poor man into the ground?"

"Because once you take his money he believes he owns you," the doctor said.

"Then it's a good thing we turned him down," Alex said.

"You said you could help me," the doctor said.

"Do you know why Harry was killed?" Alex asked.

"Something about stealing from Robert," the doctor said.

"He did," I answered, "And he passed it on to us before he died."

"That would explain Robert's search of the body and the cursing when he couldn't find whatever it was," the doctor said, "But why are you telling me this? It could get us all killed."

"We want to pass something on to Mary and learn more about what's going on," Alex said.

"What do you want passed on to Mary?" the doctor asked. Alex dug into her pocket and pulled out the third wad of money. The doctor's mouth dropped open. "That's a lot of money. Why do you want Mary to have it?"

"Because it took her husband's life to keep it out of Robert's hands," Alex answered.

"Robert got his hands on the treasure map, did he?" the doctor said, "And then Harry stole it from Robert."

"Treasure map?" I asked.

"An old miner came to town, said he had more money than anyone in the world could spend," the doctor said, "Claimed he had a map that showed the way but he needed someone willing to give him a horse and wagon. This was the latest town on his travels. He had been laughed out of every one so far. The people here just ignored him. On his third day in town his body was brought to me. I looked through his belongings, but there was no map. I figured he was just crazy and put the body in the ground. The rumours came up about three months ago that Robert was getting some men together to go treasure hunting. I thought about the map, but by then it was Robert's."

"And Harry was one of the men to go on this expedition for treasure," I said.

"Mary said Robert promised to pay off all of Harry's debts," the doctor said, "Then Harry took off."

"You ever get the name of the miner?" Alex asked.

"Sure, I have it written down somewhere," the doctor started toward his desk.

"Don't worry about telling us," Alex said, "Just put two graves stones on two graves for us," Alex said.

"Two?" the doctor said stopping.

"One for the miner and one for Harry Porter," Alex said, "We'll pay for them."

"You found the treasure then," the doctor said.

"And are doing right by the people who deserve it," Alex said.

"You will be targets the minute Robert sees you," the doctor said.

"We can return the map if he wants," I said, "There's still treasure there if he wants it."

"But you took some," the doctor said.

"Well, if he wants to be unreasonable about things, yes," I replied.

"Maybe we should take the money to Mary ourselves," Alex said.

"She'll shoot at you," the doctor said.

"That would be the point," Alex said, "And then after giving her the money we ride out of town."

"That would be a good idea," the doctor said, "He'll follow you though."

"And what's the rest of your plan?" I asked Alex.

"We'll talk about it else where," Alex said, "It's better not to involve the doctor in this any farther." The doctor looked relieved, but curious. Alex stood up. She put the money for Mary away and pulled out her own money. She counted out some and handed it to the doctor.

"That should cover the grave stones," Alex said. The doctor nodded and put it away. Then Alex and I left the doctor's office and headed back to the hotel.

The next morning Alex and I were eating breakfast in the hotel dining room when Robert came into the room and came over to our table.

"You're the two men who brought Harry back to town," Robert said.

"For all the good that did him," I replied.

"Well, he stole something from me and I was wondering whether he gave you anything or whether you took anything he had," Robert said.

"He didn't have anything to steal," Alex said, "And he didn't have anything that he could have given us. We brought him back hoping his life could be saved."

Robert nodded.

"May I ask the reason you're back?" Robert asked.

"Check on the widow and go back to where we were before we started this journey," I answered.

"Good luck with that, then," Robert said. Then he turned and left the room.

"Plan?" I asked Alex.

"Thomas," Alex answered.

"You think he can help?" I asked.

"I hope so," Alex answered. When we were finished eating we left the hotel with our stuff. After our horses were ready we rode to Mary's house. We tied our horses to a hitching post nearby and walked toward the house. We were open about it and people stopped and stared at us.

I could see a rifle sticking out of the broken window, but no shots were fired at us. We got as far as the door. Now people were really wondering, I even recognized Robert and the doctor in the crowd. Alex knocked on the door. It opened a little bit. Mary stood to one side of the door, looking dishevelled and half scared.

"We were wondering if we could talk with you for a moment," I said taking my hat off.

"You brought Harry back," Mary said.

"Yes, Ma'am," I replied.

"Come in," Mary said. We squeezed through the opening and into the room. The room was well kept and looked like you could eat off the floor or any of the furniture.

"We brought you something, because we figured you might need some help," Alex said. She pulled out the wad of money and offered it to Mary. Mary took it and slowly tears came to her eyes. Alex took Mary into her arms before Mary could collapse. Alex directed her to a chair but continued to comfort her. I took up watch at the window, but no one seemed interested in coming closer.

Once the worst of it was over, Alex let Mary go. Mary looked a lot better emotionally. She stared at the money.

"Harry took Robert's map, didn't he?" Mary said.

"I believe Robert stole the map in the first place," Alex said.

"So, you have the treasure now," Mary said.

"And now you have some of it," Alex said, "If you need any more, you can have it."

"This is more than I've ever had in my life," Mary said, "I could settle Harry's debts and live without every worrying about money again. But why?"

"Harry tried to get it all for you," Alex said, "But we have a few other things we need money for."

"I need to get the doctor to give Harry a grave stone," Mary said.

"Done," I said.

"What?" Mary asked looking at us with wide eyes.

"We talked to the doctor last night," Alex said, "Paid for Harry's gravestone and the old miner whose map it was in the first place." Mary looked back at the money and nodded.

"How can I ever thank you?" Mary asked.

"Keep it away from Robert and keep the map a secret," Alex answered. Mary nodded again. She went into the bedroom. A minute later she came back without the money. She took her post at the window again and we left the house. Everyone stood back as we mounted our horses and rode out of town.

It was a day's ride to the next town. Once there, we stopped at the sheriff's office to ask if any marshals were coming through town and then Alex headed for the telegraph office. I headed for the saloon and played poker until it closed down.

The next morning there was a knock on my door. It was Alex.

"I received a response from Thomas," she said.

"And?" I asked as I finished getting dressed.

"He'll be here in a couple days," Alex answered.

"Then what?" I asked, "As far as we know the law has no idea about what Robert has been doing and half the town is in league with him. And the other half doesn't want anything to disturb the peace."

"That means there are dead people out there who need to be heard," Alex said, "We'll talk to Thomas and see what he can do. Hopefully we'll be able to come up with a plan."

"Hopefully?" I asked.

"We can't just go in and kick them out," Alex said, "We don't have proof to be able to hang them. We need some kind of plan before we head back."

"Well, we have a couple days to think about it," I said, "In the meantime let's have breakfast."

We spent the next three days in the saloon, playing poker. On the fourth day as we were coming out of the hotel when Thomas came riding down the street.

"How'd you get on a horse?" Alex asked as Thomas stopped beside us.

"The same way I've always gotten on a horse," Thomas answered.

"Last we saw you, you were riding a cart," I said.

"Didn't think I needed it this trip," Thomas replied.

"You gonna get down so we can talk?" Alex asked.

"Of course," Thomas said. He moved his other leg to this side of the horse and dropped down, landing on his good leg. Then he limped over and tied his horse to the hitching post. Alex started back into the hotel, I followed and Thomas limped in after us. We found a private table in the dining room and told Thomas all about Robert Stewart. He didn't say anything, just listened.

"Sounds like Robert Stewart has himself a very tidy game," Thomas said once we were finished.

"Yes, but is there anything we can do about it?" I asked.

"Find evidence of crimes, so that I can arrest him and his gang," Thomas answered, "Me and an army of deputies."

"We were hoping for something better than that," Alex said.

"Then you need evidence of what Robert Stewart is doing," Thomas said.

"Then we'll go back and get it," Alex replied.

"And what about the man Robert has following us?" I asked.

"Hopefully, we'll look like we picked up a friend and are going back," Alex answered.

"He has a man following you?" Thomas asked.

"Since we left the hotel to talk to his sister," Alex answered, "Seen him a few times over the last few days. He's better than most, but not quite good enough to escape notice."

"And you think dragging me into this is a good idea?" Thomas asked.

"We've simply met up with a friend, are staying overnight and leaving the next day," Alex said, "That should give us enough time and you can telegraph for your army of deputies in the next town."

"And if he doesn't accept that tale?" Thomas asked.

"Then we run for it," Alex answered.

"This is sounding worse than ever," Thomas said.

"Let's hear a better plan," Alex said. Thomas didn't answer.

"We'll be leaving tomorrow morning unless you have come up with something better," I said after a couple of minutes. Alex and I left the hotel. We went to the saloon.

The next morning Thomas was waiting outside the hotel for us when Alex and I came out. The three of us mounted our horses and headed back to the town. The man continued to shadow us. We rode into town and got three rooms at the hotel. No one paid any attention to us.

Early evening found us in one of the rooms. I was sitting on the bed, Alex was leaning against the wall next to the window and Thomas was sitting in the chair. Thomas was talking about the collection of wanted posters he had with him. Alex was giving the occasional comment, but I could see her tiredness. I was playing solitaire.

There was a knock at the door. I looked at Alex; she shrugged. I got up and opened the door. A rifle was pointed at me with a sneering man holding the other end. I stepped back. The man followed me into the room and three friends with rifles followed him.

"Drop your gunbelts," the man in front of me ordered. I unbuckled mine and let it drop. Alex did the same. Thomas sat there not sure what to do.

"You, too," the man with a gun pointed at Thomas said. Thomas stood up and let his gun belt fall.

"Tie their hands," the man in front of me said. The fourth man set his gun down and pulled out some rope. He went over to Alex first and tied her hands behind her. Alex didn't try to fight him. Then he came over to me and tied mine behind my back.

"Looks like everything is going well," Robert said stepping inside, "Take the two gunslingers to the wagon. I'll take the marshal someplace more comfortable. Wait for me."

"Yes, sir," the man in front of me said. Then Alex and I were led out of the room, down the back way and pushed into a wagon. Two of the men climbed horses and waited, while the other two climbed into the driver's seat. One of them turned around, so that he could shoot us at any sign of an escape attempt.

Robert rode up several minutes later and led the way out of town

When the wagon stopped we were dumped out of the wagon on to the sand. I managed to get to my knees. Alex sat up. Robert and his men were still on horses

"You should've left well enough alone," Robert said, "Now you're going to die."

"Then shoot us already," Alex muttered. Robert's men raised their guns to shoot.

"Leave those men alone," the voice was strong, female and coming from somewhere behind us.

"Mary, this's none of your business," Robert said.

"It is my business," Mary responded, "Now turn around and leave. You and your men."

"Do you think that one lone rifle will scare me?" Robert said, "All I have to do is give the order and my men will shoot you and you'll no longer be a problem."

"You don't need to shoot these men, they did nothing wrong," Mary said, "They don't know anything. Take your men and go back to your town. You even have a marshal now."

"True, but leaving these two alive seems like leaving a loose thread," Robert said.

"You're just looking for more kills to satisfy your ego," Alex said, "That's really why. You want the feeling of power that ordering someone's death brings you. After all the power of doing anything yourself is far scarier than ordering it. And you would never want to chicken out of something in front of your men."

"You're asking to be shot," Robert said looking at Alex.

"Anything is better than watching you prance around," Alex said, "So, either shoot or leave us alive. Flip a coin if you have to."

"Let's go, men," Robert said, "Leave them for Mary." The men turned their horses and rode away, with Robert at the lead. Alex collapsed. I sighed. Mary came running. She started by untying my hands. Once they were free I went over to Alex.

"Is he hurt?" Mary asked.

"Just tired," I said. I turned Alex over, her hat came off and her braid fell across her face.

"A braid?" Mary asked. I checked Alex's pulse; it was strong.

"Alex is female," I said, "She dresses as a male to live as a gunslinger." I undid the ropes on her wrists. Alex started coughing and it woke her up. She sat up.

"You all right?" I asked.

"Yeah," Alex answered. I offered her my hand, she took it and I helped her up. Alex grabbed her hat and we turned to Mary.

"I didn't know what to do," Mary said, "I certainly didn't want him to kill you."

"It's fine," I said, "But now we need to figure out what to do next. We can't leave Thomas with them."

"We're going to have to for the moment," Alex said, "Unless you know of an army we could use."

"You can't go after Robert," Mary said, "He'll just make sure you're dead next time."

"But we can't leave Thomas with him," I said.

"She's right," Alex said, "Anything we do will just get us in more trouble."

"We should go back to my house," Mary said looking around, "It would be better than staying out here."

"Yeah," I said looking around. There didn't seem to be anything around but desert. Then I saw two dark spots on the horizon.

"Could be more trouble," Alex said looking at the spots. We turned and headed for town. I looked back occasionally. The spots grew into two people on horseback. At the pace they are going they would over take us before we reached to town.

The figures were silhouettes when Alex turned and looked. She stopped.

"What is it?" Mary asked stopping as well.

"I recognize those two," Alex said, "Maybe they can help us." I looked at the silhouettes. At first it was just two men on horses, then I recognized Shane and Gerald.

We waited for them to catch up.

"What are you folks doing out in the desert in the middle of the night?" Shane asked. There was a new edge to his voice and a scar that now ran down the left side of his face. "Especially without much firepower."

"Trying to think of a way to get ourselves out of trouble," Alex answered. Gerald got off his horse.

"Care to start at the beginning?" Gerald asked.

"We found a man bleeding to death in the desert and took him into town," Alex said, "He died. We left for a few months. We came back a week ago and visited Mary." Alex indicated Mary. "Then we went to the next town, contacted Thomas and waited for him. Came back here, where Robert dragged us out to the desert to shoot us. Mary stopped him. And now we have to figure out how to get Thomas."

"I hope there are a few more details there," Gerald said.

"What did you do to Robert?" Shane asked.

"Nothing, yet," I answered.

"Got any plans?" Gerald asked.

"No," Alex answered.

"How about Shane and I ride into town," Gerald said, "We'll be gunslingers for hire and see what happens. You two should lie low until he isn't likely to shoot you on sight."

"We need our stuff," I said as Gerald got back on his horse, "If it's possible to get it."

"We'll try our best," Gerald said before they rode toward the town. We continued walking.

A while later a rider came from town. It was Shane and he had two horses in tow, mine and Alex's.

"Everything was just as you left it," Shane said, "Gun belts on the floor, saddlebags on the bed and horses in the stable."

"Just like anyone else who has gone missing from this town," Mary said. Alex took her gun belt off her horses back and strapped it on before taking the reins. I took the reins of my horse before worrying about the gun belt.

"Anything else?" Alex asked Shane.

"We attracted attention the minute we set foot in town," Shane said, "But Gerald figures they are looking to hire, not shoot us for consorting with you."

"We'll be at Mary's house," Alex said, "Good luck."

"You, too," Shane said before riding back into town. We mounted our horses, with Mary on the back of Alex's horse. We rode to Mary's house, but we tried to avoid bring attention to ourselves. When we got there, Mary showed us the stall behind the house for our horses and a room inside for us to sleep.

Alex crawled into her bedroll and fell asleep. I could hear Mary getting ready for bed in the next room. When the sounds stopped the light went out. I had already blown out the lamp in this room, but I sat in the chair with my gun out.

The sky was starting to lighten when Alex moaned. I got up and went over to kneel beside her. I brushed the loose hair out of her face. Alex looked like she was in pain.

"Alex," I said quietly. Alex jerked awake and sat up. The fear disappeared from her eyes as she looked around.

"I hate those dreams," Alex said quietly.

"They're less frequent than they used to be," I said.

"I'd be happier if they just went away," Alex said. I moved back to my chair as Alex took her hair down and started to brush it out. We sat there in silence. I drifted off to sleep about the time light appeared on the horizon.

I woke to knocking at the front door. I looked out the window; it was bright outside. I heard the door being opened and a hushed voice inviting someone in.

"Where are Alex and Toby?" the voice sounded like Gerald.

"Toby is sleeping in the other room," Mary answered, "Alex went out the morning just as I was getting up. She hasn't come back."

"She hasn't been seen in town," Gerald said. I stood up and stretched.

"Good to see you awake," Gerald said from the doorway.

"What time is it?" I asked.

"Just after noon," Gerald said, "The quiet time of day."

"What've you found out?" I asked.

"Robert Stewart is hiring every gunslinger he can," Gerald answered, "I've seen Thomas."

"How is he?" I asked.

"Scared and ready to do whatever Robert says," Gerald said, "Robert is now pretending he has the law on his side."

"What's he doing?" I asked.

"Sending teams out to search for something," Gerald answered, "I'm not sure what."

"Why does that take a marshal?" I asked.

"A show of power, I think," Gerald answered, "Shane and I are supposed to be headed south tomorrow. Where's Alex?"

"I don't know," I answered.

"I was hoping she could go through Robert's office and find out the whole point of this," Gerald said, "Maybe stop it before anything bad happens. But she can't be seen, otherwise Robert will shoot her and go looking for you."

"You gonna wait or just want me to pass the message along?" I asked.

"Pass the message along, I can't stay," Gerald answered.

"Then I will," I said. Gerald nodded before turning and going back to the other room. He stuck his head out and checked the street before leaving.

Mary found something for me to eat and we waited.

It was two hours later when Alex finally came back. She was a little dirty, but otherwise fine.

"I already talked to Gerald," Alex said, "I found Shane and was talking to him when Gerald got back."

"And?" I asked.

"Robert is looking for a woman and her family," Alex said, "Looks like he'll do anything to find her. He was going to use the treasure to pay for the gunslingers and to create a palace, which from the plans looks more like a prison. Now, he's just upping the rent in town to pay for it instead."

"What's the name of this woman?" Mary asked.

"Clara Brooks," Alex answered.

"All this just for Clara?" Mary asked, "Even the shooting of people?"

"It looks like he built up his fortune and then got lonely," Alex answered, "Now, he wants her."

"Her father never approved of Robert," Mary said, "To the point that when Robert wouldn't stop courting, the whole family packed up and moved away."

"Having met Robert, I'm not sure I blame the man," I said.

"Robert always blamed it on the fact that our family had no money," Mary said, "Now that I think about it, he probably made his fortune thinking that he could win her father over. He won't be able to."

"Do you know where the family went?" Alex asked.

"South, I think," Mary said.

"What are you thinking?" I asked.

"We find this lady and trade her for Thomas," Alex said.

"But once Robert has her, she'll be a prisoner," Mary said.

"We wouldn't leave her with him," Alex said, "But we need Thomas back unharmed."

"So, we go with Gerald and Shane tomorrow?" I asked.

"Yes," Alex answered.

"What about her life?" Mary asked.

"We have to find her and talk to her," Alex answered, "Hopefully we can work all that out."

Mary nodded. Alex and I went into the other room and started a game of poker.

The next morning we joined Gerald and Shane as they rode south. The country was drier the further we went. We rode for three days before we came to the first village. The residents here had little, but shared willingly with us. Gerald had to talk them into taking payment. The next morning we were on our way. Alex had asked a few about Clara Brooks, but hadn't learned anything.

The next town was bigger and seemed a little more well-off, but there was no information on Clara Brooks. We kept going.

Two weeks after we left Robert's town we arrived at another town. This one had a small village on the outskirts. It looked like the honest citizens lived in the village and some worked in town. And the worst of the worst lived in town. I'm talking about men who see the only reason to live as money and sex. No code, no values, no morals and short life spans.

We didn't get a second glance from anyone as we walked into town. We had left the horses at a stable in the village. There were saloons in every other building, with plenty of brothels, a general store and a burnt out sheriff's office. As we stepped on to the sidewalk two men stepped out into the street. They shot at each other; one hit the other man's chest. He collapsed as he friends laughed from their place on the sidewalk. The winner went back up on to the sidewalk and was escorted back into the saloon by the men standing on the sidewalk. Two Chinese men came out of a building down the block, picked up the body and went back.

"I bet they make quite a bit of money," Shane said, nodding toward the building.

"Probably," Alex said, "But I bet the hours are bad."

"I doubt this place ever sleeps," Gerald said.

"The people probably pass out eventually," I said, "But it's unlikely they all do it at once. So, what now?"

"We start at what's left of the sheriff's office," Gerald said. We walked over. Four walls were standing and you could tell what had been furniture. The bulletin board out front had nothing up. I stepped inside the doorway. The charcoal remains of a man were lying beside the desk.

"Looks like the sheriff never made it out," I commented to Alex, who had entered behind me, "Wasn't even pulled out of here for burial."

"Let's just see if there's anything left and get out of here," Alex said.

"Don't like this place?" I asked.

"If by place you mean the whole town, then yes," Alex answered. I went over to the desk. It was scarred by the fire, but otherwise in good shape. I opened the drawers one at a time and looked through each.

"What're we looking for?" I asked.

"Information," Gerald said from the doorway.

"Well," I said, "This isn't the place to find it. These drawers were empty before the fire."

"Not a very good sheriff," Alex commented.

"I doubt the town went to hell overnight," I replied.

"Back to the village then," Gerald said. I followed Alex back out to the street. Two more men were in the middle of the street; they managed to shoot each other but not to kill each other. Their friends went back into the saloon. The Chinese men came out again, but this time they took them to a building farther down the street.

"I wouldn't trust that doctor," Shane commented.

"I wouldn't trust anyone in this town," I said.

"I think that would be about right," Shane said with a smile. Gerald started toward the village and the rest of us followed.

There was one store in the village and it sold only the bare necessities. Alex went over to the counter. The man behind it looked up at us.

"The general store in town has everything you'll need," the man said.

"We're looking for someone," Alex replied, "Her name is Clara

Brooks."

"There's no one here by that name," the man said. He had closed up at the name.

"Looks like she's here somewhere," Shane said, "Should we try a house to house search?"

"If you're looking to do damage to something, go burn down the town," Alex told Shane before turning back to the shopkeeper, "She changed her name, didn't she?"

The man didn't answer.

"We aren't looking to hurt her," Alex said, "If we wanted that we could've gone into town. We need her help with something."

"She lives in the white house," the man said, "But she's married."

"Thank you," Alex said. Then we left the store.

"Burn down the town?" Shane asked.

"Only way to improve it," Alex answered.

"People would die," Shane replied, "Those poor drunks who've passed out would be burned alive."

"Considering what we've seen, I think most of the drunks have probably done something to deserve it," Alex said.

"You go after people for committing crimes like burning people alive," Shane said.

"Only if the victim needs to have revenge," Alex replied. We stopped in front of the white house. It looked like every other house on the street, except for the white paint.

"We'll wait here," Gerald said.

"Fine," Alex said. Alex and I went over to the door. I knocked. A moment later the door opened. The woman that stood there was slightly shorter than Alex, with blues eyes and long, brown hair that hung down her back.

"Clara Brooks?" Alex asked.

"I used to be," the woman said, "Who're you?"

"We're here because Robert Stewart is looking for you," Alex answered.

"Do you work for him?" Clara asked.

"No," Alex said, "But we were hoping you could help us."

Clara looked us over before opening the door so that we could come inside.

"What can I do to help?" Clara asked once she had closed the door.

"Come back with us," Alex said.

"I can't," Clara said, "Robert is evil. I watched him shoot a man for saying good morning to me and then drag the body out into the desert. When I told my father, he packed us up and we left. I can't go back there."

"We know what Robert is," Alex said, "He tried to kill us, but we need you to come back."

"Why?" Clara asked.

"Because you're the one thing he really wants," I answered, "And we need him to release a friend."

"You're going to trade me for your friend," Clara said. She started to back away from us.

"That's what we need it to look like to Robert," Alex said, "Hopefully, we can get him to agree to let our friend go and still keep you away from him."

"How do you plan on doing that?" Clara asked. She stayed where she was.

"We're not sure yet," Alex said.

"I have to talk to my husband," Clara said.

"We'll stop by tomorrow morning then," Alex said. Then we left the house and joined Gerald and Shane.

"Well?" Gerald asked.

"She isn't sure about it," Alex said, "She said she would talk it over with her husband and give us the answer in the morning."

"Sounds like a no," Gerald said.

"If it is we'll deal with it in the morning," Alex said.

We went back into town and got rooms at the cleanest looking hotel. For us being strangers in town, no one bothered us. I watched a man punch another man for brushing passed him, but when Shane did it the man ignored him. I still slept with my gun in easy reach.

The next morning Alex and I went to Clara's house while Gerald and Shane went to the stables to get our horses.

Clara opened the door at our knock and let us in. A man was sitting at the table. He was about my height, solidly built and wore starched clothes. I believe he had been the bartender last night at the hotel.

"These're the men I was talking about," Clara told the man.

"Terence," the man said, standing up and offering his hand.

"Alex," Alex replied, shaking his hand. He turned to me, his brown eyes searching mine, like they had done with Alex.

"Toby," I said, shaking his hand.

"We talked the situation over," Terence said, "And my wife isn't going anywhere unless I go with her."

"Fine," Alex said, "We need to leave immediately." Clara looked shocked for a second before turning and starting to pack belongings up. Terence nodded and went into the other room.

They were packed in a few minutes, and then Terence went around back and got the horses ready. We met Gerald and Shane at the edge of the village.

"Who are these men?" Terence asked.

"Shane," Alex indicated Shane and then indicated Gerald, "Gerald. They're helping us. This is Clara's husband, Terence."

"Fine," Gerald said. We started riding.

"How do you plan to keep Robert away from Clara?" Terence asked. Gerald and Alex looked at each other. Alex shrugged.

"That's what the travel time is for," Gerald said, "Planning."

Two weeks later the six of us walked toward Robert's residence after dropping our horses off with Mary. We stopped in the middle of the street out front. A moment later Robert came out.

"Maybe Mary was right," Robert said, smiling as he looked at us.

"Her for Thomas," I told him.

"And the other man with you?" Robert asked.

"Her husband," Alex answered, "Where she goes, he goes. Her for Thomas or we take her back home."

"And what if Thomas doesn't want to?" Robert asked.

"Knock him out and bring him," Gerald answered.

"You were in with them all along, weren't you?" Robert asked.

"Only when it comes to business with you," Gerald answered.

"You have five minutes to produce Thomas," Alex said.

"You think you could get out of town?" Robert asked.

"Six times four is twenty-four, which is the amount of men you will lose if you try to stop us," Alex answered, "Not to mention a good chance that someone will hit her. So, bring Thomas down.

We'll switch her for him and then leave town."

"You weren't going to leave everything alone before. Why should I believe you would now?" Robert asked.

"We met up with Thomas in the next town and had to come back through to get to the job," I said, "We did nothing to interfere with your business."

"I'll go get Thomas," Robert said, and then went inside.

"Now what?" Clara asked in a whisper, "You said, you weren't going to turn me over."

"There are men all over the place," Gerald said, "If we try anything now, we'll use up all twenty-four bullets, plus knives and still never get out of here."

"You can't leave us with him," Terence said quietly.

"Toby," Alex said.

"Yes," I replied.

"How close do you think we can get to Robert?" Alex asked.

"Have to get across the street and up the stairs to the sidewalk," I said, "But if Robert will come to the edge of the sidewalk like he did before it'll make things easier."

Alex took two steps toward Robert's house, no one watching moved.

"We're waiting, Robert," Alex shouted as she took another step forward. A minute later Robert came back out with Thomas following him out. Thomas was limping under his own power, but his face looked like it was at the final stages of healing. Thomas glanced around, his eyes constantly moving under he had figured out where everyone was, and then they rested on Alex. Alex took another step forward.

"You all right?" Alex asked Thomas.

"I'm fine," Thomas answered.

"I would never mistreat a marshal," Robert said.

"What you say doesn't hold up," Alex told him, "That's why I asked Thomas."

"Let's just get this over with," Robert said, "Thomas, walk slowly once Clara has started." Gerald nudged Clara and Terence forward, neither wanted to move. Thomas took one step forward so that he was just behind Robert. Then Thomas grabbed Robert's gun right out of its holster and jabbed it into Robert's back.

"Move forward," Thomas told him, "Or I will shoot. And if any of your men shoot at any of us, I will shoot you."

Clara and Terence stopped and then stepped back. I pulled out my gun and saw Shane do the same. Alex also took hers out. Robert moved forward and Thomas followed, keeping the gun in the same position. Once Thomas and Robert had reached Alex the rest of us started to go back the way we had come. The crowd watched us, but no one moved to interfere.

When we reached the edge of town we found our horses tied to a hitching post, even Thomas's. There was an extra one that looked like Robert's. Alex tied Robert's hands behind his back and then tied him to the saddle once he was on the horse. Alex was the last to mount. Then we left town.

Clara and Terence headed south to go home. The rest of us headed back to the town where Alex and I had picked up Thomas.

"And what're you planning now?" Robert asked as we rode.

"You will be put on trial," Thomas said, "Kidnapping a marshal and attempted murder."

"And murder," Alex added, "He shot Harry Porter."

"Looks like everything is working out," Gerald said.

"You gonna stick around for the trial?" I asked.

"Sure," Gerald answered, "Don't really have anything else to do."

"You moved pretty fast for a man with a limp," Shane said to Thomas.

"As a marshal you have to be prepared to do anything," Thomas replied.

"Then how did you get caught in the first place?" Shane asked.

"Robert moved faster than first anticipated, not to mention was a lot more paranoid," Thomas answered.

"It worked," Robert said, "I could have killed you that night."

"And because you didn't, we now have you," Alex said, "Your men wanted to shoot us, you wanted to shoot us and I told you to shoot us. But you didn't."

"You told him to shoot you?" Shane asked.

"Yes," Alex answered.

"Why?" Shane asked.

"Because I was getting tired of watching his ego swell because of his feelings of power," Alex answered.

"So, what was the plan back there?" Thomas asked, "Since I

spoiled it."

"Alex had just come up with an idea, when Robert went in to get you," Gerald answered, "Other than that we didn't have one."

"You could have gotten everyone involved killed," Thomas said, "Did the couple agree to that?"

"Yes," Alex said, "They said that Clara could go with us as long as Terence was along. I think they expected us to back down rather than take both of them."

"Pity for them that we were so desperate," Gerald said.

"Why pity them?" Alex asked, "They got a vacation, about ten minutes of terror and then got to ride home untouched."

"And are probably grateful for the last one," Thomas said, "Not everyone lives for the thrill."

No one responded and the group stayed quiet for the rest of the trip. When we arrived Gerald and Shane helped Thomas escort Robert to the sheriff's office. Alex and I headed for the hotel.

Once in my room I went to sleep.

The next morning when I went down for breakfast Alex was already sitting at a table. I sat down across from her.

"Any news?" I asked.

"Haven't heard from anyone yet," Alex answered. I nodded. We didn't say anything as we sat there. Just after our breakfasts arrived Shane and Gerald came in. They sat down.

"How long do you think this will take?" Shane asked.

"The trial?" Alex asked.

"Yeah," Shane answered.

"Depends on whether there's a judge in town or whether we're waiting for one to stop in," Alex said.

"Thomas said he was leaving," Gerald said, "I thought he was the main witness."

"I don't know," Alex replied, "I haven't talked to him yet this morning."

"He should be staying here," Shane said.

"I'll talk to him before he leaves," Alex said.

"If he hasn't already," Shane said.

"I've been awake since before dawn," Alex replied, "If he was leaving that early he would have left last night."

"Having trouble sleeping?" Gerald asked.

"Some drunk was singing as he went home for the night," Alex answered, "Couldn't get back to sleep after that." Shane and Gerald's breakfasts arrived and my plate and Alex's were taken away.

"I hope this adventure isn't ruining any plans you had," Alex said.

"We were just traveling around looking for another job," Gerald replied, "So far this has been interesting, even if we aren't getting paid for it. Fortunately, our last job paid quite well so we have money until we find another one."

"Good to know we aren't causing you to go broke," Alex said.

"What about you two?" Gerald asked, "Any money problems?"

"We had a really good job," Alex answered, "We shouldn't have any money problems for a while."

"Need help spending it?" Shane asked.

"No," Alex said, "We're paying our own tab on this too."

"We told the sheriff that we would stop in and see how the prisoner is," Gerald said standing up, "We'll see you later." Shane stood up as well.

"See you," Alex replied. Gerald and Shane left. A moment later Thomas came in. He saw us and sat down in the chair that Shane had just vacated.

"Good morning," Thomas said.

"Morning," I replied.

"Gerald said you were leaving," Alex said.

"I need to talk to someone about the sheriff of that town," Thomas said, "The current sheriff bowed to Robert and that shouldn't be tolerated. I will leave after breakfast, talk to someone about the problem and be back here with news before the trial starts."

"When is it supposed to start?" Alex asked.

"A week from now," Thomas said, "The judge is currently visiting relatives in another town and that's when he is due back."

"We'll have to find something to do for a week," Alex said.

"Stay out of trouble," Thomas said. His breakfast arrived.

"We'll see you when you get back," Alex said as she stood up. We left the hotel. We headed to the saloon. It was open and there was a poker game going in the back corner. I joined it and Alex watched.

At noon we took a break and had lunch before going back to the saloon. This time Alex played while I watched. About supper time the rest of the players went off to eat. Alex was about to get up when a man sat down. He was medium height and wearing a suit with his stomach starting to hang over his belt. His brown eyes looked over at Alex and then studied me before going back to Alex.

"You're the other two gunslingers waiting for the trial," he said. He said it like it was a fact and not something we needed to confirm. "I saw the two in the sheriff's office this afternoon. I need a job done and the sheriff is busy."

"What kind of job?" Alex asked.

"There's a group of bandits who steal my horses," the man said, "I need them stopped."

"Perhaps some details would help," I suggested.

"My name is Lance Dempster, I keep a herd of horses just outside of town," the man said, "Once a week a group of bandits takes five horses from my herd. I know where they sell them, but I can't stop them from stealing them. The sheriff has tried, but he's a busy man. When I was in there today reporting the latest theft, it was suggested that I hire you two."

Alex looked at me and I shrugged.

"We'll help you," Alex said.

"Wonderful," Lance said, "When can you start?"

"We need more information," Alex said.

"Sure," Lance replied.

"When do these bandits usually strike? And what day of the week?" Alex asked.

"In the evening, I believe. And there's no specific day," Lance said.

"Then I guess we can start any time," Alex said.

"My wife should have supper ready," Lance said, "Come for supper and then I'll show you my land."

"We'll be there," Alex said.

"Wonderful," Lance said, then stood up. Alex stood up as well. And then we followed Lance out of the saloon. He led us down the street and to the next street where he went to one of the larger houses on this street. He opened the door and we followed him inside. We were in a hallway of an expensively decorated house.

Lance put his hat on the hook by the door before going into the first doorway on the left. I placed my hat on the hook beside his and followed Alex into the room. It was a parlour, again expensively decorated. Lance continued into the next room. We followed. This was the dining room. The table was set for two.

"Wait here," Lance said before going into the other room off the dining room, which I assumed was the kitchen.

"Looks like he forgot to talk to his wife before he invited us for supper," I commented sitting down in one of the chairs that didn't have a place setting. Alex sat down in the one across from me.

"I'm sure that will all be straightened out," Alex said.

"Something wrong?" I asked.

"I feel like it's time to move on," Alex answered, "Even though we aren't finished here yet."

"As soon as this trial is finished we don't have to stay," I said.

"Yeah," Alex replied. Lance came back into the room. He was followed by a woman. She was carrying two more place settings. Alex and I stood up.

"This's my wife, Charlotte," Lance said. Charlotte set the dishes on the table.

"Toby," I said offering her my hand.

"Nice to meet you," Charlotte said shaking my hand before turning to Alex.

"Alex," Alex said also offering her hand.

"Nice to meet you as well," Charlotte said shaking Alex's hand. Then Charlotte started to set the places.

"Sorry if our presence is a problem," I said.

"It isn't a problem," Charlotte said, "I just wasn't expecting guests." Charlotte went back into the kitchen. Lance sat down, so Alex and I sat down as well. We waited without talking until Charlotte brought supper out. Once it was all on the table, Charlotte sat down. Lance said a prayer over the meal and then we started eating.

As we talked during supper, Alex and I learned that Lance not only owned horses, but he owned the stable in town. And Charlotte worked for the dressmaker in town. Other than that we talked about the weather and where the railroad was being built.

After supper Alex and I followed Lance first to the stable to get our horses and then out to the land he had his horses on. He pointed out the various horses, where his land ended in all directions and where the bandits were most likely to strike. Then we all went back into town. After leaving our horses at the stable Lance went home. Alex and I headed for the sheriff's office.

The sheriff was sitting behind his desk when we entered. He looked up at us.

"What can I do for you?" he asked.

"Mr. Dempster asked us to stop the bandits from stealing his horses," Alex said, "Said he heard about us while making a report on the last theft."

"Shane and Gerald suggested you to him," the sheriff said.

"I figured that," Alex replied, "We're wondering about the horse bandits."

"They've been operating around here for at least five years," the sheriff said, "Steal horses, ride them to where they sell them and then walk back here. They've been caught twice, but escaped. But if you can stop them…" The sheriff shrugged.

"And if we have to shoot them to stop them?" I asked.

"Then room will be found in the cemetery," the sheriff answered. Alex nodded.

"Thank you for your time," Alex said. Then we left the office and headed to the hotel.

The next morning I was the first one up. Alex came down when I was halfway through my breakfast. As I was finishing up Shane and Gerald joined us.

"I thought you two would be off rustling cattle thieves," Shane said.

"No cattle involved," Alex replied.

"So, you took the job?" Gerald asked.

"It's something to do," I answered.

"Thomas told us to stay out of trouble," Alex said.

"Where did he go?" Gerald asked.

"To talk to a man about a new sheriff," Alex answered, "The current one was Robert's puppet."

"I'm surprised no one has shown up to try to break Robert out of jail," Shane said.

"Maybe they lost their head," Alex commented. Gerald laughed.

"I hope so," Gerald said.

"We have to go watch for horse bandits," Alex said, "See you when they're caught." Alex and I stood up.

"Good luck," Gerald said. We left the hotel. After a stop at the stable we headed for the horses.

We made up a camp close to where the bandits normally struck and took turns watching horses and playing solitaire.

It was the last day before Thomas was due back, when I spotted five men sneaking toward the horses. It was evening, so the men were just shapes in the dusk. I signalled Alex. She dropped the cards and came over. She nodded to say she saw them. We both pulled out our guns. I aimed at one and Alex aimed at another. The shots sounded almost like they were fired at the same time. The horses started in the opposite direction. The four men that were still standing had pulled out guns and were looking around for the source. I fired again and one man went down. Alex fired again and a third man went down. The two men left standing fired at us, but couldn't tell exactly where we were. Alex and I fired a third time and the last two men went down.

Alex and I packed up our camp before going over to the bodies. All five men were dead.

"Looks like our job is done," I commented.

"Then let's go back to town and tell the sheriff where to find the bodies," Alex said. We mounted our horses and rode back into town.

After stopping at the stable we headed over to the sheriff's office. The sheriff was sitting behind his desk and another man was sitting in the chair across the desk from the sheriff. The man had white hair, but was fit.

"And these are the other two gunslingers," the sheriff told the man, "Alex and Toby." The man turned and studied us.

"Strange time to be disturbing the sheriff," the man said.

"We only wanted him to know that we stopped the horse thieves," Alex replied.

"Does that mean we have another trial to do?" the man asked.

"No," I answered, "That means there are five more bodies to put in the cemetery."

"Where are they?" the sheriff asked.

"Near where they usually stole horses," Alex answered.

"Then I'll send the doctor and my deputy over there," the sheriff said.

"Is Thomas back?" Alex asked.

"Thomas?" the man asked.

"The marshal who was kidnapped," Alex explained.

"Shane said he came in yesterday and has been resting quietly in his room," the sheriff answered.

"Have to see what the problem is tomorrow then," Alex said.

"The trial starts tomorrow morning," the man said, "I want it to be over as soon as possible."

"Fine," Alex said, "Any attempts to escape?"

"No," the sheriff answered, "But Gerald has seen a man in town he recognized as one of Robert's men. He hasn't come near the jail, but Gerald is sleeping in the cell next to Robert's just in case."

"Then we'll see you tomorrow," Alex said. The sheriff nodded. Alex and I left the office and headed for the hotel.

We each got a room for the night. Once in bed I was sleep.

Shane was sitting in the restaurant when I came down for breakfast. He signalled to the chair across from him when he saw me. I sat down.

"So, you're back from catching horse bandits," Shane said.

"I guess you could say that," I replied, "But we didn't exactly lock them up."

"One of Robert's men is in town," Shane said.

"Alex and I talked to the sheriff last night," I said, "He told us Gerald was sleeping at the jail just in case of an escape attempt. He also said that Thomas was back."

"Came in day before yesterday," Shane said, "Saw him, but didn't talk to him."

"Alex said she was going to see what his problem is," I said.

"Trial is supposed to start in an hour," Shane said, "I told Gerald I would be at the jail after I was finished breakfast. I'll see you at the courthouse."

"See you there," I said. Shane stood up and left the restaurant. He stopped long enough to say good morning to Alex as she came in. She sat down in the chair next to mine. We were brought breakfast.

"I talked to Thomas last night," Alex said, "He was told that he had to find his own sheriff if he wanted to replace Robert's sheriff."

"Sheriff's are in short supply?" I asked.

"Certain towns go through sheriffs pretty quickly," Alex said, "Thomas asked if either of us would consider being sheriff."

"Wouldn't work," I replied.

"I told him no," Alex said, "So he was going to ask Shane and Gerald."

"The trial starts in about an hour," I said. Alex nodded. When we were finished breakfast, we headed over to the courthouse. Thomas was already there, along with two men dressed up as lawyers and the man who had been talking to the sheriff last night, who happened to be the judge.

The trial consisted of my testimony, Thomas's testimony, what Robert had to say and Gerald's observations. The lawyers also made some comments.

It was an hour until suppertime when the judge stepped out of the room to think about everything and come up with a decision. He was gone for half an hour before coming back and stating that Robert was guilty. The sentence being that Robert would be hung tomorrow morning.

Shane and Gerald helped the sheriff escort Robert back to the jail. Their plan was to eat and then sleep in the cell next the Robert's. Thomas followed them. The judge and lawyers went home. Alex and I went to the hotel for supper.

After supper Lance found us in the saloon. The poker game was full, so we were sitting at a table having a drink. Lance sat down.

"I talked to the sheriff this morning," Lance said, "He said the doctor and the deputy had picked up and buried the bodies of the horse bandits."

"They tried to steal more horses last night," I said, "So, we shot them."

"I'm thankful that they've been stopped," Lance said, "I came here to give you your pay for the job." Lance pulled twenty dollars out of his coat and placed it in front of us. Alex picked it up.

"Nice doing business with you," Alex said.

"The pleasure has been mine," Lance said then he stood up and left the saloon.

"Half your hotel bill?" Alex asked me holding the money up.

"Thanks but I think I can cover the whole thing," I replied. Thomas entered the saloon. He looked around a bit before seeing us and coming over to the table. Alex put the money away. Thomas sat down.

"I just finished talking to Gerald," Thomas said.

"And?" Alex asked.

"He is going to become sheriff and Shane will be his deputy," Thomas answered, "But they're asking that you two come along when I tell people they're now the law enforcement in that town."

"Fine," Alex said.

"And I have the funds to pay for the hotel, meals and other expenses incurred while here waiting for the trial and a week when we get there," Thomas said.

"Even better," Alex said.

"I'm surprised you aren't in a hurry to move on to the next job," Thomas said.

"First we would have to find it," I said, "With this we just have to sit back and make sure Gerald and Shane don't have too much trouble. And there won't be any expenses we have to find money for."

"I see your point," Thomas said.

"When does Gerald want to leave?" Alex asked.

"Tomorrow after the hanging," Thomas answered.

"We'll be ready then," Alex said.

"Then I'll see you in the morning," Thomas said.

"See you," I replied. Thomas stood up and left the saloon. I stood up and got a bottle from the barman before sitting back down.

Someone groaned near my ear. A weight shifted off my left side and sunlight hit my face. I groaned and rolled to the right. I managed to catch myself before I fell off the bed. As much as it hurt I opened my eyes. Alex lay on the other side of the bed with her face to the pillow. We were both dressed, and the hotel room was mine. By the sun's position I would say that we had an hour before the hanging was suppose to take place. Slowly I sat up. My head wanted to lie back down. I sat there for a while. By the sound of her breathing I'd say Alex had gone back to sleep.

Finally I stood up and went over to the washbasin. I poured

some water in and used it to splash my face. It washed away the sleep, but didn't make me feel any better. I packed up my stuff. Then I went over to the bed and touched Alex's shoulder. She didn't respond. I gently shook her shoulder. She groaned.

"Time to get up and watch a hanging before riding a day," I told her.

"Already?" Alex asked.

"Shouldn't drink if you don't want to deal with the hangover," I answered.

"I'm getting up," Alex replied.

"You'll have to get your stuff from your room," I said. Alex slowly sat up. After a moment she stood up and used the rest of the water in the washbasin. Then we left my room. We stopped at hers long enough for her to grab her stuff. In the lobby we left the keys with the front desk. The clerk said that the bill had already been paid. Then we headed to where the gallows had been set up. There was already a crowd of people standing around waiting. We found a place and waited.

It was fifteen minutes later when the procession came from the jail. First the sheriff, a clerk, Robert flanked by Shane and Gerald, and then the deputy. They reached the top of the platform. The noose was put around Robert's neck. The sheriff read out the legal stuff. And then the sheriff pulled the leaver. Robert fell through the hole.

The crowd dispersed as the doctor dealt with the body. The sheriff and deputy headed back to the sheriff's office. Shane and Gerald came over to where Alex and I were standing. Thomas arrived at the same time they did.

"What happened to you?" Shane asked looking at us.

"A couple bottles of booze," Alex answered.

"You well enough to ride?" Gerald asked.

"As long as you don't suggest eating first," I answered.

"Then let's go," Thomas said. All five of us went to the stable and got our horses. Then we headed out of town.

Once again it took us a day to get back to the town. We all took rooms at the hotel for the night, since it was too late to start trouble.

The next morning the five of us showed up at the sheriff's office so that Thomas could inform him that Gerald was taking his position. The sheriff was not happy, but left without trying anything.

After that Alex and I went back and found a quiet place to have breakfast.

Over the next week I played poker or watched the world go by from the porch in front of the hotel. Alex spent the week helping Mary figure out her brother's business and what to do with it. Thomas disappeared; I think he moved on to the next place he needed to be. Shane and Gerald cleaned up what they needed to, otherwise just kept law and order. They were good at it too. Unfortunately, Shane had to shoot the former sheriff after he got drunk and decided to take back his position.

At the end of the week Alex and I moved on.

SIMONE'S CHILD
CHAPTER 14

Toby

We travelled for six months before arriving back in Dustcloud. Alex and I stopped outside the gate to Lady Grace's mansion. After a moment the butler came out and opened the gate. We entered the compound.

"Lady Grace will see you in the parlour when you have put your horses away," the butler said.

"Thank you," I said. The butler locked the gate and went back into the mansion. Alex and I rode around to the stable. We put our horses into their stalls. Alex checked under the canvas that covered the boxes of gold.

"Looks like Lady Grace checked it out," Alex said letting the canvas fall back into place, "But nothing is missing."

"Lady Grace has her own money," I said. We left the stable and went to wash up. When we had finished we went inside.

We found Lady Grace sitting in the parlour reading a book. We sat down. Lady Grace closed the book and set it down on the table beside her.

"How are you?" she asked.

"Doing fine," Alex answered.

"Not getting into too much trouble?" Lady Grace asked.

"No more than normal," I answered.

"One day all that trouble is going to catch up to you," Lady

Grace said.

"Probably," Alex replied, "Until then we'll continue."

"I was going to ask you to escort me to visit Simone," Lady Grace said, "But I'm needed here."

"What's happening with Simone?" Alex asked.

"According to the letter that arrived last week she is pregnant," Lady Grace answered.

"We'll have to stop through and congratulate her and Sheldon," I said.

"I'll write her back and you can deliver it," Lady Grace said.

"What've you been keeping busy with?" Alex asked.

"Spending my time at the orphanage just outside the city," Lady Grace answered, "I'm enjoying seeing the children, listening to them and playing with them."

"As long as you're having fun," Alex said.

"There must be something you consider fun without being dangerous," Lady Grace said.

"Card games," Alex answered, "They aren't usually dangerous.

"Unless you cheat," I said.

"And if you aren't playing for money even that possibility is gone," Alex said.

"Just card games?" Lady Grace asked.

"There're other things, but I tend to get bored of them quickly," Alex answered.

"How long will you be in town?" Lady Grace asked.

"A couple days," I answered. The butler stepped into the room.

"Supper is ready," the butler announced.

"Thank you," Lady Grace said. The butler left the room. Lady Grace stood up and went into the dining room. Alex and I followed her.

"I hope you don't mind that I checked what you left in my stable," Lady Grace said.

"We don't mind," Alex replied.

"Now I'm curious as to where all that gold came from," Lady Grace said, "And who did you steal it from?"

"It came from a mine," Alex replied.

"I cannot see you two mining," Lady Grace said.

"We didn't," I said, "Someone else did it for us. We just found the map that led to the mine."

"Someone else had already stolen it from the body of the miner who made it," Alex said.

"How did you get the map then?" Lady Grace asked.

"It was given to us by a man who was shot and dumped in the desert," Alex answered.

"It sounds like the map is bad luck," Lady Grace said, "Are you gong to leave the gold in my stable?"

"I was thinking we could move it to my parent's barn," Alex answered, "But we can't move it yet."

"When will you be able to?" Lady Grace asked.

"Soon, hopefully," Alex answered.

"I just don't want anyone to break in and try to steal it," Lady Grace said.

"The only people who know it's there are all presently in this house," Alex said, "That makes it safe enough for the moment. We'll move it when we can."

"Very well," Lady Grace said. We switched to a different subject while we finished supper.

After supper, Lady Grace joined Alex and me in a game of poker. When Lady Grace decided that it was bedtime, we all went to our rooms.

The next morning I woke up to the sun shining into my window. I joined Lady Grace for breakfast. We didn't talk while we ate. When she was finished Lady Grace left the dining room. I was just about finished when Alex came into the dining room. She took some food from the sideboard before sitting down.

"What're we gonna do today?" I asked.

"Was there something you wanted to do?" Alex asked.

"No," I answered.

"Then let's just spend the day relaxing," Alex said, "And tomorrow we can head out to visit Simone."

"Sounds good," I said. Alex nodded before turning to her food. I stood up and left the dining room. I ended up sitting in the veranda enjoying the weather.

I was about to go in for lunch, when I heard two horses approaching. I stood up and looked. Lady Grace was riding up to the mansion with a man wearing a priest's collar. I stepped off the veranda toward them. The butler came out the front door with Alex following him. Lady Grace and the man stopped the horses. Lady Grace looked upset and the priest looked worried.

"What's the matter?" Alex asked.

"One of the children was kidnapped," Lady Grace answered, "And the sheriff is busy dealing with another matter."

"We'll get our horses," I said, "You can explain what happened on the way." Alex and I quickly saddled our horses. Lady Grace and the priest started riding with me and Alex.

"Several of the boys were out gathering wood," the man said, "They usually do that in the mornings. This morning they came running back early and without wood. The oldest one told me several men on horses had picked up Jotham and ridden off with him."

"Did he say what these riders looked like?" I asked.

"Ranch hands with their hats pulled low and bandanas over their faces," the man answered.

"Jotham is only six," Lady Grace said, "And the men didn't go after any of the other boys."

"We'll need the oldest to show us where Jotham was taken," Alex said.

"Of course," the man said, "Anything you need, as long as you can bring Jotham back."

"We will try," I said. The orphanage looked like someone had pushed several shacks together, but it looked well cared for. A young woman came out to greet us; she looked worried.

"Go get Ward," the man told the young woman. She went in and returned with a boy, who looked to be about eleven.

"Ward," the man said, "These two need you to take them to where the men took Jotham." The man pointed to us. The boy nodded and got up on the man's horse.

He led the way and Lady Grace came along with us.

We headed out from the city and into an area with scattered trees. Ward stopped and turned to us.

"There," Ward said pointing to a spot in front of us. Alex got down and examined the markings left by the horses.

"Three riders," Alex said after a moment, "Looks like they barely slowed down before speeding up again."

"When we saw them, we ran," Ward said, "Jotham couldn't get

out of the way fast enough."

"We'll try to find him," Alex said, "But you and Lady Grace need to go back to the orphanage."

"I can help," Ward said. Lady Grace didn't look happy about the suggestion to go back.

"I know both of you want to help," Alex said, "But if we catch up to these men, we don't know how the men will react. It's safer for all of us."

"Shouldn't that be our choice?" Lady Grace asked.

"You've asked us to do a job," I said, "You may not trust what we do on our own time, but can you trust us to do this job?" Lady Grace didn't respond for a minute.

"Fine," Lady Grace said. She didn't sound happy about it. "Ward, let's head back."

I could see that Ward didn't like it but he and Lady Grace turned their horses around and started back to the orphanage.

"How can you tell there're three horses?" I asked as Alex got back on her horse.

"One of the horses is having problems with a shoe and there are two sets of tracks side by side," Alex answered as we started to follow the tracks.

I studied the tracks as we went and I could see what she meant. We rode without talking for a while.

"Why kidnap a boy?" Alex asked, "Why just one? And why that particular one?"

"We'll have to ask them when we find them," I said.

"I know," Alex said. We went back to riding without talking.

As the day wore on we continued the follow the tracks. When night fell we stopped because we couldn't see the tracks. Since we weren't moving we rested the horses. About an hour later the moon rose and there was enough light that Alex could see the tracks. I could see well enough to avoid bumping into things.

We stopped to rest just before dawn. After the sun had risen, so we continued on.

About noon we could see three riders in the distance. It looked like their horses were tired. The one horse with the broken shoe also had something tied behind the rider. It was the right size and approximate shape of a six-year-old boy.

It wasn't long before Alex and I caught up with the riders. Each rider had a bandana covering his lower face and his hat pulled low. They were wearing jeans, chaps, checkered shirts, jackets, hats and spurs, but those didn't look like their clothes. They noticed us. Alex went along one side of them and I went along the other side.

"Where're you headed?" Alex asked.

"None of your business," the rider with the boy on his horse said.

"I just wanted to know, because you aren't gonna make it," Alex said.

"And why aren't we gonna make it?" the rider asked.

"Because you'll kill your horse before you get there," Alex answered.

"My horse is fine," the rider said.

"Not used to a horse, are you?" I asked, "Between the bad shoe and exhaustion from being ridden too hard for too long, your horse is suffering."

"And what business is it of yours?" the rider asked.

"We hate to see horses abused," Alex answered, "So, why don't you stop and we'll tell you a few things about taking care of horses?"

"We're fine," the rider answered.

"That wasn't a request," Alex replied as she pulled out her gun and pointed at the direction of the riders. Two of the riders paled.

"You won't shoot us," the rider said.

"It's better if you're dead than your horse," I replied also pulling out my gun. The riders stopped their horses.

"Now get down," Alex said, "All of you." The riders got down, but still held on to the reins. I could hear the boy's quiet sobs.

"How about you untie your cargo," I suggested. None of the riders moved. Alex moved her horse next to the one the boy was on. She carefully untied the boy and pulled him off the horse into her arms. The boy wrapped his arms around Alex's neck.

"Unsaddle them," Alex ordered the riders, "Then tie them to a branch over in the grassy spot." The riders didn't move.

"Now," I said shooting the ground between two of the riders. The riders jumped, but the horses were too tired to be bothered. The three riders did as they were told. Alex got off her horse and sat down holding the boy on her lap. I tied our horses in a different shady spot.

When the riders were finished, they stood there, not sure what to do next.

"Come over and sit here," Alex ordered pointing to a spot a few feet from her. The riders obeyed. I went over and checked the one horse's shoe. There was only one nail holding the shoe on. I pulled the shoe off before going back to where Alex was sitting.

"I had to take the shoe off," I said, "It would be better if the horse isn't ridden for a while."

"Figures," Alex replied. The boy had fallen asleep.

"Now what do you plan on doing with us?" the rider asked.

"Make you answer some questions," Alex answered.

"Like what?" the rider asked.

"What were you thinking?" Alex said, "You steal horses and clothing, ride flat out until you exhaust the horses and you kidnap a boy. Either you're stupid or you completely lack common sense." The riders were silent.

"We were asked by the man running the orphanage to rescue the boy," I said, "That's why we followed you. If you'd been smart with your horses we might not have caught up with you."

"But since you weren't, I think we need some answers," Alex said, "Because you aren't robbers, you aren't gunslingers and you definitely aren't ranch hands."

"And what'll you do if we don't give you answers?" the rider asked, "Shoot us?"

"No," Alex answered, "There're a lot of better ways to get people to talk. Of course if you like the option of being shot it can be arranged. We can even shoot you without killing you."

None of the men said anything. Alex and I waited. An hour went passed without anyone saying anything.

"I thought you were going to torture us until you got your answers," the rider asked.

"We are," Alex answered, "We just have to think up the one that would work best."

"Shouldn't you be talking it out then?" the rider asked.

"No," I answered, "We will think up one each and then once two of you have been tortured, then we'll discuss what to do with the third one."

"You're making excuses because you aren't gonna torture us," the rider said.

"Actually, we wanted to give one of you time to answer on your own," Alex replied, "If we don't have to do any harm then we won't." None of the riders responded. I squatted down next to Alex.

"What do you think?" I asked in a whisper.

"I think they're men with money," Alex answered in a whisper, "The only reason they aren't talking is because they don't think we'll do anything."

"So, what do you want to do?" I asked.

"At this point I'm all for knocking them out and dragging them back to the orphanage, where they can explain themselves," Alex answered, "I'm hungry and the one man is stubborn. The other two might talk, but the leader won't."

"Maybe if we knock him out first," I said.

"Might work," Alex replied. I stood up and walked toward the men. The two watched me, but the leader didn't bother. I went around behind them. The two would have turned their heads to see me if they thought they could without looking scared. I took my gun so that I was holding the barrel and used the handle to hit the leader on the back of the head. He collapsed forward. Both men started to move away.

"Let's not move," I suggested, moving forward, and switching the gun back so that I was holding it properly. They froze in place. I bent down and checked for a pulse. I found one. I stood back up.

"The question is whether you two will come quietly," Alex said, "Or whether Toby has to knock you out as well."

"We'll come quietly," the rider on my right replied.

"Good," Alex said.

I had each rider saddle a horse before putting both on one and tying them together. Then Alex helped me put the leader on the other horse and tie him into place. I put the saddle on the other horse. I gently picked up the boy and handed him up to Alex once she was mounted. Then I untied the horses. I mounted up on mine and we headed back towards Dustcloud.

We arrived at noon the next day. The leader was now awake, but thankfully I gagged him when I tied him to the horse. The priest, the young woman and Lady Grace all came out to meet us. The young woman pulled Jotham down and into a hug.

"Why did you bring them with you?" Lady Grace asked.

"We thought they might be able to answer some questions," I replied, "But they were stubborn and we got hungry."

"There's food inside," the priest said.

"Do you have somewhere we can put these men until they've answered our questions?" Alex asked.

"I guess so," the priest answered, "Maybe the stable where we keep the horses would work."

"Show us the way," Alex said. The priest led us around the house to a couple walls with a roof out back. I wasn't entirely sure that it was safe for horses, but leaving the men there would be fine as long as someone was watching them.

"Those're the men that took Jotham," Ward said. He had come over.

"Yes, they are," Alex said, "And we need to know why."

"Why?" Ward asked.

"Because then we know how to prevent it from happening again," Alex answered, "Perhaps you could help us."

"Sure," Ward said.

"We need these men watched while we eat," Alex said, "If they try to escape I need you to run in and get us."

"I can do that," Ward said.

"Good," Alex said. Alex and I left the horses tied to a hitching post and went inside. The priest and the young woman had a meal set out for us. Lady Grace was sitting at the table.

"Thank you for bringing Jotham back," the young woman said.

"You're welcome," I answered between mouthfuls of stew.

"Jotham isn't one of the orphans," the young woman said, "He's my son."

"If you don't mind me asking, who's the father?" Alex asked.

"I never knew his name," the young woman answered, "I was working at a saloon when he was conceived. I got out of that life when I found out I was pregnant. Father Gilbert was the only one willing to take me and my son in."

Alex nodded.

"What do you plan to do with those men?" Lady Grace asked.

"Talk to them," Alex answered, "Ask them questions, gather information."

"And after that?" Lady Grace asked.

"Talk them into going home," Alex answered, "Hopefully. I don't really feel like killing any of them. Even if they deserve it for the way they mistreated those horses."

"Mistreated the horses?" Lady Grace asked.

"One of the horses had a shoe that was coming off, but the man riding the horse never noticed," I said, "Instead all the horses were forced to run until they were exhausted. And they were still riding the horses when we found them. That’s the reason we caught up with the men."

Alex had finished her stew and pushed the empty dish away. The young woman took the bowl and put it in the tub of water that looked like it held the rest of the dishes. I finished mine and handed the bowl to the young woman. Alex and I went back out to the stable. The three men were still lying in the straw where we left them.

"They didn't escape," Ward said.

"You did well," Alex said.

"The one kept trying to talk around his bandana, but I couldn't understand what he was saying," Ward said.

"I'm sure we'll find out in a minute," Alex said. Ward went off. Alex knelt down and pulled the bandana out of the man's mouth.

"You’ll regret this," the man sputtered. Alex shoved the bandana back into the man's mouth.

"You should be regretting your actions," Alex said, "If you hadn't been stupid you wouldn't be tied up and sitting in a stable being forced to answer questions."

The man said something, but it was muffled by the bandana. Alex pulled out the bandana.

"I'm not going to answer any questions," the man said. Alex stuffed the bandana back in. Alex stood back up.

"What’re you thinking?" I asked.

"That this’s Jotham's father," Alex answered, "There’s a family resemblance."

I studied the man for a moment.

"You're right," I said.

"And I think he was stealing Jotham to take him home," Alex said. She knelt back down.

"Correct me if I'm wrong," Alex told the man, "You bought an hour with a whore and then never thought about it again until you saw a six-year-old boy that resembles you going around with a lady you recognized living at the orphanage. Now you don't really care that his mother was a whore, only that the boy is your son. So, you get some friends to help you. You steal some clothes and horses from workers on your father's ranch. Then you go and kidnap your son. And right now you are supposed to be home with your son, giving him the life you believe him to deserve. Not this life at an orphanage."

The man said something through the bandana. Alex pulled it out. As soon as he started swearing she shoved it back in.

"I would have to say you're right," I said.

"Sounds like it," Alex said standing back up.

"Now what?" I asked.

"Now, we deal with them," Alex answered. She turned and left the stable. I stayed right where I was. The leader said something through his gag. I ignored him. A moment later Alex came back with the priest following her.

"The wagon is back here," the priest said pointing to the back corner of the stable.

"We just need to borrow it for a while," Alex said.

"Whatever you need," the priest said. Alex and I got the wagon out. We hooked up the two horses in the stable. Then we hauled the three men into the back of it. I sat down in the back to watch the men and Alex climbed up on the driver's seat. We started moving. We went around Dustcloud and out into part forest where there wasn't any private property. After a while of dodging trees and going over uneven ground we stopped. Alex climbed down and I helped unload the men onto the ground.

We stripped them naked and tied them to a tree before putting the clothes back in the wagon. Alex and I climbed onto the driver's seat and headed back to Dustcloud. This time Alex entered the city. She stopped at a church, where we put the clothes into the poor box. Then we continued back to the orphanage.

We put the horses back into their stalls and the wagon back in its place. The priest came out.

"Lady Grace went home for supper," he told us.

"That's where we're going next," Alex said.

"What about the horses?" the priest asked, "The one needs a new shoe." Alex reached into her pocket and pulled out some money.

"You pay for a farrier to put on a new shoe and you can keep all three for your trouble," Alex answered, offering the priest the money. The priest took the money.

"If they come back, I will have to give them their horses back," the priest said.

"What ever you feel is right," Alex replied. The priest nodded. Alex and I got up on our horses and headed for Lady Grace's mansion.

When we arrived and found Lady Grace was in the dining room eating supper.

"There's no guarantee they won't come back," Alex said.

"But Jotham is with his mother for right now, which is where he belongs," Lady Grace said.

"When you are leaving?" Lady Grace asked.

"Tomorrow," I answered.

"Well, good luck on your next adventure," Lady Grace said.

"Hopefully we'll get to visit Simone without too many adventures along the way," Alex said.

"I'll give you the letter in the morning," Lady Grace said.

"All right," Alex said.

After supper Alex and I played poker out on veranda until it was dark.

I woke up to knocking at my door. Opening my eyes I could see the sun shining in the window. The knocking was repeated. I got out of bed and went over to the door. Opening it, I found Alex standing there.

"Time for breakfast," Alex said.

"I'll be down in a minute," I replied.

After closing the door I got ready to deal with the day before heading downstairs. Alex was sitting and eating. I took a plateful before sitting down.

"Lady Grace has already eaten and gone," Alex said after a few minutes.

"Did she leave the letter she wanted us to deliver?" I asked.

"Yes," Alex answered, holding up an envelope, "A letter arrived for us from Nadine."

"What does she say?" I asked.

"She's hoping that we're passing through sometime soon," Alex answered, "Because she wants an escort somewhere."

"And she doesn't want Jacob along?" I asked.

"Sounds more like he isn't around," Alex answered, "Nadine says he's been taking on a new job immediately after one is finished."

"Simone, then Nadine?" I asked.

"That's what I was thinking," Alex answered.

"Whenever you're ready to go," I said pushing away my empty plate. Alex put the envelope and the letter in her pocket before. We prepared our horses before leaving the stable.

When we arrived at the gate, the butler was already there. He opened the gate and we left the compound. The butler closed the gate behind us.

Alex and I left Dustcloud. We travelled for a week stopping when we were tired or the horses needed a rest. If we needed supplies we stopped in a town rather than bypassing it.

At the end of the week we reached Plantville. We were going to pass through, but as we came into town we could see that Fitzgerald's house had burned down. As we went farther up the street there was a gallows being built.

"It's late in the day," Alex said, "Maybe we should stop and rest."

"A drink sounds not too bad," I replied. We went to the stable. The stable master was sitting on a hay bale by the door with a half-full bottle of whiskey and there was an empty bottle at his feet. He took another swig.

"A little early in the day, isn't it?" Alex asked.

"You can put your horses in any stall," the stable master said, "I suppose you're here for the hanging too."

"The hanging?" Alex asked. The stable master finally looked at us. He studied us for a long time.

"The Bastard is gonna hang the doctor," the stable master answered.

"Who's the Bastard? And why is he gonna hang the doctor?" Alex asked.

"He showed up in town one day and said the town had

potential," the stable master said, "He started a mining operation just outside of town that has been bringing people and money into town. The lumber to build all the projects that people are talking about hasn't gotten here yet, though. But he feels that he owns the town and the people in town let him." The stable master stopped to take another swig. "Anyway, he shot a man for disagreeing with him, but didn't kill him. Doctor Fitzgerald, tended to the wounded man. Which made the Bastard furious and then Fitzgerald gave him a lecture for shooting the man. But the bastard couldn't shoot Fitzgerald because everyone was out there watching by now. Instead he burned Fitzgerald's house down in the middle of the night. Fitzgerald escaped, but the poor patient that had been shot didn't. Then the Bastard comes up with a fake charge against Fitzgerald and the sheriff arrested him and now he's condemned to hang."

"Who's the Bastard?" I asked.

"His name is Harry Cutler," the stable master answered, "But you'll recognize him by the limp."

"I agree with his new title," Alex commented.

"You know him?" the stable master asked.

"I'm the person who caused the limp," Alex answered.

"Maybe you should have hit him a little higher up," the stable master said.

"I could try again," Alex said.

"Bad idea," the stable master said, "No one in town wants to lose the money the Bastard is bringing in. There ain't been much here since the town was founded, but there was enough to keep the people that stayed employed. Now there's a boom coming, they don't want to see it gone."

"So, they're willing to forgive and forget as long as there's money coming in?" Alex asked.

"That's the way life rolls," the stable master said.

"Why don't we just annoy Harry again?" I suggested.

"That sounds good," Alex said, "Make him angry, but not the townspeople."

"What are you going to do?" the stable master asked.

"Avoid Cutler," Alex answered, "Sorry we won't be needing stalls for our horses. But thank you for the information." Alex dug into her pocket and took out a couple coins. She handed them to the stable master, who stared at them. Alex and I left the stable, but went around to the second street.

"We need a third horse," I said.

"You find the third horse, while I go get Fitzgerald," Alex said, "We'll meet up in the trees just outside of town."

"See you there," I said. Alex turned around and headed for the sheriff's office. I started to look for a horse.

I finally found a man living just outside town that was willing to sell an old quarter horse. Then I went to the meeting spot to wait. Only a couple minutes went by before Alex and Fitzgerald rode up on Alex's horse. They stopped next to me.

"That went well," Alex said as Fitzgerald got down.

"The sheriff is gonna be mad when he wakes up," Fitzgerald said as he mounted the quarter horse.

"Then let's get out of here before he wakes up," Alex said. We traveled a little faster than usual.

By the time we stopped for the evening we had slowed down to our normal speed. Fitzgerald decided to continue riding with us.

It took another three days to reach Alex's hometown. And it was late evening when we rode into town. We stopped at the stable before going to the hotel.

When I woke up it was still dark out. There weren't any noises or extra lights. I got up and went to the window. The street was empty. The first streaks of light came over the horizon. I turned from the window and washed up before going downstairs.

The clerk had fallen asleep standing at the counter. I left the hotel and went down the street to the restaurant. There were only a few other people there.

As I ate, I watched people through the window. The town was slowly waking up and going about its day. More people came into the restaurant, ate, and left. It reached the point that the restaurant almost empty.

The lunch crowd was starting to come in when Alex finally entered the restaurant. She came over to the table and sat down in the chair across from me.

"Sleep in?" I asked.

"First time in a long time," Alex answered.

"That's a good thing," I said. We were brought lunch.

"There was a message from my parents at the front desk when I came down," Alex said, "They invited us to supper. Simone and Sheldon will be there, too."

"That gives us something to do for the evening," I said.

"Relaxing this afternoon sounds nice," Alex said.

"Where's Fitzgerald?" I asked.

"He said something about spending the day with the town doctor," Alex answered, "We'll probably see him tomorrow."

"Should we stop in to visit the sheriff and see if we're wanted?" I asked.

"No," Alex answered, "If we're wanted, they can come find us. But I don't think they'll be passing out wanted posters."

"Why not?" I asked.

"Because I talked to the sheriff before breaking Fitzgerald out," Alex answered, "He didn't want to hang Fitzgerald. It was just to appease Cutler. They don't want to make him angry after everything they've seen and they don't want him to take the money elsewhere."

"So, we did him a favour," I said, "Now he doesn't have to hang Fitzgerald and Cutler doesn't think it was his fault."

"I hope so," Alex said. We had just finished lunch when there was a gunshot from out in the street. We went outside. Two men that I didn't recognize were in the middle of the street; one apparently dying from a gunshot wound and the other standing with his gun out. The sheriff was coming down the street. His deputy coming down the other side of the street followed by the doctor and Fitzgerald. The man still standing turned as if to leave.

"Stop," the sheriff yelled. The man turned back. The doctor reached the body and bent down to examine it. The sheriff had his gun out when he stopped close to the man that was still standing.

"Who are you and what do you think you're doing?" the sheriff demanded.

"He drew first," the man answered.

"In this town there is a law against gunfights in the middle of the street," the sheriff said, "So, hand over your gun and let's go back to my office."

"What?" the man asked.

"Hand over your gun," the sheriff repeated. The deputy had his gun out and had come up on the other side of the man. The man looked and saw both of them. He handed his gun to the sheriff and let himself be marched off to the sheriff's office.

Alex walked over to the doctor and Fitzgerald, who were standing over the body. I followed. The man was in a dark suit that matched his hat, boots and tie. His face had several scars on it. And there was a patch of blood on his shirt.

"Can you help me with him?" the doctor asked when he saw us.

"Sure," I answered. I took his legs and Fitzgerald took his arms. We took him back to the doctor's office. Alex and the doctor followed us. We put the man on the table that the doctor gestured to, then Fitzgerald and I withdrew to the waiting room. The doctor went to the body and searched it. He took all the weapons and brought them back out to the waiting room with him. He set them on his desk before turning back to us.

"Maybe it's just me," I said, "But he doesn't look as dead as he should be."

"The amount of blood is too neat," Alex said.

"He didn't have a pulse," the doctor said, "And it was hard to tell if he was breathing.

"If you have the right control you can stop your heart," Alex said.

"I've heard of it happening," Fitzgerald said, "But why try it?"

"If that's what he did, then we should be able to ask him in a minute," Alex said.

"Well, if he's alive he can go to the jail with his friend," the doctor said, "The law in this town says no gunfighting."

"Obviously they didn't know," Fitzgerald said, "In most towns you just have to prove that the other man shot first."

There was coughing in the other room as the 'dead' gunfighter woke up.

"Alex, cover the back door," the doctor said, "Toby, cover this door. And Fitzgerald, go get the sheriff."

Alex went to stand at the back door. Once the doctor had entered the room I stood in the doorway with my hand on my gun. The man had rolled on his side and was still coughing. The doctor waited patiently until the man had stopped coughing.

"You're very alive for someone who's just been shot," the doctor commented.

"Had to let him win," the man's voice was more of a growl.

"Well, he's in the jail right now and you'll be headed there shortly," the doctor said.

"Please don't," the man said, "He'll kill me."

"Alex," the doctor said.

"Yeah," Alex said.

"You've been around," the doctor said, "Does it sound like he's lying?"

"Hard to tell," Alex answered, "But I wouldn't put money on a plea like that."

"He's been after me for months now," the man said, "I barely stayed one step ahead of him. I decided to finally make my stand. If he believed me to be dead, he would leave me alone."

"How about now?" the doctor asked Alex.

"But no after thoughts," Alex said, "Wasn't a great plan. Especially since he would probably go after you again when he found out he didn't kill you. And that time he would make sure you were dead."

"Not having a great plan isn't necessarily lying," the doctor said.

"No, but they rode into town last night," Alex said, "Not separately, but together. Like two friends or partners. The only problem is I can't see any reward for a scheme involving what we've seen so far."

The man didn't respond, but had started looking for an escape. The door to the office opened and the sheriff entered, followed by Fitzgerald.

"I was told there was an issue with the body," the sheriff said.

"The body isn't as dead as he looked," the doctor replied. I let the sheriff passed me. He saw the man sitting up.

"Looks like another cell is calling for an occupant," the sheriff said as he pulled out restrains.

"I had to," the man said, "He was gonna kill me."

"Next time a man is trying to kill you, come to the law," the sheriff said, "That way you don't end up on the other side of the law. Now, if you fight, one of the two gunslingers is going to put a real hole in you."

The man didn't resist as the sheriff put him in the restrains. The sheriff directed him toward the door. I moved out of the way. Alex joined us as I followed the sheriff. The sheriff nodded his thank you.

We escorted them to the sheriff's office. The deputy opened the cell and the sheriff directed the man inside. The deputy shut and locked the door. Neither of the gun men looked happy.

"The question remains as to what their scheme was," Alex said.

"I'm sure we'll figure it out in the next few days," the sheriff said, "Since you'll be here for a couple days at least, do you mind helping me if I need you?"

"We don't mind helping you," Alex answered.

"Thank you," the sheriff said. Alex and I left the sheriff's office. We went up the street back to the restaurant to pay for our lunch as we left in such a hurry. Then we continued on to the Turner residence. We went up the walk and on to the porch. Alex knocked on the door. There might have been a sound but I wasn't sure. Alex looked puzzled as if she had heard it as well. She turned the door handle. The door opened. We stepped inside.

It felt like there was something wrong. I pulled out my gun. Alex gently closed the door behind us. The sound came again. I tried to figure out where it was coming from. Alex pointed to the back of the house then pointed to herself before pointed upstairs. I nodded that I understood.

I continued down the hallway. I stopped and looked into the parlour. There wasn't anyone in there. I stopped at the dining room. It was empty as well. The door to the kitchen was closed. I turned the handle and opened the door. Mrs. Turner was tied in a chair. She was gagged and blindfolded. I pushed the door all the way open until it hit the wall. There was no one else in the kitchen. I put my gun away before I went to Mrs. Turner and pulled the blindfold off. She looked scared, but when she realized that it was me, she tried talking through the gag. I removed the gag before starting on the rest of the ropes.

"You have to help Frank," Mrs. Turner said, "Those men were going to kill him."

"What exactly did they want?" I asked.

"They showed up just before Frank was about to leave for work," Mrs. Turner answered, "They tied me up so I wouldn't run and tell the sheriff. And they threatened to kill Frank if he didn't take them to the bank and let them into the vault."

I had just got Mrs. Turner loose when Alex came into the

doorway. Mrs. Turner ran to hug her daughter. Alex returned the hug.

"We need to get to the bank," I said. Alex nodded. Mrs. Turner looked like she was close to bursting into tears.

"Go to the sheriff," Alex said, "But tell him not to come to the bank unless he hears several gunshots."

"But," Mrs., Turner started.

"Go," Alex said, "You'll be safe at the sheriff's office and Toby and I can take care of this." Mrs. Turner still hesitated.

"Please, Mrs. Turner," I said, "It would be the best thing right now." Mrs. Turner finally nodded. All three of us went out the front door. From the sidewalk Mrs. Turner headed for the sheriff's office, while Alex and I went to the bank.

We went in the front door. Everything seemed to be normal at the bank. Alex went to the teller closest to the manger's office. There was a closed sign on the cage, but a woman stood behind it.

"I need to speak with Mr. Turner immediately," Alex said.

"I'm sorry," the woman said, "He's been in a meeting with a bank client all morning."

"It's the middle of the afternoon," Alex said.

"Some business takes a while," the woman replied, "Mr. Turner asked that he not be disturbed."

"Then I'll suffer his wrath," Alex said going over to the door and trying the handle. It didn't open.

"I said you can't go in there," the woman said. The guard got up from his chair beside the door and started towards us. Alex kicked the door. There was a cracking noise and it swung open. From where I was standing I could see Mr. Turner tied to his chair and gagged. The woman saw it as well and let out a scream. Alex and I went into the office. Mr. Turner seemed to be fine, but there was a gaping man-sized hole in the back wall of the bank and the vault door was wide open. Alex was already beside her father cutting the ropes that held him. The guard entered the office.

"They took off in a wagon," Mr. Turner sputtered as soon as the gag was out, "They said they would kill Marsha if I didn't cooperate with them."

"Hopefully Mrs. Turner got to the sheriff's office," I said.

"You freed her?" Mr. Turner asked.

"That's how we knew to come here," Alex answered.

I looked out the hole. There were marks in the dirt from the wagon but no other sign of it or the men. I stepped back inside.

"We need to get the sheriff," the guard said.

"I think we should all head to the sheriff's office," I said.

"Why?" Alex asked.

"Because I think the bank robbers are there or the men who're locked up are accomplices," I said.

"When did the robbers leave?" Alex asked.

"Just before noon," Mr. Turner answered.

"Let's go," Alex said. Alex and I headed for the door with Mr. Turner and the guard following us.

Alex and I reached the sheriff's office first. We entered to find Mrs. Turner explaining to the deputy what happened. The two men were still exactly where we left them. Mrs. Turner and the deputy turned to look at us.

"Where's the sheriff?" Alex asked.

"Robert came in complaining that his wagon was missing," the deputy answered, "The sheriff went to check it out." Mr. Turner and the guard arrived. Mr. and Mrs. Turner saw each other and wrapped themselves in each other's arms.

"The bank has been robbed," Alex said, "And we think these two may have something to do with it." Alex pointed to the two men in the cells.

"Also might include the missing wagon," I said.

"What?" the deputy said. The sheriff entered the office followed by Robert.

"What the hell happened?" the sheriff demanded.

"Those men broke into my home this morning," Mr. Turner said pointing to the men in the cells, "And tied up my wife before dragging me to the bank, where they had me open the vault before tying me to a chair. Then they made a hole in the wall of my office and loaded everything from the vault into a wagon that was waiting. When they finished, they left me there."

"Could the wagon have been mine?" Robert asked.

"Probably," Alex answered, "When they came into town last night they had only two horses."

"So, after hiding the wagon, they have a shoot out on the main street," the sheriff said, "And it looks like the one man is dead and the other is gone before the law is the wiser."

"Or in this case the dead one breaks the other out of jail while the sheriff learns of the bank robbery," I said.

"Looks like one of you had better tell us where that wagon is," the sheriff told the men.

"I have no idea what you're talking about," the one on the right said.

"Fine then," the sheriff said, "It isn't important to recover it immediately anyway. Mr. Turner, why don't you take your wife home? I'm sure Mr. Harlan can patch the hole in your office wall. Robert, you and Jason go search the town for your wagon. Bring it back here when you find it. Alex and Toby, I need to talk to you for a minute."

Mr. and Mrs. Turner left the sheriff's office heading towards their home. The guard headed back to the bank. Robert and the deputy took a side of the street to search for the wagon. The sheriff signalled us to step outside, but he left the door open so that he could see the men.

"Yes?" Alex asked.

"Judge Brown isn't in town and won't be back for a least a week," the sheriff said, "But it looks like these men need to be constantly watched."

"You want us to take turns with you and your deputy?" Alex asked, "Or do you want us to go find the judge?"

"The judge is in Cartwheel," the sheriff said, "Visiting some old friends. I know you're here to visit Simone and Sheldon, but it isn't that far away. I'm sure the judge will come if you explain the situation."

"Who are these old friends?" Alex asked.

"Mr. and Mrs. Hill," the sheriff answered.

"We'll leave tomorrow morning," Alex said.

"Thank you," the sheriff said. He went back into his office.

"Well that was supposed to be our next destination," I said.

"Not quite how I figured the visit would go," Alex said. We started back up the street. We went back to the Turner residence. Alex was just about to knock when the door opened. Simone was there.

"Mother is falling apart," Simone's voice was quiet as she let us in. Alex and I stepped inside. The sound of crying seemed to be coming from upstairs.

"Father is with her," Simone said leading the way to the parlour. We entered the parlour. The only change from earlier was a baby basket sitting on a chair. I could see the baby sleeping inside.

"We only recently heard that you were pregnant," Alex said. I sat down in one of the chairs and Simone sat down on the settee.

"You must not've talked to Lady Grace in a while," Simone said.

"We've been busy," Alex said. She gently picked up the baby before sitting beside Simone. The baby kept on sleeping.

"His name is Jesse," Simone said, "He's a month old now."

"Lady Grace gave us a letter to deliver to you," Alex said. She fished it out of her pocket without disturbing the baby and handed it to Simone. Simone opened the envelope, took out the letter, and read it.

"I don't suppose you're going back through Dustcloud any time soon?" Simone asked.

"Wasn't in the plans," I answered.

"Then I will just have to mail my response," Simone said. The noise from upstairs had stopped.

"Where's Sheldon?" Alex asked.

"He's been busy helping build several places that burned down last month," Simone answered, "They're just about finished, so he wasn't sure whether he would be able to join us for supper."

I could hear two people coming down the stairs. A moment later Mr. and Mrs. Turner entered the parlour. Mrs. Turner looked like she had gotten herself together.

"I'm sorry I don't have supper ready," Mrs. Turner said as she sat down.

"It's understandable," I said.

"We could go to the restaurant to eat," Alex suggested.

"That sounds good," Mr. Turner said. Mrs. Turner stood up and went back upstairs. We were all ready and waiting when Mrs. Turner came back downstairs.

We headed towards the restaurant. Sheldon joined us when we reached the main street. Since we were before the supper crowd we were able to find a table.

Our food was brought to us fairly quickly. Jesse woke up and started to fuss. Simone gave up eating to try and calm him down. After a few minutes Sheldon took Jesse to try. It didn't seem to work. Alex took Jesse from Sheldon to let Sheldon finish eating. Jesse calmed down immediately. He rested on Alex's shoulder studying the world around him with those turquoise eyes. It looked like a combination of Simone's green eyes and Sheldon's blue ones.

After supper we went back to the Turner residence to visit. When it got dark Simone and Sheldon went home. Shortly after that Alex and I decided to head back to the hotel. Mrs. Turner offered us the two spare rooms, but Alex said no. We were told that the rooms would be available if we ever needed them. Once back at the hotel I went to my room and went to bed for the night.

The sun had just risen over the horizon when Alex and I left town. We had stopped at the sheriff's office before leaving to see if anything had changed. It hadn't.

It had rained over night so everything was muddy, slowing us down. And about the time we were thinking about stopping for the night the rain started again. It rained all the way to Cartwheel.

When we arrived, Alex led the way to the stable behind Nadine's house. The rain was not so heavy after we had put our horses in their stalls. I led the way through the rain to the kitchen door. I opened it and stepped inside. There was no one in the kitchen. Alex closed the door. We removed our coats and hats, draping them over chairs to dry out.

I heard a door open upstairs. A moment later, Nadine stepped into the kitchen.

"Alex," Nadine said, "Toby. I thought it would take you longer to get here."

"We needed a place to stay overnight," Alex said.

"Didn't you get my letter?" Nadine asked.

"Yes, we did," I answered, "But we got caught up in something else."

"I understand," Nadine said, "Have you had something to eat?"

"A warm bed would be nice," Alex answered.

"Of course," Nadine said turning back to the stairs, "Both guest rooms have been made up. Jacob said something about bringing guests back. I've been waiting for the last two days." Alex and I followed her up the stairs to our rooms. I hung up my wet clothes before crawling into the bed.

I rolled over to find the sun was up and shining into the room. I packed my stuff up and went downstairs. Nadine and Alex were sitting at the kitchen table eating breakfast.

"So, you're going to find the judge and go back?" Nadine asked.

"That's the plan," Alex said, "Then we're going to come back to give you an escort."

"I should be ready by then," Nadine said, "Jacob hasn't been spending enough time home to notice whether I'm here or not."

"What's he been doing?" Alex asked.

"He took a series of jobs with the same person," Nadine answered, "The person lives here, but the jobs take him all over the place. He shows up here after supper and leaves again after breakfast. He doesn't even tell me where he's going."

"How long has he been doing that?" Alex asked.

"Since you two left for the wedding," Nadine answered.

"He'll run out of jobs eventually," Alex said. I stood up and put my empty plate in the dish pan before sitting back down.

"You two should be going," Nadine said, "The sooner you deal with the situation the sooner you can get back. And if Jacob sees you he'll convince you to join his next job."

"We'll see you when we get back," Alex said as she stood up. I stood up and we left the house. We got our horses from the stable before going to the Hill residence. The house looked perfect for a family, spacious, a garden and an excellent climbing tree. I waited with the horses while Alex knocked on the door. A man opened the door. Alex explained why she was there. The man closed the door. Alex didn't move. A moment later an older man opened the door. Alex explained what we needed. The older man nodded and then gave Alex some instructions before going back inside, closing the door behind him. Alex came back to where I was waiting.

"Is the judge coming?" I asked as Alex mounted on her horse.

"He just has to pack his things," Alex said, "Then we'll have to go to the stables and let him get his horse."

"Fine," I said. We waited ten minutes before the judge came out with a suitcase. His hosts had escorted him to the door and said their goodbyes. The judge walked and Alex and I rode to the stables.

We waited while he got ready. A few minutes later he came out of the stables. From there we were on our way.

We stopped to rest the horses as the sun was setting, but the judge decided that it was better to continue on, than to stop for the night.

It was late evening when we rode into Alex's hometown. Our first stop was the sheriff's office. The judge was off his horse and headed into the office before Alex or I even stopped our horses. I tied the reins of the judge's horse as well as my own. Then I followed Alex inside.

The prisoners were still in their cells. The judge and the sheriff were talking. Alex sat down in a chair and I leaned against the wall next to the door.

The judge and sheriff continued to talk. Alex was starting to look as tired as I felt. The judge finally said something that sounded like it was meant to end the conversation. Then he left. The sheriff looked at Alex and me.

"Go find hotel rooms," the sheriff said, "But be back here just before one in the afternoon."

"See you then," Alex said standing up. Alex and I left the office. We took our horses to the stable before getting our rooms.

I entered my room, dropped my stuff on the floor and collapsed onto the bed.

It was late morning when I got up. At the restaurant I received leftovers from breakfast.

After breakfast I went in search of Alex. I found her in her room, playing solitaire. Once she lost the game, Alex shuffled the cards and we started playing poker.

At noon we went to the restaurant for lunch and then Alex and I went to the sheriff's office.

The sheriff and his deputy were sitting at the desk finishing their lunch. Alex took a chair and I leaned on the wall by the door.

"You're here to help guard the prisoners," the sheriff said.

"You have enough testimonies?" Alex asked.

"The judge will call on either of you only if it's necessary," the sheriff answered.

"Fine," Alex said. No one said anything else as they finished eating. At ten minutes to one the sheriff and his deputy put the prisoners in restrains. Then the sheriff led the way out of the office. The first prisoner followed him with the deputy keeping him in line then the second prisoner with me keeping him in line and Alex walking along side us. The sheriff led us to the courthouse and into the courtroom, where the prisoners were seated where there was a place for a guard to sit on each side of them. Once they were seated the sheriff took the seat in front of them. The deputy sat on one side and I sat on the other with Alex sitting behind them.

The courtroom slowly filled with people until one o'clock, then the doors were closed. The judge came in a sat down in his seat. The trial started.

We heard from Mrs. Turner, Mr. Turner, the guard at the bank, Robert and the sheriff. When they had all gave their testimonies, the judge declared the two guilty. We escorted them back to their cells. Alex and I went to the restaurant for supper before going back to the sheriff's office.

For the next week, Alex and I took turns with the sheriff and deputy in guarding the prisoners. At the end of the week the marshal from the jail and four deputies showed up to escort the men to the jail.

Alex and I ended up staying an extra day to visit with Simone before heading back to Cartwheel. Fitzgerald joined us as we headed out of town.

THE KID
CHAPTER 15

Toby

This time we stopped for the nights and arrived back in Cartwheel just after lunch on the third day. Alex and I left Fitzgerald at the hotel before going to the stable behind Nadine's house. Nadine came out of the kitchen door as we came from the stable.

"Is there anything more you have to do?" Nadine asked.

"Not that I know about," Alex answered.

"Good," Nadine said, "We'll leave tomorrow morning."

Nadine led the way into the house. Alex and I sat down while Nadine dished up lunch. We talked about what was going on in the world.

After lunch, Alex and I did the dishes. Nadine had work she had to finish. Alex ended up working in the garden and I cleaned the stable.

Nadine served supper. After supper, Alex and I did the dishes and then Nadine to joined us in a couples of hands of comet until dark.

I woke up to the sound of someone going down stairs. When I came down stairs, Nadine was sitting at the kitchen table reading a letter. She was still in her nightgown and robe.

"Morning," I said. Nadine jumped a little. She looked up at me and relaxed.

"Good morning," Nadine said, "I'll make breakfast in a moment." She continued to read the letter. I started the fire in the stove going. Nadine had finished reading so she put the letter on the table and started making breakfast. I glanced at the signature and saw that it was from Jacob.

Alex joined us shortly after.

Alex and I did the dishes while Nadine dressed. When we were finished Alex put out the fire in the stove.

"Ready?" Alex asked.

"Yes," Nadine answered.

"Then let's head out," Alex said. The three of us went out to the stable. We got our horses ready. Fitzgerald joined as we went through town.

"Does Jacob know you're off to visit Jared Pearson?" Alex asked once we had left town.

"I told him before he left for the last job," Nadine answered.

"Was he listening?" Alex asked.

"He nodded and said it was fine," Nadine answered, "So, I doubt he heard me. I'm so tired of him disappearing and leaving me alone at home. If he comes home while I'm gone then maybe he'll listen next time."

"Depends on the job and the employer," Alex said.

"He talks occasionally about retiring," Nadine said, "It seems more likely I'll get word that he died and was buried in a local cemetery."

"As good as any place to be buried," Alex said, "Personally I think it's better than sending the body home."

"Some of us would like to know where our loved ones are buried," Nadine said.

"That's what headstones are for," Alex said, "But to get any kind of marker on your grave someone in town needs to know your name."

"I would rather Jacob just retired," Nadine said, "Then he could die of old age instead of being gunned down in a strange place."

"What would he do if he retired?" I asked, "Jacob seems the kind who needs something to do."

"When I met Jacob he was a carpenter," Nadine said, "He built furniture for people and he was good at it. I married a carpenter."

"How'd he become what he is now?" I asked.

"His first partner showed up after we had been married a couple years," Nadine said, "Reuben showed up shortly after Jacob's parents were killed by bandits on their way to visit us. Jacob was more than willing to learn and Reuben was willing to teach him. However, Reuben had no interest in finding the bandits who'd killed Jacob's parents. Instead he convinced Jacob to protect other people so that it wouldn't happen to anyone else."

"Which would be why he doesn't like revenge jobs," Alex said.

"They spent four years riding all over the country before Reuben was shot and killed," Nadine said, "Jacob stumbled back to me. He was drunk and looked twice his age. I almost didn't recognize him the first time I saw him. I certainly didn't want to take him back in, but after he sobered up, he begged me to take him back. I did and he went back to being a carpenter. That lasted three years and he hasn't gone back to it since."

"Being a carpenter is a good thing," Alex said, "Maybe you can convince him to retire after this job."

"I'll be trying, but I doubt it'll work," Nadine said. No one said anything else for a while.

It took a week to get to Riverside. When we arrived, Fitzgerald immediately went off to find himself a hotel while Nadine, Alex and I continued to Jared's house.

*　　　*　　　*　　　*

Matthew

Three riders came into town. The lady looked like a housewife. She was riding in a sidesaddle, which can't be comfortable for any rider for very long. The second rider was a man. His jeans, brown coat and light brown hat were covered with dust from travelling. He was starting to look like he needed a haircut and a shave. The third rider was also a man wearing jeans; both his coat and hat were black. He was also covered with the travelling dust. But he was clean shaven and it was hard to tell how long his hair was. Both men had guns holstered to their hips, but that looked like all the weaponry they had.

"What is it?" Johnny asked.

"Two gunslingers," I answered nodding toward the window.

Johnny looked over my shoulder.

"I don't know the lady or the other man," Johnny said, "But the man riding the morgan, him I know."

"Is he gonna be a problem?" I asked.

"No," Johnny answered with a laugh, "Alex might be willing to help us. I'd want to meet his partner first, but I can't see him taking on a partner who would be a problem."

"How long have you known Alex?" I asked.

"I haven't seen him in a couple years, but before that we rode off and on together for three years. Or close to that," Johnny answered.

"How is he with a gun?" I asked.

"Not quite as fast as some on the draw… more likely to hit what he is shooting at though," Johnny answered, "He's been around a while and he's usually pretty smart about things."

"Can he shoot anything besides the handgun he carries?" I asked.

"I've seen him shoot a Winchester with deadly accuracy," Johnny answered, "Seen him fire a shotgun too, but he wasn't as good with it."

"We don't have a lot of money to pay him or his partner," I said.

"Relax, Matthew. I'll talk to him," Johnny said, "We'll work things out. If he doesn't want to join us that'll be fine too."

"I'm just trying to be cautious," I said.

"And if it was anyone other than Alex I would encourage it," Johnny replied.

"You think he'll work out?" I asked.

"I know he will," Johnny answered.

*　　　*　　　*　　　*

Toby

Riverside was smaller and less crowded this time. We rode through town and out the other side to where Jared Pearson lived.

Jared Pearson was sitting on the veranda when we rode up. He stood up when he saw us.

"So nice to see you," Jared said as Nadine got down from her horse.

"Nice to see you, too," Nadine replied.

"You're all welcome to join me for drink," Jared said looking at me and Alex.

"We'll stop by later," Alex said, "Right now finding a hotel room seems like a good idea."

"Then you and Toby are invited to supper," Jared said.

"See you then," Alex replied.

Going back into town we stopped at the first hotel. Fitzgerald was sitting in the lobby. He rose and came over to us.

"What're you gonna do while Nadine is visiting Jared?" Fitzgerald asked.

"Go for supper there tonight," Alex answered, "After that who knows."

"I saw Johnny," Fitzgerald said, "He's in the saloon down the street."

"We'll have to stop in and see how he's doing," Alex said.

"I'll wait here," Fitzgerald said. Alex and I went to the front desk. We each got a room and headed upstairs to leave our stuff.

"Who's Johnny?" I asked.

"Johnny Kidd," Alex answered, "We took some jobs together a while back. He's pretty good with a gun, but picky about which jobs he takes and who he works with."

I nodded. Alex reached her room. I continued down the hallway to my room. Reaching it, I put my saddlebag on the bed. I went back down to the lobby, where Alex and Fitzgerald were waiting for me.

We walked over to the saloon. It was still fairly empty. There were a group of men at the bar, a table in the back with a poker game in progress and two men sitting at a table in another corner. Everyone, except one of the two men, ignored us. I followed Alex and Fitzgerald to the table. The man stood up as we approached. He had dark blue eyes, black hair and reminded me of Alex when I first met her. The other man who had remained seated looked more like a miner with his scruffy beard and dirty clothes. His grey eyes studied us as if he expected us to shoot him at any moment.

"What an unexpected surprise," the man who had stood up offered his hand to Alex.

"How are you?" Alex said shaking his hand.

"Busy, but fine," Johnny answered, "You're still travelling with Fitzgerald, I see."

"Actually Alex saved me from being hung," Fitzgerald said, "And I haven't found any place to settle back down."

"He's sober too," Alex said.

"There've been a lot of changes in the last few years," Johnny said.

"Speaking of changes," Alex said, "Johnny, this's my partner. Toby. Toby, this's Johnny."

"A partner?" Johnny said, "I'm not sure whether to congratulate you or offer my sympathies." Johnny held out his hand to me.

"It's worked out well so far," I replied, shaking his hand. We all sat down at the table.

"This's Matthew," Johnny indicated the man beside him," There're three of us working for a local mine owner."

"Who's your third man?" Alex asked.

"Tate McPherson's kid," Johnny answered.

"Tate had a kid?" Fitzgerald asked.

"Not a surprise," Alex said, "He slept with every woman who crossed his path, even though he kept talking about going back to his wife."

"Apparently the kid is by his wife," Johnny said.

"That's a surprise," Alex said.

"I met up with the kid at Tate's funeral," Johnny said, "Aside from one bad job, which he claims to be lucky to have escaped from unharmed, Alan has been doing pretty well."

"Sounds like you're doing well for yourself," Alex said.

"Yeah," Johnny said, "What're you doing in town?"

"With a friend who's visiting an aquaintice," Alex answered.

"Guard duty?" Johnny asked.

"Only for traveling here and back," Alex answered.

"Sounds boring," Johnny said.

"Depends on what we find to do," Alex replied.

"Maybe you can help us," Johnny said, "We've been hired to guard a mine near here against a gang of bandits."

"How many bandits count as a gang?" Alex asked.

"There're twenty in the gang," Johnny said, "They usually send five men out at a time. All twenty are good with guns. We've been on the job for almost three weeks and only Alan has hit any of them. None of us've been shot yet, but the scratches and bruises are starting to add up."

"We have to go to Jared's for supper, but after that we should be free for a couple of days," Alex said.

"Jared as in Jared Pearson?" Johnny asked.

"Yes," Alex answered.

"Is he the friend or the acquaintance?" Johnny asked.

"The acquaintance," Alex answered.

"I'm told Jared is good to have as a friend," Matthew said.

"He's smart enough to keep an eye on his enemies," Alex replied, "What he does for his friends I don't know."

"You haven't known him long?" Johnny asked.

"Met him a while back, just haven't been back here since," Alex answered.

"You're busy as usual?" Johnny asked.

"Haven't slowed down any," Alex answered. A man came into the saloon. I recognized him as the gunslinger that Mr. Howard from back in Brighten had employed. He looked over the room before starting toward the table then he hesitated.

"And here's our third man," Johnny said signalling the man to come over to the table. The man walked over. I saw the laughter in Alex's eyes that didn't show on her face.

"Alan," Johnny said once the man was pulling up a chair, "These're friends of mine, Alex, Fitzgerald and Alex's partner, Toby." Johnny indicated each of us.

"Nice to finally meet you," Alan said.

"If I had known you were Tate's kid the whole job would've been easy," Alex commented.

"My father never talked about what he did," Alan said, "But I'm starting to think I should skip telling people my name and just tell them I'm Tate McPherson's son."

"Give them your name," Alex said, "Easier to gain your own reputation. And if you run into any of your father's enemies they won't shoot you immediately."

"I'm guessing you've met Alan," Johnny said.

"Alex and Toby were the other side of the bad job I took," Alan replied.

"And you didn't shoot him?" Matthew asked.

"No reason to," I answered.

"Alex and Toby are gonna be helping us while they're in town," Johnny said.

"I'm here in case you get shot," Fitzgerald said.

"As long as you stay sober," Johnny said.

"Haven't had a drink in years," Fitzgerald said, "Don't see any reason to crawl back into the bottle now."

"The town doctor is starting to get old," Alan said, "I don't trust him to do a good job any more. You may not be good in a fight, but having a doctor around is a good thing."

"We'll have to talk the whole job over later," Alex said, "Toby and I have to go for supper."

"See you when you get back," Johnny said. Alex and I stood up and left the saloon. Our horses were still outside the hotel.

"What do you think?" Alex asked as we mounted our horses.

"It'll be an interesting job," I answered. We rode to Jared's house.

Nadine came out to meet us.

"How's your visit so far?" Alex asked once we had tied our reins to the hitching post.

"Excellent," Nadine said.

"Good," Alex said.

"You took a job, didn't you?" Nadine asked.

"We offered to help with a job," Alex answered, "We leave when you're ready."

"Good to know," Nadine said, "I was thinking a week."

"Then enjoy your visit," Alex said. Nadine led us inside to the parlour.

“Good evening,” Jared said as he entered the room.

“Good evening,” I replied.

“Supper is ready,” Jared said, “If you'll all come this way.” We followed him into the dining room. The food was already on the table. We sat down and started to eat. The conversation was mainly about what was going on in the world, how it looked like the railroad might someday go from coast to coast and how much the world was changing.

After supper we continued the conversation in the parlour. When Nadine decided it was time for bed, Alex and I went back into town. We left our horses at the stable this time before going back to the saloon.

Johnny, Matthew, Fitzgerald and Alan were still sitting at the same table, though it took a minute for Alex and me to get through the crowd.

"You're back," Johnny said as we sat down.

"We told you we would be," Alex said, "We would've been back sooner but we're too polite."

"I can't see walking out on Jared Pearson," Matthew said.

"Only if it was an emergency," Alex said, "Or he was too busy to notice."

"I thought they were gonna get caught up in their own conversation and forget about us a few times during the evening," I commented, "But they seemed to notice what they were doing before it got to the point where we could leave."

"You leave once and people start to catch on," Alex said, "Now, what're the details of this job?"

"We go sit at the mine and if the bandits attack, we defend," Johnny answered, "We take our own food, water and anything else we need. It's boring unless the bandits strike."

"Usually," Alex said.

"Bring your horses to the docks after breakfast," Johnny said, "We'll head out from there."

"Sounds good," Alex said.

"Gonna go back to your hotel?" Johnny asked.

"Sleep sounds really good," I replied. Alex nodded.

"See you in the morning," Johnny said. Alex and I stood up and left the saloon.

The sun was rising when I woke up. Getting out of bed, I washed up before going downstairs. I found a table in the dining room and was served immediately.

Alex came downstairs after I had finished eating. She sat down in the chair across from me.

"No more nightmares?" I asked.

"I still have nightmares," Alex answered, "But they're mild and I have no trouble going back to sleep after them."

"That's good," I said.

"I haven't felt this rested in years," Alex said, "But sometimes it was useful to be awake early in the morning."

"You'll figure something out," I said, "In the meantime rest is useful."

"True," Alex said. The waitress brought Alex's food.

Once she was finished we left the hotel and went to the stable. Getting our horses, we went to the dock. No one else was there yet, so Alex and I waited.

Fitzgerald arrived soon, then Alan. We waited close to an hour before Johnny and Matthew showed up.

"You should've gone to bed earlier," Alex commented.

"Shouldn't've had that much to drink either," Johnny replied.

"Don't you get in trouble with your employer?" Alex asked as we started riding parallel to the river.

"It's very likely that he isn't up yet," Johnny answered, "He lives at the mine and tends to drink himself to sleep."

"And the bandits don't attack at night?" Alex asked.

"For some strange reason, no," Johnny answered.

"Probably see it as more of a challenge to strike during the day," Alan said.

"They're taunting us," Matthew said, "They're rubbing in our faces the fact that we can't stop them during the day thus we obviously couldn't catch them at night." Alex shot Johnny a look that asked what was with Matthew. Johnny saw it and shrugged in response.

"They're probably right," Alan said.

We had left the city, but we were still travelling along the river. Three buildings that were slightly inland came into view. Coming closer, we saw two sheds and a cabin. There didn't seem to be any people around. Johnny stopped his horse at a group of trees near the mine. He tied the reins to a branch. The rest of us followed suit.

Johnny pointed out positions for me and Alex before going to the cabin. Everyone had a position where they could see anyone coming as well as any activity near the buildings.

Half an hour after we had gotten there, a man came out of the cabin. He went over to one shed. Opening the door, he pulled out some tools, closed the door, and walked over to the other shed. He went inside and closed the door behind him.

We spent the rest of the morning watching for anyone. At noon we stopped for lunch before spending the rest of the day doing the same thing. As the sun started to get close to the horizon the man came out of the shed. He put his tools away in the other shed before going into the cabin and closing the door. Johnny signalled to us that the work day was over.

All of us mounted our horses and headed back to town.

"I'm guessing the only excitement is when the bandits attack," Alex said.

"Unfortunately," Johnny replied, "But there weren't many other jobs I was willing to take."

"Some days you're too picky," Alex said.

"But I never end up with a job I hate," Johnny said.

"If it wasn't for certain associations I wouldn't either," Alex said.

"The problem there is more than half the jobs you tend to take don't pay," Johnny said.

"How much are you getting for this job?" Alex asked.

"A dollar a day," Johnny answered.

"Does that even pay for your rooms?" Alex asked.

"Room and board," Johnny answered, looking uncomfortable.

"Which means if you do anything else, like drink, you lose money on the job," Alex said.

"At least room and board is paid," Johnny replied.

"True," Alex said.

"I'm amazed you didn't ask about pay," Johnny said.

"Toby and I did one of those jobs most people won't think about doing," Alex said, "And got a good pay out."

"Drinks are on you then," Johnny said. Not much else was said the rest of the way into town.

Once there Johnny, Matthew and Alan went to their boarding house. Fitzgerald, Alex and I went to our hotel for supper. After supper we all met up at the saloon.

*　　　*　　　*　　　*

Johnny

I watched the group through the saloon window. I had stepped outside for a breath of fresh air and no one had really noticed. They were busy playing poker. In was strangest version I have heard of with the winner buying the next round of drinks. Alex, her partner and Fitzgerald seem to have gotten Alan to relax. Even Matthew wasn't as uptight as usual.

I rolled and then lit a cigarette. I turned to have my back to the window as I exhaled.

I was on my second cigarette when Alex stepped out of the saloon. She came over to where I was standing.

"What's wrong?" Alex asked.

"This's my last job," I answered.

"Why?" Alex asked.

"I'm retiring," I answered, "I have a wife and two children back home who've been waiting for me. Stopping in every few months for a week or so isn't good enough anymore."

"What about Matthew and Alan?" Alex asked.

"They have each other," I answered, "Alan needs to figure out who he is anyway."

"How long do you figure the job will last?" Alex asked.

"Hopefully less than a month," I answered, "If it takes longer I figure on finding the bandits and taking them out that way."

"Toby and I'll have to leave before that," Alex said.

"I know," I replied. We were silent for a few minutes.

"You ever think about retiring?" I asked, "Or are you going for buried in the town where you were shot?"

"Sometimes I get a tired feeling and think that maybe I should get out while I'm ahead," Alex answered.

"What stops you from doing that?" I asked.

"Something else comes along that I have to deal with," Alex answered, "And the thought doesn't come back during the rests between jobs."

"The problem with being a gunslinger is that when, or if, you reach the time when most people have settled into their lives, you're forced to make decisions about what to do with your life," I said.

"And most of us wouldn't have it any other way," Alex said.

"True," I said.

"Have you told Matthew and Alan about your decision?" Alex asked.

"Somewhat," I answered, "I told them that they're on their own for the next job."

"Are you gonna tell them?" Alex asked.

"I don't know," I answered.

"Well, in the meantime, come back inside," Alex said heading back into the saloon. I followed.

* * * *

Toby

I was sitting in the dining room staring at the food that had been set in front of me when Alex sat down.

"Too much to drink?" Alex asked.

"Apparently," I answered. I pushed my plate to her. Alex started to eat.

"Are you hurt?" Alex asked.

"Once the headache goes away I'll be fine," I answered. Fitzgerald came into the dining room and sat down.

"Good morning," Fitzgerald said.

"Morning," Alex replied.

"I wonder how Johnny and the other two make it to work if they drink that much all the time," Fitzgerald said.

"I don't think they usually drink as much as they did last night," Alex said, "I doubt they have the money to do that."

The waiter brought Fitzgerald a plate of food.

"Well, everyone seemed to have had quite a bit to drink last night," Fitzgerald said.

"Tonight will probably be different," Alex said.

"Today I'll be out with you," Fitzgerald said, "But tomorrow I'm going to spend the day with the town doctor."

"From what Johnny has said, there haven't been any serious injuries so that should be fine," Alex said. Not much more was said as Alex and I waited for Fitzgerald to finish eating.

When he was done we got our horses. There was no one at the dock when we arrived, so we waited.

It was mid-morning when Johnny, Matthew and Alan rode up. They looked about how I felt. We started toward the mine. Alex and Johnny led us and no one talked.

Arriving, we left our horses by the trees and took up our posts.

The rest of the morning went by without anything happening. At noon the man came out of his cabin, picked up his tools and went into the second shed closing the door behind him. We took a break for lunch.

The afternoon with quiet, even the pounding in my head had died down. Johnny had just given the signal that the work day was over when I could hear the sound of horses coming. Based on the fact that everyone was drawing their weapons I'd say that they could hear it too. Johnny pointed at four places where there was cover. All of us went for cover. Fitzgerald found a place where he was least likely to get hit and made himself as small as possible. Alan went to the cover that was on the right. Alex and Johnny were together behind the next cover. Matthew and I were on the far left.

Everyone was in position when the riders could be seen. I was expecting five riders and based on Matthew's language when he saw them so was he. Instead all twenty riders were headed in our direction.

All the riders had their hats pulled low and bandanas covering their mouths and noses. Even so that a couple of them looked familiar; maybe they had been at the saloon last night.

Once they were in range Alan and Matthew started shooting. The riders returned fire. I held off firing until they were a few feet short of our cover. Johnny and Alex joined in as well.

The charge was slowed and those that remained on horseback continued on around us. Both sides seemed to be equal in accuracy and dodging. I was barely getting off one shot before I had to duck again. But a few of the riders were lying on the ground. The riders that had gotten passed us set fire to the tool shed before heading back the way they had come. They continued to fire at us.

I felt a sharp pain through my left shoulder, but continued to return fire.

When the riders were out of range, Alex and Alan ran for the horses. Each mounted their own and rode off after the riders.

"What the hell are those two doing?" Matthew demanded standing up. I stood up more slowly and looked around. The tool shed was engulfed in flames. Fitzgerald was getting to his feet. I walked over to the cover that Alex and Johnny had hidden behind. Johnny was lying on his back with blood smeared around the hole in his chest.

"At least Johnny had the sense to..." Matthew cut off when he saw the body. I don't know how long we stood there in silence but Fitzgerald came over. He knelt down and closed Johnny's eyes. I turned my attention to the battlefield. There were three bodies. I walked over to the first one, knelt down and pulled the bandana off. It was the bartender from the saloon.

I started to rise when a sharp pain went through my shoulder again. It went back to being a dull pain once I was on my feet, but the world was starting to swim.

I went over and sat down on a large rock. The miner had come out of the cabin and was standing looking down where Johnny lay. Matthew was looking over the other two bodies and Fitzgerald was headed my direction.

"How bad is it?" he asked when he reached to me.

"Just got hit in the shoulder," I answered. Fitzgerald looked at the wound in my shoulder.

"It doesn't look too bad," Fitzgerald said, "But I should bandage it."

I nodded before standing up and following Fitzgerald.

"There's a chair in my cabin," the miner said as we passed him. Fitzgerald and I went into the cabin. It held a table, a chair and bed. I took off my coat before sitting down on the chair.

Fitzgerald had me take off my shirt and then he set to work. Just as he was finishing up Matthew came into the cabin.

"We got the bartender from the saloon, the man who cleans out the stables, and the night clerk at one of the hotels," Matthew said.

"Why would those three be bandits?" Fitzgerald asked.

"I don't know," Matthew answered, "But I'm sensing trouble, especially with Alex and the kid going after the rest of the bandits."

"We need to get into town," I said, "And talk to the sheriff."

"He could be a member of the gang," Matthew said.

"Doesn't matter," I replied, "What we need is to get those bodies planted in the cemetery before they start to smell."

"And why should we bother with them?" Matthew asked, "They tried to kill us."

"I was thinking about Johnny," I answered.

"Sorry," Matthew said.

"You gonna stand around or you gonna git into town?" the miner asked as he entered the cabin.

"We were just about to leave," I said as I put my shirt back on. Pain shot through my shoulder but I ignored it. I picked up my coat before following Matthew out of the cabin. Fitzgerald stayed in the cabin. I pulled on my coat as we walked to the horses. We mounted and headed for town.

"How long do you think it'll take for Alex and the kid to get back?" Matthew asked.

"I don't know about Alan, but Alex won't be back until all the bandits are dead," I answered.

"He could be killed," Matthew said.

"That's never stopped Alex before," I replied, "Especially if there's someone to be avenged."

"That's foolish," Matthew said. I shrugged and we didn't talk for the rest of the ride into town.

We rode to and stopped in front of the sheriff's office. The sheriff came out of his office before we could dismount.

"What happened?" the sheriff asked.

"We got some of the bandits who've been terrorizing Mr. Bartol's mine," Matthew said.

"Casualties?" the sheriff asked.

"Johnny and three of the bandits, who we've identified as the bartender from the Golden Drink, the man who cleans out the stables and the night clerk at one of the hotels," I answered.

"I'll get the doctor and ride back out with you," the sheriff said before going back into his office. He came out a moment later. Matthew and I headed for the stables. The sheriff and the doctor arrived a few minutes later. The sheriff helped the doctor hitch up the wagon. When they were ready we all headed for the mine. No one said anything as we rode.

Fitzgerald and the miner had placed the bandit's bodies near the remains of the shed. Johnny's body was still where he had fallen, but a piece of canvas was now covering him.

The doctor stopped the wagon next to the pile of bodies. The sheriff examined each body before the doctor placed them into the wagon. Then Matthew and I moved Johnny's canvas wrapped body into the wagon.

"Where're the other two men who were working with you?" the sheriff asked.

"They followed after the bandits escaped," Matthew answered.

"Hopefully that won't get them killed," the sheriff said. He and the doctor climbed back on to the wagon and headed back to town.

Before Matthew, Fitzgerald and I left for the night, the miner came out and told us that he didn't think he would need us tomorrow.

When we got back into town Fitzgerald and I stopped at the

stable before going back to the hotel for supper.

After supper I went up to my room. I played solitaire until I decided to go to bed.

After breakfast I sat outside the hotel.

Matthew stopped by mid-morning to tell me that Johnny had been buried and the grave had been properly marked. After this job he was going to stop in and tell Johnny's wife that Johnny had died.

Fitzgerald joined me for lunch before going to talk with the doctor. I went back to sitting outside the hotel.

I listened to various conversations and it sounded like there were about seventeen men missing. Word was also getting around about the three that were dead and what they were doing when they died.

In the middle of the afternoon Nadine rode into town. She saw me and came over.

"Where's Alex?" Nadine asked.

"Off dealing with bandits," I answered.

"Why aren't you with her?" Nadine asked.

"We were helping to guard a mine and she took off after the bandits after they attacked," I answered, "She hasn't come back yet."

"I was thinking about leaving tomorrow, but I guess it'll have to wait until Alex comes back," Nadine said.

"If you're tired of visiting Jared, you can probably stay in Alex's hotel room," I said.

"I'm more worried about Jacob getting back," Nadine said.

"How long was he supposed to be gone?" I asked.

"I'm not sure," Nadine answered.

"If you're really worried, I can leave a message for Alex and escort you home," I said.

"Thank you, but it isn't urgent," Nadine said. The sheriff came up.

"A number of bodies were found," the sheriff said, "At least one has been identified as one of the bandits. I was just about to head out there."

"I coming," I said as I stood up. The sheriff started toward the stable and I followed.

When we came out of the stable on our horses Nadine was waiting outside on her horse. The sheriff looked at me and I shrugged. The sheriff led the way with Nadine and me following.

We left the town and came in to area with several cave entrances. There were six bodies lying on the ground, all dead from bullet wounds. Some of them seemed familiar, like met on the street familiar, but other than that I didn't know any of them.

"Alex's work?" Nadine asked.

"And a kid by the name of Alan," I answered.

"So, where are they?" Nadine asked.

"After the other nine," I answered.

"The other nine?" Nadine asked.

"The other nine bandits," I answered.

"The doctor is supposed to be on his way," the sheriff said, "But I guess it'll be up to him to identify these men."

"I can't identify them," I said.

"I'll wait here for the doctor," the sheriff said. I nodded. Nadine and I turned our horses around and headed back into town.

Our first stop was the stable so that I could leave my horse there. Then we went back to the hotel. I sat down in the chair outside. Nadine tied the reins of her horse to the hitching post and sat down beside me.

"You're worried about Alex," Nadine said.

"Alex is good at what she does, but the bandits seemed to be equal when they were shooting back," I replied, "And she's only doing this to get vengeance for Johnny's death."

"She left one pile of bodies behind," Nadine said.

"Yeah, it looks like they were caught off guard," I said, "That means the last nine are running and know who's chasing them."

"I hadn't thought of that," Nadine said, "I suppose there's no way to find her."

"Not without knowing which direction she went or at least some way to track her," I replied, "And I'm not very good when it comes to tracking."

"So, you're just going to sit here?" Nadine asked.

"For today," I answered, "Tomorrow I'm going back out to the mine to see if the miner still thinks he needs help."

"Why?" Nadine asked, "If Alex is after the bandits what would the miner need?"

"I don't know until I've talked to him," I answered, "There are other dangers out there other than one gang of bandits."

"And if he doesn't need you?" Nadine asked.

"Then I sit here and worry until Alex comes back," I answered.

"You'll find me when Alex is back?" Nadine asked standing up.

"Of course," I replied. Nadine mounted her horse and headed back to Jared's house.

After supper I joined a couple other guests playing a game of poker.

The next morning I went out to the mine with Matthew. The miner was sitting on a chair outside his cabin, smoking a pipe.

"Figured you'd be back out," the miner said.

"Does that mean you don't need us anymore?" Matthew asked.

"Don't see much point," the miner answered, "But when the other two are back, come and see me."

"We'll see you then," I said. Matthew and I turned around and went back into town.

The two gentlemen were still at the hotel when I arrived for lunch. They invited me to join them and we ended up spending the rest of the day playing poker.

I spent the next day trying to find things to do.

The afternoon of the third day as I came out of the hotel after having lunch, I saw Alex and Alan ride into town. They went right to the sheriff's office. I sat down on the chair outside the hotel.

A moment later the clerk stepped out of the hotel and walked over to me.

"This came for you," the clerk said holding out an envelope. I took it.

"Thank you," I said. The clerk went back inside. I looked at the envelope. It was addressed to me and Alex, but there was no indication who had sent it. Matthew came up.

"Any sign of them?" he asked.

"They just went into the sheriff's office," I answered.

"Then what're you doing just sitting here?" Matthew asked.

"Waiting until they're finished with the sheriff," I answered.

"What's that?" Matthew asked, noticing the envelope.

"Don't know yet," I answered. I opened the envelope while

Mathew started pacing. Taking out the letter I read it. Just as I finished I could see Alex and Alan riding toward Matthew and me.

"What happened?" Matthew demanded as they got down. Neither answered as they tied the reins to the hitching post.

"We went after them, we found them, we killed some of them, the rest fled, we chased them and we finished killing them," Alan said, "What happened here?"

"Johnny has been buried, the miner wants to talk to all of us," I answered, "And a couple other things."

"Like what?" Alex asked.

"Nadine is ready to go home and this," I held up the envelope, "Just arrived." Alex took the letter. She read through it before looking up at me.

"Does Fitzgerald know about this?" Alex asked.

"Not yet," I answered, "I just received it and I haven't seen Fitzgerald since breakfast."

"What's he been doing?" Alex asked.

"Helping the doctor out," I answered.

"We'll have to talk to him about it," Alex said.

"We should go out to the mine," Matthew said, "Before it gets too late."

"Is there a rush?" Alan asked.

"The sooner the job is done the sooner I can go explain to Johnny's widow why he isn't coming home from this job," Matthew answered.

"Then let's go," Alex said. Matthew headed for the stable. I followed him. We got our horses and met Alex and Alan near the dock. Then we went out to the mine.

The miner was sitting on a chair outside the cabin. We tied our horses to the tree branches and walked over to him.

"They're all dead?" the miner asked.

"Yes," Alex answered.

"Good," the miner said. He stood up and went into the cabin. He came out a moment later with an envelope. The miner handed each of us fifty dollars then he sealed the envelope.

"This needs to go to Johnny's widow," he said, holding up the envelope.

"I'm going there," Matthew said. The miner hesitated until he saw Alex nod.

"Make sure she gets this," the miner said, handing the envelope to Matthew.

"I will," Matthew said. The miner sat back down as if he was dismissing us. We went back to our horses and rode back to town.

When we reached town, Matthew and Alan went their way. Alex and I left the horses at the stable before going back to the hotel.

Alex was already sitting in the dining room when I came down, but she hadn't been served yet.

"Morning," Alex said.

"Yeah," I responded.

"What did you stay up doing?" Alex asked.

"Playing poker," I answered.

"I suppose we should go talk to Nadine today," Alex said.

"Only if you're ready to head back," I said.

"We can go up this evening," Alex said, "Then we can head back tomorrow."

We were half way through breakfast when Fitzgerald came in and sat down.

"Good to see you back," Fitzgerald said.

"Have you figured out what you're gonna do?" Alex asked.

"No," Fitzgerald answered, "I would prefer to just go home but I know that isn't really an option."

"A letter came that was addressed to Toby and me," Alex said, "It's from the mayor of Plantville. He and the town council would like our help getting rid of Cutler."

"Are you gonna help?" Fitzgerald asked.

"We hadn't discussed that yet," Alex answered.

"If you did that, I could go home." Fitzgerald said.

"Even if we decided to do it, we have to escort Nadine home first," Alex said.

"When'll she be ready to go?" Fitzgerald asked.

"We'll go talk to her this evening," Alex answered, "And probably leave tomorrow morning."

"I'll be ready," Fitzgerald said. His food was brought. Alex and I were finished so we left him to eat and went outside.

"What do you think?" Alex asked.

"I don't see any reason why not," I answered, "We don't have any jobs lined up and no general direction to go. Unless you have something else in mind."

"No," Alex said. Alan came up.

"Matthew left this morning," Alan said.

"He doesn't waste any time," Alex commented.

"He wastes energy on other things, but seems to like having a specific purpose," I said.

"It doesn't help that he's paranoid about the rest of us," Alan said.

"What're you gonna do now?" Alex asked.

"I don't know," Alan answered, "There isn't much for jobs around here and I don't have enough of a reputation for people to come looking for me."

"We have a job," Alex said, "But it doesn't require more than one or two people."

"Do you mind if I tag along anyway?" Alan asked. Alex looked at me and I shrugged.

"Sure you can tag along," Alex said, "You have to pay your own way."

"That's fine," Alan said.

"We're leaving tomorrow," Alex said, "We have to escort a lady home and then go to the job."

"I'll be ready," Alan said. He turned and walked away.

"How is he to work with?" I asked.

"Still learning, but catches on quickly," Alex answered, "Reminds me a lot of Tate. Though once he learns enough, he'll probably be better than his father."

"What was Tate like?" I asked.

"Over eager, highly sensitive to situations," Alex said, "Usually cheerful, charming when he wanted to be and ready to follow orders of whoever he was working with at the time."

"Sounds like an interesting man," I said.

"The only problem was that he never saw himself equal with anyone he worked with," Alex said, "He always took the bottom position in the group, even when he should have had a higher one or as a leader he would have done the group more good. That's why I figure Alan will be better than Tate. Alan seems more sensitive to what is needed rather than which position he's in."

I nodded. We switched subjects and kept talking. At lunch we went inside to eat and both were invited to a poker game that lasted all afternoon. After supper we went out to Jared's house. We ended up staying and visiting until after dark. Then we headed back to the hotel for the night.

The next morning, Fitzgerald arrived at the dining room when Alex and I did. And Alan was waiting outside when we were finished. All four of us went to the stable to get our horses. From there we went to Jared's house, where Nadine was waiting. Then we headed back to Cartwheel.

The trip back took us a week. Going through town Fitzgerald and Alan broke off to find a hotel. Alex, Nadine and I went straight to the stable behind Nadine's house. There weren't any other horses there, so Jacob wasn't home. Once our horses were in their stalls we went into the house. Alex helped Nadine make supper. After supper I did the dishes. After day on the road, the bed felt good.

My eyes opened, but it was still dark in the room. I wondered what woke me, then I heard a thump from downstairs. It was followed by a muffled ‘ouch.’ I got out of bed and quietly went to the door. There was another thump. It sounded like a person had walked into a piece of furniture. I opened the door and looked out. Nadine was standing outside her door with a lamp in her hand. I stepped into the hall as Alex's door opened. She stepped into the hallway. She was wearing pants and a shirt. I also saw the light glint off the gun in her hand.

Another thump came from downstairs. I started down the stairs with Nadine following me. She held up the lamp to provide me with more light. The kitchen door opened with a creak. I went towards the kitchen. There was a thump and a yelp. I reached the doorway and could see two figures, one standing and the other on the floor. Nadine came to stand behind me. With the light I could see that it was Jacob standing in the kitchen. The figure lying on the floor was that of a boy, who looked like he might be sixteen. He was holding his leg rubbing his shin.

"What’s going on?" Nadine demanded. I moved aside so that she could enter the kitchen.

"We were trying to come in quietly," Jacob answered.

"Well, quiet woke everyone up," Nadine stated, "Who’s this?"

She pointed to the kid on the floor.

"Justin," Jacob answered, "I offered to teach him some life skills before someone killed him."

"Then the next time you want to teach him stealth do it far away from where I'm trying to sleep," Nadine roared at Jacob, "In the meantime, go back out to the barn. All the beds in here are full."

"Nadine," Jacob started.

"Both of you," Nadine shouted, "Out to the barn. Now!"

Jacob looked like he was going to say something.

"You have five seconds to get outta my kitchen or neither of you are welcome back, ever," Nadine shouted, pointing at the door. Jacob pulled the kid to his feet and both went back out of the kitchen door. After putting the lamp down on the table Nadine picked up the chair that was knocked over and sat down on it. She rested her elbows on the table and put her head in her hands.

"What was he thinking?" Nadine asked. I stepped into the kitchen.

"He wasn't," I replied. Nadine smiled briefly. Alex came into the kitchen.

"Jacob?" Alex asked.

"And the kid he has recently taken on," I answered.

"So much for talking him into retiring," Nadine said, "Why do I put up with this?"

"Because at one point you loved him enough to swear that you would stick by him through all this sickness," Alex answered. Nadine smiled again, but only briefly.

"I kicked him out," Nadine's voice was soft.

"Why don't you go back to bed?" Alex asked, "And in the morning you'll see everything in a clearer light."

"I suppose," Nadine said. She stood up, picked up the lamp and started toward the stairs. Alex and I followed her upstairs. She went into her room taking the light with her. I heard Alex go into her room. I went into mine. Lying down, I went back to sleep.

The next morning I went downstairs and found Nadine making breakfast.

"Good morning," Nadine said.

"Morning," I replied.

"I expected Alex to be up by now," Nadine said.

"She's been sleeping recently," I said.

"That's good," Nadine said.

"Except when disturbed in the middle of the night," Alex said coming into the kitchen.

"Jacob came in this morning and apologized," Nadine said.

"He decided to eat somewhere else?" Alex asked as Nadine served breakfast. All three of us sat down.

"I let him tell his side and apologize," Nadine replied, "Then I outlined his disrespectful behaviour and told him that he could come back into the house when he decided to change that behaviour."

"Hopefully he will," I said.

"He's spent thirty years trying to become who he is today," Nadine said, "I doubt it'll happen anytime soon. When're you two leaving?"

"We thought this morning," I answered, "But if you want us to stay longer we can."

"Thank you for the offer, but you have people waiting for you," Nadine said.

"We'll come back and see how you're doing later," Alex said.

"I'll be all right," Nadine said. No one said anything else while we finished eating breakfast.

After breakfast Alex and I did dishes before leaving the house. The kid was still asleep in the loft when we saddled out horses. We left the barn and went into town. Alan and Fitzgerald were waiting for us outside the hotel. They mounted and we headed out of town.

Two days later we rode into Plantville. We went down main street. People stopped to stare when they saw Fitzgerald.

"Why do I feel like I have a target painted on my back?" Alan asked.

"Because Cutler tried to have Fitzgerald hung," Alex answered, "And last time we were through, Toby and I sprung him from jail."

"And you didn't think that maybe we should sneak in?" Alan asked.

"We want Cutler to know we're here," Alex answered.

"And you don't think he'll just shoot you?" Alan asked.

"He might try," Alex said, "But he prefers to have an unfair advantage." We went over one street. This one was mostly houses.

"If he ever challenges you to a fight, follow him out and don't wait until you're in position to take out your gun," I said, "He knows all the ways to cheat without getting charged."

"You fought him when you came through last time?" Fitzgerald asked.

"We met him before that," Alex said.

"Why didn't you kill him then?" Alan asked.

"I figured the limp was good enough," Alex answered. We stopped in front of a house. The house was new enough that it hadn't been painted yet. There were two posts that looked like the start of a hitching post. We left our horses there and went to the door. Alex knocked.

It took a few minutes before the door opened. A woman stood there.

"We're looking for the mayor," Alex said.

"This way," the woman said. She turned and led us into the house. Alan closed the door behind us. The woman led us down the hall to a door. She opened it and gestured that we should go inside. The office took up nearly a quarter of the main floor. An older man sat behind the desk and there were at least a dozen chairs placed around the room.

The mayor stood up as we entered the room. The woman closed the door behind us.

"Alex and Toby?" the mayor asked, "And Fitzgerald?"

"And Alan," Alex answered, "You wrote a letter saying you wanted help getting rid of Cutler."

"I did," the mayor said. He indicted that we should sit. We all found a chair and he sat down.

"Now you want to get rid of Cutler?" Fitzgerald asked, "Why couldn't you do this back when he was destroying my life?"

"The whole council has seen the error of our ways in letting Cutler do that to you," the mayor answered, "And we're glad you avoided being hung."

"What's happened here since?" Alex asked.

"Cutler decided he's in charge and offers to shoot anyone who doesn't agree with him," the mayor said, "We didn't want to do anything before because he was bringing in money. Now the building supplies are here and everyone has work. The council figures that it can take over the mine and keep the money coming in."

"So, you've determined that you no longer need Cutler and now you want to get rid of him," Alex said.

"That is correct," the mayor replied. The door to the office opened and the sheriff stepped inside.

"Is there something wrong?" the mayor asked the sheriff.

"Cutler is outraged that wanted criminals could ride openly into town and not be arrested," the sheriff answered.

"Are you wanted criminals?" the mayor asked.

"Not that we know about," Alex answered.

"It's probably for springing Fitzgerald," the sheriff said.

"I'm sorry about what by the way," Alex said.

"A mild headache is a lot better than a guilty conscience," the sheriff replies, "But if I don't do something…"

"This's why we need to get rid of Cutler," the mayor interrupted.

"Both cases have to go before the judge, correct?" I asked.

"Yes," the sheriff answered, "That was why we were still holding Fitzgerald."

"Then arrest Alex and Fitzgerald," I said, "If you are seen taking them to the jail then Cutler should leave you alone."

"For the moment," the sheriff said, "But the judge'll be here in about a week."

"That gives me and Alan a week to get rid of Cutler," I said.

"Cutler will try to have you two arrested as well," Alex said.

"Then we have to be careful in what we say and do," I replied.

"It should work," Alex said.

"Are you sure?" the mayor asked.

"No, but this's what we do," I told him. Alex stood up. She undid her gun belt and handed it to me. Fitzgerald stood up. The sheriff took out his gun and escorted them out of the room.

"Your rooms and food will be paid for while you stay here," the mayor said.

"We'll be staying at the new hotel on main street," I said.

"Very well," the mayor said. He took a sheet of paper and started to write. It was a few minutes before he looked up again.

"Show this to the owner," the mayor said, holding out the fold piece of paper. I took it. I stood up and left the office with Alan following me. We went out the front door. I mounted my horse and took the reins of Alex's horse. Alan mounted on his, taking the reins of Fitzgerald's horse. Our first stop was to leave our horses at the stable. Then we went to the hotel.

The owner took one glance through the letter and immediately gave us two of the best rooms, which he showed to us himself. He assured us that if we needed anything all we had to do was ask.

I closed the door, dropped my stuff and Alex's on the chair. Soon I was sound asleep.

The next morning I spent time talking to various people. Alan went into the saloon.

After lunch I went up to my room to think. I stood by the window and watched people come and go.

I had learned bits and pieces of information, but nothing seemed useful in getting rid of Cutler. I would have to see if Alan had any ideas.

I saw Cutler walk into the saloon. A moment later he came back out and went to stand in the middle of the street. A full minute later Alan came out of the saloon. As soon as Alan was on the street, Cutler started to shoot at him. Something seemed to be in Alan's favour because none of the six bullets hit him. Finally Alan shot back. Cutler dropped his gun and his hands grabbed at the growing blood stain on his chest. He fell to his knees and then toppled forward. The sheriff went over to the body and checked to see if Cutler was alive or dead. His body language as he straightened up confirmed that Cutler was dead.

I left my hotel room and went downstairs. A man was arguing with the sheriff. The man wanted Alan locked up for murder. Alan just stood waiting to see what the final decision would be. It seemed to take the man forever to wind down.

"I saw the whole fight," the sheriff finally interrupted the man, "There wasn't any murder, it was self-defense."

"He waited until Cutler was out of bullets," the man said.

"At the risk of being shot himself," the sheriff said.

"It was murder," the man said.

"If you wish to discuss this further you can take it up with the judge when he returns." The sheriff went back to his office. The man stalked off and the rest of the crowd went about their business. Alan came over to where I was standing.

"I wasn't sure what else to do," Alan said.

"It worked out better this way," I said.

"Now what do we do?" Alan asked.

"Follow the mayor," I answered. Alan looked confused. I pointed to where the mayor was going into the sheriff's office. Alan nodded in understanding.

We went over to the sheriff's office and stepped inside.

"I had hoped that you would join us," the mayor commented.

"Are the charges dropped?" I asked.

"Yes," the sheriff answered, "With Cutler dead there isn't anyone who cares about the charges."

"Who was the man who wanted to charge me with murder?" Alan asked.

"Richard Charters," the sheriff answered, "He was Cutler's assistant."

"Will he talk to the judge?" Alan asked.

"I don't know," the sheriff answered.

"Is he gonna be a problem with taking control of the mine?" I asked.

"I doubt it," the mayor answered, "He doesn't own any of it. And the workers are local so they'll listen as long as they get paid."

"Richard might blow a lot of hot air, but he's harmless," the sheriff said.

"I hope so," Alan said. The sheriff took the key out of his desk drawer and went into the back area where the cells were. A moment later he came back with Alex and Fitzgerald.

"That was fast," Alex commented.

"He decided to challenge Alan," I said.

"This's to thank you for your help," the mayor handed Alex an envelope, "And Fitzgerald, I was wondering if we could talk."

"Certainly," Fitzgerald said before following the mayor out of the office.

"Sounds like our work here is done," Alex said.

"I wouldn't go too far until the judge arrives," the sheriff said, "Just to make sure there aren't legal consequences that we missed."

The door opened and a young woman stepped inside. She looked like she had been beaten and her ripped dress was streaked with dirt. She collapsed once she had stepped inside.

Alan was helping her into a chair before anyone else could move.

"What happened?" the sheriff asked moving closer to the young woman. Alex and I moved out of the way.

"The stagecoach was attacked," the young woman said. She sounded on the verge of tears.

"You're safe now," the sheriff said handing the young woman his handkerchief. She burst into tears. We waited until she was calm enough to talk.

"My parents and I were going to visit my aunt," she said, "The stagecoach slowed down even though there wasn't anything around. Then it stopped. My father was just about to check what was going on when three men with guns appeared. They demanded we all get out. They kept demanding money. We didn't have anything. They hit me because they thought it would make my father give up the money. The stagecoach driver did something, I'm not sure what, but the men turned toward him. I ran away. I don't know if anyone chased me or not. I ran until I got here. You have to help my parents."

She broke down crying again. Alan looked up at us with a pleading look that asked us to help her. I looked at Alex. She shrugged.

"We can go and help your parents," I said, "But there are a few things we need to know."

"Like what?" the young woman sniffled.

"How about we start with your name and your parent's names?" the sheriff suggested.

"Sarah Thompson," the young woman answered, "My parents are John and Ruth Thompson."

"Which way did you come into town from?" Alex asked. Sarah thought for a minute.

"That way, I think," Sarah answered, pointing in a direction.

"Good," Alex said, "We'll find your parents." Alex, Alan and I left the sheriff's office. We stopped at the stable to get our horses before going off in the direction Sarah had pointed.

It was early evening when we found what was left of the stagecoach. It was a burnt out shell. We looked around. Between the stage and the trees was the half burned body of the driver. Inside the stage was the burned body of a man. The smell of the recent fire was still strong.

"This looks bad," Alan commented.

"I think the man is probably what's left of John Thompson," Alex said.

"Then where's Mrs. Thompson?" I asked.

"Based on footprints and scuff marks," Alex said, "It looks like she was dragged into the trees."

"How many are we expecting?" I asked.

"Four," Alex answered.

"Four?" Alan Asked, "Sarah said there were only three."

"Probably the fourth man was riding shotgun," I replied, "It makes sense if the stage slowed and then stopped before the men appeared."

"But why attack the stage?" Alan asked.

"Most stages that employ someone to ride shotgun are transporting money," Alex answered.

"Do you think we'll find the men?" I asked Alex.

"Looks like they aren't expecting anyone to follow them," Alex answered, "The trail should be easy to find."

"Then let's go," I said. Alan and I followed Alex's lead into the trees.

When night fell, we stopped to rest before continuing. The moon was full, making it easy to see the larger objects. Alex still followed the trail. At dawn we stopped to rest.

It was a few hours after dawn when we came across the body of Mrs. Thompson. It looked like she had been raped and beaten. She was dead, but with so much damage it was hard to tell what killed her.

"Ruth Thompson?" Alan asked. He seemed to have a hard time looking at the body.

"Based on the similarities to Sarah, I would say yes," Alex answered.

"How can anyone do something like that?" Alan asked.

"Only the people who do this kind of thing know the answer to that," I replied.

"We'll get her on the way back," Alex said, "Finding the men before they get very far is more urgent." We continued on.

It was mid-morning when we found the campsite. There was stuff scattered all over the clearing: clothes, supplies and guns. We stopped and tied our horses to a tree.

"They didn't take anything, if they've moved on," I commented as we looked around the campsite.

"I'm not sure where they are," Alex said, "But they haven't moved on."

A few minutes later we could hear voices coming towards us. All three of us took out our guns. Four men came into view. At first they didn't see us. The moment they did all of them turned and started running. Alan was the first to fire, I was second and Alex was the last. Five shots rang out and all four men fell to the ground. Alex and I walked over to the men. Three of them were dead and the fourth one was bleeding badly from his abdomin.

"You're so stupid," Alex told the man.

"But it was fun," the man smiled. He spit up some blood and then quit breathing.

"Let's get back to town," I said, "We can bring back a wagon and people to help."

"Yeah," Alex said. We went back to where Alan was standing.

"Are they dead?" Alan asked.

"Yes," Alex answered.

"Good," Alan said. We mounted our horses and rode back to town.

We dismounted outside the sheriffs office. The sheriff stepped out of his office.

"Sarah is inside," the sheriff said. Alan went into the office.

"They're dead," Alex said, "Her parents as well as the bandits."

"I'll get the mortician and the four of us can ride out," the sheriff said, "My deputy can look after things here."

"Whenever you're ready," Alex replied. The sheriff went behind his office and came back a few minutes later on horseback. Alex and I mounted and followed him to the mortician's office. The sheriff went inside. Five minutes later he came back out and mounted his horse. The mortician came around in his wagon. And we started off to where the bodies lay.

We picked up the driver and Sarah's father; then her mother and finally the four bandits. The sheriff took the guns, but everything else was left where it was. Then we headed back to town.

The mortician went back to his office, the sheriff went to his office and Alex and I went to the hotel.

We spent two more days in Plantville. Alan spent the time with Sarah and once he was allowed to leave, he planned to escort her to her aunt's place. The judge showed up, heard the whole story and let us all go. Alex and I headed back to Cartwheel.

ALEX'S LAST JOB
CHAPTER 16

Toby

When we put our horses in the stable it was obvious that Jacob was still sleeping out there, even though he wasn't there at that moment. There was no sign of the kid.

Alex and I went into the house. Nadine was not in the kitchen. She wasn't anywhere on the main floor as far as I could tell. Alex and I went upstairs and each took a guest room. Leaving our stuff there we went back downstairs.

"It seems no one else is here," I commented.

"Then we'll wait for Nadine to come home," Alex said. We sat down at the kitchen table and started playing poker.

It was almost time to start making supper when the front door opened and closed. Nadine entered the kitchen.

"You're back already?" Nadine asked hanging up her shawl.

"It wasn't a difficult job," Alex answered, "We would have been back sooner but we had to wait for the judge to show up."

"You stayed for a trial?" Nadine asked.

"There wasn't a trial," Alex answered, "The mayor and the sheriff wanted to make sure that there weren't gonna be any legal ramifications for us."

"What did you do?" Nadine asked.

"Alex sprung Fitzgerald out of jail because the sheriff was going to hang him," I answered, "The sheriff was willing to forgive and forget but the mayor wanted to make sure that Alex wouldn't be considered a wanted criminal."

"And it all worked out," Alex said.

"What about the man you were going there to deal with?" Nadine asked.

"He challenged Alan and lost," I answered.

"How are Fitzgerald and Alan doing then?" Nadine asked.

"Fitzgerald is back as the town doctor," Alex answered, "The town now owns the mine, so there's a steady source of money in town. As an apology, Fitzgerald was given the house that Cutler was building for himself. The town council has volunteered to finish the construction and to furnish it."

"He's happy about it all," I said, "He hadn't wanted to leave."

"Alan is busy," Alex said, "He found a girl in need of a hero and quickly stepped in to fill that role. And unless something happens I think his gunslinging days are limited."

"And the girl?" Nadine asked.

"Is sad that she lost her parents, She wasn't letting Alan too far out of her sight," I answered.

"Sounds like everything worked out," Nadine said.

"Leaving us with nothing that we need to do," Alex said, "How're things here?"

"The same as when you left, with the exception that Jacob has sent the kid to stay somewhere else," Nadine answered.

"How're you feeling about it all?" Alex asked.

"Tired," Nadine answered, "But not tired enough to give in. Every other day he's at the door asking to come back, but he hasn't changed and if I let him back in nothing will change. After everything, I need the changes, but Jacob doesn't want to understand that."

"I'm sure he'll get the message," Alex said.

"If he finds out you two are around and don't have a job, he'll find you one," Nadine said.

"He can try," I said, "But a break sounds nice right now."

"He will try," Nadine said, then started supper. Alex and I continued to play. After supper, Nadine joined us for a couple of games of comet. When we were tired all three of us went to bed.

The next I do jobs that Nadine needed help with around the

house. Alex spent the day working in the garden. Jacob wasn't seen at all. Overall it was a quiet day.

The morning started out the same way. After breakfast, Nadine found a job I could do that Alex could help me with.

Nadine was making lunch when there was a knock on the kitchen door. Alex and I stopped moving, but stayed in the parlour. I heard Nadine open the door. It was Jacob's voice but I couldn't distinguish any words. Then Nadine answered. I'm pretty sure that someone standing on the front path could have heard every word clearly. As soon as the door slammed shut, Alex and I went back to what we had been doing. We finished just as Nadine called us for lunch. After lunch, Alex and I went to the hotel and joined the poker game. When we arrived back, Nadine had gone to bed.

By the end of the week Nadine's house had been cleaned, everything that had been broken was fixed, the garden was looked after, and even the furniture had been rearranged. Jacob had disappeared once the door had been slammed in his face. Now that the week was over, he had shown up again, but he hadn't come to the house.

Nadine had decided to work on a quilting project that evening, so Alex and I sat out on the porch. There was no feeling that we had to fill the time with conversation, we just sat and enjoyed the evening.

It was starting to get dark when Jacob came around the house and stopped at the bottom of the steps to the porch.

"You need to talk to Nadine for me," Jacob said.

"No, we don't," Alex said, "If you want to talk to Nadine, you have to do it yourself."

"She won't listen to me," Jacob said.

"Why don't you try listening to her first," I suggested, "Then you might understand the reasons behind why she won't listen to you."

"You two aren't going to help me at all, are you?" Jacob asked.

"I think he's deaf," I said the Alex, "We give him help and he thinks we're against him."

"Not a surprise," Alex said to me, "He's never liked to listen to ideas that go against the way he has chosen to live."

"Well, I hope he gets used to living in the stable then because that appears to be the way he's chosen to live," I said.

"Stop that and help me," Jacob said. Alex and I didn't say anything. Jacob took that as a good sign.

"All I need you to do is talk to Nadine for me," Jacob said.

"No," Alex said.

"You can talk her out of being angry," Jacob said.

"No," Alex said. Jacob looked like he was going to say something else.

"And the response to that is no," I said. Jacob stood there unsure what to say or do. Alex and I sat there and watched him expectantly. Finally Jacob turned and walked away.

"I think we need to do something about the situation," Alex said.

"We need to find some way to get Jacob to listen," I said.

"That seems to be the biggest problem," Alex said.

"We could tie him to a chair and gag him until he agrees to listen," I said.

"That has possibilities," Alex said.

"The only question there is how many days it would take," I said.

"Looks like we have time," Alex said.

"No itch to get out of here?" I asked.

"No," Alex said, "Might come back if I sit here too long, but it's nice to sit and relax without it. If you have the itch to move on you can."

"I'm fine right here, thank you," I said.

"Should we tell Nadine before we tie him to a chair?" Alex asked.

"How do you think she'll react to her husband being bound and gagged?" I asked.

"We should probably tell her," Alex said. We sat there a few more minutes without talking. Finally Alex stood up and started toward the door.

"Good luck," I told her.

"Coward," Alex said.

"Yes, ma'am," I replied. Alex shook her head, but I saw the imp twitch. She went inside.

Lamps in town were slowly being lit just as the stars were

starting to appear. The moon had started on its journey across the sky when the door opened and Alex stepped out.

"How'd she take the suggestion?" I asked.

"Calmly," Alex answered.

"Is that a consent?" I asked.

"Pretty much," Alex answered. I stood up and we went inside. Alex took out some rope and I picked up a kitchen chair before we went through the kitchen door. When we reached the stable Alex went first to see if Jacob was there and whether he was asleep. After a moment she signalled me to come in. I did. Jacob was sleeping in the loft. I placed the chair in the middle of the stable.

"We need to give it some time," Ale's voice was quiet, "When he starts talking in his sleep then, no matter what we do he won't wake up." I nodded.

We waited about five minutes before we could hear him muttering. Alex and I climbed to the loft. Alex searched him for any weapons. She pulled a knife from his boot. Then she bound his wrists. We carried him down like that and set him on the chair. I held him in an upright position while Alex tied him up. When she was finished I used his bandana to gag him. He was still trying to talk in his sleep through the gag, but he was definitely still asleep.

Alex and I left him there and went into the house. Once in my room I went to bed.

After breakfast the next morning Nadine asked about Jacob. Alex figured that it was a good time to check on him. So the three of us went out to the stable.

Jacob was in the same position that Alex and I left him in last night. Except that he was awake and glaring at us. He yelled something through the gag.

"What did he say?" Nadine asked.

"He told us to untie him," Alex answered.

"Is he going to be able to get free?" Nadine asked.

"Jacob taught me to tie someone up without them being able to get free," Alex answered.

"I doubt he meant it to be used for this," I said.

Jacob said something through the gag.

"What did he say?" Nadine asked.

"That he isn't interested in listening to anyone yet," Alex

answered, "We can look in on him later."

"Very well," Nadine said. We left the stable.

By the second day Jacob started to smell, but we didn't dare untie him for anything. On the fifth day we undid the gag and gave him some water. Nadine was there. But Jacob didn't feel like listening so we put the gag back and left the stable.

He had been there a week and smelled like it, when the three of us tried again. Alex undid the gag and gave him some water. When she was finished, he started swearing at us so Alex put the gag back. Then Alex and I left Nadine with Jacob and went into the house. We sat down at the kitchen table and played poker.

An hour later Nadine came in and sat down on the other chair.

"I talked to him," Nadine said, "I told him how I feel about his behaviour and what I would like to see change. I also told him that I had a better offer than sitting around here and waiting on him. I also said that if he didn't straighten up after this I was going to take that other offer. Then I ungagged him and we discussed it. We agreed that he could continue this lifestyle for two more years and, after that, if he didn't retire, I was gonna leave. I also told him that he wasn't allowed back into the house until he didn't smell anymore."

"Did you untie him?" Alex asked.

"No," Nadine answered, "He needs to apologize to you two for his behaviour before he can be untied."

"Should we go out now?" I asked.

"Give him a few minutes to think about it all," Nadine answered.

"Comet?" Alex asked as she shuffled the cards.

"Sure," Nadine answered. Alex started dealing the cards out.

After we had played a while we put the cards away and went out to the stable. Jacob was sitting there without the gag.

"Nadine said you wanted to talk to Toby and me," Alex said.

"Yes," Jacob said, "I want to say that I'm sorry about my recent behaviour."

"If that's it then we can go back to our game," I said, "Because there's a lot of not recent behaviour that hadn't been to our liking." Alex and I turned as if to leave.

"I'm sorry about that as well," Jacob said, "And it won't happen again."

"Fine," Alex said. She pulled out a knife and cut the rope that was holding Jacob. Then Alex, Nadine and I went back into the house and started playing comet again. Jacob came in as Nadine was dishing up supper.

The next week was quiet. Alex and I spent a lot of time in town. The first day of the next week two letters arrived, one for Alex and one for Jacob. Alex was at the house when they arrived so she was able to read hers right away. After reading it, Alex became thoughtful and withdrawn. When Jacob home he had been he read his letter. Apparently it was a request to hire him for a job. Jacob asked if Alex and I would like to help if there was two hundred dollars each and expenses paid. Actually he offered it to Alex while they were in the stable. I overheard it. Alex said she would talk to me before agreeing, but either way this would be her last job. Jacob started asking questions before Alex told him to shut up and mind his own business.

Alex told me later about the job that Jacob needed help with. I figured why not.

The next day we said goodbye to Nadine, saddled up and rode out to where the kid was staying. There Jacob traded his horse in for the loan of a horse and wagon and Justin joined us.

Three days out, we hit rain for the next two days and mud on the sixth day. Jacob managed to get the wagon stuck in the mud. In getting it out, Alex became covered in mud and we wrecked a part of the wagon. When we reached a place that was semi dry we stopped to fix the wagon.

Alex came back to camp wearing just her shirt and pants. Her hair was still dripping and she was carrying her boots, hat and coat. She looked beautiful. Once again my heart did the flip-flop and I had to go back to what I was doing so I wouldn't to stare.

"You're female," Justin said, staring at Alex. Alex just glared at him briefly before dropping her stuff on her saddlebags and going to help Jacob.

"Alex is female," Justin told me.

"I saw," I replied without looking up. Justin continued to stare after her.

"She shouldn't be with us," Justin said, "Women don't belong in this work."

"She does everything you do, only better," I told him, "And she doesn't talk half as much as you do. So shut up and get back to work." He went back to work.

"How can you be willing to ignore what is proper?" he asked.

"Because proper is bullshit that people stuff up your ass to keep control," I told him, "Now shut up already." He was quiet, but the type of quiet that you know the person wants to keep talking. I ignored him and kept working.

Alex finally braided her hair and put her hat back on. We finished everything by the time that night fell. Then Jacob cooked supper, we ate in quiet. Once supper was finished I went and sat by myself for a while.

Alex came over after some talking around the fire.

"So?" I asked.

"Jacob set Justin straight about me going back," Alex said, "The kid has some serious relearning to do before Jacob can let him go out on his own."

"Every time he opens his mouth I want to jam something in there before he can start speaking," I said, "Never had that reaction to anyone before."

"He's just a kid who needs to learn how the world works," Alex said, "With any luck he'll learn when to keep his mouth shut. Or he'll die because he didn't." I half smiled and then let it go. Alex let the quiet grow.

"You told Jacob that this was your last job," I said.

"I did," Alex replied, "He was talking about two more years worth of work and helping to train the kid. I'm tired."

"Last job ever?" I asked.

"I was still hoping to take a trip out to the mine," Alex said, "See how much more we could bring back."

"And after that?" I asked.

"I might take a job here and there to relieve boredom, but I bought Peterson's apple orchard and Mr. Peterson isn't as healthy as he once was," Alex said, "I was going to tell you."

"I know," I said, "I just overheard you say that to Jacob and my mind has been running overtime."

"Thinking about retiring?" Alex asked.

"Something like that," I answered.

"And do what?" Alex asked.

"I'm not sure, but I think I have to go home first," I answered, "From there I'm figure something out."

"Good luck," Alex said.

"All I have to do now it get through this job without killing the kid," I said.

"Now that he knows I'm female we won't hear the end of it," Alex said.

"Challenge him to a pissing contest," I suggested, "If he wins, say you'll stay out of danger. If you win, he has to keep his mouth shut."

"Are we shooting at each other or an object at a distance?" Alex asked.

"Jacob would veto shooting at each other," I answered.

"Pity," Alex said. The other two appeared to be going the sleep. We went back over to the fire and into our bedrolls. I went to sleep.

The next morning I was the first up and making breakfast when Alex woke up. Then Jacob woke up. We were eating and the kid still hadn't woken up. We cleaned up the dishes and packed up camp. The kid still slept. Alex loaded her gun and started target practise with things on the far side of the kid from her. The first three shots had the kid blinking and groggy. The next two had him out of his bedroll and in a squat looking for the person to shoot. Alex stopped.

"Glad to see you decided to get up," I told Justin. He looked confused.

"We already ate breakfast," Alex said, "And we packed up the camp too." Alex started to put her gun away.

"Reload first," I reminded her. She shrugged, but reloaded her gun then put it away.

"That wasn't funny," Justin said.

"When you get to be the experienced gunslinger you'll understand," Alex replied.

"And then you'll laugh," I added. Justin grumbled as he put away his bedroll.

"You missed the fourth target," Jacob told Alex. Alex looked.

"I did, didn't I? Oh well, it isn't really important," Alex said, "Since I wasn't exactly aiming at them."

"Those would be easy to hit," Justin said, looking at trees Alex had hit.

"Then hit a different tree each time and hit with all six bullets," Alex told Justin. Justin took out his gun. He checked it over and then took aim.

"Have to do it all in less than a minute," Alex added. Justin readjusted him aim and fired off all six of his bullets. Jacob went over and checked the kid's accuracy. Then he came back.

"Got two in one tree and missed another tree altogether," Jacob said.

"Not that easy," Alex said.

"Then you do it," Justin said. Alex pulled out her gun and fired six bullets in rapid succession at the trees. While Jacob went to check she reloaded her gun. Jacob came back.

"Six for six," Jacob said.

"Can we go now?" Alex asked. The kid just nodded. We got underway. It was another day and a half before we reached the town where we were supposed to meet the person that hired us.

Coming into town, I could see a group of men gathered around objects they were using as cover that had been placed around a house at the end of the street. We stopped our horses in front of the general store, which was the second building on our way into town.

"I wonder what's happening down there," Alex said looking down the street before getting down from her horse.

"Better to stay out of it," Jacob said before heading into the general store. Alex and I followed him inside with the kid trailing along behind us. The shopkeeper looked up from the ledger he was studying. Jacob went straight to him.

"Good afternoon," Jacob said.

"Afternoon," the shopkeeper responded.

"I received a letter from a Mr. Pontisso," Jacob said, "And it said that if I came in here and asked I would be directed to Mr. Pontisso."

"He even told me to expect you," the shopkeeper said, "but it's going to difficult to talk to Mr. Pontisso."

"Why?" Jacob asked.

"You see what's happening down the street?" the shopkeeper asked.

"Yes," Jacob answered.

"Well, that's the house of Mr. Pontisso and his wife," the shopkeeper said, "And they're in there. Whether they're alive or dead is unknown."

"What exactly is happening down there?" Alex asked.

"Five men stopped in town to rob the bank," the shopkeeper said, "They succeeded, but the sheriff tried to prevent them from getting away, so he had men at every way out of town. The bank robbers instead went into the Pontisso residence and took the couple hostage. Been a stand off out there for three days now with the occasional exchange of gunfire."

"Sounds like they need someone to intervene," Alex said.

"That may not be a good idea," Jacob said, "We can wait and see what happens."

"Where would I find the sheriff?" Alex asked the shopkeeper.

"Out front of the house," the shopkeeper answered.

"Thank you," Alex said. She left the store. I followed Jacob and the kid outside. The shopkeeper also came out.

Alex walked down the street. As she got close to the men one man asked her to stop. I could see the light reflect off the left side of his vest. They talked for a couple of minutes. The sheriff shook his head, but didn't stop Alex as she continued forward. She walked through the gate and up the path to the door. She pushed it open and stepped inside. Every eye was on that door and every person was waiting to find out what was going to happen. Five minutes passed. Ten minutes passed. People were starting to move, but not far and not fast. Fifteen minutes passed. The shopkeeper started to turn to go back inside when the door opened. Five unarmed men came out with their hands up. Alex and a man came out supporting a woman between them. I guessed that they were Mr. and Mrs. Pontisso. The sheriff and his men rushed forward to arrest the men and help the couple.

In no time Mr. and Mrs. Pontisso were in a comfortable place, the four of us were given hotel rooms until the Pontissos were ready to go, and we had all been bought a drink.

We stayed for three days. Then we escorted the Pontissos to visit their daughter and then back. Then we headed back to Cartwheel.

Jacob had another job offer before we had brushed out horses down. I got stuck helping. Alex told me that I could find her at Peterson's orchard when I was ready to go after the rest of the treasure. Then we parted company.

* * * *

Lady Grace

I was sitting in the dining room of the hotel in Cartwheel when Alex came into the room. I was here visiting Nadine and she had told me that Jacob, Alex and Toby had gone on a job. Apparently they had just gotten back. Alex came over to the table. I signalled her to sit down.

"Where's Toby?" I asked.

"Jacob dragged him off to get ready for the next job," Alex answered.

"Why are you visiting me then?" I asked.

"I'm not going on this job," Alex answered, "But I had heard that you were going to visit Simone."

"I am," I said, "In about a week."

Alex nodded.

"You and Toby going separate directions?" I asked.

"He has a job and I have other things to do," Alex answered, "Being partners doesn't make us inseparable. Besides we're only going to do one more job after he's finished with Jacob."

"Then what?" I asked, hardly believing what I was hearing.

"Then I retire," Alex answered, "And I don't know what Toby is going to do."

"And that's it?" I asked.

"Why not?" Alex asked.

"You and Toby are in love, that can't be all," I answered.

"Nothing in this world happens exactly like we think it should," Alex said, "You should know that. If we're supposed to be together then we will, if not then we won't." Alex stood up.

"So, you're going to let go and hope for the best?" I asked, "The world is what we make of it."

"I'm tired of making it. Now is the time to for leaving it and hoping for the best," Alex said. She put her hat on and left the hotel. I stared after her. Finally I stood up and went after her. When I reached to the street I could see her already on her horse and leaving town. I turned and headed for Jacob's house.

I found Jacob taking care of his horse.

"Where's Toby?" I asked. Jacob looked up at me and then went back to what he was doing.

"Toby took Justin and is doing a job guarding a goods wagon," Jacob answered, "In the completely opposite direction from Alex, who's heading home. Ain't nothing to do about them."

"You don't think it's wrong that they are going opposite directions?" I asked.

"They will get back together, without any help," Jacob answered, "Anything else would be putting our noses in where they don't belong."

"You're always putting your nose in their business," I said.

"Only when it came to jobs," Jacob replied, "Now Alex is retiring, what she does is her business."

I studied him for a full minute, but as far as I could tell he was telling the truth. I turned and left the barn. As I was walking away, I thought I heard Jacob start whistling.

*　　*　　*　　*

Mr. Peterson

I was sitting on the front porch resting when I heard a horse coming up the road. I sighed and readied myself to tell off who ever it was when Alexandria came into sight. This old body was glad to see her. I had figured five years, but I'm getting too old to do this. The girl stopped just below the bottom step.

"I received a note from a concerned citizen," Alexandria said, "You don't look quite as dead as it made you sound."

"I might as well be as far as the town folks are concerned," I replied, "I collapsed one day in the orchard. Someone saw it, now they realize I'm old. Every lady in town is bringing me meals, I've got pickers coming out my ears, someone even took the apples off for me and sold them, offers to fix my house, and doing my chores for me. Why can't people just leave an old man be?"

"I'm sure they're just trying to be helpful," Alexandria said.

"Helpful? Why don't they just shoot me like you would a lame horse?" I demanded. I started to cough, but the fit was mild and passed quickly.

"What would you like me to do? And shooting you is not one of the options," Alexandria said.

"I'd like you to take over the orchard. I'll show you how to do it. Maybe they'll leave me be if you're here," I said, "You need to learn how to treat your land anyway."

"Fine," Alexandria said, "But I have one more job that I'm waiting on someone else to do."

"We'll deal with that when we get there," I said, slowly getting out of the chair. I went down the stairs. Every other person who had come up had offered to help me going down the stairs. Alexandria just stepped back and waited for me. I knew there was something I like about her. Once I was on the ground, Alexandria followed me as I led her though her land.

*　　　*　　　*　　　*

Toby

I will never know how Jacob gets those jobs or how he gets so many, but I was relieved when I managed to get out of Cartwheel. Now it was three months since I had seen Alex and I was standing in the hotel in her hometown. I already had a room and was headed for the saloon when Simone and Sheldon came into the hotel.

"Hello, Toby," Simone called. She looked like she might be pregnant again.

"Hello," I replied.

"So, you and Alex are here for a visit?" Simone asked.

"Actually, she's been here for a while," I answered, "I'm supposed to meet her here and then we have one more job together."

"I haven't seen her," Simone said.

"She's probably busy," I said.

"Busy doing what?" Simone asked.

"There've been rumours that Alex is helping Mr. Peterson," Sheldon said.

"And you didn't tell me?" Simone asked.

"Thought you'd heard," Sheldon answered.

"Well, she should've at least come to say hello," Simone said.

"I don't know," I said. Then I headed into the saloon, where I played poker until it closed down for the night.

I slept till noon before getting up. I went to the restaurant and ate lunch. Then I headed up to the Peterson place. Mr. Peterson was sitting on the porch when I got there.

"What do you want?" he demanded.

"I'm looking for Alex," I answered.

"She'd be up a tree in the orchard you passed on your way up here," Mr. Peterson said.

"Thank you," I said then headed back down the road. I stopped at the orchard and climbed the fence. I started to wander until I saw which tree she was sitting in; I went to it. She seemed to be staring at nothing in particular.

"Simone is mad at you," I said. She woke out of the trance and looked at me.

"If she was paying any attention, she would have known I was in town," Alex said climbing down, "I've been staying in my parent's barn."

"They let you?" I asked. We started for the far side of the field and the Turner property.

"I've done it before, why shouldn't I do it again?" Alex said, "They know, but I'm not going to move back into their house and I don't have one of my own."

"Ready to go?" I asked.

"Been waiting," Alex answered, "What took you so long?"

"Jacob kept the jobs coming until I slipped out back," I answered, "He would still having me doing them if I hadn't. And Justin is a very slow learner, especially when it involves keeping his mouth shut."

"You predicted that would happen before I left," Alex said.

"He's as green as when you left," I said.

"Jacob is gonna have his hands full then," Alex said, "His fault." We climbed the fence on this side and headed for the barn.

"So how is being an orchardest?" I asked.

"Not bad," Alex said as she opened the barn door, "There's a lot to do some days and not much other days. Take care of the trees and then pick the apples when they're ripe."

"Sounds pretty close to farming," I said.

"Probably," Alex said, she went to her horse and got it ready for travel. Then we walked with her horse to the stable in town where I left mine. I got mine ready and then we both mounted and headed out of town.

At the town just before we headed into the desert, we purchased a horse and cart. Then we headed for the mountain pass. No adventure this time, just the trail and lots of sunlight. We stopped at the same small town as before to get water and supplies. We continued on to the mine. We loaded boxes on to the cart until it wouldn't hold anymore. There were still some boxes, but we left those behind and started back. We stopped in the town again. This time Alex stopped in front of where the sheriff was leaning on a post watching us. He looked curious. Alex got down and walked over to him.

"Need some help?" the sheriff asked.

"No, we just felt that you should have this," Alex said, holding out the map to him. The sheriff's eyebrows went up. He took the paper. Alex came back and climbed into the driver's seat again. Then we left town. We went back through the mountain pass. And back to Alex's hometown, where we stored the cart in her parent's barn.

I stayed the night in the barn with Alex. After breakfast the next day I went up with her to see Mr. Peterson. The man was sitting on his porch, looking like he could die any minute.

"You're back," the voice was still gruff, but it was losing volume. Alex climbed the steps on to the porch.

"We came in last night," Alex said.

"They say I should move into town," Mr. Peterson said.

"Up to you," Alex said.

"I'm not going to town, I'm gonna die right here where I belong. I wrote to my son," Mr. Peterson said, "He'll never get here in time, just like him to miss all the important events in my life." The old man paused. "So, you tell him that all he gets is the contents of the house and maybe the house if he wants to move it. I paid for the plot next to my wife when she died. I better be buried there."

"There's nowhere else to put you," Alex said.

"With people these days you can never tell," Mr. Peterson said,

"Always mess up what you tell them." He paused again. "You be good to this orchard and it'll treat you right. You were always the one who cared, don't forget who you are, ever."

"I won't," Alex said. She came down the stairs and we started for town. If he lived to see the doctor I would be surprised. We went to the doctor's office. The doctor was sitting out front reading. He looked up at us.

"What can I help you with today?" the doctor asked.

"Mr. Peterson is dead," Alex said.

"What happened? Where is he?" the doctor asked standing up.

"He died on his front porch," Alex answered.

"He should've moved to town," the doctor said.

"Why? He died where he wanted to and how he wanted to," Alex said, "As long as he is buried next to his wife, he gets everything he wanted. There's no better way to die."

"There's no good way to die," the doctor said.

"Then I'm sure you'll spend all your life running from death and it will get you worse because it had to chase you," I said. The doctor gave me a funny look.

"Some of us have accepted that we'll die, we just hope it's peacefully," Alex said, "Roderick Peterson managed that. Bury him according to his instructions, please."

A stagecoach rolled into town and stopped in front of the hotel. One man got off and carried his bag. The man's black hair was starting to be streaked with grey and his eyes looked like Mr. Peterson's.

"Looks like Thayer Peterson arrived too late," the doctor said.

"We'll be around," Alex said. Then we headed back to the Turner's barn.

Alex was sitting on the edge of the loft, while I was getting my horse ready. The door opened and Thayer Peterson came inside.

"Alex?" he asked.

"Yes," Alex answered.

"I'm Thayer Peterson. Roderick Peterson was my father," Thayer said, "I was told you're the one who found him this morning."

"He said he was expecting you," Alex said.

"Then you talked to him before he died?" Thayer said.

"Yes," Alex answered.

"Did he say anything about his belongings?" Thayer asked.

"The contents of the house and the house, if you want to move it, are yours," Alex answered.

"And the land?" Thayer asked.

"Belongs to me… has for a while," Alex answered.

"Very well," Thayer said, turning away.

"Make sure your father is buried next to his wife," Alex said.

"Why?" Thayer asked, turning back.

"Because that's what he asked to have done," Alex answered. Thayer nodded and then left. "What other reason is there?"

"Some people don't care what happens once someone is dead," I said.

"They should," Alex said. I led my horse out of the stall and into the main area.

"I'm headed for home now," I said. Alex stood up and came down to stand near me. The urge to hold her was there, but I restrained myself.

"Not gonna take your half of the treasure?" Alex said.

"You'll keep it safe," I said, "I don't have any place where it would be safe. I'll be back for it though."

"Then I'll see you when you do," Alex said. She stepped closer and I took her in my arms. We kissed. When we came up for air, we broke apart and I left the barn. I left town without looking back.

Forever later or a day later, I'm not sure which, I was riding toward the farmhouse where I grew up.

It was six months later I rode back into Alex's hometown. Everything seemed the same. I rode up to where Mr. Peterson's house used to be. Now there was a much larger and new house. Alex had been busy since I left. I tied my horse to the porch railing and went up the stairs. I was just about to the door when Alex opened it. She was wearing a skirt, a man's shirt and her hat.

"Hello," I said.

"Hello," Alex said with a smile, "Come back for your share now?"

"And see how you're doing," I answered, "Looks like you've been busy."

"It was finished yesterday," Alex said. She came outside and closed the door behind her. I sat down on the rail. "The orchard needs tending regularly and I have a nephew who likes to come and help. And Simone is pregnant again."

"I knew that from last time," I said.

"Well, she's due any day now," Alex said, "You ever figured out what you're doing?"

"I've been thinking about it," I answered, "I keep coming back to wanting to settle down."

"You have money to buy any land you want," Alex said.

"True," I said, "But I don't know where."

"That's a problem," Alex said.

"This past six months it wouldn't have mattered where I was or what I was doing," I said, "All that seemed to really matter was that I wasn't with you."

"And here I was just thinking about how lonely this house is," Alex said as she smiled. I took her hand and pulled her to me. We kissed. This time when we stopped no one moved.

"Alexandria Turner," I said, "Will you marry me?"

"Yes."

ABOUT THE AUTHOR

B. Heather Mantler is a student of psychology. She lives in Prince George, British Columbia and is a member of the writing group Scribblers Unanimous. Heather is always working on another story as she hopes to finish every story idea she has ever written down. She was a nominee for the fiction category of the 2012 Prince George Regional Arts and Cultural Awards and short listed for the 2013 John Harris Fiction Awards. Heather encourages all her readers to post their reviews on Amazon.com or Good Reads.

www.ingramcontent.com/pod-product-compliance
Lightning Source LLC
Chambersburg PA
CBHW030930020726
47498CB00001B/193

* 9 7 8 1 9 2 7 5 0 7 0 6 3 *